LONDON *dynasty*

LONDON DYNASTY

Copyright © 2021 by Geneva Lee.

Estate Publishing + Media

www.GenevaLee.com

First published, 2021.

Cover design © Geneva Lee.

Image © soup studio/Adobe Stock.

THE DYNASTIES
BOOK ONE

LONDON
dynasty

GENEVA LEE

ESTATE
PUBLISHING + ENTERTAINMENT

To the Loves,
You are my safe place

And to their fearless leaders,
Shelby,
Elsi,
Christina,
Jami, & Karen

CHAPTER ONE

"**G**irl, you aren't going to win the lottery."

I flinched at Sheila's sharp voice, burying a frown when I spotted her watching me. Her eyes had narrowed so much that she looked like a hawk, save for her thick, sky-blue eyeliner. She snagged a lipstick tube from her pocket and popped off the lid to reveal the mauve shade she'd chewed off her lips earlier, during the match.

"It's a waste of time," she continued, applying the lipstick in a mirror she'd propped up near the dish sink. "You might as well flush your money down the toilet."

I ignored her. That was always the safest angle to take where Sheila was concerned. As far as I knew, the sixty-year-old had worked at Hare & Hound since the day she was born. In the six months I'd been working here, she hadn't taken a day off—not once. Sheila might be right about wasting my money, but I wasn't going to spend my whole life working in a rundown pub in Berkshire.

Business had died down since the match ended. Only a

few regulars remained, nursing the wound of the local football club's defeat. Most were blaming the sky-high August temperatures for the loss. As it was, I'd propped open the walk-in freezer to cool off. The heatwave had suffused the air with a heavy humidity that verged on suffocating. I craned my neck in an attempt to cool off before looking down at my last chance at salvation. The scratchcard wasn't about getting rich or getting out, though. Even West Bexby, with its one traffic light, had double the cost of living of other small towns—due mostly to its location between Oxfordshire and Greater London. Rent and the electricity bill were due tomorrow. I had enough tip money for only one. I flipped the ten-pence I was holding, sent out a prayer for luck, and scraped off the last silver box.

I sank against the wall and stared like I might be able to will the clover outline I'd uncovered to be the horseshoe I needed.

Shelia chuckled before making a clucking noise. "I told you—"

Before she could dish another serving of advice, the swinging door that separated the kitchen from the bar burst open. Eliza, the pub's only other waitress and one of the few people who seemed comfortable in the small town, swayed in with a tray of dirty dishes. She dumped them in the sink with a teeth-rattling crash.

I shoved the ticket into my apron before she could turn to see it.

"Hanging out without me?" She wiped her hands on her checkered apron as she studied me. Eliza could have left the Berks. She was smart enough to go to university, pretty enough to be a model, with her glossy brown hair and dark, round eyes, or curvy enough to have landed a husband. Instead, she seemed content to follow Sheila's example and work at the pub. Like me, she transplanted here. Like me, she didn't want to talk about why. It made her an ideal flatmate and friend. "Everything good, Kate?"

"Yeah," I forced a smile. "Shelia was just giving me a little advice."

"Again?" Eliza glared at her with a look as frosty as the air wafting from the open freezer.

Sheila opened her overly lipsticked mouth, but before she could respond, a bell clattered over the entrance, alerting us to incoming patrons.

"Your table, Sheila," Eliza said with a grin that spread like the Cheshire Cat's. Sheila grumbled as she saddled toward the dining room, but she kept her eyes downward. As soon as she was gone, Eliza pulled a pack of cigarettes from her apron. She held it out, but I shook my head. She opened the backdoor a crack and stepped one foot out as though this counted as being *outside* before lighting one. "So, did you win?"

"What?" I asked. "Win?"

"That scratchcard I saw when I came in—did you win?"

Shit. Apparently, my sleight of hand hadn't been fast enough. There was no point in hiding it now. Besides, facing her tomorrow when I was short on what I owed wouldn't be any better than admitting it now. "Nope."

"How much?" She flicked ash from the end of her cigarette.

"A hundred pounds." Shame spiked inside me, burning molten in my chest and throat. I tried to ignore it, but I felt the heat seep across my skin. The trouble with being fair-skinned was how easily it reacted. My chest. My neck. My cheeks. By now, they were all red and splotchy from all that escaped shame. It was a map of my failures painted for her to see.

"I got you," she said, as though this was both not a big deal or an ongoing problem. It was both.

"You had me last month, too," I said sullenly.

"Business is down," Eliza lied smoothly.

"Business isn't down. I'm a shit waitress." That was the truth, and we both knew it. I suspected Ron had hired me because he thought I was pretty. Actually, he'd told me as much, couching it as a treat for his customers, mostly working men who haunted the pub between other responsibilities like work and wives. I'd turned out to be a disappointment when it came to waitressing. It had taken me the better part of a month to lift a tray with an entire order of pints. I had to make two trips when I started waiting tables. I'd yet to successfully remember the usuals' orders or when to drop off the bill. Eliza pitied me, showing me little tricks to help me remember orders and names. That had helped, but I'd bet money that Sheila could greet a customer, take an order, deliver it, and cash out the table wearing a blindfold. Eliza probably could, too.

"You're still learning," Eliza dismissed the truth like she did any of my more negative self-talk. "You'll get better. It's your first job, right?"

It was one of the few facts I'd bothered to share with

her, and only then because her own work history had come up one night over a bottle of cheap wine from Tesco. She'd been waiting tables since she could drive. I didn't ask where and she didn't offer. I had confessed, however, that the pub was my first job. Eliza had raised one thinly-plucked eyebrow, waited a moment, and moved on. I supposed she'd paused to give me a chance to explain my lack of real-world experience. I was relieved she didn't press me harder. The last thing I wanted was for her to feel sorry for me. But now it was clear she did anyway.

The bell clanged again, and Eliza tossed her cigarette out the back door. She patted my arm as she walked past. "Don't worry about it, Kate. I got you."

"Thanks." I forced the gratitude out so hard that I practically chirped. After growing up with nothing, I still didn't know what to do when people were nice to me. Eliza seemed to sense this and only nodded. I needed to do something to make it up to her. "I'll take the table. You can still have the tip."

I owed her that much.

The wide grin came back, and she reached into her apron for another cigarette. "You're the best."

I paused at the sink to wash my hands before going back to the floor. It was a habit, but it also gave me a chance to check myself in Sheila's mirror. My hair had managed to stay reasonably secure in the tight knot at the top of my head. Pulled up this tightly, it looked darker than it was. There was almost no hint of the red tint it held when I wore it loosely. The rest of me looked about the same. I didn't bother with much make-up. Between going back and forth to the kitchen and the overworked dining room aircon, I would wind up sweating it off within minutes. Not that there was much it could do for me anyway. My eyes were set a little too wide, and my mouth matched. My cheekbones were so high and sharp they seemed to swallow my face. Ron, the skeevy pub owner, might think I was pretty, but I felt mismatched. If anyone bothered to look, they would see it, too. That hadn't stopped anyone from trying to grab my ass as I passed, though.

Backing through the swinging doors, I pulled out my notepad and a stubby pencil. A group had taken the table in the corner. As I walked toward them, light bounced through the window, nearly blinding me. I looked outside to find a shiny silver Jaguar was parked by the curb. I surveyed the group more closely and didn't recognize a single face. That wasn't a surprise since people in Bexby didn't drive luxury cars. All three of them were busy on their mobile phones. When I reached the table, they barely looked at me.

"Pints all around. Hell, pints for the bar to celebrate the win," one said, still busily dashing out a text on the screen.

There was no point writing that down. Even I couldn't screw up delivering pints on the house. I'd been right that the group wasn't from around here. They obviously had money if they were buying rounds, even if there were only a few other souls in the place. That money might buy beer and fancy cars, but it hadn't done them any good in the common sense department. "Might keep the celebrating down," I advised, tucking the notepad back in my pocket. "Most folks around here are wallowing."

"What did they expect going up against the..." the man stopped as he finally glanced up at me.

"Kerrigan! What the hell?" He lounged back and hit his friend on the shoulder. "I thought you were in New York for the summer or France or some shit?"

My head tilted, and I shook my head, but before I could point out his mistake, his friend jumped in.

"Yeah, why are you working in a shitbox like this place? Daddy cut you off?"

"I'm sorry I've never met you. I'm not..." I was so taken back by having the pub insulted that I couldn't remember the name he'd used. I mean, Hare & Hound was, as he put it, a shitbox, but I didn't need some entitled wankers coming in and pointing it out. "My name is Kate, actually."

"No fucking way." He stared at me before looking around the pub like he expected a camera crew to jump out. "You serious? Kathy?"

"*Kate*, and I am." I pushed a strand of hair off my sweaty forehead with my pencil. "What else can I bring you?"

But he wasn't listening. His hand stretched out and snapped a picture of me with his phone's camera.

"I didn't say you could do that," I said quietly as my blood went cold.

"It's cool." He dismissed my concern like it was his right to do so. " Just no one is going to believe that we met Kerrigan Belmond's twin or doppelganger in...where the fuck are we?"

"West Bexby." I resisted the urge to pluck the phone

from his overprivileged fingers and smash it. Instead, I tucked my pencil behind my ear. "I'll grab those pints."

I circled around and left before they could take any more photos. My heart began to pound. My fingers splayed over the worn oak of the bar to steady myself. Instead of ducking behind it to the taps, I continued on to the kitchen. My vision swam along the edges. By the time I'd pushed through the swinging doors, I couldn't breathe. Suddenly I no longer felt the oppressive heat; I was cold like I'd been plunged into an icy river. The world blurred around me, water closing in overhead and pressing down. I tottered forward, reaching for the wall, but I was too far. My fingers closed over empty air as I stopped breathing.

CHAPTER TWO

I wasn't close enough to the wall to catch myself. I was falling, losing control, and for a second, I wanted the panic to win. I wanted it to overwhelm me and wash me away. My knees gave way, surrendering, just as Eliza's arm dipped around me and hauled me upright.

"Whoa, maybe you should sit down," she said.

I shook my head. "I'm fine."

"Is it the heat or another panic attack?" she asked.

"The heat," I lied. I didn't have an explanation for the panic attacks. They came out of nowhere and rendered me nearly helpless. So far, I'd managed to keep myself from having one in front of customers, but Eliza had witnessed plenty of them.

"Let me get you some water," she coaxed.

"No," I said quickly as the drowning sensation roared inside me again. "I'm fine. I should get back to the assholes at table four."

"Did they say something to you?" Eliza asked, her eyes turning to steely flint.

"No. They just thought I was some friend of theirs. They were rude about it, like they couldn't believe she would work here."

"Lovely," she sneered. "I'll take care of them. Did they order?"

I was suddenly thankful I hadn't gotten their food order yet, because I had a feeling Eliza would have dumped it on their heads. She didn't take well to rude men. Regulars knew to toe the line around her.

"Just a round for the house. No food. They were busy taking my picture to show Kerrigan someone or another. Some rich bitch, I'm sure, " I muttered. My breathing had finally returned to normal, and the pressure had faded entirely. At least the attacks, while inexplicable, ended as suddenly as they started. Unfortunately, I almost always wound up with a migraine after.

"Kerrigan?" Eliza replied. "Like Kerrigan Belmond?"

I pressed a palm to my forehead as the first throb hit. "Yeah. I think that's it. Do you know her?"

"Do I know Kerrigan Belmond?" She laughed at the question, staring at me like I was playing a prank on her.

I shook my head to let her know I had no idea why she found this amusing. "Who is she?"

"Socialite. Family is worth a fortune."

"What do they do?" I asked. No wonder the guys had acted like idiots. I couldn't imagine a socialite working at the Hare & Hound. I couldn't even imagine a socialite in West Bexby.

"The internet or railroads or something." She sighed as if to say it didn't matter how they'd gotten rich, only that they were.

Her sigh mirrored my own feelings. It wasn't fair that some people had everything while I was gambling on lottery tickets to pay my electricity bill.

"I can deal with them," I promised her.

"You let me know if they step over the line again, though?"

I nodded as I backed out of the kitchen and turned toward the bar. The guys were probably too busy spewing their celebration all over their social media accounts to care about me, but I studiously avoided looking their way. I was reaching for the first glass when Sheila dropped a fifty-pound note on the worn wooden counter.

"Those boys left, said to give you this," she told me. "They also said sorry about the picture." Sheila waited for me to explain myself.

"Thanks," I grabbed the money and shoved it in my pocket instead.

Sheila huffed away. I had no idea what annoyed her more: that I hadn't explained what had happened or that I'd been rewarded with a massive tip for doing absolutely nothing. All I knew what that having my photograph taken was a small price to pay for an easy fifty pounds. I dashed in the back to give it to Eliza.

"Nice!" She pushed it back toward me after I explained what happened. "Keep it for a rainy day."

"Okay," I said, deciding to slip it into her pocket when she wasn't looking. There was no way I would let her cover my share of rent while I kept this, but I knew better than to try to argue with her.

"Hey, check this out," She turned her phone toward me. "You really do look like Kerrigan Belmond. If you put on some make-up, you could be her twin."

I took the mobile and scrolled through the socialite's account photos. She'd documented her life and posted it on the internet for all to see. I could see what the men and Eliza were talking about. We did look a little alike, but it was more than just the make-up that set us apart. Every picture was oozing the elite life she enjoyed. In one, she was sipping champagne stretched across a chaise lounge, the Mediterranean providing a stunning backdrop. In another, she was blowing a kiss behind the wheel of a Road-ster. Picture after picture showcased her in designer clothes living a life I could only dream of. I scrolled to the top and read her bio. There wasn't much, just a passing mention of recently graduating from Oxford and the link to some phil-anthropy. As far as I could tell, her whole life was spent taking things off silver platters and lowering herself for the occasional charity work. It was as far from my life as I could imagine. I wasn't even sure I could imagine something that wild. I bet Kerrigan had never worried about an electricity bill in her life.

"I guess I should be flattered," I said for Eliza's benefit as I passed back her phone.

"She's probably a bitch," Eliza said. "What do you want to bet?"

I waved the cash I was still holding. "How about fifty pounds?"

"Nice try, Kate," she said with a laugh. "Tell you what? Let's stop at Tesco and buy ourselves the cheapest champagne we can find. We can drown our lowly sorrows and take selfies drinking out of plastic cups."

I couldn't help smiling at that. Tomorrow was Sunday, and the pub would be closed. We might as well have a little fun. I suspected Kerrigan Belmond would agree.

FIFTY POUNDS BOUGHT US THREE BOTTLES OF CHEAP wine and a week's worth of cheap groceries. The groceries lasted until the following morning; the wine did not. I woke the next morning to a pounding headache and sun streaking through the blackout curtains I'd failed to close in my drunken haze. It took a minute for me to process that the pounding wasn't just in my head. I heard Eliza yell something, her voice muffled by the walls between us. I grabbed my phone off the nightstand and checked the time, groaning when I saw it was only a quarter to nine. Meanwhile, the pounding continued. I had no idea what wanker showed up to beat down a door on a Sunday morning, but I knew they either had a poor sense of timing or a keen sense of torture. Untangling my legs from the sheets, I pushed myself up a bit too fast, which earned me a brain-splitting slice of pain behind my eyes.

"I'm coming," I yelled to the unwanted guest at the door.

This had better be good.

CHAPTER THREE

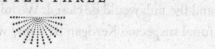

A s soon as my fingers closed over the lock, I hesitated. Whoever was pounding this loudly was both pissed and strong. After a moment, I turned the lock but not the chain. I opened the door as far as the chain would allow and peeked outside. Two dark eyes stared back at me, glaring through the crack.

"Can I help you?" I asked, coating the words with as much rudeness as possible.

He cleared his throat with obvious annoyance. "Do you work at the Hare & Hound?"

"I'm sorry. What is this about?" I asked. If he was going to answer my question with a question, I would do the same. I had no idea what had brought him to my door, but he was in no posi

tion to act like he was the frustrated one. The stranger stepped back, allowing me to get a better look at him. He was dressed in an expensive suit, the kind men bought on the High Street in one of London's ritzier neighborhoods.

The kind that was far too expensive for him to be a police officer coming round to ask questions. His salt and pepper hair, coupled with the lines creasing his forehead and eyes, only made him look more distinguished. He didn't belong in Bexby. He didn't even belong in this postcode. So, why was he here nearly breaking down the door to my flat?

"I'm looking for a woman who works at that pub," he said flatly, craning his head to get a better look at me through the chained door. He slid his hand into his breast pocket, and I fought the urge to slam the door in his face. Maybe I was wrong. Perhaps he was a police officer with good taste, and he was simply reaching for his badge. He drew out a phone, and I relaxed. "This woman."

He held the phone screen out so I could see it. It was a picture of me from the pub. I looked flustered, and the angle was terrible. It was the photo the jerks had snapped of me yesterday without asking permission.

"Why do you want to talk to her?" I asked, hoping he couldn't see much of me through the opening. My heart began to race, and I wished Eliza had answered the door. She would have known how to handle a strange man showing up on our doorstep.

"I need her help," he said curtly.

A brilliant idea occurred to me. Something told me I needed to get him out of here and fast. I needed to distract him long enough to figure out what to do. Eliza had an ex-boyfriend who might provide some backup muscle. I just needed to get rid of the stranger long enough to call him. "Maybe you should try the pub."

"The pub is closed today, and I need to return to

London as soon as possible. If you know this woman, I would be very grateful for any information. In fact, allow me to show you how much." His hand reached into his pocket again and drew out a billfold. A moment later, three crisp 100-pound notes were in his hand. "Do you know her?"

"Just a moment," I stammered. Closing the door, I leaned against it and tried to breathe. It was a remarkably stupid idea to open the door to a man, no matter what he was offering. He was probably a murderer who sought out women who lived in shabby flats, knowing they'd open the door for the right price. The smart thing would be to lock the door, call the police, and hope he went away.

I didn't move from the spot.

But three hundred pounds meant I wouldn't have to take Eliza's handout again this month. I could do my part. I could even buy some groceries or set some aside in case my shitty waitressing skills kept me from earning enough for next month's bills. If he left, I'd regret it. Good fortune didn't usually find itself on my doorstep, and it might not bother calling again if I slammed the door on it now.

I straightened and drew my robe more tightly around my waist. There was no time to check the mirror, and after a night of drinking, I couldn't imagine the state I would be in. I slid the chain free with my index finger and opened the door.

The man had turned away as though he was about to leave, but he spun toward me now. His mouth was opened but whatever he was going to say died on his lips.

"How?" he breathed before shaking his head. "I'm sorry. You look like..."

"I'm Kate," I interrupted him. "That picture is of me."

I didn't know what else to say or what to expect. A few moments passed in stony silence as he stared at me as though trying to process these two facts. Finally, he held out the money. "I'd like to talk to you, Kate. May I come in?"

I stepped back, prayed he wasn't concealing an ax in his tailored suit jacket, and waved him inside. He stepped through the door, his eyes searching the flat as though he was looking for something. They stopped on the small table in the front room cluttered with empty wine bottles. Then landed on the ashtray full of Eliza's cigarette stubs. Other than that the place was very tidy, owing in no small part to our lack of worldly goods. The flat had been spartan when I moved in, and I hadn't brought more than a bag of clothes with me. Since then, we'd picked up a few cast-off pieces of furniture, accumulated a stack of newspapers, and not much else.

I spotted Eliza's bra peeking out from behind a pillow on the sofa, and I scrambled over to grab it. "Please have a seat," I said, sinking down and shoving it deep into the cushions.

He took an armchair we'd found in the second-hand shop around the corner, his fingers grazing over its worn arms. A look of distaste curled his upper lip, but he said nothing.

"Would you like a cup of tea?" I offered.

"Don't go to the trouble," he said, somehow making it

sound both polite and condescending at once. "I came to speak to you."

"Why?" I asked. I was nobody. He was sitting in the very proof of that fact now.

"That photograph I showed you," he began, hesitating for a moment before continuing, "to be honest, I'd hoped to find someone else here."

"Kerrigan?" I asked and his eyes widened.

"Yes..."

"That's what the ass who took that photo of me, without permission I might add, called me."

"Then, you haven't seen her?" Disappointment colored the question. When I shook my head, his shoulders slumped like branches sagging under their own weight. "I suppose I had hoped you might be..."

"Her?" I couldn't contain my surprise. "No, and I told that guy yesterday that." Had he really come all the way from London to see if I'd been lying? "I looked up Kerrigan last night. I doubt you're going to find her anywhere this...humble." It was the nicest way I could put it. It would have been more accurate to say that I doubted she would lower herself to even stepping one pedicured foot into West Bexby let alone take a cheap flat over a hair salon.

"You must forgive me. I'm just rather desperate to find her."

"Did you lose her?" I thought of the recent photos I'd seen on Kerrigan's social media accounts. Most of them included snow and Christmas decorations. It was late summer now, which meant she hadn't posted recently. No doubt her hundreds of thousands of followers were disappointed. Maybe one had finally tracked her down. "I'm sorry, but I don't know her or where she is."

"Neither do I," he admitted.

"Maybe that's what she wants."

"One would assume so since she ran away."

"Ran away?" I repeated.

"Yes. Around the holidays. Her stepmother and I assumed she wanted a break from all the parties. She left a note saying as much, but she hasn't returned," he said.

My mouth fell open as I realized who he was and why he was here. Instantly, I felt horrible for giving him so much attitude. "I'm so sorry. I didn't know she was missing, Mr..."

"Tod. Tod Belmond. Not missing exactly," he said. "We've had word. She's just left out some important details about when she plans to return home. I apologize. This probably all sounds very unusual."

Unusual was not the word I would use to describe it. Did rich people just do this? Check in and out of their lives on a whim? And over what? Growing bored going to tiresome parties? "I'm sorry that I couldn't help you."

"Actually, you might be able to, Miss...?"

"Kate is fine," I said.

"We believe Kerrigan might have cold feet, and I'm concerned that by the time she faces her fears, she may have done irreparable damage to her future," he started.

I nodded, trying to keep my eyes from rolling. There was nothing I could do about them. It sounded to me as though his daughter was a bit of a spoiled brat. "Why would she have cold feet?"

"We have an arrangement—it's very common among

families in our circle," he explained, choosing his words with obvious care. It hardly mattered. I could translate the meaning he was trying to skirt so delicately. Whatever the arrangement was, it was common between filthy rich people. People like him and his daughter. Not me. "Kerrigan is practically engaged to Spencer Byrd."

He paused as if expecting a response. Finally, I shrugged. "Good for them?"

"The Byrds hold a hereditary peerage and Spencer will be Duke of Wellesley when his grandfather passes. Our family and the Byrds have been planning this marriage since before Kerrigan was born," he informed me.

My mouth gaped open. "Seriously? An arranged marriage?"

"People like us do not marry without purpose. We must see to our estates and duties."

"You mean, keep rich people rich without actually doing anything?" I suddenly understood why Kerrigan had run away. Being forced to marry someone purely to uphold some agreement, made with no regard to my feelings, would make me want to run, too.

"If that is how you like to think of it." His smile was tight and forced. In the entire time he'd been here, he hadn't relaxed in the slightest. Maybe he was worried being poor would rub off on him.

"Regardless, I find myself in a predicament. The Byrds wish to announce the engagement, but my daughter refuses to come home. Arrangements need to be made. Introductions—"

"Introductions?" I interrupted him. "Do you mean she hasn't met the man you're marrying her off to yet?"

"Kerrigan is familiar with the Byrd family. Of course, she's met Spencer before, but it was years ago. They attended different universities, and haven't met since."

"I don't really see how I can help you." It was hard to feel sorry for him given that he was basically willing to sell his daughter to some random man with little thought to her feelings. Still, he had to be at least a bit worried about her well-being.

"You're wrong. You can help me," he said to my surprise. "You look just like her..."

"So, I've heard," I said slowly, a chilling sense of dread welling in my stomach.

Despite my body's warning, I wasn't prepared for what he said next. "I need you to pretend to be Kerrigan."

"What?" I shook my head, feeling a little dazed by this revelation. "I don't think I understand."

Be Kerrigan? Like it was a role I could just drop into? He was mental. I stared at her father, noticing for the first time the purple bruising under his eyes, a sign he wasn't sleeping well. He hid the truth behind an expensive suit and businessman manner, but it was there. He was worried. But I couldn't decide if he was worried about his daughter or his plans?

"Kerrigan will return," he said firmly. "It's simply a matter of biding time until she does. You really do look exactly like her. It would be easy to fool anyone into believing you were her."

I snorted at the thought. "I doubt that."

I might look like Kerrigan but I didn't know the first thing about her life. It wouldn't take a genius to see through me.

"You will be coached," he continued as if he knew what I was thinking. "We will arrange for you to have access to Kerrigan's friends."

"We?" Was there more than one insane person behind this idea?

"Myself and Kerrigan's assistant. Kerrigan told him everything. He is the perfect person to guide you, and he is the soul of discretion." His eyes pinched as if this last fact both impressed him and infuriated him.

"Her assistant?" I balked. Now I knew I was right. I was not the type of person to rely on an assistant. I wasn't even qualified to be an assistant myself.

He ignored me again. "It will be quite easy to extend the wedding planning, given the grandeur expected for the event, for over a year, which will give my daughter enough time to come to her senses. In the meantime, you will live in our family home in London, attend social functions, and serve as Spencer's companion in the upcoming social season."

"Wait." I held up a hand to stop him. This was an even crazier plot than I thought. "Mr. Belmond, are you telling me that you want me to pretend to be your daughter for an entire year?"

"If necessary. You will be compensated of course."

"That's never going to work," I said, unable to hold back a peal of laughter. "I don't know anything about your world or your family. People will see right through me. And what about Spencer? Don't you think he'll be a little upset if suddenly the real Kerrigan returns and he discovers he's been lied to?"

"That's why it's important that he not discover that," he said simply.

"I don't know what makes you think I can con someone like him for that long, but —"

"As I said, you will be groomed to do exactly what Kerrigan would do and say what Kerrigan would say. It might sound overwhelming now, but I think you'll find it worth your while."

"And why is that?" I asked defiantly.

"Because in exchange for one year of your cooperation, I will pay you ten million pounds."

CHAPTER FOUR

T he room seemed to shrink around me, closing in like
it was on the verge of collapsing. The offer rang in
my ears, but I couldn't seem to process what he said. I
stared at him, waiting for him to laugh or tell me I was on
camera. Across from me, Mr. Belmond waited patiently for
me to respond and showed no sign that this was some type
of trick.

"I'm sorry but did you say ten million pounds?"

"I believe it's more than fair compensation for what I'm
asking you to do. Of course, perhaps you enjoy your job at
the pub and your life here." He looked around the flat, his
eyes sparking with naked disdain.

Why would he offer me so much when it was clear that
he didn't have to? Anyone could see that I barely scraped
by on what I made. Ten million was an unfathomable
amount to someone like me. He could have tempted me
with much less. Unless...

"This is about more than playing dress-up and going to

some parties," I guessed in a low voice. "You wouldn't pay me ten million for that."

"Astute observation," he said, the disdain in his eyes shifting to flinty coldness. "While this marriage has been arranged, and is all but a done deal, no one can guarantee that Spencer won't back out of the arrangement."

Of course, poor Kerrigan was expected to do exactly as she was told, but the man could do as he wished. If he'd already agreed to the match, what might change his mind? Maybe he wouldn't like her company or he had a girlfriend or... A terrible thought occurred to me. Even if the marriage would occur after my ploy ended, there would be expectations before that.

"And you need me to make sure he doesn't," I whispered.

"It seems you understand me perfectly," he said, confirming my fear.

"You expect me to sleep with him?" I asked in a strangled voice. If that was the case, he was asking me to do more than simply play pretend. What he asked of me had a lot of other terms, none of which were particularly polite.

"That is at your discretion," he said, but a current of desperation ran through his words. "I simply ask that you encourage an attachment and keep him happy. I need you to keep his interest."

"I doubt that will be possible without—"

"As I said, it will be at your discretion to decide what needs to be done. I don't need to know any particulars in that regard," he said, turning slightly puce as if the thought of sex made him queasy. "I'm assuming you can handle those decisions for such generous compensation."

I swallowed, but my throat felt like the desert. My tongue seemed stuck in my mouth as I tried to work up the courage to respond.

He seemed to sense my hesitation. "If he wanted to sleep with you, would that be a problem? You aren't a virgin, are you?"

"No," I said quickly, hoping he didn't spot the lie. The reality was that I didn't know if I could sleep with a complete stranger in exchange for money, even ten million pounds, but I wasn't ready to say no to his proposal yet, either.

There was no way around it. The money would change my life. It would change almost anyone's life. I couldn't believe I was actually sitting here considering selling myself —selling my virginity—to some rich Londoner so some rich heiress could sip cocktails on a beach. But did I really have any other choice? Was I willing to say no and continue to scrape by, not making enough to live on and keeping my head down in a pub in the middle of nowhere? Still, I couldn't bring myself to say yes.

"Why are you doing it?" I asked him. That's what I needed to understand.

"I'm sorry?"

"The arranged marriage," I told him. "Why bother?"

"It is in the best interest of Kerrigan," he explained. "My own title won't pass to her."

"Because she's a girl?" I never understood how that little caveat had continued to exist amongst most of the aristocracy. Someone should write the king and tell him it was the twenty-first century.

"That would be the case under most circumstances. But as I'm only a Baron, my title isn't hereditary," he said. "A union between her and Spencer Byrd will ensure that she continues to rise in the London circles."

"Is that what she wants?"

There was a moment's pause as this hit him. It was clear he'd never considered the question.

"Of course it is," he said in a low voice, fury hiding in it as if he was offended that I might understand his daughter better than he did. "Why wouldn't she? She spent her whole life in this world. She must know how important it is to our, I mean, her future."

I suspected his interests were not as altruistic as he tried to make them out to be, especially after that little slip-up. But on the surface, I couldn't fault a father for wanting the best for his child. I just wasn't sure that marrying her in exchange for a title and fortune would make her happy in the long run.

"Can I think about it?" I asked him.

"Think about it?" He blinked as if he heard me wrong. "You need to think about an offer of ten million pounds?"

But I didn't budge. "I need to think about it. Is that a problem?"

"No. Of course, not." The strain in his voice said otherwise. "You have twenty-four hours."

I nodded. Surely, I didn't need more time than that to consider. "And if I say yes? Should I pack my bags?"

"That won't be necessary. You'll need to look the part as soon as you arrive in London."

I read between the lines of what he was saying. Nothing I owned from my well-worn plum-pink handbag to my underpants would help me pass as Kerrigan Belmond. "I understand."

Mr. Belmond stood from his seat and slipped a card from his pocket. I was beginning to wonder what else he had hiding in there. "When you've made a decision, please call me. I will remain in the area in the hopes of hearing from you."

I showed him to the door and said goodbye. As I closed it behind him, I studied the business card. It was printed on heavy, linen cardstock. Tod Belmond was printed in an elegant script. Under his name was his phone number and email address. I turned it over to find a coat of arms emblazoned with *Pertinacia, Patria Et Rex* on the back. I should look up what it meant. Maybe it would give me some insight into the Belmonds and whether I should say yes or no. I was so wrapped up in my thoughts I didn't hear Eliza enter the living room, not until she interrupted my thoughts and answered for me. "You'd be crazy to say no. Kate, you can't seriously be thinking about saying no."

CHAPTER FIVE

I nearly jumped out of my skin, dropping the card in the process as I shrieked, "You scared the shit out of me."

"Sorry," she said, sounding not at all apologetic. "Ok, let's back up a step and deal with the most important decision? Do we drink all the wine? Or something harder? I think we need a drink."

"It's nine in the morning," I told her as I bent to pick up Belmond's card from the floor.

"I think when you're propositioned for ten million pounds, alcohol is called for, regardless of the time of day." She picked up a few bottles off the table until she found one that still had some liquid sloshing around. She screwed off the cap and took a swig before passing it to me.

I took it and dropped onto the couch beside her. "What am I going to do?"

"Tell me everything," she said. "I only heard the ten million pounds part."

I filled her in on Kerrigan's father's strange proposal.

Eliza didn't say anything as I went over the specifics. When I finally stopped, she frowned. "And?"

"And what?" I asked, feeling as confused as ever.

"That's all you know?" she said with exasperation. "He just wants you to pretend to be his daughter for a year, date some rich guy who's going to be a Duke or something, and in the end pay you ten million pounds. What am I missing? Why are you hesitating? There must be something wrong with the guy she's supposed to marry."

She'd put into words all the thoughts tumbling around my own scattered brain with a clarity I envied. Right now, I probably couldn't remember what was up and what was down.

"I was wondering the same thing," I said grimly, considering her last point. There must have been a reason the real Kerrigan ran away, and it had to come down to the arranged marriage.

"Clearly, it's time to stalk him," Eliza said. She bounced up from the sofa and ran into her bedroom, returning with her mobile. Her thumbs were already tapping out his name on the screen. "Let's see... Byrd with a Y, right? That must be his grandfather. Here he is—oh wow!"

"What? How bad is it?" I asked anxiously, reaching to grab the phone.

"I mean..." She passed it to me and waited for me to take a look. "Do you think I could pass for Kerrigan? Because I have no qualms about being paid ten million pounds to pretend to be engaged to that. In fact, I might pay them to let me."

It wasn't hard to see what she was talking about. I'd

expected something else entirely. Tod Belmond had been clear that Spencer was about my age, so I knew he wouldn't be some disgusting, old guy about to kick the bucket, but I hadn't expected him to be...well, sexy. I scrolled through pictures of him from the search engine, ignoring the captions as I saw glimpses of the man Kerrigan was meant to marry. He had a strong straight jawline that was angular and powerful. In most photos, it sported a slight stubble that seemed to skirt the line between clean-shaven and a closely cropped beard. It was impossible to see the color of his eyes in most photos, particularly due to the dark lashes framing them. He always seemed to be cast in shadow or slightly turned from the camera, but there was no denying that he was handsome. Even in the photographs, he exuded a sort of primal masculinity that suggested he knew exactly how wealthy and privileged he truly was, and that he planned to enjoy everything that privilege afforded him.

I stopped on a photo of him on a beach, coming out of the waves, water rippling down his golden, muscled chest, and my mouth watered. Eliza peeked over to look at the screen and gasped.

"Now you've got to say yes," she said. "You cannot say no to that."

"It's not that simple," I said, tossing her phone back to her. It was too tempting to consider Belmond's proposal with Spencer's gorgeous face staring back at me. "I mean, am I really going to just waste a year of my life pretending to be some rich bitch?"

"Do you have better plans?" Eliza asked with a snort. "I mean, by all means, stay in Bexby, drink crap wine from

Tesco, and get evicted with me in a few months when we can't pay rent."

"That's another thing," I cried, latching on to the excuse she'd given me. "I'm your flatmate. I can't just leave —"

"Yes, you can," Eliza said in a firm voice that left no room for me to continue down that path. "I know we were joking before, but now I'm being serious. You have to say yes. You can't walk away from that kind of money."

"But he expects me to... you know..."

Her eyes widened, glinting with suppressed laughter. "Is that what you are worried about?"

"I've never done it before," I confessed.

"Trust me, you could do worse than giving your virginity to someone like Spencer Byrd." She sighed. "Much, much worse."

"But how could I go through with it?" I asked.

"It will be easy, darling." She looked at his photo on her mobile again. "Just close your eyes and think of England."

CHAPTER SIX

"Are you sure?" Eliza asked me for what must have been the hundredth time.

I shrugged my small duffel higher onto my shoulder and nodded. "Weren't you the one who wanted me to do this?"

"I don't want you to feel forced," Eliza said as we waited outside our building for the cab that had been arranged to drive me into London. Mr. Belmond had seen to all the arrangements as soon as I called him with my answer. "You'd be crazy to turn down ten million quid, but..."

"I'm crazy for thinking I can pull it off," I said, voicing the concern I knew was on both our minds. She had a point. I couldn't exactly say no to the offer, but that didn't mean I was prepared to fake being an heiress for an entire year. "What's the worst that can happen?"

"I can't believe you just said that!" Eliza shook her head, looking terrified at the question. "Let's see. You could say the wrong thing. You could offend someone. They could find out. You—"

"I get it," I interrupted her before she talked me out of getting in the car. "I didn't expect you to actually come up with a list." She'd clearly been putting some thought into this. Still, I had considered all of those things myself, and I'd come up with a solution. I would keep my head down and keep my mouth shut. How much trouble could I get into if I stayed quiet most of the time?

"So, have you thought more about... you know?" Eliza arched an eyebrow suggestively and made a gesture with her hands.

"What?" Trying to decipher her meaning.

"You know..."

"I don't," I said with confusion.

"About sleeping with Spencer." She dropped her voice to a low whisper, so no one passing us on the street would overhear.

"Oh. That," I said flatly. "Nope." That was a lie. I hadn't thought of anything else. The truth was that I was less afraid of messing this up, or saying the wrong thing—or even being found out—than I was at the prospect of going to bed with a man I'd never met. "Am I a terrible person for doing this?"

"People sleep with people for money all the time," she said, waving off my concern.

"Yeah," I said with a hollow laugh that seemed to echo in my chest. "They're called prostitutes."

"And trophy wives and gold diggers," she giggled.

"You're not helping." But I couldn't help laughing with

her. It was so utterly absurd to be in this situation. Only a few days ago I was worried about making my half of the rent, and now I was off to London to live in the lap of luxury for a year. I kept waiting to wake up from this insane dream I was having and discover I'd fallen and hit my head.

"I need to get to the pub," Eliza said, checking her watch. "Unless you want me to wait with you."

I did want her to wait, but I understood that Ron was expecting her. Given that he had found himself down a waitress, I couldn't keep her here without making his life harder. Eliza was pulling double duty until they could straighten things out at the pub. "No, you go. I feel terrible you have to cover for me."

"You'd cover for me if I had a chance at ten million pounds," she said, and I didn't disagree. Friends did not stand in the way of success. They helped you clear a path to it. Eliza had done just that. "Just buy me a tiara or something when you get your money."

"Done," I promised her. "And he said there will be a stipend, so I'll send rent."

"You don't have to do that," she said automatically, shooting me a tight smile. We both knew she meant it, even if it wasn't true. She did need me to help out, and I would. I couldn't just leave her behind without a second thought. Eliza lurched forward and gave me an awkward hug, whispering in my ear, "Call me and let me know you're okay."

"As soon as I get there."

"You're doing the right thing," she said, pulling away, her eyes shining like she might cry. "Even if it feels crazy."

"Are you sure?" I asked, echoing her earlier question.

"Life isn't worth living if you don't do something crazy now and then." She smiled brightly at me as if to drive the point home. "You've got this."

"I'll call you tonight," I called after her as she started down the block toward the Hare & Hound. It was strange to watch her walk away. She'd only been part of my life for a few months, but I couldn't help thinking as she disappeared around the corner that my old life was vanishing, too. It already felt like it was slipping away. Almost like I'd never existed. I hadn't exactly put a dent in the world. That was changing. I might not be Kerrigan Belmond, but in a year's time, I would have more money than I could even fathom. Considering that most of the time there was a negative symbol in front of my bank account balance, it was hard to imagine what it would be like on the other side of this arrangement. I could buy a house. I could travel. I could shop. I'd never really thought about any of those things before. My life had been about getting by and staying alive for as long as I could remember. What would my life look like when I wasn't in survival mode?

Before I could consider that question, a black car with windows tinted so darkly that I couldn't see inside pulled up to the front of my building. I took a step back from the street to allow whoever was inside to get out. It wasn't every day that a Mercedes found its way to Bexby. Actually, I'd never seen one in the sleepy village before. To my surprise, the driver opened the door and stepped out. He was dressed in a black suit and sporting a cap, which he tipped in my direction.

"Miss Belmond?" he asked me.

It took me a second to process two things: the first was that he wasn't wearing a suit. He was wearing a uniform. The second was that he was talking to me.

"Yes," I said, turning on a million-watt smile. "Sorry, I was expecting a cab."

"I think you'll find this more comfortable." He grinned at me as he opened the back passenger door.

I slid inside, doing my best to look like this wasn't the first time I'd done so. "Thank you."

"There's water and bourbon in the console," he informed me before closing the door and returning to the driver's seat.

I appreciated his suggestion. The back of the sedan was broken in two by a glossy center console that housed a small tablet. The seat's quilted leather nearly swallowed me as the seatbelt moved automatically within reach. I took it, wondering what I'd discover next. I studied the thin grooves etched into the gleaming surface before reaching to tap one. It opened and a cupholder rose in its place. Looking around I found another between the seats. It opened to reveal a refrigerated section that held water bottles and a bottle of the aforementioned bourbon. I took a bottle of water and placed it in the cupholder.

"Please let me know if I can see to your comfort," he told me as he started the car with a push of a button.

I did my best not to ogle as I took in the elegant stitching along with the leather upholstery. An emblem emblazoned with the word Maybach informed me what kind of car I was in. I made a mental note to consider buying one of my own when my money came through in a year's time. I would be responsible with most of it, but maybe a splurge or two wouldn't hurt. Then again, this wasn't exactly a low-profile vehicle. Once the ruse was over and I no longer had the cover of Kerrigan's name, I needed to keep myself off the radar. My hand skirted over the buttery leather armrest to the tablet, discovering that offered me a variety of options from extending a footrest to a massage. I chose both, feeling that I might as well spoil myself while I had the chance.

The drive to London was largely pastoral when we reached the edge of the village, complete with rolling hills and cattle. Between the massage, which went all the way to my calves, and the smooth ride, my eyes were growing heavy. I glanced at the shiny new mobile phone that had arrived at my flat this morning with a note that I should read a collection of dossiers that had been loaded onto it. I'd planned to spend the journey doing just that, but as I relaxed into the first moments of my new, temporary life, I decided a nap couldn't hurt.

A LOUD HONK WOKE ME AND I BOLTED UPRIGHT, ONLY to be dragged back by the seat belt fastened around me. It took me a moment to remember where I was. Looking out the window, I gasped to see myself surrounded by traffic and buildings and people. The streets outside the car were teeming with activity. How long had I been asleep? A quick check of my phone told me that it had been over an hour. Panic gripped me as I realized the bustling scene outside the car was London. We were already here, and I hadn't done a thing to prepare.

After coaxing the belt to loosen, having panicked itself when I jolted forward and locked me in place, I leaned forward and called to the driver, "Are we close?"

"Nearly there, but it will be a bit with traffic," he said over his shoulder. "I trust you had a nice nap."

"Too nice," I muttered, wishing I had a breath mint. I tapped a few more consoles and found some. I guess I wasn't the only one who had fallen asleep back here.

"We had to make a small detour due to road work, but we should be in Hampstead shortly."

"We've reached London, though?" I asked, peering outside. The city was starting to give way to quieter stretches.

"Kinda," he said with a shrug. "That was Watford. We don't have to go into the city proper, thankfully. It would be hours, but they reopened the M25. This construction makes getting anywhere impossible, but we're nearly to Hampstead."

We hadn't even been in London proper? My memories of London were loud and jarring, full of flashing colors and swarms of people. I was surprised we'd only passed through a suburb, but I was also grateful for the construction delays. It gave me time to cram some of the information I'd neglected to study.

Grabbing my mobile from the console, I opened the folder marked Kerrigan on the home screen and began to scan through the notes. A sinking feeling dragged at me. This wasn't just a few collected facts, there were pages and pages of information. It was like someone had been writing her autobiography. Instantly, I regretted sleeping. I'd promised myself I would arrive as prepared as possible. According to Mr. Belmond, only a few people were to know the facts of my arrangement with him. Even his new wife was being kept in the dark. Given that she was nearly my age and had barely known him a year—thank you, Google—he didn't seem worried about my ability to fool her. Considering that I was expected to live in the same house as her, I didn't share his certainty.

I was only on the second file—a play-by-play of Kerrigan's private primary school days—when the car slowed in front of a gate.

The driver rolled down his window and spoke into a callbox, "Miss Belmond is home."

I ignored the shivering thrill that raced through me at that proclamation and turned my attention to the gates. The wrought iron groaned and began to swing open, affording me a glimpse of the place I'd agreed to call home.

CHAPTER SEVEN

When I'd been told I would move to London and live in the Belmond family home, I hadn't expected a mews but I wasn't prepared for an estate. It wasn't the sort of place I pictured people living when they claimed to live in London. Hampstead wasn't full to bursting with people, houses and shops stacked on top of one another. Nor was it a sleepy village. It was practically a different world. I thought only the King and Queen lived in large residences with gardens and endless rooms. Apparently, I was wrong—very wrong.

I swallowed back the gasp that threatened to escape my mouth as I took in the behemoth before me, reminding myself that the real Kerrigan would never be so impressed by a place she'd been tens of thousands of times. But it wasn't easy. The house, if it could be called that, sat behind a tall brick wall, which afforded privacy by obscuring the estate from view. Panels had been cut and secured to the iron gates to block out even the nosiest of passersby.

Considering what lay beyond those gates, I could understand why. Most people in the city lived in cramped flats
and visited parks to enjoy green space. That wasn't necessary for the Belmonds, it seemed. They had space both
inside and out.

The Mercedes continued, once the gates were fully
open, down the private drive. Behind me, I heard the gates
close with an ominous rattle as we were swallowed into a
lush garden. It was a riot of flowers, blooming in colorful
masses. Large trees towered along the perimeter of the wall
blocking the residence from the street leading to it. We
continued along the drive only a short way, even the
wealthiest Londoners had to put up with some limitations,
I supposed. Maneuvering the long car around a fountain,
the driver parked and got out to open my door.

I did my best not to get caught staring as I stepped into
the afternoon light and took in the grand expanse in front
of me. Neatly trimmed hedges ran the length of the house,
a large brick Edwardian home greeted me, complete with a
small tower, circled with windows, overlooking the front
garden. It was imposing: far grander than any place I'd ever
been. My pulse quickened as I studied it.

"I'll bring this inside," the driver said, holding up the
bag he'd retrieved from the boot.

"I can do—" But he was gone before I could tell him I
would handle it. Quickly, I realized it would be a mistake to
carry my own bag. I assumed Kerrigan didn't do such
things. She had probably never carried anything heavier
than a Chanel handbag in her life.

I found myself frozen to the spot, staring at the house

and listening to the tinkling spray of water from the nearby fountain. I'd expected someone to be there to greet me. Did Tod Belmond just expect me to walk inside, kick off my shoes, and make myself at home? I took a cautious step forward as if I might discover I'd simply found myself in a mirage. The paving stones were firm under my foot. Solid. Real. As real as I was, but I was playing a part. Perhaps, that's why I couldn't get a grip on my new reality.

As I took a second step, the front door burst open and a statuesque woman appeared.

"Kerrigan!" she called, and my stomach flipped.

I'd seen her photo in the files I'd skimmed through quickly. Tod Belmond's third wife. My stepmother. I knew a few facts about her. She was only four years older than Kerrigan and me, which made me a little nauseous. They had married less than a year ago after a whirlwind romance. She'd been a dancer, ballet or something respectable. I'd thought she'd look pretty in her picture. In real life, she was gorgeous. Easily the most beautiful woman I'd ever met. Her dark, yet luminous eyes were set over regal cheekbones. Her deep brown skin was flawless, made all the more striking by the ivory silk she wore. The clothing draped over her with sophisticated ease, rippling across her flawless figure as she strode toward me.

"I'm so delighted you're back at Willoughby Place," she said, and then, to my shock, she threw her arms around me. "I feel certain we're going to be the best of friends."

"I'm glad to be home," I murmured, feeling more confused than ever. "It's been..." I cursed myself for napping instead of preparing.

"Too long," she said. "You didn't even come home for Christmas." She looped her arm through mine and continued, leading me inside, completely oblivious to my discomfort, "I was concerned that you might be angry—about the elopement, I mean. It was so last minute, and Tod felt—"

"I'm not angry," I cut her off quickly. I wasn't, but Kerrigan might be. That was her problem to sort out. I was just grateful that she seemed nice and blissfully ignorant that I was a fraud.

"Oh, I'm so glad! And you must call me Iris. I know there was never a discussion about the stepmother thing," she said in a lowered voice, "but I hope it won't be awkward. It will be so nice to have another woman in the house."

"Okay, Iris," I said, trying on the name. I was grateful I wouldn't have to call her mum. That would have added a layer of weirdness to a situation that was already teetering on too surreal to maneuver.

"Are you tired?" she asked as we stepped into the marble entry.

I gawked for a moment as I drank in the opulent setting. The interior of the house was vastly different than the exterior. Everything had been remodeled into a sleek, modern mansion. Overhead a cluster of starburst chandeliers hung at varying lengths. Sliding doors were open on each side, revealing glimpses of luxurious sitting rooms, and a grand staircase waited in the center, leading to the upper levels of the home.

"I fell asleep in the car," I confessed after I managed to get ahold of myself.

"It's too comfortable!" she exclaimed with a laugh. "I can't stand being driven if I'm alone, because I start to doze. But if you're not tired, then I hope you won't mind lunch. You can say no. I promise not to be offended."

My stomach grumbled at the idea of food. "Lunch would be good."

"Wonderful. I'll let you change." She managed to say this without a hint of judgment, but I realized then that although I was wearing a nice pair of black trousers and a simple t-shirt, I looked woefully out of place.

"Thanks," I offered, wondering if I might be able to find my room without drawing suspicion.

"I made sure your closet was changed for the season. It seems no one got around to doing so since the fall. Of course, we'll pick up some new pieces. I've been dying for a shopping partner," she gushed.

I nodded, starting toward the stairs and hoping I hadn't made a calculated error. Before I reach the bottom step, a ding stopped me, and I turned to see the lift doors slide open. I'd been so caught up in all the other spectacular elements of my new home that I hadn't even noticed it. A man in a well-cut linen suit stepped out.

"Good, I caught you," he called, his deep voice bouncing off the marble floor and booming around me.

"Giles is quite pleased you're back, too." She smiled warmly at him. "He's been helping me get ready all morning for your arrival."

"Yes, Miss Belmond," he said, moving toward me in a businesslike clip and ignoring Iris altogether. "I have an itinerary for you to review. Perhaps, I can accompany you to your quarters."

I flipped through the mental files I'd managed to absorb and remembered that Giles was Kerrigan's assistant. I nodded enthusiastically at my savior. "Of course. I do have lunch with Iris, though."

"Of course," he repeated my own words, continuing past me on the staircase without a backward glance at either of us. "This won't take long."

"I'll be in the library," Iris said. "Take your time and get settled."

I gulped, forcing a smile in response, and started up the stairs, toward my new life.

CHAPTER EIGHT

I caught up to Giles, who had already started down a hall, and opened my mouth, only to have him hold up a hand.

"Perhaps, we should wait," he said. It was perfectly polite, and he was right, but I had the oddest sense of being a child told to hold her tongue at the table.

I followed him in silence, padding across plush Persian runners, past art that looked dangerously expensive until he stopped in front of a door. He turned the knob and opened it for me.

"Your rooms," he said with the slightest emphasis.

Rooms? I managed to swallow the question since we weren't inside and safely behind a closed door. It wasn't a bedroom that we entered but rather a sitting room, taste-fully decorated in shades of light blue. Heavy, silk drapes in icy silver were drawn, allowing the late morning light to filter into the space. A velvet couch, a small table with a stack of magazines, and two upholstered chairs were clustered around an unlit hearth. There wasn't a spec of dust anywhere. It looked as though the occupant might have left this morning, not months ago.

"Mrs. Belmond will want you to change," Giles said, looking me up and down with an expression that said he understood why and agreed with the request.

My gaze fell on the duffel I'd brought with me from Bexby. It had been delivered to the rooms ahead of me. I had a few outfits in there, even a nice dress. Despite what Iris had said I wasn't certain I could literally step into Kerrigan's shoes. Not yet, at least.

Giles followed my gaze and rolled his eyes. "Don't even think about it. If this ensemble is any indication, nothing in that bag is suitable."

"You don't know—"

"Kerrigan Belmond has never worn an item of clothing that cost less than a hundred pounds," he informed me.

My mouth formed a small O. Of course she hadn't. She'd probably never checked the sales rack at Zara or worn a hand-me-down like the dress I'd been considering, a gift from Eliza.

"This way," he said impatiently.

I barely had time to process the bedroom he led me through, complete with a sumptuous four-poster bed and too many pillows to count before I found myself in an octagonal room. Mirrors lined every wall and it was empty save for a pin-tucked stool and fur rug in the center of the room. Giles walked up to a mirror and waved a hand over it. Instantly, a crack appeared in the glass and it opened to reveal rows and rows of shoes.

Glossy, patent-leather black shoes. Prim, round-toed suede heels. Sky-high, strappy sandals. There had to be over one hundred pairs of shoes, all neatly lined up on shelves, waiting for their owner to return.

"The first rule to passing as Kerrigan," Giles said, "is looking like her. She always chooses her shoes first and then creates her outfit around it."

He said this like she crafted a work of art. I shook my head. "I don't really wear heels."

"You do now," he said dismissively. "Pick a pair."

"That's it?" I asked. "Then what?"

"I will help you pick an outfit that Kerrigan would put together."

"Did she always have you do this?" I asked, trying to buy myself time. I had no idea which shoes Kerrigan would pick or what was appropriate for a lunch date with my twenty-six-year-old stepmother. It felt like a test, and I was going to fail.

"Rarely. Kerrigan had impeccable taste," he said. "She didn't require me to dress her."

"Had?"

"Has," he corrected himself.

"I don't want her to be angry when she comes back. What if I break a heel?" *Or my ankle?*

This earned me an eye roll that was neither inconspicuous nor good-humored. It was clear that while Giles might know Kerrigan well enough to help me, he wasn't thrilled at the prospect. "She'll buy new shoes. Just pick."

I ran a finger along the shelf, stopping on a pair of relatively stable-looking wedges. They weren't nearly as sexy as most of the others, but they had the benefit of a bit of a platform. Most of Kerrigan's other shoes could be used as murder weapons. Still, the white leather straps were thin and delicate and the platform would easily push me five inches off solid ground. Before I could look for something less tall, Giles noticed my pause and seized them.

"These will be fine."

I stepped back and watched as he opened more doors hidden within the mirrored walls, picking hangers with practiced ease. He stopped and arched an eyebrow.

"Are you going to change or..."

"Oh, um." I shifted uncomfortably.

"Kerrigan is very comfortable with her body," he advised.

"And if I'm not?" I asked defensively.

He resumed pillaging the closet, talking over his shoulder. "I would suggest you become comfortable. There's a party tomorrow night. Spencer will be there. I expect things will progress rapidly."

Apparently, Giles was going to force me to read between the lines. Except that I needed more than that from him. "Look, you don't have to treat me like I'm her, but I'm not an idiot either. Just tell me what you're trying to say."

"Alright." He stopped and turned to face me, clutching something lacy. "If you can't get naked around me, how do you plan to do so around Spencer?"

"I—I—" I'd pushed him to be honest, but now I wished I hadn't. The surreality of my situation was wearing off quickly, and in its place was a rather harsh reality. I'd agreed to act as Kerrigan. I'd known I would be expected to sleep with Spencer. I suppose I'd imagined a lights-off, under-the-sheets experience. "You're right," I admitted finally. "I guess this is a lot to digest. Thank you for being honest with me. It's nice to have an anchor in the storm."

For the first time, Giles smiled. Stretching out one hand, he offered me the lingerie he'd gathered. My outfit was draped over his other arm, which held onto the shoes that had inspired his choices. "This is a rather unusual predicament. I promise to help you navigate it as Kerrigan would."

"And she would already be down to her birthday suit?" I guessed.

"If it makes you feel better, I've seen her naked a thousand times. It's hardly anything exciting."

"Am I terrible if that makes me feel better and worse?" I asked him.

"Not at all."

I took a deep breath and closed my eyes, remembering what Eliza had said. This was the first of many uncomfortable situations I'd signed up for when I agreed to her father's plan. I thought of the ten million pounds. Once I had it, I could slip away, start over, and finally start a real life. That was enough incentive.

A short while later, I stood in front of the mirror, processing the transformation Giles had achieved. When he'd first handed his choices, I'd been skeptical. To go with the wedges, he'd chosen a pair of airy, wide-legged linen pants in a summery white. They rose high on my waist, tapering in at the narrowest point with two precise, sophisticated pleats. The silk blouse he'd selected was thin and nearly sheer, cropped to showcase the highrise of the pants.

"Less is more for a luncheon," he told me, handing me the largest pair of diamond solitaire earrings I'd ever seen.

"Are these real?" I asked, nervously, as I poked them through my lobes.

He paused and considered. "Do you want to know?"

"No," I said swiftly. If one of them fell out, I didn't want to think about losing a diamond approximately the size of a small boulder.

Giles finished putting a few items into a handbag and passed it to me. I took it, studying the quilted leather and its interlocking CC logo.

"Lipstick, keys, identification, and I put my number in your mobile," he informed me.

"Identification?" I repeated with surprise. I opened the clasp and found a driver's license. Kerrigan's face stared at me. I scanned it quickly. "But why wouldn't she take this..."

"She took her passport," Giles said. "Wherever she went, she didn't need to drive, it seems." He reached over and fluffed my hair over my shoulder. I'd sat still long enough for him to show me how she curled the dark locks we shared with an iron. He'd even walked me through her daytime cosmetic routine, which I was grateful turned out to be relatively low maintenance for someone who planned her wardrobe around her shoes.

I looked in the mirror one more time and found a stranger staring back at me. I'd seen her pictures, but until this moment, I'd questioned how everyone else saw such a resemblance. This morning, I'd shoved unruly hair into a ponytail and slipped into what I thought was a dressy outfit. Then I'd been whisked away from Bexby in the safe confines of the Belmond's car and delivered here, where Giles had overseen the final stage of my physical transformation. The reflection showed no sign of Kate. I'd emerged from my cocoon with bouncing curls, full, painted lips, and the kind of sophistication that could only be bought. I'd become Kerrigan Belmond.

It had taken me nearly an hour to dress, so by the time, Giles went over a few more, important points and led me back downstairs to the library, I was starving and ashamed. I darted inside, the Chanel clutch under my arm. "I'm so sorry that I made you wait."

Iris looked up from the tablet she was holding—apparently, the hundreds of books surrounding her on the walnut shelves weren't to her taste—and blinked. "I expected you to take longer."

I drove my lips into a smile and shrugged, realizing that Kerrigan wasn't likely to apologize for taking too long getting ready. "I suppose I'm hungry."

"Well, our reservation isn't for two more hours, but we could hit the shops near Hillgrove's," she said brightly. "But if you're terribly hungry, I can call and have them move it up."

"I can wait," I said. After visiting Kerrigan's closet, I sensed she was unlikely to turn down a shopping trip.

"Excellent! This is going to be wonderful."

Within an hour, I'd realized two things: Iris had meant everything she said about wanting to be friends and that I had never really been shopping in my life. Not by Belmond standards. When we'd reached Sloane Street in Belgravia, I'd recognized the designer names gracing the shop doors. Inside the first boutique, I'd made the mistake of peeking at a price tag and nearly fainted, uncertain if it was the item's cost or the phone number to a helpline for shopping addicts.

Iris seemed more suited to this life than I was. If she saw a piece she liked, she just picked it up and handed it to the shop girl charged with attending to the every need of the two of us.

"Aren't you going to get anything?" she asked me as we stood admiring a collection of silk scarves.

"I don't really wear scarves," I said without thinking and instantly wished I hadn't. Maybe Kerrigan loved scarves. There were several parts of her closet that I hadn't seen inside yet.

"They're such lovely accessories," Iris said, fingering the edge of one. She didn't seem surprised by my proclamation. "You can never have too many."

"Which one should I get?" I asked her. The truth was that I had no idea where to start and without some help, I was going to just have to start pointing at random things and hope I chose wisely.

"This is a lovely shade of blue," she said, holding it up. "Your father mentioned it's your favorite color."

I tucked that bit of information into my brain for safekeeping. "It is," I agreed. "I'll take this one."

"I'll wrap it up for you, Miss Belmond," the shop girl said, moving to place the scarf in an orange box.

"You'll have to show me how to wear it," I told Iris.

She beamed back at me. "I'd love to. I think—"

Before she could finish the thought, a hand appeared on her shoulder as an older woman with silver-blonde hair cut into a short, chic bob stepped beside us. "Iris! What a pleasant surprise." She turned and gasped when she saw me. For a heart-stopping moment, I thought I'd been found out. Instead, she reached to squeeze my arm. "And Kerrigan! Your father mentioned you were back in town, but I hadn't expected to see you until tomorrow night. Spencer is looking forward to it."

"S-so am I," I stammered as I started to piece together what was happening.

"I wish we could stay, but I'm heading to lunch with my daughter at Hillgrove's."

"Oh, we're on our way there," Iris said without missing a beat.

"You must join us," Spencer's mother said, and my heart sank as she waved to a younger girl, who was examining a pair of sunglasses. "Evie would be delighted for the company."

For a moment, I considered faking a stomach cramp. I wasn't ready. Giles had barely scratched the surface of what I needed to know. I wasn't prepared to impress his mother or speak to his sister. Going with them now could only end in disaster, but before I could come up with an excuse, Iris grinned widely.

"We'd love to join you."

CHAPTER NINE

As soon as we reached Hillgrove's, which proved to be nearly as posh as the nearby shops, I excused myself to the loo. Iris was busy seeing to a larger table than she'd reserved, and the Byrds would be joining us after they finished with their purchases down the street. I was hoping that might buy me some time to send a plea for help. Locking myself inside a stall, I sent a panicked message to Giles on the mobile he'd given me. I sank onto the toilet and waited. After five minutes I gave up. Placing my mobile back in my handbag, I reminded myself that this meeting was inevitable. So what if I was supposed to have one more day? Was twenty-four hours going to do that much to ready me?

Gathering my lone shopping bag and purse, I reached to unlock the door as a sudden bang shook the thin wall shared by the adjoining stall. I bit back a yelp as a breathy giggle floated through the air.

"Here? Someone might hear us," the voice behind the giggle said.

"I can't wait," a gruff voice, oozing with sex, replied. "I need to fuck you now."

I froze, too embarrassed to interrupt whatever was going on in the adjoining stall. The wall between us ran from ceiling to floor, but the material was flimsy enough that I could hear every movement. I wouldn't be discovered unless I made noise and opening my door would definitely make noise. Clutching my purse against my chest, I sent up a prayer that someone else would walk in and scare off the couple.

"They're waiting for you," she simpered but there was no fire behind her argument. She'd agreed to whatever he wanted from the moment they'd ducked into the ladies' room.

"And I'm so bored I'm about to fall asleep. I need to do something that gets my blood pumping." The wall shook with a sudden jolt, and I heard the woman moan.

"We need to hurry," she whispered at the sounds of rustling fabric and ripping foil. Something slammed into the wall, followed by a throaty groan of pleasure that sent a gush of molten desire between my legs. I couldn't see anything, but I could hear the slap of bare flesh colliding and the primal sounds of pleasure.

A string of filthy encouragement started as the wall vibrated with their thrusts. "That's right. Ride my cock. God, I love the way your tits bounce when I'm fucking you," he grunted.

"Oh my god," she cried out, and suddenly I found my own hand reaching to unfasten the waistband of my trousers. I slipped a finger down the lacy knickers I was wearing, more delicate and sexy than any I'd ever owned before. Propping myself against the far wall, I closed my eyes and imagined I was the one with my legs wrapped around the stranger, taking his cock. I circled the swollen bud frantically, building alongside them, too desperate to soothe the ache ravaging me to feel ashamed for what I was doing.

A choking sound, as though a hand was being used to muffle a scream of pleasure, pushed me over the edge, and I threw my own arm over my face, biting down on my skin to keep from being heard as I came on my hand. I rode out the lingering spasms in silence, my hips bucking wantonly to the sound of their final climaxes.

"Whoa, steady there," I heard a low warning as the sound of feet hitting the floor echoed in the otherwise empty restroom.

"Just a little shaky. How do I look?" the breathy woman asked.

"Like you just shagged a patron in the loo." Arrogance replaced the gruff sexiness.

I found myself wanting to see the man on the other side of the stall, wishing it was me in there with him.

"Maybe you won't be so bored at your lunch meeting now," she said with a giggle.

"Well, I won't be complaining about the wait staff's attention to detail."

Another giggle.

It was a waitress in here, screwing a businessman. A

surge of envy roared through me, unexpected and over-whelming. Why couldn't I be that open and willing? Why was I the one afraid to get undressed in front of a stranger? Why was I the one pleasuring myself in muted silence to the sounds of other people's orgasms?

"Let me sneak out first, and I will make sure you get that fresh bourbon you ordered," the woman said. "Thanks for the shag, Mr. Byrd."

My hand was still in my pants when she said his name and I barely bit back a cry of surprise. It had to be a coinci-dence. I hadn't just sat here and got off on listening to the man I was expected to court screwing someone else. I with-drew my hand shakily as I made to button my pants. I'd wait for them to leave, slip quietly into the restaurant, and casually ask Mrs. Byrd if her son was here. But would that give me away? Surely, she would say something. There had to be plenty of people with that surname in London. I'd almost convinced myself as I heard the door open and close. I waited for a moment and breathed a sigh of relief.

"Hello?" the man's voice called, and I realized my error. The waitress was going out first, probably to avoid being spotted.

I stayed perfectly still, hoping he let it go, and waited, but there were no sounds of footsteps or opening doors. It worked.

"Once more unto the breach," he muttered to what he must now believe an empty room. I held my breath, distracting myself by trying to place the quote. Just a few more seconds and he'd disappear into the busy restaurant and back to his business.

Footsteps echoed in the air, moving toward the exit, just as a chime broke the silence, alerting me to an incoming text. I scrambled to get my mobile out of my bag and silence it but the damage was done.

"I thought I heard someone." There was a predatory edge to his voice now that made me want to be caught, followed by a low chuckle that made me shiver. "You could have joined us."

I bit my lip and kept my eyes clenched shut, clutching my mobile like a life raft.

"I hope you enjoyed it, dirty girl," he said before finally leaving me alone with my hammering heart and wet panties.

CHAPTER TEN

I was ravenous by the time I reached the table where Iris sat chatting with Mrs. Byrd and her daughter. The two had finished their shopping while I was trapped in the loo. They looked up at me as I joined them, and I did my best to act normally.

"There she is!" Iris said. "I ordered you your favorite. At least, according to your father. I hope you don't mind. I know I made you wait to eat."

"Thank you," I said softly, taking the empty seat between Iris and Spencer's sister. I had no idea what Kerrigan's favorite was, and I prayed it wouldn't turn out to be something disgusting like snails or whatever places like this served to people with too much money. Picking up the linen napkin at my place setting, I laid it on my lap.

"I'm so chuffed to meet you. I'm actually shaking, see?" She held up her hand to demonstrate.

"Oh! Me too." I hoped that any lingering color on my cheeks would be excused as excitement or nerves.

"I've always wanted a sister and—"

"*Evelyn*," her mother cut her off sharply. "Kerrigan doesn't want to hear about that. There's still a lot to be decided. Let's give her a few hours to settle into being home again."

The youngest Byrd looked very little like her mother. Whereas the elder exhibited the poise of a woman accustomed to walking amongst the highest rings of society, Evelyn seemed about to bubble over at any moment like a kettle left on the heat too long. They shared the same fair skin, but age had hewn the older woman into sharp angles that were polished with expensive clothes and jewelry. Evelyn was curvy and round, her cheeks as rosy and warm as her artless smile. She wore a simple floral dress that had been chosen to flatter her ample figure but had none of the tailored couture of her mother's structured, navy blue sheath.

"I don't mind, Mrs. Byrd," I said, taking a sip of water from a crystal goblet.

"Please call me Caroline," she corrected me. "We are practically family."

"I don't mind, Caroline," I backpedaled, starting to feel as though I was suffering from whiplash. Things needed to be decided, but we were practically family? Next to me, Iris fidgeted in her chair a little as if she was thinking the same thing.

"You must tell us what you're wearing to the reception tomorrow," Caroline said, tipping her chin as her eyes narrowed ever so slightly. She was appraising me. It was the first day of class, and she was here presenting me with a pop quiz.

"I haven't really thought about it," I admitted.

Iris went rigid beside me, telling me that I had answered incorrectly.

"But it's tomorrow," Caroline pressed.

"Mum, let her alone." Evie shook her head, rolling her eyes with the passion only a teenage girl could muster. "Not everyone cares about clothes."

"Someone must, Evie darling." She turned to Iris conspiratorially. "If I didn't put clothes in her closet, this one would go about naked—and that would be disastrous."

I saw the glide of her daughter's throat as she swallowed the subtle insult her mother had lobbed in her direction.

"I like clothes, but I prefer shoes," I said, trying to shift the topic of conversation before Caroline could toss another dart at Evelyn. "I already chose those. I always start my outfits by choosing my shoes."

"Oh, I like that," Evie said.

"You and I should go shoe shopping," I said. "What are you wearing tomorrow?"

"Um," she hedged, glancing toward her mother, "I was thinking about this rose-colored gown that—"

"It doesn't suit you, darling," Caroline stopped her. "I had Lana steam that new black dress I picked up for you at Harrods."

Evie nodded, her smile cracking at the edges.

"Perhaps, I'll wear black as well," I said, trying to lift

her spirits without insulting Caroline. I was having a hard time not rounding the table and dumping my water over the woman's head. She deserved it, but Kerrigan Belmond would never do such a thing. "We could be twins."

"Oh, I've always wanted—"

"Black will wash you out," Caroline said to me. "I was thinking something ivory or perhaps white."

Something bridal, I realized, because those colors wouldn't wash me out.

"Then we'll contrast each other," I whispered to Evie, and she grinned.

"Of course, it would be nice if you'd gotten more sun while you were away," Caroline continued, her eyes skirting across my arms. "You're fortunate that you have that lovely olive undertone in your skin, but I would imagine it would be even lovelier if you sunbathed. I know I can never get enough sun when I'm in Cannes. That is where you went on your little pre-marital gap period?"

I could almost swear I saw a glimpse of claws under her careful questioning. Kerrigan's absence had been noted by the matriarch. What questions had that raised?

"I was there for a bit," I lied. I'd never been to France in my life. "But then I found myself just wandering where my heart took me."

"How bohemian." To her credit, she managed to make this sound only mildly insulting. I had no doubt she'd muzzled her disdain.

"I think it's so smart for a woman to take time to get to know herself before she gets married," Iris interjected.

"Life changes so much after saying 'I do.' It's important to know who you are before you make such an important commitment."

"I suppose that's how it's done now. When I married my late husband, I wasn't even out of university, but that was ages ago. You should listen to your stepmother, she's been down the aisle more recently than I." She smiled at Iris, but no hint of the sweetness of her lips reached her eyes. They remained narrowed and wary.

I was starting to understand the game we were playing. Caroline Byrd had positioned herself as the head of the table, a spot she intended to keep by bullying and making casually cruel remarks.

"I will. Thank you." I turned to Iris. "I really do want to hear all the details of what I missed while I was away. I'm still adjusting to father being married again."

Caroline snorted into her water goblet. "That man is a serial groom."

"He believes in love," Iris said with quiet courage. "As do I. We're lucky to have found each other."

I found myself wanting to know the man Iris had fallen in love with. Kerrigan's father hadn't struck me as a particularly sympathetic or loving soul, but Iris was one of the sweetest people I'd ever met. If she saw that side to him, might it be there?

Our lunches arrived, saving us from more of Caroline's passive-aggressive tactics. I breathed a sigh of relief when a simple omelet was put in front of me.

"Would you like some bread?" the waiter asked, and I

nodded. He placed a fresh roll on the rim of the china plate and turned to offer one to Evie.

"No, thank you." She kept her eyes trained on the filet of chicken and roast vegetables that had been placed before her.

I looked over to Caroline who was watching the interaction like a hawk, prepared to swoop down and attack should her daughter make the wrong choice. She relaxed in her seat a little, opening her mouth to refuse the bread before the waiter had even asked.

"Nonsense," I spoke up, stopping him. "Without bread, how are you going to help me eat this butter?"

"She makes a good point," Iris said, latching on to what I was doing. "I'll have two please."

Across the table, Caroline seethed quietly, shaking her head when the waiter finally asked her. The rest of the meal was fraught with a number of pointed questions and barbed remarks. I managed to dodge the traps she laid for me and began to perfect the art of subtly sticking up for Evie. It helped that Iris was there to back me up.

"Thank you for inviting us to join you," Iris said graciously as the waiter arrived. She beckoned for the bill.

"Oh no, I insist that you let me pay," Caroline started.

"Actually," the waiter turned to his cart and produced a bucket and champagne, "the gentleman over there has already paid and sent this as his compliments along with this note."

Caroline looked over at the table the waiter indicated and laughed. "It seems your brother is here, but couldn't be bothered to join us."

I got my first glimpse of the man I was expected to marry across a crowded room. He'd stood to leave and he paused, his hand reaching to button his suit jacket. I'd seen his picture online, but it hadn't captured the raw sensuality he possessed. It radiated off him. All around him, eyes turned, but his eyes met mine and an electric current seemed to crackle through the air. Had everyone else felt that? I turned away, my cheeks flushing. I was on edge after the luncheon with his mother and after what I'd heard in the loo. The thought of the loo sent the dizzying sensation in my stomach crashing down. I wanted to believe it was still a coincidence. Then, I remembered that it hardly mattered. His marriage was an arrangement. He owed nothing, especially not to me. I wasn't even the woman he was destined to marry.

Caroline held her hand out for the note, but the waiter shook his head. Instead, he passed it to me. "It's for you. He asked you to read it in private."

His mother turned a puzzled look in his direction. Then, directed it at me. "How odd."

"But they knew each other as children?" Iris pointed out.

"Yes, but it's hardly appropriate given the arrangement for—"

"Mother," Evie interrupted, "it's just a note."

My heart started pounding as I took it and continued to do so during our farewells and all the way home while Iris discussed tomorrow's event—the night where I would be formally introduced to a man I already felt I knew intimately.

As soon as we reached Willoughby Place, I headed to my rooms to put away my shopping. Stepping inside, I closed the door and unfolded the note.

Next time, dirty girl.

CHAPTER ELEVEN

Despite its lush comfort, I didn't sleep well in Kerrigan's bed the first night. Instead, I laid in the silky sheets, pillows around my entire body like a fortress, and rehashed the day's events. Tod had stayed late in the office, working to secure a multi-billion dollar real estate parcel, according to Iris. After barely managing to keep my cool with Caroline Byrd, I was glad to have one less person watching my every move. Iris had continued to be kind and welcoming. The staff had given me a wide berth. But none of those things kept me awake, eyes staring blankly at the vaulted ceiling. No, my insomnia was the direct result of four simple words.

I don't know how he knew it was me in the loo. Or why he'd felt the need to point it out. It wasn't exactly the warmest start to our relationship. Still, every time I thought of the way he'd spoken to me while I hid in the stall, I felt a hungry tick between my legs. I'd listened to a man I'd never met, who I'd practically sold my soul to, fuck another woman. My rational half wanted to be angry about it. My emotional half was confused, jealous even. The confusion seemed to stem from the fact that I had no legitimate claim on him. And underneath my reason and my feelings, something else boiled. It was primal. It clawed inside me, wanting to be unleashed, and rattled the cage of my conscious efforts to contain it. The feeling sent my hand dancing between my legs again and again, but no matter how many times I pleasured myself, I wasn't sated.

I was still lying in bed when the room lightened at dawn, sunlight filtering through the drawn curtains, and I was awake when someone knocked on the door.

"Yes?" I called not bothering to rise from my pillow fort but pulling the covers over me more tightly.

Giles entered, carrying a tray, and brought it to the bedside table. "Having a lie-in?"

"Something like that," I muttered. Struggling to sit up, I tugged the old t-shirt, one of the few things I'd brought along with me, down, so I was presentable.

"I have your schedule for the day," he informed me as he made me a cup of tea. He paused when he lifted the lid of the sugar jar. "How do you take this?"

"Two sugars," I said. "But you really don't have to do that for me."

His head cocked. "Interesting, but no, I really do."

I supposed this was more of the expectations I needed to absorb and adhere to if I was to pass for Kerrigan. "What do you mean by schedule?"

"Your father—pardon me, Mr. Belmond—would like to leave sharply at seven. Your hairdresser and make-up artist are scheduled accordingly, and your facialist will be here in an hour. Iris would like to hang out with you after your facial while you're getting ready." He shifted uncomfortably, lifting his glasses from his tipped nose and then cleaning them on a handkerchief. "Her words. Not mine."

"Of course," I said, breathing in the floral scent of the black tea.

"You should know that Kerrigan didn't approve of her father's romance with Miss Adler."

I frowned. "So I should ignore her?"

"You're the one present, Miss..." he trailed off and I realized he wasn't sure what to call me.

"My name is Kate," I said softly.

"It would be better not to get in the habit of using it. If I were to slip up and use it in front of the wrong person, the consequences could be messy." He spoke apologetically, and I appreciated the difficult position he was in.

"What about K?"

"K?" he repeated.

"Just call me K, like a nickname. I'll tell everyone that I picked it up while I was traveling," I added the last pointedly. Later, I planned to drill Giles for as much background on Kerrigan's whereabouts as possible. I didn't want to be caught off guard—like I'd been with Caroline—again.

"I suppose, Miss...K," he self-corrected. "How you proceed within this social circle is up to you. I am only here to offer insight."

"Then I'd like to get ready with Iris." That was an easy decision. It was understandable that Kerrigan had bristled at her stepmother's closeness in age, but I had to believe if she'd gotten to know her that she might feel differently. "But am I seriously, just getting pretty all day?"

"It is a rather important day. We should go over who will be in attendance—"

"But you'll be there, right?"

"If you would like," he said, his eyebrows lifting in surprise. "I can attend with the driver and stay in the car."

"You can't come to the party?" I shook my head, abandoning my tea to the bedside table as panic began to take hold of me. I needed someone there. Someone who was on my side.

"I am not an invited guest. It is a very exclusive occasion. However, should you like me to remain nearby..."

"No. I won't ask you to wait in the car. I can't believe they're that snobby." I paused and recalled how Caroline had acted at lunch. Maybe I could believe it, but there had to be others like Iris and Evie who were different. Still, I wouldn't ask Giles to sit around while I sipped champagne and danced. "What happens if I forget something or need help?"

"Your father...bloody hell, I did it again. Pardon me, Mr. Belmond will be nearby, but there's a simpler solution."

I clutched a pillow to my chest and nodded.

"Keep a glass of champagne with you. Whenever you need to avoid someone or some question, take a drink and nod or smile."

"That's your advice?" I said flatly. I was going to make a mess of this. "I'll just wind up drunk."

"One thing I've learned about the wealthy is that they love to talk about themselves, let them. Your silence will be rewarded with all sorts of inane chatter. Being drunk is just a bonus," he said with a shrug.

He continued on, giving me a rundown on the foods likely to be served and what Kerrigan might eat, the dancing, the drinks, the dazzling company. I was to spend the evening in the presence of politicians, aristocrats, and billionaires. This wasn't some casual gathering at the local pub. This was a gala event.

"So, what are we celebrating?" I asked.

Giles frowned, puzzlement written over his face. "Your engagement, of course. Or Kerrigan's, rather, but you take my point."

"What?" I blurted out. "I thought I was meeting Spencer for the first time in years."

"You are, but agreements have been reached."

Images of handshakes and private meetings held in rooms filled with men and cigar smoke popped into my head. I'd bet that was close enough to what had happened.

"So he's not going to propose?"

"I suppose he might, but he's agreed to the arrangement as well."

Something about that fact struck me. I'd been thinking a lot about how Kerrigan must be feeling, but now I realized Spencer had been dragged into this as well. After the encounter in the bathroom, I was certain he wasn't looking for a wife out of necessity. It was a business arrangement, plain and simple.

"Why?" I pondered out loud.

"Pardon?" Giles called as he disappeared into the nearby ensuite bath. He returned carrying a silk robe.

I scrambled out of bed, hoping that getting up would clear my head. Slipping into the robe, I wrapped it around me, tying the belt tightly. Long kimono sleeves draped gracefully to my wrists, and I admired the elegant crane print of the fabric for a moment before I found the right way to posit my question. "Why does he need an arranged marriage? What does he get out of it?"

Mr. Belmond had been clear on his reasons for selling his daughter off to the Byrds. They had a title that would convey to her as well as her children someday. He was buying privilege and status and willing to pay with his daughter's freedom.

"Like all aristocratic families, there's never enough money," Giles told me.

"They're poor?" This surprised me, given the shop I'd met Caroline and Evie in yesterday.

"Not by any standards but their own," Giles said dryly.

"Do I detect a hint of disdain?" I couldn't help smiling. I doubted Giles could be this open with the real Kerrigan, but we were something more of equals—each of us being paid to perform services for the Belmond family.

"Perhaps," he admitted before straightening his back, "but that's not my place to say. The Byrds are very influential and they're worth millions of dollars. A union with the Belmond name will give them more power."

"How much power do they need?" I asked in exasperation.

"A man never has enough power if he senses there is more to be had." Giles passed me the itinerary. "Do you need help picking your gown for tonight?"

I took a deep breath. "No. I want to try myself, but I would like your thoughts on my choices."

"Very well." He tipped his head. "In that case, I will leave you to it and check in on you when the facialist arrives."

When he left the bedroom, I tip-toed to the closet, still feeling as though any minute someone might burst in and drag me off for being a fraud. I felt like a thief going through Kerrigan's clothing and belongings.

"It's part of the job," I reminded myself as I poked around looking for how the mirrored doors opened. When I found the first one, I discovered another section filled with shoes. How many shoes did she need? Given that she used them to pick her daily outfit, I guessed a lot. The first thing I needed to do was know what I was working with. Walking the perimeter of the oddly-shaped room, I opened each door until I was staring at Kerrigan's complete wardrobe. I'd expected to discover a lot of clothes, but it was mind-boggling how much was hiding behind those mirrors. Half of Harrods must be hanging in there and all of the clothing had been organized by color. I took a step back and surveyed the shoe sections. There had to be hundreds of shoes for me to choose from. No wonder she was able to start with her shoes.

I felt a bit like Cinderella as I picked up a pair of silver shoes with a heel so high it looked dangerous. I wasn't sure which would be trickier to walk in—these shoes or glass slippers. Sliding it on my foot, I reached for the other shoe. Instantly, I was half a foot taller than before. I took a cautious step forward followed by another, surprised to

discover they were much easier to walk in than I'd
expected. Still, I suspected the unnatural height would
make it impossible to last the evening wearing them. I
studied my choices until I landed on a pair of impossibly
beautiful heels. The sheer black fabric had been sculpted
into a sensual silhouette, gathering ever so slightly at the
heel. It looked like lingerie for feet, and I was in love. Their
heels were slightly less extreme than the others. As soon as
I slid them on, I understood why Kerrigan started with her
shoes. No matter what I wore with them, I would feel sexy.

It turned out, though, that picking a dress that I felt
equally enthralled with was impossible. Caroline wanted
me to wear something bridal, which made sense now that I
knew they were planning to announce our engagement this
evening. But Kerrigan's closet had very little white or ivory.
There was a champagne gown that had an intricately
beaded bodice studded with silver crystals as well as a
number of black dresses ranging from cocktail length to full
ball gown. None of them felt right. Because the truth was
that no matter what I wore tonight, I was a liar. How could
clothing cover up that?

What could I wear that would make me half as glamorous as Kerrigan Belmond? How could I step into her
shoes?

CHAPTER TWELVE

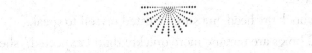

I ris discovered me half an hour later, sitting in a pool of silk, tulle, and sequins, near the point of tears. She stopped at the threshold of my closet and stared for a moment. Like me, she was wearing a silk robe but hers was a light gold color that brought out the natural luster of her dark skin.

"Kerrigan?" she called without moving. "May I come in?"

"Yes," I said, choking back a sob. I didn't want the first thing she told her husband to be that she'd found his *daughter* crying in her closet. "I'm sorry. I know I should have this sorted by now. I just can't figure out what to wear. I don't know what's wrong with me."

Iris moved closer, gathered her robe carefully, and sank down across from me onto the floor. She looked around at the dozen dresses on the floor. "I see what you mean, but I think I know exactly what's wrong."

I blinked up at her, hoping she couldn't see my watery eyes.

"Nerves," she pronounced it like a doctor delivering a diagnosis. "Tod told me that your engagement is being announced tonight. Honestly, I was shocked. Did they warn you?"

I shook my head, not sure I trusted myself to speak.

"Things are moving more quickly than I expected," she said with a sigh. "I'll admit that I don't quite understand this match. I didn't even know people did things like this, but he assured me that you were on board." She paused and met my eyes directly. "Kerrigan, you can tell me if you're being forced to do this."

I shot her a strained smile. "I did agree." That wasn't a lie, exactly. I'd known this was part of the arrangement, which made it easier to fudge the truth a little. "I suppose it's all happening so fast. I thought I had a bit more time."

"Listen, I know what happened," she said in a lowered voice. "I know why you left, and I think you did the right thing for you, but it's not too late to change your mind."

That definitely was not part of my arrangement with Tod Belmond, but her words struck me as odd. Kerrigan's father had admitted that she had run away from her duties. He'd assured me that she just needed more time, but what had scared her so badly in the first place?

And what happened if she didn't come home?

What would they do? I'd promised a year. Nothing more. I'd even signed a contract. I was under no obligation to continue to be Kerrigan Belmond, but what would happen in a year if she hadn't returned?

"I'm sorry." Iris interrupted my thoughts. "I think I'm making this worse. I should—"

I reached out and grabbed her hand. Clutching it, I told the truth. "I'm scared about tonight—scared that I'll mess everything up and disappoint...my father. I'm scared Caroline will be nastier than she was at lunch. But mostly, I'm just afraid of what happens next."

"You'll never disappoint him," she promised softly. "I may not understand why your father is pushing through this marriage, but I know he loves you more than anything."

"Not more than you!"

She laughed at this, smiling warmly. "Definitely more than me, and that's okay, he should. A father should love his daughter more than anything in the world."

I found myself wishing I knew that kind of love. I couldn't admit that to her, so I returned her smile and forced myself to take a deep breath. "They're going to have their work cut out for them making me pretty."

My skin always got splotchy and red when I cried. I could only imagine how I looked now after a panic attack and a night without sleep.

"You're going to look gorgeous," Iris said firmly. "Now let's figure out a dress."

"I don't have anything bridal," I told her miserably.

She arched an eyebrow.

"Sorry, Caroline wanted me to wear ivory or white, remember? It feels like she wants to send a message," I explained to her.

"That woman is a bit too opinionated for my taste," Iris

said in a voice that made it clear what she thought of Caroline Byrd. "You should wear what you want."

"I have no idea what I want," I admitted. None of this was mine. Yesterday, Giles had transformed me into Kerrigan. I'd spent the day feeling like I was in someone else's skin. It hadn't been what I expected. I hadn't felt bad or even wrong, just not like myself. But not in a bad way.

"Well, none of these," she decided. Standing, she reached down to offer a hand. I accepted it gratefully. Following at her heels she bypassed the neutral gowns I'd been looking and at went straight to a rack filled with bold shades of red.

"You're going into battle, and clothes are your armor," she advised me, sifting through the contents of the closet, one hanger at a time. "Your wit is your weapon. Wield both wisely."

I stayed silent, considering her words, as she held up one dress followed by another until she finally held one to me and smiled widely.

"This one."

She held it against me as I turned to study the mirror. It was nothing like what Caroline had suggested. I expected it would upset Spencer's mother to have me wear it. But there was no denying that it was a statement.

"This will send a message," Iris whispered.

"Which is?"

"That you're a queen, and queens hold all the true power."

I stared at the mirror, wondering if it was possible for a dress to convey all of that. Somehow, though, I knew she was right. Without me, Tod Belmond would be screwed, and the Byrds would lose out on my family's fortune and connections. I was the most powerful player on the board because I had nothing to lose.

"YOU HAVE AN EVENT TONIGHT, NO?" CAMILLE, THE facial expert as she'd been introduced to me a few moments ago, asked with a heavy French accent.

"Yes. I mean, no. I'm sorry, what was the question?" I stammered, still feeling anxious about what waited for me this evening.

"You are going to a party tonight?" she repeated a little more slowly.

I nodded. "A dinner or a ball." God, she probably thought I was an idiot. I prayed she didn't ask me about my skincare regime or my travels. I was struggling enough with facts that I didn't want to have to make up lies. "I just know it's important."

"I will be gentle then." She stood behind me, her eyes watching mine in the colossal bathroom's mirror. Her hand reached and took my chin, tilted my head to study me. "Have you been wearing sunscreen?"

"I try to avoid the sun," I said without thinking and my stomach flipped over. Where was it that everyone thought Kerrigan had been? New York? The South of France? I had to remember that. No one would believe that a wealthy, beautiful woman had gone to the Mediterranean and stayed out of the sun.

But Camille didn't seem to think anything of my

answer. "Good girl. The sun will ruin your skin. Hats and sunscreen, remember?"

I suspected she'd given this lecture before, but I nodded anyway.

"Thankfully, your skin is quite clear, so we will make you glow." She lowered her voice, a hint of a smile reflected by the mirror. "Just like you've woken up with a lover."

I bit my lip and hoped I wouldn't blush.

I didn't know what to expect as I climbed onto the small table she had set up near the sunken tub. It had been covered with crisp, white sheets. As I laid down, she covered me with a fresh one, tucking it around me before gently placing a rolled towel under my neck.

"Good?" she said softly.

"Hmm." I sighed more than answered.

Camille wrapped another towel around my head, this one slightly warm. "Relax, *cherie*. You seem very tense."

"It's a big night," I admitted to her. "I'm announcing my engagement." Maybe confronting this sudden change in circumstances would make it easier to handle later this evening. The words felt funny coming out of my mouth as if they belonged to someone else. In a way, they did. But nothing could change the fact that I was the one who would be accepting well-wishes and taking Spencer's arm tonight. I had to be ready for it.

"Congratulations! We will make you extra beautiful." She clapped her hands lightly. "Close your eyes."

I did as she instructed and she placed two cool gel pads over them. I relaxed into the comfortable situation I found myself in, hoping I didn't fall asleep but already feeling tired.

Camille lifted my hand. "Do you have a ring?"

"Not yet," I murmured. Would I? Would he give it to me tonight? Would others ask? I couldn't imagine a diamond on my finger and yet, it was another almost certainty confronting me.

"We will do a little something for your skin here." She massaged cream into my hand. "You must moisturize. It looks as if you've been doing dishes." She laughed. No doubt the thought of Kerrigan Belmond with her hands in soapy water, was hilarious to those that knew her. I, however, had been washing dishes only a few days ago. She continued to rub the lotion into my skin. When she finished she wrapped a steamed towel around it. She repeated the process on the other side. By the time she was finished, I'd nearly fallen asleep.

Camille worked quietly, humming slightly under her breath, while she applied serums and lotions and whatever other magic she carried with her to appointments. She paused occasionally to place a warm towel on my face, wrapping it so only my nostrils were exposed. I drifted between sleep and awake as she worked.

When she finally removed the last towel, she applied one final lightweight liquid to my skin.

"Miss Belmond," she called through my bliss-soaked haze, "you're finished."

"Call me Ka-K," I managed to correct myself in time, choosing the nickname I'd given Giles to use. I took my time sitting up. My whole body felt loose and relaxed as she handed me a mirror.

"I think you are going to give your fiancé indecent thoughts this evening," she told me with a wink.

My skin radiated a subtle glow that made my whole face look brightened and flawless. "Was that the creams you used or magic?"

She laughed. "A little bit of both."

Camille reached into her bag and brought out a jar. Placing it on the counter, she pointed to it. "Use that on your hands morning and night. It will make them soft again."

"I will," I promised, reaching to rub them and finding they already felt silky soft.

"And let me know when you have set a date for the big day. I will put it on my calendar."

I swallowed, doing my best to look excited at the idea of my *upcoming* wedding. Thankfully, she was already packing up her things and didn't seem to notice. A year from now, it would be Kerrigan here getting a facial before her big day. It almost made me jealous, considering how good it felt. Then I remembered that a year from now I would be able to afford facials and other luxuries. I made up my mind then that a year from now I would celebrate my newfound independence by booking facials for myself and Eliza before I finally fled England.

I found Iris waiting for me in her own room.

"I had a light lunch brought up."

"Thanks. I'm starving." I took one of the sandwiches and nibbled delicately.

"I'm always hungry after a facial. I think it opens my pores and my stomach," she said with a giggle.

"Thank you for helping me with the dress," I said, taking a seat on the opposite side of her sofa.

"Of course. I imagine you're feeling all sorts of emotions today. I was a nervous wreck when we announced our engagement. I can't imagine having all of this thrown at you at the last minute." She sipped from her teacup thoughtfully. "You can talk to me about it. Any time."

I nodded, wishing that were true. I found myself wanting to open up to her and spill the strange situation I'd found myself in. I wanted to admit how worried I was that I'd find myself drowning before I realized I'd accidentally gotten in over my head. But Iris didn't know about my arrangement with her husband or the truth about Kerrigan. Not only would it jeopardize the agreement, but it might also cause problems for her own marriage if she found out she'd been lied to. Still, I felt terrible keeping it from her, especially because part of me very much wanted to be her friend.

She can't be, a cool voice told me in my mind. A year from now, I would be gone. This was temporary. I couldn't allow myself to build a real relationship with anyone here, even her.

When the hairdresser arrived, I placed my trust entirely in her hands. I didn't have the slightest idea what to do with my hair. Usually, I threw it up in a messy bun or a ponytail. It had been months since I'd bothered with a trim, a fact the stylist must have noticed based on the way her nose wrinkled as she analyzed the challenge before her.

"I'm glad we came early," she announced to us. "You need the full treatment."

For the next two hours, she cut and colored, chatting nonsense with her friend, who was busy applying a special treatment to Iris's closely shorn locks. I joined in when I could, but spent most of the time listening. Iris spoke of her family, who lived in Paris. Her mother had been a model, which was no surprise given her daughter's beauty. Iris herself had split her time between the French capital and London, where she performed with the Royal Ballet until Tod Belmond swept her off her feet at a charity gala.

"I wondered how you met," I said with a sigh.

Iris cocked her head with a strange expression. "You were there. Although, I don't believe we met."

"That's right," I said quickly. "One gala bleeds into another."

Iris snorted. "I had no idea the wealthy spent every week saving something endangered by throwing money at auctioneers."

I could almost picture the scene of which she spoke: women in beautiful gowns sipping champagne but not daring to have too much, men in tuxedos making business deals, a dance floor and crystal, and a whole different world that I'd only ever experienced in fairy stories. After tonight, I would have firsthand experience with that world. Tonight I would be the innocent princess offered as a willing tribute to a stranger. Next week there might be another ball, another dinner, another spectacle to attend. Why did my first event have to shine such a light on me? I wasn't ready. I wished Tod had asked me before he agreed to this evening. Then again, maybe he'd known all along and that was why he'd been so desperate when he sought me out in Bexby. He could have warned me, though.

Each second that ticked by seemed to press against my shoulders, forcing me under its weight. Each minute was like a surge of water battering me as the riptide dragged me down. I fell silent as I battled the panic attack threatening to overcome me. Iris fell into an easy conversation with the stylists and I tuned my attention to it. After a few minutes, the terrible sensation of drowning began to ebb away, evaporating as quickly as it had overwhelmed me.

My stylist had proceeded to teasing and curling my hair while she gossiped with the others and when she finally let me see what she was doing, I discovered another transformation had been made. My hair was slightly darker, or at least richer in color. There was no sign of dullness or frizz. Instead, it had been swept into a loose, but elegant updo that showed off the curve of my neck.

"I can change it," she told me when I remained silent too long.

"No," I cried out. "I love it."

"It will show off your shoulders in that dress," Iris added.

We spent the remainder of the late afternoon, being plucked, lined, and painted by yet another crew of make-up artists. I wanted to ask if I would be expected to put this much effort into every event I attended, but I decided it was safer to wait and ask Giles.

When the time finally came for me to slip into my dress, every remnant of Kate was gone. I had completely morphed into Kerrigan now. I had her hair, her clothes, even her precious shoes. But would I actually pass for her?

As I left my room, I made my way toward the staircase, pausing near the banister when I heard voices below.

"We're going to be late," Tod Belmond stormed, pacing the length of the foyer and checking his watch.

"It's not even seven, darling," Iris said in a soothing voice. She'd opted to wear a gold gown that showed off her dancer's body and brought out the deep tones of her skin. It definitely wasn't as daring as the gown she had chosen for me to wear tonight.

Caroline had wanted me to wear white, but Iris had pushed me towards the opposite end of the spectrum. I smoothed the black lace down and hoped I looked alright. My dress had long sleeves that stopped at the wrist, the lace showing flashes of my pale skin. It dipped low, carving an elegant but slightly provocative line from my cleavage to my arms, leaving my shoulders bare before dipping even lower in the back. It flowed along the curves of my body flaring slightly around my ankles. Unlike the arms, the gown itself was lined with a thin nude fabric that made it look as though I was wearing nothing else beneath. I reached down and lifted my skirt at the thighs ever so slightly so I could see my feet as I began my descent down the stairs. The dress went perfectly with the peekaboo heels I'd chosen early, and I'd been surprised to find that despite their height, they weren't difficult to walk in. Still, after wasting an entire day getting pretty, I wasn't going to fall ass over tea kettle down the steps and wind up in an ambulance.

When I reached the fifth step down, Tod stopped and turned, his mouth open as if to call out. But whatever he planned to say to me died on his lips. I nearly froze myself, worrying that I'd already messed up. Had I done something his daughter would never do? Worn my hair the wrong way or chosen the wrong shade of lipstick? I'd trusted the people that came here today, assuming they would treat me as they had always done to her. Maybe I shouldn't have assumed.

But when I stepped onto the landing, Tod caught my hand. "You look beautiful, Kerrigan. Spencer will be pleased."

"Thank you," I murmured, feeling suddenly shy.

He must have noticed because he released my hand and crooked his arm to his wife. "You'll follow behind us in the Maybach."

"I'm not going with you?" I blurted out. "Why did you wait for me?"

"I simply wanted to be certain you got out the door on time. Punctuality hasn't always been your defining characteristic. And you may wish to stay longer than us."

I tried to ignore the implication of those words. I might want to seal the deal with Spencer—or rather, he might expect me to go to his bed. Then there was the other reason, Tod had waited. He wanted to see me himself, to know if his scheme would work or if he had to call everything off. I made a mental note, though, that Kerrigan favored tardiness. It was little things like that which might help me pass for her.

A driver helped me into the back of the Maybach as Tod helped Iris into the backseat of a black limousine. Their car had already started down the drive as my driver took the wheel of the Mercedes.

"Ready, Miss?" he asked.

Part of me wanted to say no and run back into the house. I could change and be gone before Tod Belmond realized I wasn't behind them. Despite all that I had done so far, I sensed that tonight the final line would be crossed. After this evening, there would be no turning back. I would be trapped in the arrangement until time or my double set me free.

I thought about the ten million pounds. One year of taking orders. One year of playing a part. And then I would never belong to anyone again.

"Yes," I said. As he drove away, I didn't bother to look back.

CHAPTER THIRTEEN

It turned out that I wouldn't have gotten far had I decided to run because in less than five minutes' time the car turned into a drive and paused to speak with the security guard at the gate. A moment later, the gates opened revealing my first glimpse of Sparrow Court, the Byrd's family home. If I had been impressed with Willoughby Place, this residence actually intimidated me. The house itself sat a good way from the road, far enough that it might have looked small in the distance if it weren't so terribly palatial. The drive had been lined with spotlights that were turned on despite it still being twilight, giving the feeling of making a grand entrance from the moment we drove onto the property. The drive itself was paved with bricks, but I didn't feel the slightest bump thanks to the smooth ride of the Maybach. We rounded the circular drive, pulling past a fountain featuring three female statues, breasts bare, holding large pots from which water flowed to the pool below. Flowers floated in the water next to small candles which flickered romantically. The Mercedes paused and a gloved attendant opened the door.

"Miss Belmond." He offered me his hand and I took it.

Rising out of the car, I swallowed a gasp at the scene in front of me. The staircase leading into the main entrance had been draped with white flowers of all types. Roses, lilies, peonies, and other varieties too exotic for me to name mixed with twisting ivy vines. Even from here the delicate floral bouquet perfumed the air. Lanterns had been placed at the far end of each step. Suddenly, I understood why Caroline had wanted me to wear white. She wanted me to look the part of the innocent, blushing bride. I found myself wondering if this was simply a party to announce an engagement, what would the actual wedding be like?

I glanced around looking for Tod and Iris, but they were nowhere in sight. Other than a few others arriving, I was alone. I thanked the attendant for his help and took a single step toward the party, hesitating for a moment and wishing I had made Giles sit in the car, after all. I turned my head slightly at the sound of an engine in time to see the driver pull away, off to wherever he was expected to wait until I called for him. I had no choice but to go inside and hope I didn't trip down the staircase or make an unintentional blunder. A group that arrived after me chatted animatedly as they went ahead, entering without so much as a pause. I could do that, I decided. One foot in front of the other until I was inside, and then I would make the next right move. But as the partygoers climbed the stairs, a man stepped around them, wearing a tuxedo that showcased his broad shoulders and athletic build. I blinked when I saw him, but the rest of my body refused to budge momentarily. It was him. I'd seen him for only a moment across the restaurant, but I recognized him both from that distant encounter and my shameless internet stalking.

You are Kerrigan Belmond tonight, I told myself as I plastered a dazzling smile on my face. I looked like her. I was dressed like her. I merely had to act like her. She wouldn't freeze at the prospect of facing a childhood acquaintance no matter how circumstances had changed since her youth. I continued on until I was close enough to touch him.

He extended a hand. "You look lovely tonight, Kerrigan. It's been too long since we saw each other. It almost makes me wish I'd chosen Oxford over St. Andrew's."

"Good evening, Spencer. You look lovely—I mean, handsome, too," I said flummoxed by the gentleman before me. Was this how he wanted to play it? Were we to pretend that nothing had happened yesterday? If that was what he had wanted, why go to the trouble of sending a note over to me? Why point it out?

"Shall we?" he asked stiffly, crooking his arm.

I accepted it, and we went silently up the stairs. Every inch of my body was aware of his presence. I'd spent last night imagining what it would be like to feel his hands on me, to have his weight crushing my body as he took me. But if Spencer felt a physical attraction to me, he showed no sign of it. He barely looked at me as we made our way to the party and his demeanor remained stiff and detached like he was simply another attendant sent to guide me into the house.

As soon as we were through the double entrance doors, carved from solid wood, the scene changed from romantic tranquility to a crowded room buzzing with people. The foyer looked like it could fit half a row of mews inside it, and there were people everywhere. My hand gripped Spencer's forearm a little more tightly, earning me a curious glance. He led me inside and I found myself trying to take it all in. If a mansion was impressive, one filled with rich and important people was even more so. Women dressed in elegant gowns, dripping with priceless jewelry, hung from the arms of men in tuxedos, sipping from champagne coupes. A string quartet played Mozart in one corner, and waiters wove through the crowd offering canapes and drinks. Before I could process the busy setting, Spencer pulled his arm away. I started, looking at him with a panicked expression and feeling as if my life raft had just been yanked out from under me.

"If you'll excuse me, I see my grandfather. I'll find you in a moment." He nodded his head at an older man with bushy white hair and a face lined with signs of age and frustration. I'd done enough homework on the Byrds, thanks to the internet and Giles, to know that the elder Byrd was a member of the House of Lords, a Duke, and one of the few remaining persons that held a hereditary seat in Parliament. He was in a sense a dying breed and judging by his age, I meant that quite literally.

Spencer left me standing there, wondering exactly what to do. I was surrounded by strangers who all thought they knew me. A few heads turned my way and several people nodded hello. I returned the greetings, hoping no one came up and tried to talk to me.

"You're here!" an excited voice squealed to my right.

I turned in time to see Evie's bright smile as she threw her arms around my shoulders. "Mum sent Spencer to escort you in. Where is he?" She peeked around my shoulder as though he might be hiding there.

"He went to speak with your grandfather," I told her.

"That cad! He left you here all alone?" She slipped her arm through mine and tugged me toward a nearby waiter.

"I suppose he thought I could take care of myself." And why wouldn't he? It occurred to me that once again I needed to act as Kerrigan would. I shrugged, hoping I appeared nonplussed about being left to my own devices. "It's been so long since I attended one of these. I'm dreading having to make boring small talk all night."

"This will help." Evie swiped two glasses of champagne from the waiter's tray and handed one to me. "The only perk of these blasted parties is drinking as much champagne as I can before my mother finds out." She followed her confession with a small giggle.

I tapped my crystal coupe to hers. "I'll drink to that."

She lowered her voice so only I could hear her as she continued, "It's even harder when half the men bring their new wives every six months. Just when I'm starting to remember names, they change again."

I seized on her innocent observation to turn it to my advantage. "Honestly, I don't recognize half the people here."

"Well, there's my brother and grandfather. No doubt,

they're talking about some political crisis. Oh, there's your father!" She waved at him. Tod tipped his head in acknowledgment but raised a questioning eyebrow at me as he joined Spencer and Lord Byrd. "And there is Brock Quinn and his new girlfriend."

I followed her gaze to a powerful-looking man, surrounded by other important-looking men, and was surprised to discover his attention was acutely focused on the beautiful blonde at his side. The heat between them was palpable, even from a distance. I felt myself growing warmer as I watched them. Would a man ever look at me like that? As though he was torn between devouring me and protecting me?

"They're going to announce their engagement any day," she guessed.

"I don't think we've met." I kept my response purposefully vague, hoping Evie would continue to fill in the blanks.

"He was her boss. Infamous bachelor. Now that he's off the market, everyone is wondering which of his brothers will fall victim next."

"Victim?"

"To love," she said. "It's obvious when you look at those two that they're truly in love."

"How can you be sure?" I asked.

"Because you see it so rarely around here. Everyone just marries to please their parents or secure a business deal. Well, that's what first marriages are for on Billionaire's Row." She stopped chattering, and her hand flew to her mouth. Evie shook her head, loosening the blonde curls that had been pinned neatly up. "I'm so sorry. I hope I didn't offend you. I know our parents have an understanding about you and..."

"No offense taken," I promised her. In all honesty, I was glad she saw through the games the people here played. Maybe it would save her from falling victim to one when she was older. "What exactly is—"

Before I could finish my question, I spotted Tod Belmond striding toward me and I fell silent. A muscle ticked in his jaw and his lips were pressed together in a hard line. He was unhappy, and although I had no idea what I might have done, I knew I was to blame.

"Excuse me, Evie," I said softly. "I think my father needs a word."

She nodded, looking nervously between us, and whispered "good luck" before disappearing back into the crowd.

Tod caught my arm, his fingers gripping my elbow tightly as he led me away from the party. I didn't speak as he opened a pair of doors to an unoccupied solarium. When we were finally alone, he rounded on me. "What did you do? Five minutes with Spencer and you've ruined everything."

"Me?" I jerked in surprise, staring at him. "I didn't do anything!" I racked my brain for some mistake I might have made—a glib comment or an insult—but came up with nothing.

"Spencer just told me that he's asked his grandfather to hold off on the announcement. He says he's not ready to tell people that he's engaged to you. So, I'll ask again, what did you do?" Tod hissed before pacing the length of the room.

I stood in mute shock for a moment. I hadn't done anything to discourage Spencer. Not today, at least. He'd made no mention of yesterday at Hillgrove's, but it had to be that. There was absolutely no way that I was going to confide the details of that event to Tod Belmond, though. "I really didn't do anything. He escorted me inside and then excused himself to speak with his grandfather. I've barely spoken to him."

"What about this dress?" He gestured to my gown. "Perhaps, it's too suggestive. Caroline mentioned that she asked you to wear white."

"Your daughter doesn't have a lot of white in her closet," I said, trying to stay calm while inside I was seething. Everyone wanted me to dress up and play pretend like I was a doll, but somehow it was my fault when the game went poorly.

He pointed his index finger at me, brows raised, and leveled a command. "Fix this."

He didn't wait for me to respond. Instead, he stormed away. I didn't follow.

The inside of the solarium was full of plants. Exotic ferns and flowers sat in pots on over-filled tables. The air was humid, warmer than the climate-controlled house, and stuffier than outside. The space had been cultivated into a lavish greenhouse rather than another showy living space. It was clear that whoever kept it spent considerable hours tending to the plants. The only light inside the glass room came from the lights of the party which had spilled into the garden. I could hear laughter and conversation, too distant to make out. Outside people were having a good time, and I found myself dreading my eventual return to the champagne and gossip and curious eyes. Reaching out, I ran a finger down a large green leaf, its rubbery surface squeaking softly at my touch. Behind me, footsteps approached but I didn't turn to see who had disturbed my temporary sanctuary. I knew by the way my body responded—as though it sensed him before it saw him. My nipples tightened, pushing against the fabric of my dress, my pulse quickened, and goosebumps rippled across my bare skin.

"Monstera albo," Spencer's voice called. "It's incredibly rare to see that depth of variegation."

"It's different," I murmured.

"Different?" he repeated. "You don't like it? It's considered a beautiful specimen by most people who see it."

"Different can mean beautiful. I think it would be a disservice to dismiss it with such a general term as beautiful, though. Don't you think?" I asked.

There was a pause, and I wondered if I'd screwed up again. Obviously, I'd done something that had upset him or he wouldn't have delayed announcing our engagement. When he finally spoke, his words were thick with meaning. "You aren't what I expected."

"Is that why you're having second thoughts?" I studied the leaf more closely, suddenly finding myself intensely interested in the nearby plants. I couldn't bring myself to face him. I was afraid that away from the glittering lights and distractions of the soiree, he would see right through me.

"I saw your father drag you off. I thought I should come and explain myself." He reached out and took my hand. "It's not second thoughts."

"But you don't want to marry me," I pressed. I needed to understand why. That was the only one I could fix.

"Do you want to marry me?" He tugged gently on my hand, urging me around to finally look at him.

The darkness cast shadows across his handsome face, making it impossible to read anything in his eyes. He had a drink in his hand and the heat of bourbon warmed his breath. I could smell it lingering on him. He was going to keep asking questions instead of answering mine, thus making it impossible for me to decide what the right answer was. That only left me one choice: honesty. "I don't know."

Well, as honest as I could be. If I were Kerrigan, I wouldn't be sure, even if I had committed to the arrangement. Isn't that why she had run away?

"Exactly," Spencer said. I gawked at him for a second before composing myself. "How can we know?"

"But you agreed to this," I pointed out.

"So did you," he said.

"What changed?" I asked. "Was it yesterday?"

Even in the dimness, I spotted his confusion. "Yesterday."

I swallowed, feeling an anxious lump forming in my throat. "At Hillgrove's when I accidentally...you know..."

"I'm sorry I have no idea what you're talking about, Kerrigan. I had business in the city all day."

"You had a lunch," I stammered, wondering if I was losing my mind. "I was there with my stepmother and your mum and sister. You sent champagne. The note?"

I couldn't bring myself to raise the issue of what had happened in the loo. If I'd dreamed up the whole experience, the last thing I wanted was to confess that I'd had some sort of waking fantasy about getting off while he fucked another woman.

"Hillgrove's?" He snorted, shaking his head. "That bastard."

"I'm sorry?"

"I was in the city, but trust Holden to be in the right place at the wrong time. My brother conveniently forgot to mention seeing you," Spencer said. "Mother might have mentioned it, though. I'll have a word with her."

I closed my eyes, trying to fit together all the puzzle pieces he'd just handed me with what Giles had told me about my fake fiancé. "Holden? Your brother? But why did he send me a note?"

"That is a very good question," Spencer admitted, studying my face. "You must have caught his attention."

I was suddenly grateful for the lack of light so that he couldn't see me blush. I felt my cheeks heat.

"We're confused for one another all the time. That's one of the reasons having an identical twin is a pain in the arse."

A twin. I found myself relieved and curious and strangely angry. I knew that Spencer had a sister and a brother, but no one had mentioned Holden was more than just his brother but his identical twin. It seemed like a fairly important detail to leave out.

"What did his note say?" Spencer asked, cutting into my thoughts.

"Nothing," I said too quickly and his eyebrow shot up.

"I see," he said in a cold voice. "Of course, he would think it funny if he got to fuck you first."

"Excuse me?" I blurted out. Yanking my hand away, I stared at him, waiting for an apology.

But he didn't look remotely sorry. "Would you prefer to ignore the rather large elephant in the room?"

"I'm not just some slot for you to stick your cock into," I said angrily, ignoring the small voice that laughed inside me. Wasn't that exactly what I was? Hadn't I agreed to be just that? A placeholder until Kerrigan returned?

His lips twitched at this, but his expression remained moody. "I've offended you."

"Yes." An alarm went off in my brain but I ignored it. Now I was willfully disregarding the mission I'd been sent to perform, but I couldn't help myself. I had expected Spencer to romance me a little, perhaps flirt, but he didn't seem to care about any of those things. His expectations were clear. I'd already been bought for him. It was up to him to decide if he wanted to keep me.

"Given that you agreed to our families' wishes, I thought you were comfortable with being transparent about this situation." He shrugged, emphasizing his strong shoulders. I fought the urge to grab hold of them and haul him toward me.

Instead, I dug my heels in and shot him a haughty look. "Who said I was given a choice?"

He paused, tilting his head, and then said the last thing I expected him to say, "I did. Why do you think I called off the announcement?"

CHAPTER FOURTEEN

y mind was spinning so quickly I was finding it hard to breathe. The humid air was stifling, leaving me feeling too hot and sticky. I refused to believe it was more than the greenhouse effect. But the truth was it was him. Spencer flustered me. He confused me. His motives were cryptic, given his directness about other issues, such as going to bed together. I didn't know what to think of him.

"But you expect to fuck me?" I struggled to bring the words to my lips, but my voice was clear and strong when I finally spoke.

"I'll admit that I didn't think you would be so opposed to the idea, given that you'd agreed to marry me." If I'd expected him to be angry, Spencer surprised me again by sounding *amused*. "Married people usually sleep together."

"But we aren't married," I hedged.

"I had no idea you were so innocent." He was definitely

holding back laughter now. "Tell me, Kerrigan, are you a virgin?"

I could tell what he thought of that possibility.

Annoyance flared inside me along with a sensation that felt dangerously like arousal. "Does it matter? You seem to think my body belongs to you."

"And you seem to be under the impression that I'm going to force myself on you." He moved closer, bringing his face into a shaft of moonlight, revealing an expression that bordered on interest. I had no doubt the wind would shift and he'd be back to his brooding boredom in no time.

"Isn't that how arranged marriages work?" It popped out of my mouth before I really thought about it. I wasn't engaged to Spencer. The announcement I'd been dreading had been postponed. I was beginning to wonder if it would come at all.

His eyes narrowed, his pupils so wide they looked almost black. "I don't see a ring on your finger, Kerrigan."

"K," I blurted out. "People call me K."

"I'm not most people. Nor am I looking for an arranged marriage with someone who thinks I'd force myself on her." He tapped the edge of his glass and waited for me to respond.

"I'm sorry. That came out wrong. I just thought after..." I stopped short of letting another assumption slip.

"Yes?" he prompted.

"Nothing," I said with a swallow. "'I suppose none of this matters if you don't want to marry me anymore."

"I didn't say that. Regardless of your father's concerns, I expect to move forward according to their wishes." He paused, giving time for this to sink in. When I didn't respond, he continued, "I simply want this to progress on our terms."

"What if our terms are different?"

"I expect they will be, so let me be frank. If we're going to marry each other, there are a few things we need to get clear on, Kerrigan." He emphasized the name, letting each syllable drip suggestively off his wicked tongue. It made me wish it was mine. "This is a merger of two powerful families. We both need something from one another. I'm content to give your family the title and reputation your parents are after. Your family's wealth will help shore up various estates that need a cash influx. In those ways, this is an arranged marriage. But I have no interest in forcing you to do anything but be a good wife."

My mouth went dry at the suggestion in those words. "And how will I do that?"

"Smile. Be pretty. Hold a conversation in private and your tongue in public." He paused as if giving me time to process this.

"You assume we'll go to bed together, but you don't want to sleep with me?" I asked in confusion. A ripple of displeasure rolled through me and landed between my legs. My traitorous body didn't seem confused about this development. It seemed upset as if it had feelings and I was ignoring them. My skin wanted his hands on me. My thighs wanted his fingers to dip between them.

"Any man would like to fuck his wife, especially if she were as beautiful as you are."

My eyes flashed and found the ground as heat crept over my cheeks.

"Don't act coy," he advised. "You must know you're beautiful. So the answer to your question is no. I want to sleep with you. I plan to sleep with you and so much more."

"I don't understand," I admitted, finally daring to look up at him. This whole night was supposed to be about sealing the deal, but I felt more like I was running in circles. Spencer had sent me spinning—spiraling into a heady state of agitation. My skin felt too tight. It prickled with hot awareness the longer I stayed in his presence.

"Some men get off on forcing women." He picked an invisible bit of lint off his sleeve before turning his dark eyes on me. "I do not. Quite the opposite, actually. I'd like to fuck you, Kerrigan, but only when you beg me for it."

I opened my mouth to respond but no words came out. Instead, I swallowed. Spencer rose to his feet and took two steps toward me. There was nothing predatory in his approach. Instead, he moved toward me with a casual ease that said he knew that I wanted him, too. His hands slid into his pockets and he tilted his head, an amused smile curving across his handsome face.

I found myself frozen to the spot, wishing that he would act. I'd known my virginity was a thing of the past when I'd agreed to the arrangement with Tod Belmond. It's why I had lied about it in the first place. I'd expected Spencer to simply take it based on what I'd been told about the situation. I'd prepared myself for that. Now it was like he expected me to crawl onto a silver platter and spread my legs.

Spencer finally spoke, his voice low as though he didn't want to be overheard. "Do you know why I have no interest in forcing you?" He walked around me like he was surveying an object in an art gallery. He paused behind me and I felt one finger trace down my bare shoulder.

"No," I whispered.

He stepped closer, leaving only a small gap between us. His breath was warm on my neck and every inch of my body was aware of him even though the only place we touched was where the pad of his finger still rested on my shoulder. "Ask me to touch you, Kerrigan. Let me show you."

"Here?" I burst out. "Shouldn't we go to a bedroom or..."

"I'm not sleeping with you tonight," he stopped me. "I only want to make a point."

"Which is?" I breathed.

He leaned closer and whispered in my ear. "That I won't ever need to force myself on you, because you're going to give yourself to me in every possible way...freely...wantonly. You are going to measure your life by the moments of pleasure I give you. Now *ask me to touch you*."

It was part of the arrangement. I'd known that. I hadn't expected to actually want him. Somehow it made it worse and better at the same time. Spencer didn't expect me to sleep with him tonight, which meant my panic attack had been unwarranted. I was torn between feeling stupid, over-whelmed, and *hot*. God, I felt hot like my body was on fire. Each word he spoke seemed to add fuel to the inferno burning inside me.

"Touch me," I said. Relief washed over me. I was still burning but now that I'd given him permission, he would extinguish me. But nothing happened.

"You need to ask me," he repeated, a smile coloring his voice. "*Nicely.*"

Was he fucking serious? I spun toward him, tripping on my heels and careening into him. He was closer than I expected, my sense of spatial relation completely frazzled by his mere presence. I righted myself quickly and glared at him. "Do you want consent or a fucking engraved invitation?"

"I told you that I like begging." He stepped back, widening the gap between us, and I fought the urge to go after him.

"I'm not going to beg." I crossed my arms over my chest.

"Not tonight." He smirked at my aghast expression. "But you could ask nicely. It's the polite thing to do when you're getting to know someone."

"Or maybe you're all talk," I hedged. His grin vanished and I felt a surge of triumph.

"Like I said, fucking you is not a requirement for this marriage," he said coldly. "It was a pleasure to see you again, Kerrigan. I'm certain our parents will continue to arrange as many of these damned gatherings as they can."

I balked, watching as he made his way toward the door of the solarium. He wasn't really going to leave. Was he? Was that it? Was it possible that I could get away with playing pretend until Kerrigan came home and fulfilled her end of the bargain? But the triumph I'd felt moments before faded. I'd worked myself up over tonight. I'd sold my virginity for ten million pounds to a man I'd never met. I hadn't expected to find myself wishing something had happened between us. I hadn't expected to want him. This arrangement had an expiration date. Still, there was no way I was going to beg.

But something else was weighing on my mind. If he was leaving, then something must have happened between him and Tod Belmond. "What did you say to my father? He seemed upset by you asking to hold off on the announcement."

Spencer paused at the door and turned to me with cold, hard eyes. There was no smile on his face and his confidence now sent an icy chill down my spine. "I told him that I'd like to get to know you better before I agree to marry you. That's what I told your father. He's given us two weeks, but then both our families will expect to make this public."

"You want to get to know me?" I asked, startled by the idea that Spencer had expectations that felt too much like romance.

"Yes, I'd like to get to know you. I'd like to know what's going on in your head when you watch the room with those wary eyes. And I'd like to fuck you," he added darkly. "Is that a problem?"

I swallowed and shook my head.

"Good. Now, that we've settled that. I have a request to make of you," he said. "Tonight, when your hand is between your legs and you're touching yourself, remember that it could have been me."

"You're certain of yourself, aren't you?" I bit out, hoping he didn't hear the quiver in my voice.

"Yes," he answered to my surprise. "You have so many questions. I have one of my own."

"What?"

"How wet are you right now? I bet you're drenched."

My mouth fell open, but I closed it quickly. "I'm not going to beg."

"We'll see," he said with a dismissive laugh before returning to the house, leaving me behind with regret and a soaked pair of knickers.

CHAPTER FIFTEEN

When I stepped out of the solarium, I was coated in a thin sheen of sweat that had nothing to do with the sultry air. Spencer had gotten under my skin and lit a fire. It simmered inside me and I had no idea how to douse the smoldering embers. I shouldn't want him. He'd been nothing but an asshole, bullying me one second and toying with my feelings the next. Even if he claimed he wouldn't take me against my will, there was something sinister about his expectations. He knew I was attracted to him and I suspected if I'd offered myself to him tonight, he would have taken me with little to no concern for getting to know me, just like his brother had done at the restaurant yesterday afternoon.

Was that what privilege bought you? A free pass to claim whatever and whoever you wished? I should hate that he acted like he did, instead I found myself turned on. I wanted to be disgusted, not aroused by the way he wielded his power. Instead, I was intrigued and left wondering what his next move would be.

"Already sneaking off, dirty girl?" A familiar voice drawled and I whipped around to find Spencer's face staring back at me. "I suppose we can expect the happy announcement any moment. Shall I start calling you sis?"

"Holden." He looked exactly like Spencer save for a few small differences. His bowtie was already undone and his collar loosened. He lounged against the wall with a drink in his hand. There was nothing of the polished, poised politician to him. His hair was combed but untidy, stubble dusted his jawline. He was all rough edges where Spencer was smooth.

"I've been looking forward to this evening since we shared that special moment yesterday," he said with a lowered voice. "Tell me, have you been thinking about me?"

"I don't have time for this." I pushed past him.

"So, are you engaged to my brother?" His question stopped me. "I promise not to spoil the big announcement."

I squared my shoulders, lifted my head, and reached for the most disinterested look I could muster. "No. We're taking some time to get to know one another."

Holden smirked, not bothering to hide the wicked gleam in his eyes over the calculated coldness Spencer had used to keep control of the situation. How could they be so alike and so different? My mind wandered to thoughts of how else they might be different.

"Are you blushing?" he asked, pushing away from the wall.

"No," I said quickly. "I'm just annoyed."

"At me?" he guessed. "Or my brother?"

"Both of you. I'm a woman. I can multitask," I shot back, crossing my arms over my chest.

"I see Spencer has riled you up." He took a swig of his drink, then held it out to me.

I started to refuse, then reconsidered and took it. I downed the rest of it in a single gulp.

"Don't be offended by Spencer putting a pin in things. It's not you. It's a power play. Grandfather is absolutely salivating at the idea of your father's bank account."

"Why wouldn't that offend me?" I snapped back. "Everyone is too busy masturbating to each other's bank balances and titles to remember I'm a person!"

I was beginning to understand exactly why Kerrigan Belmond had run from this life. In a world that placed so much value on wealth and possession, what woman would want to be simply another object collected and kept in a glass case?

Holden's eyes widened, and I braced myself for another dismissive remark. Instead, he started laughing. "Spencer doesn't deserve you. He certainly won't know what to do with you. I'm going to have to have a talk with my dear brother."

"Am I an actual participant in this conversation or may I leave?" I rolled my eyes.

"Oh, don't leave." His hand lashed out and caught mine. Electricity shot through me where our skin made contact and I found myself unable to pull away. "I'm rather enjoying your company."

"That would make one of us." I hoped he didn't hear the slight tremor in my voice or spot how my hands shook.

He didn't release his grip on me. Holden stepped closer and lowered his voice to a whisper, "But yesterday, you enjoyed my company."

"I wouldn't call it enjoyable being trapped in the loo while you screwed some random waitress." I glared at him.

"You're not a very good liar." He took another step closer, trapping our clasped hands between our bodies. "Tell me what you did in there. Listen? Did you bite your lip to keep quiet?" He pressed his groin against the back of my hand and I felt the hard proof that he was enjoying himself now. "Did you imagine what this looked like? How it would feel to be the one pinned against the wall?"

"No," I said in a low voice, not trusting myself to say more.

He leaned closer until he was so close that any movement at all would bring my lips to his. I held entirely still, my breath caught in my throat. "Was that because you were too busy touching yourself?"

"Fuck you," I breathed, catching his heady scent and feeling dizzy.

"Let's not get ahead of ourselves." He lifted my hand, and kissing it, winked at me. "Until next time, dirty girl."

He left me there with those words—an echo of the ones he put in my head yesterday—bouncing around in my pheromone-soaked brain. I was still processing my separate encounters with the Byrd brothers when Iris appeared.

"There you are!" she cried. "I've been looking...darling, what's wrong?"

I closed my eyes, gathering all my strength before meeting her concerned expression. "Nothing. Father's angry with me about the announcement being postponed."

"That's not your fault. I'll speak with him."

"Don't," I said quickly. The last thing I wanted was to cause problems for her. I just needed to get my head on straight and remember what was at stake. I was nothing more than a paid performer. I'd been given my role and agreed to the terms. If I expected Tod Belmond to fulfill his end of the bargain, I had to uphold mine. "I just need to find Spencer. Maybe I can talk to him."

I needed to get this on track. Everything depended on it.

"That's why I'm here," Iris said, looking pleased to be of help as she delivered what she assumed was an innocent request. "Caroline insists you two dance together. She went to find Spencer and I promised I would get you."

"He says he wants to get to know me, but he acts like I'm just a pawn. His brother told me he's trying to piss off his grandfather, " I confided my misery to Iris.

"Be careful around Holden Byrd," she advised me. "As for feeling like a pawn? Do you remember why I chose this gown?"

"Because I'm a queen?" I smiled sheepishly at the reminder. "I'm not sure that it matters if no one else sees me that way."

Iris turned a blinding smile on me. "Let them underestimate you, but never forget the power you hold. If they think you're a pawn, you have the upper hand. A queen moves freely. Don't forget that."

I nodded as we stepped into the drawing-room, and, as if to prove her point, the crowd parted before us, opening a path for me to pass. As we reached the far end, Spencer stepped into view. Iris faded from my side as he extended his hand.

"Shall we dance, Kerrigan?"

I offered him a demure smile, remembering what Iris had said. I took his hand and told him exactly what he wanted to hear, "Whatever you wish, Spencer."

CHAPTER SIXTEEN

E very head turned to watch us as we stepped onto the dance floor. Sparrow Court's drawing-room had been converted into a ballroom since we arrived. A man in a tuxedo took a seat behind the grand piano in the corner of the room and a moment later, the first notes of Chopin's Nocturne No. 2 filled the air. Spencer placed his hand on my waist and began the first steps of a waltz.

"Everyone is looking at us," I murmured, keenly aware of the fact that the room had stopped to watch as we spun slowly to the languid melody.

"Everyone is looking at you," he said. "And I can't blame them."

I arched an eyebrow, searching for a clue as to his sudden, mercurial shift in attitude.

"I apologize for earlier," he continued. "I shouldn't have said what I did."

"And to what do I owe this change of heart?" I asked. With each step we took, I became more aware of the spots where our bodies touched: his hand on my waist, the other clasped with mine, the strong shoulder I gripped as I allowed him to lead me in the steps of the waltz.

"I can't simply apologize?"

"You don't strike me as the type to be sorry for anything," I answered honestly, wondering if he would be offended. Instead, he smiled. It was the first time I'd seen a genuine smile on his face. The shadows that seemed to cloud his features lifted for a moment, allowing me my first glimpse at the man underneath.

"It's just that I didn't expect you to be..."

"Yes?" I prompted as we whirled past a group of onlookers who whispered as we passed.

"I didn't expect you to be a virgin," he admitted.

I stiffened in his arms, my eyes fluttering away from his. It wasn't as though I had no experience with men, and I wasn't certain why it seemed to matter so much. When it came down to it, I think I was more bothered by the fact that it seemed obvious to everyone. "Do I have a tattoo of *virgin* stamped on my back somewhere?"

"It was a hunch, which you just confirmed," he admitted.

Of course, I had. There was something about Spencer that seemed to find its way under my skin. He was an itch I couldn't scratch, and the longer he lingered, the deeper the itch burrowed into parts of me I wasn't sure were reachable.

"I'm actually quite turned on by it," he said.

"Really?" I craned my face back to his, unable to hide how his words made me cringe. "I don't really see why it matters. It's not a defining fact of my existence. Just something that is true for the moment—like being a certain age or having braces."

Spencer's perfect lips twitched, restraining another smile, but it danced in his eyes. "I suppose it's leftover from some primal urge to possess and protect the female. You'll have to forgive the primitive bits lurking in my DNA."

"I guess I don't understand what men find so fascinating about virgins. All I know is that I won't enjoy my first time, it will hurt, and ..." I trailed off before I could confess the truth: I was dreading it. I'd never met a man who made me want to face that rite of passage. Eliza had told me about her first time once. She'd laughed about it, but it sounded terrible to me.

"Is that what you think?" He pulled me a little closer, dipping his head so that his lips were near my ear. "I can only speak for myself, but knowing that no other man has penetrated you—been inside you—is consuming my every thought. Knowing that you saved the most intimate parts of yourself for me makes me so hard. That's why you waited, isn't it?"

His breath tickled across my ear lobe, sending a jolt of awareness through me. My eyes fluttered closed, and I soaked up the way he made me feel with his strong body pressed against mine, his hand holding me protectively. We continued to waltz, the music shifting to a rhythmic pulse in the background. I was dimly aware of the eyes on us even with my own closed. Each step we took, each turn we made, each word we exchanged was part of some esoteric ritual. We were binding ourselves to each other for all of

London society to see, but beneath the ceremony of the moment, something else was stirring inside me.

Spencer spoke as if I'd made a conscious effort to wait for him—the man destined to marry Kerrigan Belmond for years. He had no idea that I'd never thought of him before this week, so how could he be right? Because as his question lingered in my thoughts, I kept returning to the same inexplicable answer: "Yes."

There was a slight vibration in his chest as though the single word had roused more of that primal beast inside him. He managed to keep it locked away, but I sensed it there, hiding behind the sophisticated demeanor and expensive tuxedo. I shivered as I considered what it would be like to unlock Spencer's cage and set him free.

"I won't make you wait much longer," he promised. He straightened and I missed the heat of his breath on my flesh and the closeness of his body. The music began to fade, and our pace slowed. "Kerrigan?"

My eyes snapped open to meet his green ones. They pierced through me, already penetrating me in ways I'd never experienced before.

"Don't be scared," he murmured, still holding me in his arms. "Your pleasure is my pleasure, and I promise you'll enjoy every minute of it."

I LOST COUNT OF THE TIMES MY FINGERS FOUND themselves between my legs that night. Memories of the sensations Spencer had introduced me to kept me in a state of low, insatiable need. He'd told me that I would think of him and whether that was merely an idea he planted in my mind or the unavoidable truth, I thought of nothing else until I was too exhausted to keep my eyes open. I awoke the next morning, covered in sweat with the naked lower half of my body twisted in the sheets. I'd dreamed of him— dreamed of his mouth and hands on me. I felt a thrilling dread and ravenous ache as he moved to claim me. But every time his body covered mine, the dream shifted leaving me unsatisfied.

Sitting up, I grabbed my mobile and checked the time, surprised to see that it was so early in the morning. Dawn streamed through the windows, and I realized that I'd forgotten to draw them last night when I went to bed. I'd been too turned on to think of anything else but relief.

Despite the early hour, I found myself too high-strung to fall back asleep, so I wandered into the attached bath. After washing off a few lingering remnants of make-up I'd been too distracted to see to last night, I knotted my hair up and turned on the shower. The water felt good on my skin as I reached for a bar of soap and lathered it in my hand. Sliding my hand between my legs, I washed away the wet heat that had built there overnight and did my best to ignore the thrum of longing that remained. I was beginning to understand that there was only one way to deal with the way Spencer had gotten under my skin. The itch I'd felt— the one too deep to reach—could only be relieved by one thing. Something he promised to give me even as he made me wait.

I closed my eyes and let the water wash over me as I processed the subtle shift that had taken place overnight.

When I'd agreed to take Kerrigan's place, I had decided I was willing to sleep with Spencer. It was a part of the arrangement I hadn't lingered over. It made me feel dirty like I'd sold my soul for the money Tod Belmond had dangled over me. But last night, that had changed.

I wanted to sleep with Spencer. Every part of me yearned to be in his bed. I longed for him to make good on the dirty promises he had made.

By the time I stepped out of the shower and dried off, my arousal had ticked up again, reminding me that I never managed to quench the desire I felt.

I explored the closet, somewhat relieved to have the space to myself without Giles or Iris picking out options and overseeing every choice. I'd barely paused to look at Kerrigan's intimates yesterday. Now I opened every drawer and reveled in the delicate lace and skimpy garments I discovered. While Kerrigan didn't own many white gowns, she had a surprising array of white lace undergarments. I found myself drawn to them, imagining myself stretched across Spencer's bed in nothing else but the white lingerie, a symbol of the final offering of my innocence.

I chose a matching set in a dainty white mesh that had roses embroidered across the cup of the bra and along the waistband of the thong-style knickers. Perhaps, Kerrigan had picked her outfits starting with her shoes, but I found myself inclined to start here. Iris had told me that what a woman wore was her armor. It seemed to me that what I wore beneath was mine.

I did, however, begin choosing the rest of my ensemble with my shoes. Opting for a pair of canary-yellow

Louboutins that laced at the ankle, I placed them on the stool and went from there. It was surprisingly easy to employ her method. The shoes were a statement that had to be matched but not overwhelmed. A few minutes later, I'd decided on a pair of wide-legged silk pants in a bold floral print that had pops of yellow and a cropped silk tank in a deep, complementary blue. The high waist of the pants revealed only a sliver of skin and paired with the shoes were just the right length.

Opening Kerrigan's jewelry drawer, I paused, momentarily struck that every item in it was *real*. Real gold. Real silver. Real diamonds. I'd been entrusted with all of it.

"In a year, you can have real jewelry, too," I reminded myself. It was mind-boggling to consider I might be glimpsing my future.

I opted for a simple pair of gold hoops and a necklace with a golden lock pendant. As I exited, I heard a faint knock.

"Come in," I called, expecting Giles.

Iris peeked inside and her eyes widened. "You're already dressed!"

"I woke up early and couldn't fall back asleep."

"Something weighing on your mind?" she asked as she stepped inside, leaving the door cracked behind her. "Or rather, someone?"

A smile escaped me, and she lit up.

"I knew it! When you two were dancing, I half expected something to catch fire." She plopped onto my sofa and patted the cushion. "I want details." I blushed, and she laughed. "Okay, you can keep *some* of the details to yourself but tell me what you can."

I walked her through the evening, rearranging small bits of the story so as not to give anything away.

"So Holden let you think he was Spencer?" she repeated after I finished.

"Well, in a way," I said. That had been the trickiest part to explain. I'd done my best to push Holden away from my thoughts. He had tried to creep into my fantasies but I'd shut the door every time. Spencer was the man I was meant for, and the man who wanted me as well. I suspected with Holden I'd be nothing but an afternoon snack.

"He sounds like trouble," she said.

I nodded. I had no doubt that was true, which was the number one reason I needed to steer clear of him. There was enough for me to keep straight without adding a variable to the mix.

Before I could tell her that, the door opened wider and Giles stepped through, carrying a towering arrangement of flowers half as tall as he was and looking mildly surprised to find us sitting there.

"These were just delivered," he informed me, placing them on the coffee table in front of us.

I paused for a moment to appreciate the large white roses, already in full bloom, and complemented by sprays of Queen Anne's Lace. Then, I spotted a small gold envelope tucked into the bouquet. I plucked it out and tore open the flap.

"What does it say?" Iris asked in a giddy voice.

I snorted a laugh as I read it. Apparently, the flowers

were the romantic gesture. The note was to the point, instead. "He wants to have dinner this evening."

"Shall I send back your response?" Giles asked.

I realized then that I had no way to contact Spencer. He wasn't saved in my mobile phone yet. I didn't have his email address. Did that mean he didn't have mine either? Is that why he'd sent the flowers? The whole thing felt like an archaic courting ritual, as though I'd stepped into a Jane Austen novel. It seemed at odds with the erotic charge I felt toward Spencer Byrd, and somehow, completely normal. As if that was just the way things were in a powerful London dynasty.

I had a lot to learn about my new life, but for now, I would continue to let Spencer take the lead. "Tell him I look forward to it."

CHAPTER SEVENTEEN

I allowed Giles and Iris to pick out my dinner dress after it became clear to me that neither of them was going to give up until I acquiesced. After thirty minutes of listening to them squabble, I had a headache. Ducking out of the room, I decided it was time to explore my new home. I'd been on the official tour with Giles, but there was plenty I hadn't seen. I'd always found I needed to get to know a place on my own. Most of the employees I encountered were too busy to do more than nod quickly as they passed, off to whatever task they were in the midst of. But I couldn't help noticing that none of them met my eyes.

The entire house was as picture-perfect as Kerrigan's bedroom. The kitchen was updated and immaculate with high-end appliances and pristine white cabinetry. The sofa and chairs in the drawing-room looked like they had never been sat upon. Everywhere I turned a magazine-worthy spread waited for me, but underneath the glossy finishes and expensive furniture there was a coldness that left me feeling ill at ease. It was all too perfect, as though it had been contrived to create an impression and not a home.

I paused in the sitting room on the first floor and studied a framed photograph of a little girl and a woman, both of whom looked so similar my breath caught.

"That's Marissa and Kerrigan," Tod called, and I turned to find him standing in the doorway.

"Marissa?" I already knew who she was. It was glaringly obvious, but I found myself wanting to hear what Tod had to say about her.

"My first wife." He stepped into the room, offering an uncomfortable smile. "Kerrigan's mother."

"She's very beautiful." My heart pounded as I considered the possibility of meeting her. I'd never known my own mother. I'd never known either of my parents. I didn't have a single memory of either of them. It wasn't rational to want to meet her simply because she looked so much like my mother must have, but I was beginning to understand that love and sentiment didn't operate according to reason.

"She was," he said meaningfully. "She died a few years ago."

I gasped, still staring at the photograph. The woman in the picture was so full of life, her arms wrapped around her daughter as both beamed at the camera. There was no sign of illness. "What happened?"

"A boating accident. She drowned. Thankfully, Kerrigan survived."

"Kerrigan was there?" I repeated. I'd born the loss of my own parents as an orphan who'd never known anything else. I'd ached to know them, building impossible narratives of who they had been and what they were like. I couldn't imagine the pain that came with having one's mother snatched away. I wondered if it was deeper or the same. I wondered if one day I might be able to ask Kerrigan about it or comfort her.

I put the picture back on the mantle, feeling silly.

"She was a better swimmer than her mother. The Coastguard found her clinging to some of the wreckage. She was in the hospital for weeks with hypothermia, and after that..." He trailed away, shaking his head. "I'm sorry this is too depressing a story for a Sunday afternoon. I came to talk with you about Spencer."

"I'm having dinner with him tonight." I was actually relieved to shift the conversation to one of a business nature. Some gut instinct told me to keep Tod at a distance. It was best if there were clear boundaries between myself and Kerrigan's father, even if I didn't understand why.

"I heard. Good job. I was concerned after he delayed the engagement yesterday evening," he admitted. "I apologize if I was harsh on you."

"You were quite clear on the expectations," I said coolly. "I'll do my best to see that his interest remains piqued."

"Not just his interest." Tod leveled a hard look at me. "The sooner he puts a ring on your finger, the better."

"I'm sure it's just a matter of time," I said with a shrug. I didn't need to tell Tod about Spencer's desire to get to know one another or that I'd managed to capture his full attention by admitting to him that I was a virgin. Tod didn't need to know that. It was the part of our indecent arrangement that I felt we both preferred to keep him in the dark regarding. I might not be his daughter, but I looked enough like her to pass as her. I couldn't imagine he wanted to think about me in bed with Spencer anymore than he wanted to imagine Kerrigan there.

"We'll see," he said, his eyes unreadable. "Let me know how dinner goes." Then, he turned and left me to plan my attack.

I WASN'T EXACTLY SUN TZU, BUT WHEN GILES CALLED up that evening to tell me Spencer had arrived, I felt like I'd spent the day preparing to go into battle. Tonight my armor consisted of a fitted red dress with a caged bodice that functioned a bit like a bustier. Two cups barely contained my breasts, and the neckline—if it could be called that—plunged between them. My hips looked especially curvy in the tight skirt. It might have been too sexy if it weren't for its length, the skirt extended to my knees, and the accessories that Giles had chosen. A simple choker of diamonds circled my neck complemented by diamond teardrop earrings. I carried a classic Chanel clutch that matched my black heels, which featured a classic, but exaggerated silhouette that made my legs look especially long.

I left my hair down after it was curled and opted for little more than a few coats of mascara and red lipstick. The effect was simple but sexy.

I'd been a little concerned about the message that wearing red sent, particularly after my intimate discussions

with Spencer yesterday, but as soon as I starte
staircase I knew I'd made the right choice.

Spencer stood in the entry, discussing something
quietly with Tod, but he turned when he heard me. Whatever he was saying died on his lips as he drank me in. He
met me at the foot of the stairs, completely abandoning
Tod, who looked pleased by the snub rather than offended.

"You are a goddess," Spencer murmured in a low voice
meant only for me.

"Which one?" I teased.

"I'm still trying to decide." He grinned. "I'll tell you
when I figure it out." He looked over his shoulder. "I will
take good care of your daughter, sir."

Tod tipped his head. "I'll see you tomorrow, Kerrigan."

"Dad," I forced the term of endearment out, earning me
a flash of shock from Tod who quickly covered it. He left us
then and I felt a flutter of excitement to find myself alone
with Spencer.

Would tonight be the night? I'd done my best to avoid
worrying about whether I would go to bed with Spencer
this evening. Now that he was standing before me, I could
think of nothing else.

"I have something for you." Spencer reached into his
pocket and blood pounded in my ears as I waited. But the
box he retrieved was too long to be a ring box. Apparently,
he'd meant it when he said he wanted to get to know each
other before we got engaged. He flipped open the lid to
reveal a dazzling bracelet made up of two strands of
diamonds and an intricate clasp like none I'd ever seen
before. "May I?"

I didn't trust myself to speak so I merely held out my hand.

"There's a little trick to this," he said. "I'll show you later." He wrapped it around my wrist and fastened it.

I admired it for a moment. "Thank you."

"I know you're expecting a ring, but—"

"I don't expect anything, Spencer." The truth slipped out of me. My words. Not the ones I should use as Kerrigan. I'd never expected anything in my life. It made things easier.

"That changes now," he said darkly and I looked up, startled, by the bleak current in his voice. "If you're to be my wife, you should expect to be treated well, to have expensive things, to have strangers admire you."

"And what should I expect from you?" I asked, trying to puzzle out his suddenly stormy mood.

But his answer was as cryptic as the clouds in his eyes. "Nothing and everything."

Spencer extended an arm and I took it, unable to tear my eyes from how the diamonds glittered with every movement. Outside, I discovered just how important appearances were to him. A cherry red McLaren sports car was parked in front of the house. Before I could stop myself, I giggled.

"Is something funny?" he asked as he led me toward it.

I pointed to the car and back to my dress. "We match."

"So you do," he said slowly. He studied me for a second before catching his lower lip in his teeth and looking away.

I swallowed at the lingering hunger I'd glimpsed before he turned away. There was no denying the white-hot intensity blazing in his eyes. He'd been thinking about my dress and his car. I had no idea what wicked thoughts my innocent observation had produced, but the effect they'd had on him had, in turn, tightened my core and dampened my knickers.

"Where are we going to dinner?" I asked, desperate to break up the tension stretching between us.

"Dinner. Right." He opened my car door and helped me inside. "We better go before I lay you across the hood of the car and see how well you match."

My mouth fell open.

"Even your damn lips match," he muttered gruffly. "I bet your cheeks would, too...Christ, we need to go."

He slammed my door and circled to the driver's side, getting in without a word.

I was beginning to see what Iris meant when she said what I wore was armor. Not only did it strengthen me, but it also had quite the effect on my intended, it seemed.

"Dinner," he said as he hit the ignition button like he was going to walk himself through step-by-step. Whatever internal struggle he was dealing with wasn't giving him any slack.

That's why I couldn't help myself when I added, "And after—dessert."

CHAPTER EIGHTEEN

It was a mistake to bring up what might happen after dinner, given the enclosed space we now found ourselves in. I couldn't help but notice how tightly Spencer gripped the steering wheel. Five minutes into our drive, I realized that if I didn't distract him, this evening would turn into another disaster. I turned my attention to the window as we merged onto the A502 and watched as the world whizzed past with dizzying speed. I had no idea how fast we were going, but Spencer's driving was a mix of reckless-ness and anger like he was pissed at the road for some unspeakable sin.

"What's your favorite color?" I blurted out. It took effort to resist the urge to unfasten my safety belt and fling myself from the moving vehicle. Was that the best I could come up with?

Spencer glanced over, tension fading into puzzlement. "Are we five years old, Kerrigan?"

I had two choices: to be offended or to double down.

"Well, since you're being so conversational, I am forced to start at the beginning. Spoiler: I'm going to ask what you want to be when you grow up next. Think of your answer."

"Red," he bit out.

"Hence the car." I nodded. No wonder he liked my dress. "I think mine is blue, but it depends on the day. And what do you want to be when you grow up?"

"You already know the answer to that one." This time he didn't look at me.

"Prime Minister. That's...ambitious," I admitted to him.

"When we marry, my grandfather will pass his seat in parliament to me. From there, it will be a few years. Although I am expected to be the youngest man elected to the position."

He spoke of it in a curiously detached manner like he was reading from a map he'd been given. None of the passion that sometimes inflamed his words was present. It was a clipped, specific response.

"Spencer, do you want to be Prime Minister?" I asked.

"What?" He threw an insulted look in my direction. "Of course. What man wouldn't want to be the most powerful man in the country?"

"I think the king is the most powerful man in the country," I pointed out.

"Not once I'm in power," he muttered.

"Isn't your family more traditionally leaning when it comes to politics?" I asked.

"My grandfather is." He didn't offer any further clarification on this point.

I sensed it was time to move on. I wondered if he would

ever open up to me about how he really felt about being groomed to be Prime Minister. But maybe our first date wasn't the place to start. "Football team?"

He exhaled as if relieved to be talking about anything other than colors or careers. "West Ham."

"West Ham?" I couldn't contain a laugh.

"I'm a glutton for punishment," he admitted.

"They've had a rough go of it for..." In truth, I couldn't remember the last time that the team had been highly ranked in the Premier League. In another lifetime, probably.

"Since they first stepped foot on the pitch?" He shrugged. "It was my dad's team. I guess I just have a soft spot for them. He used to say that you don't love football for the wins. You love it for the game."

"Your dad sounds wise," I said softly.

"I don't honestly know," he said. "He died before I was old enough to know what kind of man he was. I only knew him as my father."

"I understand that."

"Your mother?" he guessed.

Of course, he knew that Kerrigan's mother had passed away. I thought of the picture I found earlier today. Kerrigan had known her mother, but had she known her as a woman like Spencer said? Or only as a mum? I had no idea, but I did know what it was like to be left with bits and pieces of memories to put together where a person once was. "Yeah. I don't think I really knew her."

"What about your father?"

"I didn't really know..." I cut myself off, realizing my

mistake. Panic rose in my throat with a surge of acid. "Sorry, I was still thinking about my mum. Dad? I guess I don't know him that well, actually."

Spencer nodded like he understood and a weight lifted off my shoulders. "I feel that way about my mother. I suppose I know her. She's been hovering over me her whole life, making plans and choices, but it's like...that's all she is."

"What do you mean?"

"I'm not sure I even know." He grinned at me. "Maybe we should go back to talking about our favorite colors before we're too depressed to enjoy ourselves."

I laughed in agreement. We were in serious danger of ruining our night. "I already know your favorite color. What's your favorite food?"

"There's this little pasta shop in Venice," he told me as he turned on a side street near Covent Garden. "It's sort of hidden, but it's incredible. You take it to go and then you just wander around and get lost."

"That sounds magical," I murmured, wondering what it was like to go places. I'd imagined Venice and so many other cities, it sometimes felt as if I'd been there. But I'd only seen them on television and in magazines.

"I'll take you there," he said instantly.

"Now?" I asked.

"I'm sure they'd be closed before we got there. Someday, though, when you least expect it, I'll throw you over my shoulder and whisk you away to eat pasta."

It was strange to plan a future for someone else. Every decision I made would affect Kerrigan's life. When I'd agreed to the arrangement, I worried that I might accidentally ruin her life by making a poor choice. Now, I envied the life I was creating for her. She would be the one to wander Venice with Spencer's favorite pasta. Not me. She would crawl into his bed every night. I was just a stand-in.

"You're quiet," he noted, breaking into my thoughts, as he pulled up to a valet stand.

I forced a bright smile. "I was just trying to decide my favorite food."

"Okay." He studied me for a moment as if he didn't believe me, before getting out of the car.

An attendant opened my door a moment later, and before I was on my feet, Spencer was at my side, taking my hand as the attendant got behind the wheel of the McLaren.

"So what did you decide?" he asked me as we walked toward the entrance of the restaurant.

"I don't think I've found mine yet," I said. "At least, part of me hopes I haven't because that means I get to keep looking."

His head tilted, a curious smile spreading across his face. "I like that answer. How about we start looking for it together?"

He gestured to the sign hanging over the restaurant that read *Jardin Fiore*. The outside was far from impressive, simply another place to eat it seemed. The only clue that suggested otherwise, up to this point, was the presence of valet parking. As soon as we stepped foot inside, everything changed. It was as if we'd stepped through a magical portal and been transported into an enchanted garden. We proceeded under an ivy-covered arch into the dining room where flowering branches hung from the ceiling, dangling their blossoms romantically over tables with white-linen cloths and plush leather chairs. On the far side of the room, a fireplace crackled giving a warm glow to the room, the only other light coming from candles placed strategically around the space.

"I feel like I just went through the wardrobe," I said with awe.

"Narnia has more snow, I think."

"Mr. Byrd, we have your table waiting," a host said, two large, leather-bound menus in her arms.

We followed her across the room quietly. The whole place reminded me a bit of being in a library. There was a sort of hushed reverence in the room as if every soul there had lowered their voice to a whisper out of respect. A small table, tucked in the corner, next to the hearth, waited for us.

"I was going to ask if you've been here before," Spencer said as we took our seats, "but judging from your reaction, I think I have my answer."

I accepted a menu from the girl and thanked her. "I'm glad the first time was with you." Spencer's eyes sparkled in the firelight at my choice of words, and I blushed. "You know what I mean."

"I do," he said with mock solemnity, before adding, "but I think you'll be glad that the first time is with me no matter the occasion."

I reached for my water with shaking hands and took a quick drink. I suddenly wondered if sitting so close by the fire was a good idea if he was going to insist on getting me hot and bothered.

"I'm sorry," he said, sensing my discomfort. "I'll behave. Would you like me to tell you what I like on the menu?"

I nodded, forcing my eyes away from his and opening mine, surprised to find a collection of both Italian and French dishes. I thought of the restaurant's name, a curious mix of both languages.

"The Foie Gras, obviously. I also love the risotto, and I see the venison is back on the menu. It wasn't the last time I was here."

I closed my menu, unable to keep up with him. "Would you order for me?"

"If you wish," he said.

"I trust you. Surprise me."

It turned out to be the right choice. Spencer didn't disappoint and he seemed to take his role in helping me search for my as-of-yet undiscovered favorite food very seriously. First, he ordered oysters on the half shell, which tasted like the ocean on my tongue. Then Foie Gras, which I had serious reservations about, but was surprised to find rich and delicious. Spencer watched me take every bite without much commentary. Instead, there was a sort of quiet contentment that overtook him. I had never seen him like this before. When our main courses arrived, I took a bite of veal and moaned. The dish had been new to the menu but Spencer was certain I would like it. He wasn't wrong.

"You have to try this," I said, spearing another bite on my fork and holding it out to him.

Spencer brought his perfect mouth to my fork and slid it off with his teeth, a hungry look in his eyes that had nothing to do with the food or the restaurant. He chewed slowly, his eyes hooded and he groaned a little. "Delicious."

I looked down at my plate, feeling heat spreading across my chest and up my neck toward my face. The glimpse of what he looked like when he was experiencing pleasure sent my pulse rocketing. I wanted to see that face again. I wanted to be what made him make that noise.

"Try mine," he commanded, holding out a bite of his filet.

Our eyes locked as I slid it off his fork with my mouth, and a vein ticked in his neck. I was reminded of the dreams I'd had the night before. Like those, I felt keyed up with no relief in sight. Every word, every moment that passed between us seemed to ratchet my desire up a notch while taking me farther away from what I really wanted.

Him.

There was no denying that the music and the wine, the food and the flowers all conspired to remind me that the one thing I wanted wasn't on the menu.

Spencer's hand brushed over mine. "Would you like another bottle?"

I shook my head. Any more and I might get drunk. I wanted to be present every moment I spent with him, especially if he kissed me.

"Kerrigan, come—"

"Would you like to see the dessert cart?" Our waitress interrupted us, and I resisted the urge to throttle her for her poor timing.

Spencer inclined his head. "Shall we?"

"I think I'm finished." I drained my wine glass to prove it.

"The check, please." He reached into his pocket and produced a money clip, straining to hold the stack of pound notes folded between its prongs. I waited for him to return to what he was about to say before we were interrupted, but he seemed to have forgotten.

I sucked in a breath, almost wishing I had opted for at least one more glass of wine and decided to make the first move. "Spencer."

"Yes?" he asked, drawing out a hundred-pound note, which was followed by four more.

I watched, realizing what different worlds we were from, and that he didn't even know it. He had no idea that I'd never eaten french food or tried veal or sat next to a fire with a man at a romantic dinner. He never would know that he'd just given me so many firsts that I'd lost count. Maybe he was simply following the prescribed courtship rituals of society, and I was the one caught up in the romance, dazzled by the candlelight. And somehow, none of it mattered. I knew what I wanted next—what I wanted more than anything. "Take me to bed."

CHAPTER NINETEEN

Spencer's hand moved to his tie and he tugged at it, a silent battle being waged in his eyes. "Are you sure? We don't have to move this fast."

"I'm asking you to sleep with me, not marry me," I told him, taking his hand in mine.

He raised his eyebrows. "Now *you* don't want to marry *me*?"

I opened my mouth to protest, wondering how I'd managed to fail so spectacularly at my seduction attempt.

"I'm fucking with you," he said before I could mount my defense. "I think we need to have a sense of humor about this arranged marriage thing. It will keep us both sane. To be clear, I want to take you to bed, and, as far, as marriage..."

I nodded, narrowing my eyes and staring directly at him. "Kiss me. Fuck me. Marry me. Just do one of them before I explode."

Spencer leaned forward and cupped my jawline,

drawing my lips roughly to his. The kiss was rough and gentle, promising and consuming, fire and ice. He forced my mouth open, capturing my tongue with his as he tasted me. The agonizing arousal I felt doubled until I forget where I was and who I was. There was only him and the place where our mouths touched and all the places I wanted to be touching him.

A nervous clearing of the throat alerted us to the return of the waitress.

Spencer pulled back, his palm still holding my face, and handed her the money without looking at the bill. "Keep the change," he told her, "and have them pull my car around *now*."

"Yes-s-s," she stammered, adding, "Thank you, sir."

"I think we befuddled her," I said with a grin.

His thumb stroked my cheek. "Befuddled, huh? Or maybe it was the two hundred pound tip."

I swallowed down this revelation. "Are you always so generous?"

"No," he confessed. "Only when I want something, and right now, the only thing I want is my bloody car so that I can take you home and fulfill your request."

I swallowed again, my mouth going dry at the directness of his words. I'd offered, and he had accepted. Only a short drive and some clothes stood between me and the other side of virginity.

We barely spoke as we made our way out of the restaurant to the pavement as an attendant zipped around the corner with the McLaren. He got out and handed the keys to Spencer with the speed of a man who understood exactly why he'd been summoned to perform his job with breakneck speed. The only thing that could have been more obvious was if he'd given him a fistbump. Spencer didn't seem to notice. His eyes didn't leave me until he'd helped me into the passenger seat and closed the door.

But when we pulled away from the restaurant, he turned the opposite direction from which we had arrived.

"Where are we..." I watched as we drove deeper into the heart of London towards the shops and people and busy streets.

"My flat," he said in answer to my unfinished question.

"Oh."

"Is that a problem?" he asked, looking from the road to me.

"I thought you lived in Hampstead."

"I do," he said as he shifted gears and flew down the street. "Some of the time. I keep a flat in the city to crash when I'm here late and for...privacy."

"It's where you take women," I said, understanding what he really meant.

"Does that bother you? We can go to Sparrow Court, but I can't guarantee my mother won't descend on you the moment we step foot through the door."

"No," I said quickly. Tonight, more than any other, I wanted this to be about him and me without anyone else there to spoil it. "I was just surprised."

"I assumed you knew about the flat." He flipped on a signal before roaring around a corner. A group of tourists jumped back onto the pavement to avoid being hit, but he seemed to neither notice nor care. "I'll be certain to have my people send over a full list of my assets."

"That's not necessary." I felt stupid for asking him about the flat. "I didn't mean to pry."

"You didn't," he cut me off. "You should know about my holdings. What's mine will be yours someday."

A knot tightened in my stomach at his words. Nothing of his would ever be mine. Not really. I was only playing pretend. I pushed away the thought.

"Except what you keep in the prenup," I teased, trying to lighten the mood.

"No prenup," he said swiftly.

"What?" I asked, staring at him.

"No prenup," he repeated. "If you marry me, that's that. Unless *you* want one."

"But..." I struggled to express my surprise. Foregoing a prenuptial agreement was the kind of thing that poor people with nothing to lose did. People like me. Not men with titles and money, mansions and sports cars. Not men planning to be the future Prime Minister.

"Kerrigan, your family has more money than mine. I suppose I'd understand if you want a prenup, but your father...Look, if we get married, I'd like one thing between us to be based on trust—not just a transaction. I know it's old-fashioned, but a prenup feels like an escape clause. I suppose I've never believed marriage was something you could take back."

"No prenup." It slipped out of my mouth. It wasn't really my place to promise that, but he was right. It was how it should be, and somehow, I was certain it was Kerrigan's one true chance at happiness. If her husband loved her and if they trusted each other, maybe going through with her father's wishes wouldn't be so bad.

He released the gearshift and took my hand, bringing it to his mouth. He kissed it and then let it go to shift the car into second. My head was still moving as swiftly as the car had been when we slowed down and turned into a private parking garage.

Spencer took my hand as soon as I climbed out of the car and led me toward a lift. As soon as we were inside, he was on me. He crushed me against the wall of the lift, his mouth capturing mine while his hands bunched my skirt at the hips, raising its hem enough for him to push one leg between mine and urged them open as far as my restrictive clothing would allow.

He loosed a groan of frustration against my mouth. Nipping my lower lip, he glared at me with mock annoyance. "I have a love-hate relationship with your dress."

"Oh?" I murmured, wondering how his presence could be more intoxicating than wine. I felt drunk or stoned or some blissed-out combination of the two. Spencer was a heady combination when he wasn't touching me. Add his lips and his hands and I was done for.

"I love how it looks on you," he muttered. His hand slipped around and fingered my zipper. "How it shows off every one of your delicious curves. How it draws attention to every place I want to kiss." He brushed his lips over mine, painting a tingling thrill across them. "But I hate that I can't touch you."

"You're touching me now," I said softly, pushing my

chest against his, savoring the increased contact. There was no part of Spencer that wasn't hard it seemed. His chest was like a brick wall, solid and strong. His arms held me in place. I was a lark, captive in his cage. By choice. My unclipped wings didn't flutter, only my heart did. It was the wild thing trapped. My body was a willing prisoner. I wanted to be kept and petted.

Spencer's head bent and captured my earlobe, sucking it between his teeth before he whispered, "I can't touch you *where I want to touch you.*"

That cleared things up while sending more blood rushing from my head to the swollen ache between my legs. I clutched his broad shoulders, surrendering to his possession.

I was only dimly aware of the flat as we entered. Spencer didn't bother to turn on any lights. Instead, he guided me down a hallway and into a room. The only thing I could process was the presence of a king-sized bed. Spencer turned to me, gently taking my shoulders, and waited until I was looking at him.

"Are you sure you're ready?"

I licked my lower lip, my mouth going dry. I appreciated him asking, but each time he did it marred my desire with doubt. I met his questioning gaze. "Yes."

He kissed me, his shoulders relaxing as if my answer had finally freed him of some pent-up tension. His index finger tipped up my chin and he spoke softly, "I'm going to undress you now."

In the lift, he'd torn at my clothes with a frenzy, but he didn't rush now. Spencer circled around and stopped behind me. His lips brushed my shoulder as I felt my dress's zipper slowly descend. His mouth followed, claiming each inch of skin as it was revealed. I locked my knees, afraid I might give in to the dizzying effect of his touch and fall over. Spencer paused when he reached the small of my back before tugging the zipper the last few inches, revealing his first glimpse of my thong.

"Fuck, never wear anything else," he muttered, running one finger along its white waistband.

I giggled nervously as his hands moved to slide up my arms. I'd never been undressed by a man before. It wasn't what I expected. Spencer's fingers hooked the straps of my dress and he peeled it down with a deliberation that made me hold my breath.

"You're so fucking beautiful," he said. "It's like you're a gift meant just for me." When the dress was past my hips, he released it to puddle on the floor.

I closed my eyes, feeling vulnerable and powerful at once, as I stood before him in nothing more than a pair of lacy knickers and bra that did nothing to hide my body.

"As much as I like this," he murmured as his hands skillfully unfastened my bra, "and I do, I spent the entire evening wishing your breasts were in my mouth. I don't think I tasted a thing."

"That's a pity." I swallowed as his arm reached around, grabbed the front of my bra and drew it off me. It joined my dress on the floor.

"I don't think so. It only made me want you more." His arms wrapped around me and he covered my breasts with his hands, massaging them tenderly. "I don't think I can wait any longer to taste you, Kerrigan. Come to the bed."

Spencer stopped the sensual massage and took my hand, leading me toward the bed. He nodded to it.

I dropped on all fours, instinctively, and crawled toward the pillows. I paused, uncertain what to do next. He reached out, rubbing circles on my bare backside.

"The things I'm going to do to your ass," he said in a strained voice that made me bite my lip. "But not tonight. Lay down on your back."

I did as he commanded and Spencer dropped to his knees at the foot of the bed. He crept slowly up my body, stopping when his face reached my breasts.

"Finally," he said darkly, his eyes glinting up at me before he bent to take a nipple in his mouth.

I gasped at the new sensation. Hot. Wet. Circling. Circling. His mouth sucked greedily until I was writhing beneath him. By the time he'd done the same to the other, my hips were bucking against him, seeking relief from the throb I felt at my core. Spencer smirked wickedly at me as he moved down, dropping kisses across the flat plane of my stomach along the crease of my hip.

"Now for dessert," he growled, rearing up to his knees. His hands gripped the waistband of my thong and yanked it down. He lifted my leg and slipped them off.

My pulse quickened, my heart pounding, as I lay spread bare before him. Spencer pushed my thighs apart, studying me for what felt like an eternity, with a smugness that made me catch my breath.

"Perfect," he announced like he'd been grading me silently.

Then he dove forward and before I could process what was happening, the wet suction of his mouth had found the bundle of nerves pulsing between my legs.

Stars exploded in my vision.

There was a cry.

My cry.

And shaking.

I shook and shook and shook.

But Spencer continued, unsatisfied by my swift climax. My legs pressed against his head, my body rebelling against the assault on the tender spot. That didn't stop him. My hand tangled in his hair. I wasn't sure if I wanted to yank him away or hold him in place. He decided for me, burying his face as I rode out another wave of pleasure. When I finally collapsed, boneless, he sat up with a look of purely masculine satisfaction on his face. His tongue ran along his lower lip.

"You taste so fucking good," he rasped.

I threw my arms over my face, overwhelmed and panting.

"Is that the first time a man has pleasured you?" he asked slowly.

I swallowed before answering with a meek "yes."

"Fuck, I get off knowing that. I love knowing I'm the only mouth that's been on you."

I peeked out from my arms to see him prop himself on his elbow. He was still between my legs, but now he was simply looking at me.

"You're wet," he said, "but I want to do everything I can to make this good for you."

I nodded. Spencer's hand covered my sex, stroking it with feather-light touches that still sent tremors through my body.

"Relax," he said soothingly as he coaxed a finger between my folds. I felt it slip inside me. It felt foreign but not unpleasant. He worked it deeper until I found my thighs falling open, welcoming the touch. Then I felt the tip of another finger push in as well. This time it felt as though he was lighting a fire. It didn't hurt exactly, but I found myself biting down on my arm.

"You're tense," he said in a low voice. "I want you to take a deep breath and let go."

I did as he said, inhaling deeply, and then exhaling. It felt as if I was melting into the bed. The pressure between my legs eased and his fingers began to move more easily.

"That's it." His fingers slipped all the way out and back in, each time he thrust them inside me I felt a slight strain as he loosened me with patient strokes. I became lost to the sensation, until he said, "I've got three fingers in you now. How do you feel?"

There were no words. I could only moan. Something was building inside me and when it burst it would take all my defenses with it. I would be at Spencer's mercy, and there was nothing I wanted more. Then without warning, the sensation vanished and I was left empty.

"Please," I cried out, finally lifting my arms from my face to find he'd stood up and begun to remove his clothes.

Each piece he removed revealed more of his strong, athletic body.

"Are you ready?" he asked as he shrugged off his shirt.

My mouth fell open at the sight of his muscular chest and I whimpered, pressing my legs together to fight the ache consuming me. He turned away as he took off his pants. Then he reached into a drawer in the nightstand and produced a foil wrapper. "Are you on birth control?"

I shook my head.

"Get on it," he demanded. I heard the foil rip and I craned my neck curious to watch him roll it on. My eyes widened when I saw the size of his cock. It jutted out from a thatch of dark, neatly trimmed hair. I gulped, realizing that no amount of preparation would be enough to make it easy for that to slide inside me.

Spencer followed my gaze and offered a smile. "It might hurt a little."

"A little?" I croaked. His dick had to be seven inches long. There was no way it would fit.

"At first, and then"—he climbed on top of me—"you'll want every inch of it." He positioned himself between my legs, stroking its broad crown along my warm, wet seam. "It's not too late to..."

"I want you," I stopped him with a breathless whisper.

"Put your arms around my shoulders," he directed me as he lowered himself against my body. His hand was pinned between us, guiding him toward my virginity. Fire ignited as he pushed the tip of his cock inside me.

I hung on to him, burying my face against his shoulder as my body burned.

"The next bit is the worst," he said, kissing the top of my head. "Ready?"

I nodded without lifting my head. I felt safe tucked against him.

Spencer pushed farther in. This time more forcefully, and I felt a slight pop as my body gave way to his invasion. He slid in until I was sure no more of him could fit and then stilled, giving my body time to acclimate to this intrusion. I felt full of him. My skin stretched taut by his length and girth until I felt like I might snap. I took another deep breath and exhaled. It helped a little, but not as much as last time.

"God, you're tight," he said, sounding as strained as I felt. He withdrew slightly before thrusting slowly back inside. With each movement he seemed to bore deeper.

A curious thing had happened in the process. The pain lingered along with a smoldering ring of fire, but with each deliberate thrust, the pain mingled with the sensitivity lingering in my nerves. Spencer must have known that the more I orgasmed, the more likely he would be able to stoke my arousal back to life. I gave myself to him, trusting him entirely, as he took me to someplace I never travelled.

Deeper.

Farther.

The journey carried me up a summit. When at last his hand knitted through mine and his body stiffened with impending release, we leapt together. It wasn't the explosion of pleasure he'd given me earlier. It was a freshly lit fire that warmed me. I lingered in it as we collapsed together.

Neither of us spoke for a few minutes. We just laid

there, our hands clasped together as we stared at the ceiling.

Spencer was the one to finally break the silence.

"Was it terrible?" he asked gently.

"It was wonderful." I'd taken the first step into his world, and I knew, without a doubt, there was no turning back now.

CHAPTER TWENTY

The sun woke me the following day. Spencer was asleep. He'd kicked one leg free from the sheets, which seemed to be caught on something. I tilted my head, blinking sleepy eyes, and then I realized what the unusual tent pole was. I swallowed back a giggle at discovering yet another new thing about sex.

Slithering down the bed, I climbed carefully between his legs, doing my best not to wake him.

Although my sexual experiences were limited, I'd given more than a few blow jobs in my life. No one had bothered to return the favor. Spencer had shown me last night what I'd been missing. I suspected there would be no selfishness like that on his part. He'd gone down on me again after our lovemaking as though to soothe any pain he'd caused.

I owed him—big time.

I gathered my hair loosely and pushed it behind one shoulder before lowering my mouth to take him into my mouth. He was already rock hard, which meant I didn't need to linger, but I found myself wanting to anyway. I ran my tongue along his length to his balls and back up. I licked the tip, catching a creamy bead of pre-ejaculate in the process. Spencer groaned in his sleep and shifted, giving me a better angle.

I seized the opportunity and lowered my mouth over him. Remembering his advice yesterday, I relaxed, allowing him to slide deeper into my throat before I closed my lips and sucked lightly.

"Am I dreaming?" he asked groggily. He propped an eye open and found me looking up at him, his cock down my throat and my lips planted at its root. "*Fuck.* How are you doing that?"

I lifted my mouth slowly and brought it back down until I'd swallowed him again entirely, keeping a steady pressure with my tongue the whole time.

"Don't stop," he grunted as I continued to bob up and down over him. His hand fumbled for my hair, got a handful, and urged me faster. "Fuck. Fuck. *Fuck.*"

He erupted in my throat, his cock still buried so deeply inside it that I felt only a hint of the hot lashing of his climax. When he finally stopped twitching and grew soft, I released him and crawled back up next to him.

"How does a virgin do that?" he asked me, suddenly alert and staring at me with pride and curiosity.

"I'm not a virgin," I reminded him.

"You were yesterday."

I nuzzled against him, wondering how much he would

ask about my past. It was full of moments I'd rather not relive. "When you don't put out, you learn to get good at blow jobs. I had to keep my boyfriends happy."

"You learned to do that because some wanker was upset you wouldn't sleep with him?" Spencer shook his head in disgust.

"It kept them happy for a while." But never for long.

"I can't believe any idiot ever let you get away." He kissed my forehead, then sighed. "I suppose we can't stay in bed all day."

"Probably not," I agreed, feeling as sad as he sounded.

"I need a shower. Join me?"

"I need coffee before I can be trusted to do anything," I told him.

"There's a bag in the cupboard." Spencer sat up, and I missed his body immediately. He swung his legs over the side of the bed, threw one more impressed look my way, and then disappeared into the bathroom.

I laid in bed, covers pulled to my chin, and studied the room for the first time. Last night, I'd only had eyes for the bed and Spencer. This morning, I noted how spartan the room was. There was a large television mounted opposite the bed, but otherwise, nothing hung on the walls. No artwork or mirrors or anything that conveyed a sense of Spencer's private life. The bedside tables held nothing but a lamp on each, and a remote on his side for the tv. I opened the drawer next to mine and found it empty. Between the hollowness of the space and the neutral grey decor, it felt more like a hotel than a bedroom. My stomach grumbled, reminding me that it was also empty, owing in no small part to last night's activities. Getting out of bed, I found Spencer's shirt, abandoned to the floor the night before. I slipped it on, buttoned it up, and continued my exploration.

The rest of the flat, which I'd only glimpsed in passing, was equally bare. The whole place was the definition of a bachelor pad down to the pristine, and obviously unused kitchen with its stainless steel appliances and white quartz countertops. It opened into a large sitting room. A U-shaped couch sat in front of a fireplace. Alcove shelves held a few volumes of leather-bound books that seemed more for show than reading. I opened cabinets looking for dishes. I found the glasses and mugs along with a coffee maker and a bag of beans. A quick check of the fridge revealed nothing more than a few bottles of champagne and some leftover containers. I moved them around, crossing my fingers that I might find some eggs—anything to tide me over until Spencer was out of the shower—but it was no use. I'd given up and turned to make coffee when I heard his footsteps behind me.

"Is your fridge always a wasteland? I'm starving. Aren't you?" I called as I measured the beans into the grinder.

"It's always like that," a high voice that was both too feminine and too curious to be Spencer answered.

I spun around, spilling some beans on the floor. They skittered across the tile floor in every direction as I stared at the pretty blonde watching me from the end of the kitchen island. A short silk robe was tied around her waist and her hair was piled on top of her head. It was clear she'd also just gotten up. A hundred questions occurred to me at the same time, but only one seemed important enough to lead with.

"Who are you?" I demanded, too shocked to care about sounding like a bitch.

"Rose," she said like this meant something before sauntering into the kitchen. She bent to pick up the beans, displaying a perfect, and totally bare, backside to me. Straightening she pulled open a drawer to reveal a hidden rubbish bin and dumped the ruined beans into it. "You must be Kerrigan. I've heard a lot about you."

"I can't say the same," I said slowly.

She turned and leaned against the counter, shrugging her thin shoulders. "Spencer never brags about his conquests."

"You're with Spencer?" I asked in a strangled voice. The room started to spin as I tried to process Rose and who she was. Had he brought me back to a flat he lived in with another woman?

"No, I'm here with Holden. Spencer and I are ancient history." She waved me off like I should know better. "I don't think Holden knew Spencer would be here or we would have gone to my place instead of his."

Things were beginning to make sense. "This is their apartment then?"

"I see Spencer failed to mention that, too," she said dryly.

"We were in a bit of a..." I searched for the right word. One that conveyed my intimacy with Spencer without making me sound cheap. I finally landed on "rush."

Rose's blue eyes sparkled. "I bet you were." She nodded to the coffee maker. "Tell me there's enough for us. Holden had me up all night. You know how it is."

I bit my lip and nodded. I supposed I did know, but it felt wrong sharing something as special as last night with her, no matter how nice she was being.

"Rose," a familiar voice yelled and my body tightened. A moment later, he walked into the kitchen, stopped in brief surprise, and grinned.

His mouth opened, but he stopped himself from saying whatever was about to come out. Instead, he greeted me with a simple, "Good morning, Kerrigan."

"Holden?" I said, half greeting and half question.

"Didn't know you'd be here." He opened the fridge and snagged a takeout container. He tipped his head. "It's from last night if you want some. We ordered enough for an army."

Rose moved to his side and wrapped an arm around his waist, smiling up at him adoringly. When she looked back at me there was warning in her eyes. She was staking her claim on him. I wanted to tell her that she had nothing to worry about. I wasn't the least bit interested in Holden.

"Wait," she said, blinking a few times, "is she the one from the loo?"

"The one and only," Holden said, digging a fork into the container. He spun it around, capturing a large bite of noodles.

"I guess we have kinda met," Rose said. She popped onto her tiptoes and whispered something in Holden's ear. He barked with laughter.

"I doubt it," he said.

"You work at Hillgrove's?" I guessed. I ignored the heat that rushed to my cheeks. They both knew I'd heard them fucking in that stall.

"I think you know the answer to that," she said with a smirk.

"I was just using the toilet," I said flatly. "I felt bad interrupting. Thankfully, it didn't last too long." I crossed my arms and shrugged.

Rose let out a whoop of approval. Holden, meanwhile, clutched his chest. "You wound me, but I hope you enjoyed yourself."

"Holden," Spencer said, coming out of the bedroom, "stop torturing my girlfriend." He was wearing nothing more than a pair of jeans. Without a belt they hung at the waist, showcasing the hard angles of his body, particularly the deeply hewn v-shape that started at his hips and continued under his waistband. His hair was still damp from the shower, but his jawline was peppered with stubble.

"Apologies," Holden replied, glancing between us. "Moving up the ranks quickly, are we?"

"Why wait?" Spencer asked. He walked over to me, paused, and planted a kiss on my forehead.

I resisted the urge to melt into a puddle on the spot. There was a tenderness to it that was unexpected but welcome. I tilted my head back and accepted his lips on mine.

"Come back to bed," he whispered. Letting me go, he poured himself a cup of coffee and stalked out of the room. Holden followed after him, leaving me alone with Rose.

She watched me as I busied myself making my cup of coffee. There was no milk or cream in the fridge but I found some sugar in a cupboard. When I turned to look for a spoon, Rose opened a drawer, pulled one out, and passed it to me.

"Thank you," I said, trying to keep things cordial. So what if I had heard her with Holden or she had been with Spencer in the past? All that mattered was this moment. I had no past with either of the Byrd brothers, and I had no future as well. Rose didn't know that, and she didn't need to know.

"Spencer isn't the type to settle down," she warned me.

"We'll see." I smiled at her over the rim of my coffee mug.

"You think if he puts a ring on your finger, he'll belong to you?" she asks, shaking her head. "You'll never be a part of their world, even if you marry him. Don't believe otherwise, or they'll just break your heart."

I paused and considered her for a moment. Was this just an astute observation or personal experience speaking? It was hard to tell, and I knew, without a doubt, I couldn't trust her to be truthful with me.

"I know what's going on," she continued in a low voice. "That he's going to marry you for money. That your parents arranged it, but there's something you should know. Holden told me—"

"Rose," Holden's voice cut her off sharply. He rounded the fridge, his face a stony mask. It was impossible to know if he'd heard what she was about to say. "We should let the lovebirds have their nest for the day." He looped an arm around her shoulders, towering a good foot over the petite blonde, and guided her toward the hall.

But his eyes never left mine.

CHAPTER TWENTY-ONE

Spencer had gathered my dress and shoes and laid them out over the freshly made bed. My bag was sitting next to it. He looked up at me as I entered with my cup of coffee and smiled. "I hope you don't mind, I added my number to your phone."

"It feels like we did this a bit out of order, didn't we?" I dug my mobile out of my purse. Scrolling down, I found his entry. "Smile."

I snapped a picture of Spencer, standing there shirtless, caught completely off-guard.

"Don't use that."

"Too late," I said as I added to his profile. Then I dashed off a text. "Now you have mine."

"Like a proper boyfriend and girlfriend. Let's see. What else are we supposed to do? Do you want to get some breakfast?" He glanced back at the dress. "I probably have something you could wear in the closet."

I couldn't imagine going for breakfast in the wrinkled

dress I'd worn to dinner last night. If that wasn't enough to scream *walk of shame*, my bare face and tangled hair would do it.

"I think maybe I should head back to my place," I said. "I don't want my father to worry about me."

Spencer shrugged dismissively. Clearly, he wasn't worried about what Tod Belmond thought. "I should think he'd be happy. It's a step in the direction he wants us to take."

"I suppose. Although, things are moving more quickly than I expected," I confessed, hoping that he would understand. I didn't regret going to bed with Spencer, but even I was surprised that after twenty-three years of waiting to sleep with someone, I'd slept with him after knowing him only a few days. Still, part of me felt it was only right. I'd known it somehow. I'd been sure. But that tiny voice in the back of my mind kept whispering that everything between Spencer and I was a lie. How could I have gone to bed with a man who didn't know who I really was? I had slipped into Kerrigan's life too easily. I needed to clear my head, and there was no way I could do that around Spencer. He had a way of muddying up my brain.

"Well, it's not as if it will take a year to get to know each other. I simply wanted more time before the press descended upon us and my mother started in on invitations and all that nonsense," he explained, opening a drawer. He found a pair of jeans and held them out to me. "They'll be loose on you."

"Thanks," I said as I took them. I pulled the pants on over my bare legs, not bothering to figure out where yesterday's knickers had landed. "At least we have time before they make us get married."

"The longer we give them, the bigger the spectacle will be. I think when we are ready, we just elope," he said as though he'd given it some thought.

I swallowed back a cry of surprise at this revelation. Part of my arrangement with Tod Belmond was that the wedding would take a long time to plan — long enough for him to convince Kerrigan to come back and take her rightful place at the altar. That timeline was going to have to be significantly shortened if Spencer decided he wanted to run off to get married. I felt torn. I knew I was going to have to tell Tod about this development, so he would have time to work on tracking Kerrigan down before it was too late. For some reason, I couldn't imagine taking wedding vows for her. Not only because it wasn't my place to do so, but because I feared what would happen to my own heart in the process. I liked Spencer. Maybe I liked him too much. I was certainly attracted to him. I had never considered what would happen if we became emotionally attached to one another. I thought of this relationship as more of a business transaction, like the one I'd made with Kerrigan's father. But things were getting much more complicated than that—much more quickly than I could process.

"I'd always imagined a large wedding." In truth, I'd never thought about getting married. It'd never really crossed my mind. I didn't know why. Weren't girls supposed to think about their wedding days? I hadn't, but the lie was easily delivered and even more easily swallowed.

"We'll do whatever you want, of course." He grabbed the shirt I wore and pulled me to him. "Are you certain you need to go home?"

"Don't you have work or something?" I didn't actually know what Spencer did on a daily basis, which was yet another reason things were moving too fast. It wasn't as if preparing to be Prime Minister in ten or fifteen years was a full-time, paid occupation. Still, no one had mentioned him doing anything else but that.

Spencer checked his watch and grimaced. "I really should be getting into the office. My grandfather tends to be a bastard on Mondays. Secretly, I think he hates taking weekends off. If the man could spend every moment working, he would."

"If you don't have time to drop me off, I'm sure I can call a car," I offered. Each second I spent with him, my brain felt more muddled, as if I had taken a very strong drug. The sooner I could get some space to clear my head, the better.

"Nonsense. I'm not sending you away in a car after last night." He wrapped his arms around my waist and studied me for a moment with a worried expression, mistaking my confusion for pain. "Holden distracted me from checking on you. Are you okay? Is everything all right *down there?*"

Despite the anxiety clouding my brain, I giggled. "I think I'll live."

"That's exactly what a man wants to hear after the first time he sleeps with a woman."

"Sorry. I'm new at this, remember?" I teased him.

"Actually, that reminds me." He angled his face so that his mouth covered mine, and I forgot about anything but him at that moment. "I hope you enjoyed yourself as much as I did. I promise it only gets better."

"Promise, huh?" I whispered. "You're talking a big game."

"I'm more than willing to back it up right now," he said, huskily, and his mouth crushed against mine again. I was lost to him, completely drowning in his taste. I wanted more of it—more of him. It took effort to push him away.

"Office, remember?" I said, panting heavily as I pulled away from his arms.

"Right." He scratched his head as he stepped away, putting some necessary space between us. "I have a feeling I'm going to be late to the office a little more often in the future."

I hated the thrill that raced through me as much as I loved to hear him say it.

CHAPTER TWENTY-TWO

As soon as I reached Willoughby Place, I raced to Kerrigan's bedroom. I hadn't bothered with the shoes I'd worn the night before, going barefoot in Spencer's car during the ride. I wanted to make a quiet entrance. I wasn't sure that was even possible, given that I had to be let in through the security gate. Still, I didn't relish the idea of running into anyone while I was holding my Louboutins and last night's dress in my arms. As soon as I was inside my private sanctuary, I locked the door and breathed a sigh of relief. I tossed the dress and shoes on the couch, making a note to ask Giles what I should do with things that needed to go out for cleaning. Then I looked down at myself. I was still wearing Spencer's shirt and jeans. Part of me wanted to stay in them all day, but I knew that wasn't a good idea. I stripped his clothes off as I walked into the closet and dug out more lacy undergarments followed by a pair of Kerrigan's jeans and a tank top. Since I'd been here, I spent every waking moment dressed like I just walked off the runway. Today, I needed to feel more like my old self. Changing was the first step to that. I had thought of the second step as Spencer drove me home.

Crawling into Kerrigan's oversized bed, I dialed a familiar number on my mobile. It was early enough in the day that the pub wouldn't be open. Eliza's sleepy voice greeted me.

"I'm only answering because I was worried you were dead," she told me groggily. "But unless you are dead, don't call me so early in the future."

I didn't bother telling her that didn't make much sense. I'd learned after months of living with my roommate that it took her a while to process things in the morning. Usually, there were only three things that could be counted on to wake her with a jolt: a cigarette, coffee, or gossip. I only had one at my disposal.

"I lost my virginity," I confessed.

That did the trick.

"What?" she exploded. "You've been there like ten minutes. He must be really hot."

"It's not like that," I said.

"Then tell me what it's like," she said. In the background, I heard the familiar flick of a lighter and then a long drag as she lit her first cigarette of the morning.

"He's not what I expected." I didn't know how to explain it. Not without sounding crazy. That was the trouble with this whole situation. It was inherently mental.

"How was the sex?" Trust Eliza to get straight to the point.

"Phenomenal," I admitted softly. "Better than I imagined."

She giggled. "I had a feeling it wasn't going to be as bad as you thought it would be."

"He made sure that I enjoyed it," I said, feeling a bit guilty for sharing the intimate details. There was no one else I could talk to about this openly. Only a few people knew the truth. I wasn't about to talk to Tod Belmond about the things I was doing while bearing his daughter's name. There was no way Giles and I were going to discuss my sex life. That only left Eliza. But Eliza had something else I needed. She was a bridge to my old life. She was a reminder of who I really was. After a night with Spencer, I needed that connection.

"At least you're enjoying yourself," she muttered. "The pub is full of wankers coming to the country on summer vacation. I wish I were you."

I hesitated long enough that Eliza finally said, "Kate?"

"I'm here." It was the slap in the face I needed. Hearing my name was like a bucket of cold water poured over my head. I'd been living a dream. I'd been playing at a fairytale. It was time for a dose of cold, hard reality. "I think I like him too much."

"Oh." I heard another long drag. "Look, think of it as a perk. You don't have to go to bed with some guy you hate. You're not the one being forced to marry him. It's not your life that's on the line."

"I think that's the problem," I admitted with a sigh, sinking into the pillows on my bed. *Kerrigan's bed*, I silently corrected myself. "I can't help but feel like I'm making choices for her, and that's not my place."

"Think of it like you're an actress," Eliza said brightly. "You're playing a character. Someday she'll come back and take over the role."

"That's what I was afraid you would say. Doesn't that mean I should think about her future?"

"Why? She's not. And it's not like she can't come back and refuse to marry him or divorce him or whatever," Eliza said casually, and I envied her easy dismissal of the ethical concerns at stake. "You do what's best for you. And ten million pounds is best for you. If you get to enjoy some hot sex at the same time, why feel guilty about that? Just focus on the moment and enjoy yourself."

"Eliza," I said in a soft voice, "what if I fall in love with him?"

She took the longest drag off her cigarette I'd ever heard. "Don't."

"I wish it were that simple," I said flatly.

"You barely know him, Kate. You can't be in love with him."

"I said *what if* I fall in love with him," I pointed out.

"And I told you not to do it," she said, repeating her advice. "Look, enjoy the sex, but keep it casual. Don't open up to him. Don't share who you really are with him. Don't let him open up to you. Keep it shallow. I'm talking wading pool deep."

"I'll try," I said, but I wasn't convinced I could.

"Okay, tell me the rest," she said. "Is the house huge?"

I filled her in on the details of Willoughby Place and

then described Sparrow Court. When I reached the description of Spencer's flat, she stopped me.

"Wait! He has a brother?" she asked after I mentioned my run-in with Holden and his lady friend.

"A twin brother," I said.

"You didn't mention that until now?" she shrieked. "Is he available? Because Spencer is really hot. Oh my God, are they identical? Or is Spencer the hot one and then Holden is like the Picasso version of him?"

Despite the worry that had weighed me down all morning, I burst out in laughter. "The Picasso version?"

"Yeah," she said. "Like his face is a little wrong. He looks like Spencer but his eyes are different colors or his ears are lopsided?"

"They're completely identical, as far as I know," I said, still laughing.

"There you go. Problem solved."

"What do you mean?" I didn't see how having two men as handsome as Spencer and Holden in my life was going to make anything any easier.

"Use the brother," she told me. "Mess around with him."

"I'm not sure Spencer would like that," I said, my amusement fading.

"Not judging by what that Rose chic said," Eliza reminded me. "You want to keep things casual with Spencer? Divide your attention between the two of them. I'm sure it will just be a huge burden to be sleeping with two handsome aristocrats."

"You're crazy," I told her.

"I'm right," she corrected me. "Oh shit, babe, I have to go. I promised Ron I would get to the pub early. Don't wait so long to call me next time. I want to know all the dirty details."

I hung up with her, still shaking my head at her solution to my problem. I couldn't get involved with both Spencer and Holden.

Could I?

CHAPTER TWENTY-THREE

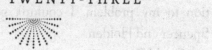

Before I had a chance to really consider it, a text message showed up on my phone.

Hey, Holden and I are going to watch the West Ham match tonight at our place. Care to come and see why they should be your team, too?

I hesitated before typing my response. I wanted to see Spencer.

Holden?

He promises to be on his best behavior, but I can kick him out if you want me all to yourself. I just thought the two of you should get to know each other.

I thought of what Eliza had said. This was my opportunity to feel out the situation. It was a crazy idea, but I wasn't sure I had any other choice. I had to find a way to keep myself from getting too involved with Spencer. That didn't leave me many options. So I responded with the only viable one.

What time?

SPENCER HAD A LATE MEETING WITH HIS grandfather, so I arranged to have the driver take me to his flat. Tod had seemed positively giddy at the news. And if he noticed that I hadn't come back to the house last night, he didn't say anything. I supposed it was easier not to worry about someone who wasn't your daughter. I didn't bother to change from my tank top and jeans. A night watching football seemed like something that should be kept casual, but when I arrived Spencer opened the door, still wearing his suit.

His necktie hung loosely around his collar, and he breathed a sigh of relief when he saw me.

"Long day?" I asked.

"The longest. But I'm glad to see you," he said. "I'm just going to change out of this."

"You hungry? Maybe I could order some take-out?"

"There are some menus in the kitchen. Holden will show you where they are." He disappeared, leaving me with his brother while he went to change. Holden appeared as if summoned.

"I'm told my assistance is required," he said to me.

"I'm sure I can find the menus on my own." I began opening drawers, doing my best to ignore him. The trouble was that Holden was as hard to ignore as Spencer, no doubt owing to their having the same face. But where Spencer sent heat flashing through my body, turning my skin slick with sweat, Holden elicited a trembling chill. Being near him filled me with a cold-but-thrilling dread that heightened my awareness of my whole body.

"They're here." Holden reached for a drawer at the same time I did, and our hands brushed. Goosebumps rose along my arm where our skin made contact, sending a tremor through me. I took a step away from him.

"I won't bite," he said, noticing my reaction, "unless you ask me to."

"That's exactly what someone like you would say," I said haughtily.

"Someone like me?" He smirked and moved a step closer. I took another back. "What does that mean?"

"I think you know exactly what it means," I said in a low voice. Where was Spencer? What was taking him so long?

"But I want to hear you say it," he murmured, moving even closer and sending me backward until I hit the counter. I reached behind and gripped its edge, realizing I was trapped. Holden leaned forward planting his hands on either side of me. "You've got nowhere to go now."

I swallowed, refusing to look at him. "I told Spencer I would order food. I'm hungry."

"I think I can help you with that." He was close enough now that any movement would bring us into contact. His lips—Spencer's lips—stared back at me in invitation. I wondered what it would be like to kiss him. Would it feel like it did when I kissed Spencer? Would it be different? Would it be better?

"What did you order?" Spencer's voice called from down the hall. Footsteps approached and Holden straightened up. He handed me the menus then walked to the couch.

The menus shook in my hands, betraying how flustered I was by the encounter.

"I haven't decided," I told Spencer as he entered the room. "Curry or Chinese?"

"Curry."

"Chinese."

They both answered at once and I wasn't sure which one wanted what.

Spencer shot me a lopsided smile that made my heart flip. "My brother and I always want the opposite thing when it comes to food. It's one of the few ways we're different."

"Naw, I'm better looking, brother," Holden said as he dropped onto the sofa and spread his arms along its back. He spoke to Spencer, but he looked at me. I turned away.

"You'll have to be the deciding vote," Spencer said. "Choose wisely."

I swallowed, wondering why all decisions had to be left up to me. My brain was swimming, so I looked down and chose the menu on the top of the stack. "Curry."

"Yes!" Spencer pumped his fist and shot a victorious look at his brother. "Clearly, we belong together."

Holden studied me for a moment as if trying to decide if that was true, but when he finally spoke, he only said, "Get me some Chicken Tikka Masala."

I placed the order while Spencer grabbed a few beers out of the fridge. It was late enough that the match had already started, and by the time I joined them on the couch, settling in closely to Spencer, they were already yelling at the screen.

"That's a fucking terrible call!" Spencer yelled as a referee threw a flag on the ground.

"So you both root for West Ham?" I asked Holden, feeling more comfortable speaking to him with Spencer at my side.

"Like he said, we pretty much agree on everything but food. We definitely have the same taste." Holden winked at me.

Next to me, Spencer was too busy yelling at the television to notice his brother's flirtations. I took a long swig of my beer followed by another. It was going to be a long match.

Apparently, during any Premier League match, food delivery was couriered by snails. Our dinner still hadn't arrived as the final minutes were counting down on the clock, and I was three beers deep and beginning to feel buzzed. Spencer and Holden weren't much better off. Each bad call seemed to result in more drinking. I was too tipsy to know if the referees were as bad as the brothers both thought or if the team was simply living up to its reputation.

"I'm going to use the loo," I told Spencer, kissing his

cheek. He grunted a response, his eyes never leaving the match. I left them discussing whether West Ham would finally be relegated this year.

I'd had enough beer that it felt good to relieve myself. When I finally stood to wash my hands, I looked in the mirror and found my face blurring slightly at the edges. Food needed to arrive soon, or I ran the risk of getting far too drunk. I retied my hair, straightened my shirt, and returned to the living room.

The couch was empty and the match over. I looked around, wondering where they had gone. Opening the fridge door, I pulled out another lager and began looking around for the bottle opener. I finally spotted it sitting next to the sink, surrounded by nearly a dozen other bottle caps. Moving to open it, I felt two strong arms wrap around me.

"You smell good," Spencer said, nuzzling the sensitive spot behind my ear. A soft moan slipped out of me and I felt his cock stiffen in response. Twisting in his arms, the beer forgotten on the counter, I offered my lips to him. The kiss was deep and slow. My mouth parted and his tongue slipped inside, flicking lazily over my teeth and sending an icy thrill racing up my spine. Somewhere in my drunken haze, I thought I heard an alarm ringing. But I was too lost to him, to lost to this slow, purposeful kiss. It wasn't like the others. It was full of a longing he had never shown me rather than the hunger with which he'd devoured me the night before.

"Well, then," his voice interrupted, and I broke away from him as I tried to process how he could be kissing me and speaking to me at the same time.

I stumbled backward as my eyes fell on Spencer standing in the open entry, holding a paper bag. My hand flew to my mouth as my brain caught up with the situation.

"You bastard!" I smacked Holden in the chest. I turned pleading eyes on Spencer, hoping he could see the mistake I'd made, but his face was shadowed. "I'm sorry—"

"Don't apologize," Spencer said, his words slurring slightly, as he placed the curry on the kitchen island. "I told you my brother and I have the same taste in everything but food."

"That doesn't mean that it's okay for me to kiss him. I thought—"

"That it was me?" he guessed. There was a sort of detached interest on his face as he watched me fumble for an explanation. Meanwhile, Holden was lounging against the counter, looking neither guilty nor ashamed. Instead, he seemed amused.

"I didn't know if you were going to share this one with me," Holden said to his brother.

Spencer abandoned the food and took a spot equidistant to us. "That's up to her," he said. "She isn't like the others."

"I can see that." Holden continued to speak to his brother like I wasn't there.

"Wait?" I stopped them. "Share me?"

I did my best to muster an appropriate amount of disgust at this suggestion, but I was beginning to feel feverish with them both here. This is what Eliza had told me to do. She told me they would be into it. Why hadn't I believed her? Because I didn't want to? Because I wanted Spencer to keep me to himself?

That was dangerous. I knew that. And standing here with both of them in front of me and alcohol swimming in my veins, I couldn't think of a reason not to have both. Hadn't Eliza said to enjoy myself while I could? The time would come when neither Spencer nor Holden Byrd was beholden to me. But for the moment, they were.

"I thought you said she was a virgin," Holden said, and I felt the sting of betrayal. Somehow, the fact that Spencer had told his brother made it easier to make my decision.

"She's not sleeping with you," Spencer said with a finality that dared him to be questioned.

"I thought that was my choice?" I was tired of standing here while they treated me like a toy they were negotiating custody of instead of a person.

Spencer arched an eyebrow in surprise. "I thought you might want more time before..."

"You're right," I said to him, taking a step toward Holden. "I'm not sleeping with him. *Tonight*." I stopped in front of his brother and looked between the two of them. The alcohol was making me brave and I slipped into the role of someone much more liberated than I had ever been. Maybe that was how Kerrigan was in real life. Maybe I was channeling her. "How does it work? Does one of you watch? Or...?"

Spencer stepped closer, his tongue darting over his lower lip. "Sometimes. Sometimes, we both...but I don't think you're ready for both of us at the same time."

I felt a gush of arousal between my legs at the thought

of both of them touching me, both of their mouths on me, of... I turned hooded eyes on Spencer and simpered, "Did you tell him how good I am at giving blow jobs?"

His jaw clenched as he shook his head.

"Come now, boys. Am I supposed to believe you don't kiss and tell? You said you share everything." I tossed my hair over my shoulder, daring one of them to contradict me.

"We haven't gotten around to talking about it," Spencer said slowly. He continued to move with caution as though he was trying to approach a wild animal.

"Do you want me to show him instead?" I was drunk, and out of control, and somewhere I knew that. The trouble was that I didn't care.

"It's nice to share," he agreed, crooking his finger for me to come closer.

I moved toward him, swaying my hips, feeling emboldened by newly discovered empowerment. When I reached him, Spencer grabbed my face and delivered a rough kiss. He was marking his territory, erasing the kiss I'd just experienced with Holden. Flames burst inside me, turning my core molten at the demanding show of affection. This wasn't the kindness he had shown me in bed the night before. It was harsh and dominating. When we broke apart, he grabbed the waistband of my jeans and dragged me to the sofa.

Spencer sat down on the edge of the coffee table and pointed to my clothes. "Take them off."

I bit my lip, dimly aware that Holden was watching. Was Spencer calling my bluff? Did it matter?

I leveled my gaze at him, reached down, and pulled my

shirt over my head. It wasn't as bold of a move as I'd anticipated since it got stuck on my ponytail. When I pulled it off
triumphantly, Holden had joined us and taken his seat on
the couch. My eyes darted to him, trying to gauge his reaction to what was happening. I had no idea if Spencer would
keep encouraging this. I had no clue how far this would go.
But with their eyes on me, I wanted to see it to the end.

I savored the lusty glint in Spencer's eyes as I removed
my bra. Holden shifted in his seat a bit to get a better view.

"The jeans, Kerrigan," Spencer said like he was
running down a checklist.

I unfastened them, pausing only a moment in case he
wanted to stop me. When he said nothing, I pushed them
to the floor, along with my thong. Then I stepped one foot
at a time out of them.

I was completely nude in the middle of a flat with two
men watching my every movement. I glanced between
them, pleased at how their eyes trailed over every inch of
me. But I made no move.

Spencer's throat slid, and finally, he gave his next
command. "Show my brother what you can do with that
wicked mouth."

I walked to Holden. His trousers strained against his
erection. Holden relaxed back into the corner of the seat
and spread his legs wide, so I could lower to my knees
before him. He threw both arms over the back of the couch
and smirked, his eyes darting down expectantly. Out of the
corner of my eye, I saw Spencer shift. Then I felt him sit
down on the table behind me.

I had their full attention. At that moment, I was the

center of their universe. They orbited me like planets did the sun. Only I could give them what they wanted—what they needed.

I undid Holden's fly with ease, my fingers moving with the brazen self-assurance pumping through me. I slipped my hand into his pants and freed his cock. It felt heavy in my hands.

"You are identical," I breathed. How nature had created not one but two perfect specimens of men was beyond me, but I was going to enjoy it.

Leaning forward, I planted my hands on his thighs for balance before delivering a slow, languid lick from Holden's balls to his tip.

"That's right," he urged.

I circled the tip, licking and sucking it lightly until I was sure he was more than ready. Then I took him into my throat.

"Fuck me," Holden said, sounding like Spencer had this morning. "Christ, are you...fuck!"

When I hit his coarse hair, I tightened my lips around him and drew up his length before slamming my mouth back down. This wasn't the slow, deliberate torture I'd delivered to Spencer in bed due to beer, so I gagged slightly.

A hand skimmed over my backside as though Spencer had heard the mistake. But I didn't let up.

"You like sucking his cock, don't you?" Spencer whispered, sliding his palm down between my legs. "She's so fucking wet, Holden. How's that feel, brother?"

"Fucking amazing," Holden grunted.

"Pull her hair," Spencer said, and I shuddered with pleasure as Holden grabbed my ponytail and yanked. He urged me up and down.

Spencer bent his mouth to my ear and murmured, "Someday, if you want, we'll fuck you both together. You want that, don't you?" He slid a finger inside me. "I can tell by how wet you are. No resistance at all."

I whimpered, the sound muffled by Holden's dick.

"You're not ready yet, though, but I think you should be rewarded. Right, brother?"

"Fuck" was Holden's only response. He jerked my ponytail up and down, fucking my throat savagely. My own need built with each thrust.

Spencer slipped two fingers inside me, plunging roughly in and out. I was so close. I wiggled toward his hand, wanting more, but he denied me. Rather than a reward, he seemed to be playing with me. Taking me close to the edge and then pulling me back until he finally withdrew altogether.

When Holden's release hit the back of my throat, I swallowed it and then lurched back on my knees. I shoved my hand between my legs, driven to the point of frenzy, and rubbed furiously until I shattered in front of them. I cried out, head falling back.

Crashing. Crashing. Crashing back to earth.

When my hand finally stilled, I hung my head, panting. Before I could make another move, Spencer picked me up off the ground and carried me to his bedroom. He kicked the door shut so forcefully that it rattled on its hinges. He set me down on my feet in front of his bed.

"I want to fuck you," he said harshly.

"Yes," I mewled. Coming at my own hands didn't hold the same power now that I knew the pleasure he could give me.

"Ask me to," he bit out.

"Fuck me, Spencer. Please fuck me."

He pushed me to the mattress, then flipped me roughly over onto my stomach. My core tightened as I heard the swift swish of his belt being pulled free of his pants, followed by the rip of foil. There was no cautious pause or tender attention tonight. I'd rattled his cage, and the beast inside him wanted satisfaction.

Spencer drove into me with one punishing stroke, and I cried out in pain. His hands gripped my hips as he thrust harder and deeper and faster each time. The pain shifted, and I wept with pleasure each time he plunged inside me. His skin smacked against mine, calling out one word.

Mine.

Mine.

Mine.

The message was loud and clear. He had shared me with Holden, but I belonged to him.

When he finally came with an angry roar, he pulled out and threw himself on the bed.

It had been too rough and fast for me to join him. That wasn't going to work for me.

I dropped down and coaxed his softening cock into my mouth, sucking until it began to harden again. Spencer crossed his arms behind his head and watched with muted interest as I worked.

When he was hard again, I dug another condom out of the drawer and rolled it over him. Then, I climbed onto him and sank down. I had to stop midway to adjust to the deep angle.

I rocked back and forth, pinned to him, my throbbing center dragging across his skin until I felt the slow tightening of my muscles. Pleasure spilled from me as I rode him.

Spencer reached to me and gripped my hips, coaxing me faster. He drove deeper into me until I was wound around him so tightly I thought I'd break. "I'm the only one who can make you feel this way."

His words snapped my taut core, and I unraveled like a spool of delicate thread.

CHAPTER TWENTY-FOUR

I woke up to the sound of Spencer snoring softly next to me and a mild headache. Untangling myself from him, I got out of bed as quietly as possible, not wanting to wake him. In the harsh light of dawn, all my choices seemed wrong. Flashes of the prior evening hit me as I gathered my clothes and snuck into the living room. I was relieved to see that it was empty. The curry rested, forgotten, on the counter. I waited for my stomach to remind me that I hadn't eaten, but it was too knotted up for me to feel even an ounce of hunger.

Shame flooded through me as I considered what I'd done. How was I supposed to feel toward either of them now? How would I look them in the eyes? Eliza had been wrong. This had not made things easier. It had only made them more complicated. I might not have slept with both brothers, but I'd never done anything like that before. I'd never even considered doing something like that before. I wanted to blame the alcohol for my rash decision, but I couldn't help wondering if it had only made it easier to do exactly what I wanted to do all along. I ignored the pang of desire I felt at the memory of how it felt to have Spencer's hands on me while Holden's cock was in my mouth. I remembered everything I had said to them. I remembered how I egged them on. Last night, the words felt brave and confident. Today I wondered if I had made promises that I couldn't keep. I wasn't really going to sleep with both of them, was I? Have a threesome? I stopped dead in my tracks as I considered it.

But despite the fact that Spencer had acted into it last night, there had been something in the way he fucked me — and it couldn't be called anything else—that told me it wasn't as simple as brothers sharing everything. He had liked watching me with Holden. He had gotten off. But then he had taken me to his bed and claimed me repeatedly —*possessively*. Which one was the real Spencer? I didn't have the courage to wait around to find out. If this was supposed to make it easier to walk away from this life and hand it to Kerrigan Belmond, it didn't feel that way. It felt like I was actively destroying her world.

I slipped on my shoes, considering whether to write a note, but decided better of it. I didn't bother to call for a car. I simply gathered my things and left as quickly as possible. The last thing I wanted was to face either of them. I would have to, eventually, but I knew I needed time before then. As I stepped from the lift into the private lobby, my time ran out as I came face-to-face with Holden Byrd.

"I thought you'd want some coffee. We used the last of it yesterday," he explained, holding out a to-go cup.

I took it cautiously and stared at him, waiting for a reckoning that didn't come.

"I didn't poison it," he said dryly, sipping his own to provide proof of its safety. "You're leaving awfully early. Does Spencer know?"

I shook my head. "I needed some fresh air."

Holden's eyes fell to the floor, and he nodded in understanding. "Are you going to take a cab?"

"I haven't decided," I admitted. "Maybe. I might take the Tube."

"Let me drive you home," he said.

"I don't think that's a good idea." *Not after what happened last night.*

"Look, Spencer will kill me if he finds out I let you take a cab or the Tube. Plus, we should talk."

"About what?" I said quickly.

He shot me a look as if to say *are we really going to play it that way?*

I took a deep breath and considered my options.

"Or I can go upstairs and wake Spencer up," Holden added, "and he can drive you home."

"Fine."

He'd played the one card he knew would win the hand. It was hard enough to face Holden this morning. There was no way I could face Spencer. We took Holden's car: a vintage Jaguar that was as different from Spencer's McLaren as possible.

"I thought you said you two have the same taste," I commented as I got inside and buckled the safety belt.

"That's just a line," Holden confessed. "The truth is

that we're as different as night and day. Spencer's the serious one. The Prime Minister." He flourished his hands across the horizon like he was picturing the future. "I'm the rake. We are, however, best friends. At least, as much as you can be best friends with your biggest rival."

"Rival?" I repeated. I had expected him to say that.

"It's obvious, isn't it? Although, I suppose he looks like he's winning. I'm not certain that being forced to carry on the Byrd name and inherit all that responsibility is much of a prize. I'm much happier being the one with no expectations resting on my shoulders." He paused before adding, "We do have the same taste in women though."

I kept my eyes trained on the scenery out the window, not daring to look at him as he said this. "That must be complicated."

"It's never been a problem."

"It hasn't?" I said, not able to hide my disbelief.

"Not yet," he said with meaning.

"Because you share them," I said, realizing the truth. They took turns, so neither had to make any hard choices.

"It's always been better than fighting with each other," Holden said in a dark tone.

"Has it?"

His eyes flashed to me and I saw a muscle tense in his jaw. "You wouldn't understand."

I needed to drop this topic. I knew that, but I couldn't bring myself to do it. There was something about the way that Holden spoke which made me think of the secrets that lingered in Spencer's eyes. There was more to the story.

Holden sighed, drumming his thumbs on the steering

wheel, before he finally began to speak. "When my dad was alive, we did everything together. Spencer loved nature. We could never get him to come inside."

"And you?"

"I was into books and painting and sculpting. Big nerd," he admitted sheepishly, "and then I discovered girls."

"Did you discover them first?"

"I've always been an early bloomer," he said with a smirk. "And then Dad died, and everything changed. He was supposed to be the one to inherit the title and the responsibility. He'd been groomed for it. Suddenly, my grandfather had to consider which one of us was more suited to take his place."

"How old were you?" I asked softly.

"Thirteen," Holden said miserably. "We went from being best friends to being pitted against each other at every opportunity. Grandfather made our family move into Sparrow Court, so that he could make sure we were raised with a proper male role model." Bitterness coated his story, and without thinking I reached out and placed my hand over his on the steering wheel. His eyes flickered to it, but I didn't let go.

"Why? What was the point of doing that to you? You were children."

"You know better than to think any of us can be children. We're heirs and heiresses. All the money in the world and none of the choices, right?" he said with a hollow laugh. "Grandfather's excuse was that he could die any moment and he had to know that the family name and title would be passed to the right one of us. It was relentless. We went to the strictest boarding schools. We were forced to abandon any interest we had that didn't align with politics. We hated every minute of it, but the worst part was that we were starting to hate each other."

"And then Spencer won?" I understood now why Holden was bitter. Why he played the part of the charismatic scoundrel of the family. It was easier than admitting defeat.

"No," he said, surprising me. "I lost."

"You didn't lose," I started to say, feeling a rush of sympathy, but Holden laughed.

"It was the only way to win," he explained. "I chose to lose. I knew what was at stake. I could grow up hating my brother and being forced into a life that neither of us wanted, or I could be the failure no one bothered with. So I took the easier road. I became the fuck up. I got into trouble. I got kicked out of schools. I was uncontrollable. Wild. And somehow that was easier for all of us. It was easier to write me off and let me do as I please. Grandfather put all of his time and attention into Spencer, and I simply became the charming bachelor you see before you."

"Is that what you are?" I asked him quietly. More and more, I could see the cracks in his act.

"I think you'll find that in our family, we all have our roles to play. I hope you understand that."

"I understand what's expected of me," I said simply, withdrawing my hand. My heart hurt for him. It hurt for the boy that had lost his father and nearly lost his brother. I understood what it was like to feel trapped with no options. I understood what it was like to become what they wanted you to be rather than what you might have been if given enough time and respect.

"At least you can't say I didn't warn you." He didn't look at me the rest of the way to Hampstead. I got out of the Jaguar in silence. Before I was through the gate, he rolled down the window and called after me. "Kerrigan?"

I stopped and waited.

"If you were mine, I would never share you." Then he threw the car in reverse and drove away.

CHAPTER TWENTY-FIVE

A week passed, and I ignored Spencer's calls and text messages. I couldn't face him. Not after what happened with Holden. Not after what I'd learned. What kind of life was I consigning Kerrigan to? What kind of life was I consigning myself to? I didn't have any answers. I simply knew that it was dangerous to be around either brother. I needed a plan. A way to keep my emotions detached from the situation. Eliza's had backfired. Instead of spreading myself between the brothers, I now felt more divided than ever. Spencer had shown me glimpses of the man he would become, but Holden had bared his soul to me. I didn't expect he would do so again, and yet, I couldn't forget what I knew.

Like me, they had taken their roles as if they had no choice. There were tens of millions if not billions of reasons in their future. I knew it was impossible to walk away from that kind of money. How much harder would it be to have never had any choice at all?

I spent most of the week avoiding social activities by claiming a terrible bout of menstrual cramps. Iris had taken to checking on me every day, bringing me a cocktail of pain relievers she swore up and down would get me on my feet in no time. But there were no cramps. No reason to take them. The last thing I wanted was to be on my feet. I wanted to hide. At least until I could figure out what to do. But each day that passed made me more anxious. I'd agreed to a year pretending to be Kerrigan Belmond. The only thing that would deliver me from that contract was the passage of time or her return. I was beginning to understand that I couldn't survive a year torn between the brothers. Not without losing something I couldn't replace. They were never mine. I needed to remember that. I needed to get away before I forgot that fact entirely. But I had no idea where to start.

The following Monday, Giles arrived with my coffee and found me on my couch in front of the fire.

"I hope you're feeling better," he said pointedly.

I wouldn't be surprised if he kept track of things like menstrual periods for Kerrigan. Either way, it was clear he knew I was lying. Still, he hadn't called me out on my bullshit. If he took issue with what I was doing, he said nothing to me. Even Tod had given me space. If there was one thing a girl could count on, it was that men got squeamish when female problems came up.

"I am. I think it's behind me now." I needed another excuse. Something to buy me time. It wasn't like I could pretend to be on my period still. Not unless I wanted them to push for medical attention.

"Good, there are some matters to attend to. As you requested, I canceled any social engagements last week, but it will be important for you to make an appearance soon."

I read between the lines of what he was saying. Tod would be asking questions soon. I had a responsibility to uphold. I had obligated myself to fill Kerrigan's shoes, and I couldn't back out now. Not without losing the ten million pounds I'd been promised and my only chance of finally being free of my past.

"Of course." I reached for the itinerary he held out for me.

"What is this about going to Surrey?" The entire week revolved around it. There would be no getting out of it.

"The Belmonds are taking the next fortnight at their country home," he explained. "You are expected to travel with them unless you have business keeping you here."

I gawked at Giles for a moment. He had to know I was avoiding Spencer and this entire situation, yet, here he was giving me an out. Tod and Iris would be traveling to the countryside. I could go with them and avoid Spencer and his family so long as Tod didn't invite them to join us. *Or* I could stay here under the pretense that I wanted to be near my boyfriend, which would please Tod Belmond to no end.

"I'm afraid I can't," I said, taking my cue.

"You should speak to Iris," he advised meaningfully. "She'll be disappointed, but surely she'll understand. I assume you need to be near Spencer."

I nodded. "I'll talk to her."

A short while later, I found Iris in the kitchen going over a menu with the cook.

"There you are." She gave me a big hug. "I was just going over the menu for our holiday. Is there anything you'd like to see on it? I was wondering if Spencer might be joining us at any point. If so, we should plan a special dinner." She turned, now speaking to the cook.

"Iris, I can't leave London right now," I said with as much disappointment as I could muster. "I'm so sorry I wasn't thinking about the time. I promised Spencer that I would attend several events with him over the next two weeks. He's been so patient while I dealt with these terrible cramps."

"Of course," Iris said sympathetically. Her lips turned down as she patted my arm. "I was looking forward to spending time with you, but it's obviously more important for you to be here with him. I know you two are enjoying getting to know one another."

I looked to the ground, hoping it came off as embarrassment. "I know I didn't come home a few times."

"It's none of my business," Iris said quickly. She wrapped an arm around my shoulder and dropped her voice to a whisper. "But I'd love to hear the gossip. It seems like things are really heating up between you two."

"Between whom?" Tod's voice boomed through the room.

We startled apart, looking guilty at being caught.

"This is girl talk. Shoo!" She waved him off.

"I just spoke with Giles. What is this about you not coming to the country with us?" Tod asked.

For the first time, I considered this through his eyes. I

was a virtual stranger, pretending to be his daughter. Now, I expected to stay behind while he packed up his household staff and his security and went to the country for two weeks. I couldn't blame him for being suspicious. It was the perfect opportunity for me to gather up whatever I could carry and leave, robbing them blind in the process. Except that despite the number of priceless items in the house, there was no way I could make off with anything that was worth close to what he promised me.

"I just think it's more important for me to be here with Spencer. He wants to spend time together. We're getting quite close."

"Still," Tod said, cautiously. "I don't feel good about you being at the house alone."

"She's an adult, Tod," Iris interjected.

"I'll ask Giles to stick around. He'll be disappointed, of course. He loves Surrey."

Suddenly, I understood why Giles had been eager to get me to stay behind. He'd known Tod wouldn't leave me here alone. I suspected Giles didn't like Surrey nearly as much as Tod Belmond believed.

"You can't do that to him," I said as dramatically as possible. I might as well really sell it.

"If it's important for you to stay here with Spencer, then you should have a chaperone."

"I didn't take you to be such a prude," Iris said, poking her arm through her husband's. "Don't stand in the way of true love."

"I don't care if he sleeps here," Tod said with exasperation. "I just want to be sure that someone who has Kerrigan's best interest at heart remains."

The gauntlet had been thrown. The question he must have been asking himself had finally been spoken. Did I really have Kerrigan's best interests at heart? It was then I realized that not only did Tod Belmond not trust me. He never would. I couldn't blame him. I was a mercenary — a woman who'd agreed to take millions of pounds to perform what amounted to con artistry. If that's how he saw me, I couldn't change that.

"I'm sure Giles will understand."

"What will Giles understand?" he asked, joining us. Giles looked expectantly between Iris and Tod then to me. "Is this about the country?"

"I'm afraid I have to stay behind, and father feels that I should have a chaperone."

Giles took his glasses off his face and began wiping them down, heaving a heavy sigh. "You know how I love the countryside."

"I know, can you forgive me?" I did my best to sound sincere, but it was hard given I was holding back laughter over the scene I was performing. Everyone in this house had their own intentions. Iris might be the only innocent one of the lot.

"It's fine. I'll get theater tickets," Giles said glumly and stomped off.

Tod looked pleased with himself as though he had just maneuvered the situation exactly as he wanted. If he saw how he had been played, he showed no sign of it. "It's settled then. You'll stay here, so you can be there for Spencer—and we'll have some time alone."

He patted Iris's bottom, and I cringed.

"Now, now," Iris said with a wink. "You're not the only one who's in love."

CHAPTER TWENTY-SIX

Giles and I fell into an easy rhythm after their departure. He did not seem concerned that I would make off with the family silver, and he kept mostly to himself. There were no morning itineraries or forced social encounters. He didn't come in to approve what I was wearing. In fact, he treated me exactly like I assumed he wanted to be treated—like I was an adult fully capable of making my own decisions.

I barely saw him.

Spencer, on the other hand, had not given up. It was clear from his messages that he suspected things had gone too far that night in his flat with Holden. I knew I couldn't avoid him forever. But I needed to take advantage of the Belmond absence. There was no way that a man with the money and resources that Tod Belmond had wouldn't know where his daughter was. I hadn't believed him when he showed up on my doorstep acting like I might be her. I'd been a convenient out.

But someone had to be funding her lifestyle. It wasn't as if she had disappeared without a trace. She needed money. I'm sure she hadn't been going without all this time. That meant that somewhere there had to be a clue. A bank account. A credit card. Tod had told me he was actively tracking her down and attempting to get her to return home. Had he hired a private investigator? There had to be some clues in the house. And if he hadn't found them. Maybe it was time I started digging around in Kerrigan's room. On the surface, it felt strangely devoid of personality. She had her shoes and her clothes, but there was little else to give me insight into who Kerrigan Belmond really was. It felt more like I was staying in someone's guest room than someone's bedroom. There had to be a diary or a computer or *something*. She had to have left some part of herself behind when she took off.

But the more I searched, the less I found. Despite the wide berth Giles had given me, he'd been around the house most of the week. That meant I didn't feel comfortable trying to get into Tod's office or bedroom to look for clues. When Giles finally announced that he was taking in a matinee of a new West End production, I finally found my opportunity. After he left for the theater, I made my way downstairs and discovered Tod's locked office door.

So, he wanted to keep me out of his office.

The problem was—like most men of his status—Tod Belmond was dependent on other people to do everything for him. It only took me half an hour to find the spare set of keys someone on the staff had stashed in the kitchen.

I let myself in and began to look around. It was a pretty

typical office, full of expensive furniture and leather-bound
books he probably hadn't read, no doubt meant to impress
those he deemed important enough to enter. I searched the
shelves for a moment before deciding they were a dead end.
The desk was much more likely. Every drawer but one
opened easily. I paused, trying to decide if jimmying it
open would leave marks. I couldn't risk it. But there was no
way that a locked desk drawer in a locked office didn't have
anything hiding in it.

Sitting back in his chair I grasped the arms of it and
blew out a deep breath. I had to find Kerrigan Belmond, but
I had no idea where to start. No friends had called. I only
had a collection of pictures she'd posted on her social media
accounts.

I sat there, studying the pictures on Tod's desk. Like a
good, newly married man, he was smart enough not to have
pictures of his late wife there. He did have pictures of his
daughter, though. There was a picture of him and Iris at a
party that must have been to celebrate their engagement.
Kerrigan stood glumly behind them. It was strange to see
my face there, looking sour, as though I disapproved. I loved
Iris. She was one of the most genuine and warm people I'd
ever met. I wondered what Kerrigan had against her.

I closed my eyes, picturing myself in the blue dress
Kerrigan had worn for the event and tried to imagine what
it must've been like for her to accept a woman closer to her
age than her mother's marry her father. I suppose I could
understand why she was biased against her. It wasn't as if
Tod Belmond was a huge catch, though. In fact, I couldn't
see what Iris saw in him—other than his billions. I couldn't

fault her for that, since it's what had drawn me to him as well.

Was that why Kerrigan disliked her? Did she see Iris as another gold digger? It was strange how women always judged other women for taking advantage of male nature. In my opinion, Kerrigan should be upset with her father for marrying someone as young as Iris—not Iris herself.

There was another picture of Kerrigan riding a horse. I searched it, hoping it might contain some clue that would open up who she was to me. I closed my eyes again. I could almost feel the horse beneath me and the wind in my hair as we rode along the countryside. But it offered me no insight into who she was either. These glimpses of her life were as nondescript as the room upstairs. I was just about to give up when I noticed a bag tucked in the corner. Its glossy yellow leather seemed an odd fit for Tod Belmond.

I picked it up and placed it on the desk. Unzipping it, I withdrew a laptop computer and opened it. Powering it on, I waited, holding my breath, until a lock screen appeared, prompting me for a password. I had no idea what the password was, but the lock screen was enough to confirm my suspicion. Because above the password request, two words told me all I needed to know: *Welcome Kerrigan.*

Why was her computer here, if she wasn't? I started to look in the bag again when the security system alerted me that there was someone at the gate. I replaced the computer, zipping it closed, and put it back where I'd found it. I'd have more time to dig into this later. Maybe even try to guess her password. But I didn't want anyone to know what I was up to.

Did Giles know this bag was here? I couldn't risk removing it from the office. I would have to see to whoever this was at the gate, send them on their way, and come back. I hoped I had enough time before Giles returned from the theatre. It was important that I covered my tracks behind me. Forcing Kerrigan to come home early was not something I wanted to discuss with Tod. I didn't want to give him a chance to renegotiate our deal, or back out of it entirely. I shut the office door behind me and pocketed the key. Making my way to the security monitor near the front entry, I clicked on the feed and groaned when I saw Spencer waiting at the gate. He was standing there, no car in sight, pressing the intercom button.

I wondered if it was a coincidence that he'd shown up when there was no one around to send him away but me. Silently, I cursed Giles. There was no way he *happened* to be at the theatre at the same time that Spencer *happened* to show up here. That meant that Spencer knew I was inside, hiding from him, and that left me no choice.

I hit the button to respond.

"I don't want to see you," I told him.

"Kerrigan, we need to talk."

My core clenched as his voice filled the empty space. It was enough to prompt the feelings I so willfully ignored to roar to life.

"Let me in. Please."

"No way," I said, standing my ground.

"I just want to talk to you. I know things went too far with Holden."

"I'm sorry, but I need time to think.

"You have had a week to think!" He roared, banging his fist on the brick security shack and wincing. "This is ridiculous. I didn't make you do anything you didn't want to do."

"That's not what this is about."

He hit the wall again. "Look, I'm sorry. I'm going crazy here. I have to talk to you."

"Then you'll have to wait until I'm ready," I said.

"Okay. Then I'll wait."

He couldn't mean that literally, could he?

As if he knew what I was thinking, he slumped onto the ground and stared in the direction of the camera.

Apparently, he could. I turned on my heel, but instead of going back to the office, I raced upstairs and buried myself under the covers. I didn't trust myself to listen to Spencer calling over the intercom or to see him sitting there. Just hearing his voice had been enough to weaken my resolve.

I waited what felt like hours. Outside, this sky grew dark, tricking me into thinking it was later than it was. But it wasn't evening, it was simply a storm. Clouds blocked the summer sun and before long, rain lashed against the windows. I'd lost track of time. Between the rain and the waiting, I was sure Spencer had given up. Instead, when I tiptoed downstairs and checked the security feed, he was still there, sitting in the downpour.

"Give up," I called over the intercom.

I watched him shake his head on the security feed. He raised his hand and hit the response button. "I will stand here and drown in this rain before I leave, Kerrigan."

"I don't think you can drown in the rain," I replied.

"Then I'll die of starvation," he said with a shrug. "Or exposure. Or heartbreak. I'm at your mercy."

He didn't mean that. He couldn't. I fought the hope that swelled inside me that he did. I closed my eyes, shutting out the sight of him drenched on the security feed and slumped against the wall. Something told me that Spencer Byrd had it within him to do exactly what he said. A vision of him, lying dead at the front gate, when Giles returned from the theatre swam to mind. It wasn't long enough of course for any of those terrible things to happen to him, but he would wait until Giles returned. And Giles would let him inside the house. And then we'd have an audience for whatever row we were about to have.

I let out a frustrated scream, reached over, and opened the gate.

CHAPTER TWENTY-SEVEN

Spencer sprang through the gate as soon as it had opened far enough to allow his body to fit through. I didn't wait to watch him run toward the house.

Planting my hands on my hips, I paced the length of the foyer and back. Then, I opened the front door. Spencer stood there, his white shirt pasted to his skin, wet hair dripping into his eyes, but he didn't blink. He didn't wipe it away. His arms stretched out, bracing the doorframe as if to prevent any sudden attempt at escape.

"Have you lost your mind?" I asked him. It was still warm outside, although the rain had cooled the summer day considerably. I pressed my fingers to my temples and rubbed circles as I tried to figure out what to do.

"Can I come in?"

I looked him up and down, grimacing at the puddle forming at his feet. He had to have been out there at least two hours, so I believed him when he said he wasn't going to leave until we talked. I didn't feel like going out there, and I doubted he would settle for a quick conversation at the door. Not after waiting so long.

I swung the door open the rest of the way and stepped to the side to let him in.

He stalked in, trailing water behind him, and stopped to face me. "You haven't been returning my calls."

"So, you thought you should come over here and catch pneumonia to get my attention?" I shut the door behind him and settled against it, crossing my arms over my chest. I needed him to understand that things weren't right between us. We needed distance. I needed time to find Kerrigan. I was already beginning to regret letting him into the house. "Did you plan this with Giles?"

He studied me for a moment before shrugging one waterlogged shoulder. "What if I did?"

"I knew it!" I exploded. They had probably hatched the plan before Tod and Iris left for Surrey. The whole thing had been orchestrated to get Spencer access to me. So much for thinking Giles was on my side. Of course, he wasn't. He worked for Tod, and Tod wanted Kerrigan to marry Spencer. That was all that mattered. It didn't matter who got in the way. It didn't matter who got hurt. All that mattered was this arranged marriage.

"I'm sorry," he said, interrupting my thoughts.

"For what?" I tried to sound as detached as possible, but my voice quavered, giving me away. "I didn't do anything I didn't want to do."

"We were drunk," he said. "I shouldn't have let things get that far."

"And if we hadn't been drinking? And I wanted to do that, would you let me?"

"I don't own you, Kerrigan."

"Are you sure? Isn't that what this is all about?" I stormed, feeling the hot prickle of tears forming in my eyes. "I'm just a commodity to be sold to a man with the right title and the right family."

"I don't think of you that way." His sincerity was obvious, but that didn't change the facts of the matter.

"But you agreed to it," I pointed out.

"I did," he admitted.

"Why? You could have anyone you wanted." That was the thing I had never understood since the moment I'd seen his picture.

"The first time I saw you I wanted you."

"What? When we were five?" I tried to sound glib, but my heart was pounding against my chest like it was trying to get out. Kerrigan and Spencer had known each other before boarding schools and universities sent them on different paths.

"Not when we were kids. The first time I saw you grown-up," he said softly. "I didn't even speak to you. It was at the Queen's garden party last summer. I looked across the lawns and you were laughing."

My heart began to slow, restricted by a sudden tightness in my chest. The truth was that he hadn't seen me last summer. He hadn't wanted me last summer.

It had been her.

"When I realized it was you, I thought finally something good was coming from my fucking family name and this sodding title. I didn't want any of this. I didn't ask for any of this. But someone had to do it when father died, and Holden made it quite clear he didn't want it to be him." He pushed a hand through his dripping hair, showering the floor with more water droplets.

I wished I could tell him the truth. That Holden believed he was doing the right thing for his brother. But I wouldn't betray Holden's confidence. Both of them thought they had sacrificed for the other. There was a beautiful irony in it that was equal parts sad and sweet.

"I'm sorry," he repeated, searching my face for a sign that I would forgive him. "I'll never put you through something like that again. Just give me another chance."

I shut my eyes and decided to be as truthful as I could with him. "It scared me."

"I didn't mean to make you afraid," he murmured, hanging his head.

"No, it scared me because I liked it." I forced the words out of my mouth.

Spencer's eyes flashed up in surprise, but he didn't say anything.

"I don't want to be the thing that comes between the two of you," I continued. "Of course, I find Holden attractive. You look exactly the same. But I don't trust him. And I just shared something incredibly intimate with you, so how am I supposed to feel when suddenly I can't seem to control myself?"

We stared at each other for a moment, neither of us speaking. The only sound in the space was our breathing and the steady drip from his wet clothes onto the marble floor.

"He said you always share women."

"I don't want to share you," he said in a harsh whisper.

"He said the same thing."

Spencer's nostrils flared and I wondered if I had done permanent damage to the brothers' relationship. I only knew it couldn't go on like this. They had to face the rivalry that lingered between them and stop pretending that everything was okay. "I won't be a prize."

"I don't want you to be my prize." He took a step toward me tentatively as if waiting to see if I would run. I stayed still. "I spent the last week afraid of losing you because I couldn't admit what I was really scared of."

"You're scared?"

He nodded, closing the gap between us. "I'm scared I could fall in love with you."

He meant it. I knew, because, at that moment, I felt the exact same way. "So am I."

"It's kind of stupid to both be scared of wanting the same thing, don't you think?" he murmured as he brushed a hand down the side of my face. His skin was cold from standing in the rain, but his touch still lit a flame of desire inside me.

"You're freezing," I noted.

"I didn't notice," he said honestly. "I'd rather die fighting for you than live without you."

"We barely know each other." It was happening too fast. I knew that. But even as I attempted to pump the brakes on our runaway relationship, my heart sped along at breakneck speed to whatever lay around the corner. I had no idea if it was happiness or heartbreak. For some reason, it didn't matter.

"I know what's in here." His hand moved to press against my chest. "That's obvious. That's what matters. The rest is details that will come with time."

"Even if it's scary?" I asked.

"Even then." He nodded, cupping my chin as he spoke. "Especially then."

"This is crazy. This was supposed to be an arrangement."

"It wouldn't be crazy to fall in love with you," he whispered. "It would be crazy not to."

I turned my face up to his, unable to keep the truth from radiating off me. I felt the same way. I had no right to the emotions swirling inside my heart. He wasn't mine. He never could be. None of that stopped how I felt.

Spencer angled his face down, hesitating for just one moment to see if I would resist, before crushing his lips to mine. His wet clothes soaked through my thin shirt, but I could think of nothing but the way his strong body felt against me. I didn't care that he was soaked through or that I was getting wet. When he lifted me and carried me into the next room, I made no protest. He kicked a chair from the head of the table and placed me on its edge, yanking down my jeans with one swift stroke. My hands fumbled with his zipper, as our tongues tangled together, and I freed his cock.

He broke free of the kiss, pressing his damp forehead to mine."I don't have anything."

"Pull out," I murmured between panting breaths.

He didn't need further encouragement. The tip of his cock pushed gently against my seam, breaching it slowly. My head fell back, a moan spilling from me as I savored the sensation of being stretched open. "Yesss."

"I'll be gentle," he promised as he pushed in an inch more.

"Don't be," I said through gritted teeth. The incremental delivery was torture. I needed him inside me. Spencer answered by plunging inside me and I cried out in agonized relief. I clung to him as he stroked in and out, taking each of us closer and closer to the edge.

"Come for me, Kerrigan." The hand gripping my hip moved between my legs, and he slipped his thumb to my throbbing clit. I arced back, losing my hold on him but he held me steady as I fell.

Fell.

Fell.

Into him.

Into us.

Into sweet oblivion.

Spencer groaned, his body tensing, and he pulled out, spraying my belly with his warm release. His hand pumped the last of it while I watched with hooded eyes. My core ached from his sudden abandonment until his eyes finally opened and the promise I saw there filled the emptiness I felt. Spencer scooped me into his arms, and I nuzzled against him, while he carried me upstairs.

. . .

WHEN WE FINALLY MADE IT TO MY BEDROOM, I excused myself to wash his seed from my skin. Spencer followed behind me, stripping off what remained of his wet clothes. I watched him in the mirror, drinking in the sight of his incredible body. Then I noticed, his lower lip trembling slightly.

I bit back a laugh when I realized he was cold. There was something so ridiculous about this muscular, powerful man shivering.

"I'm going to run your bath," I told him, walking toward the tub.

"That sounds good," he admitted, "but only if you join me."

I nodded. That sounded even better. Turning on the faucet, I waited for it to heat up. I added some oils sitting nearby and soon, steam was rising from the glassy surface of the bathwater. Spencer climbed inside and groaned as he sank against the porcelain, his eyes shuttered with pleasure. He propped open one eye and beckoned me with his index finger.

It was all the invitation I needed. I stripped off my damp tank top and bra.

I paused and considered the mess we'd left behind us. "I should probably go pick up the trail of clothes we left downstairs."

"Leave it."

"Giles will love that," I muttered. I wasn't sure his proper sensibilities would survive finding my thong in the dining room. "Of course, it serves him right for setting me up."

"It's my fault. Not his. But I wouldn't worry about shocking him," Spencer advised. "Staff sees the worst of us. It's why we pay them so well."

His words sent a lump forming in my throat. I shook myself free of the gloomy thoughts trying to break past the lingering happiness in my mind.

Spencer reached his hand out to help me, and I took it, the sudden darkness vanishing as swiftly as it had arrived. I stepped into the water carefully, lowering myself to sit between his open legs. My breasts bobbed on the water as I relaxed against him, peace settled over me. There were still obstacles in our path. There was still a deadline for our relationship. Somehow, though, in his arms, none of that seemed to matter.

His hands strayed up my body, cupping my breasts. He swirled a finger absently over my nipples, which pebbled at his touch. "Have I told you how perfect these are?"

"One or twice," I said, thinking of the nights we'd spent together.

"I'll be sure to tell you more often." He kissed the back of my neck, and my eyes closed. "You deserve to know how perfect you are every moment of every day."

"I'm far from perfect," I muttered even as his words made me ache with longing for his vision of our life together.

"What are you thinking about?" he whispered in my ear.

"The future," I admitted.

"What if we only think about right now?"

"If I could only turn my brain off, I would," I said with a bemused smile. This earned me a slight laugh.

"How about I distract you then?"

He reached over and grabbed a sponge sitting in a tray by the side of the tub. Plunging it into the water he lifted it and brought it to my shoulders. The warm water relaxed me further as he gently massaged away my distraction.

"That feels good." I allowed my head to loll against his shoulder. There was nowhere else I wanted to be than here with him.

"Kerrigan," he said. "Can I ask you something?"

I bobbed my head slightly in agreement, too mesmerized by the deliberate tenderness of his touch.

He tossed the sponge which landed with a wet plop on the tile floor. I peeked to see his hand reach toward the soap dish. Apparently, I was getting a full bath. I didn't mind in the least.

"I know we don't know everything about each other," he began, "but there's one thing I'm absolutely certain of."

"Which is?" I murmured.

"I want to spend the rest of my life learning everything I can about you. Marry me?"

I stiffened for an instant as his words hit me. Then, I sat up and twisted around to meet his eyes. He couldn't be serious. An uncharacteristic vulnerability was written across his face, the shadows that usually clouded his eyes had lifted, and in his hand, he was holding a ring.

There were ten million reasons to say no.

There were ten million reasons to say yes.

I'd been given my answer before we ever met.

But that wasn't what I thought of now. I didn't care about the ring. I didn't care that it could never work. I only knew one thing. "I want that, too."

Spencer exhaled and leaned forward to kiss me. I felt the ring slip onto my finger as our lips met.

The kiss deepened becoming a silent vow. Spencer broke away and stood, rivulets of water streamed down the stacked plane of his abs toward his well-defined hamstrings and over the length of his rapidly stiffening cock. He reached down and helped me to my feet. Then out of the tub. Spencer didn't pause to reach for a towel as he lifted me and carried me into the bedroom. Our wet flesh collided, skidding across one another as our bodies entwined.

This time when he moved between my legs, there was no hurry. We had promised each other forever. Now we had all the time in the world. Our eyes locked and I opened myself to him, allowing the fear and hope and guilt I felt to spill out. He answered with a raw vulnerability, his hands pinning mine over my head as he rocked against me. We both had secrets, ones we weren't willing to share, but in some unspoken way, we admitted to them and made a promise that one day we would strip off all of our armor. Someday we would set each other free.

It was a lie.

It was the truth.

It was everything.

CHAPTER TWENTY-EIGHT

"Oh my God!" Evie squealed as she grabbed my hand and inspected my engagement. I couldn't blame her. Since Spencer had put it on my finger, I'd caught myself staring at it on more than one occasion. I was beginning to get used to the small boulder Spencer had given me to seal our engagement.

We had kept the news to ourselves for a few days, basking in the last moments of privacy we were likely to have. It was easier to do with Kerrigan's parents out of town. But now they were back, and we had arranged a family dinner to make the official announcement. However, an announcement turned out to be wholly unnecessary, because everyone had guessed why we had brought them together.

Evie dropped my hand and threw her arms around my neck. "I've always wanted a sister."

"That's enough," Caroline said with exasperation at the sight.

Considering Evie was squeezing me so tightly I could barely breathe, I had to agree. She begrudgingly released me, and Caroline offered me a polite hug herself. Then, she turned to Iris and the two shared a knowing smile. "It looks like we have a wedding to plan."

And with that statement, they were off, rattling off ideas for flowers and cakes and whatever else went into a society wedding.

"Wonderful," Spencer muttered under his breath. "I hope they make a tent big enough for this circus."

Despite his feigned annoyance, he grinned at me. I'd managed to convince him that an elopement was out of the question after pointing out that everyone—especially the tabloids—would assume that I was pregnant. That had been enough to convince him to allow the wedding. It was a hollow victory, but it gave me time to figure out my next move.

"Excuse me." Spencer's Grandfather called to the gathering, holding his pre-dinner cocktail in the air. "I'd like to propose a toast to the couple and to the joining of two powerful families. Spencer has always taken his duty to the Wellesley title with a solemn and admirable sense of responsibility. I'm sure that sense of obligation will continue into his marriage."

Everyone raised their glass and murmured in agreement.

"How romantic," Evie whispered with a giggle. Spencer pushed her playfully from behind, just enough to stop her from laughing.

The rest of the evening was a blur of questions from

everyone. The women wanted to know all the details. How Spencer had asked me. When we wanted to get married. If I'd thought about my dress. I found myself overwhelmed trying to give the right answers. It didn't seem appropriate to tell them we'd been naked in a bathtub when he finally proposed, so I left that part out. Meanwhile, the men clustered together, talking in low voices. Holden was with them, listening but not speaking. I couldn't help noticing that Spencer seemed to deliberately ignore him.

Dinner was no better. Spencer's attention was on a new policy that Parliament was considering to stem the power of the monarchy. He kept a hand on my thigh as he discussed it. On my other side, Iris and Caroline were already proposing dates. I sat in silence, torn between both groups. I didn't belong to either of them. Thankfully, the server kept my wine glass filled. The only other person who remained quiet throughout the courses was Holden. The most he offered was a few poisoned glances thrown at me from across the table.

I excused myself as the group finished dinner and the men headed off to the study for brandy. I needed a moment to compose myself. I was on my way back from the loo when Caroline cornered me in the corridor. "A word?"

"Of course." I forced a smile. It would only make things more difficult if she decided to cause trouble. That didn't mean I liked her, though.

"You need to know what you're getting into." Her tone was surprisingly gentle, conflicting with the aggressive authority she usually displayed. "You're here because your father and my father-in-law arranged this, which means you have some sense of how deep familial obligation can run."

"I do," I said warily.

"But you need to understand that once you're a member of this family, that's it. You will always be a member of this family."

"That's what I want." I wasn't sure what she was trying to say exactly. On the surface, her words might have sounded like a threat, but they were anything but. It was a well-intentioned warning, pure and simple.

Caroline inhaled sharply, her face clouding with pain. "When Jack died, that was it for me. I had my children to raise, and now that they're grown, I will stay here and be the lady of the house until it's your turn, and then I will sit in a chair as I pass my days until I draw my final breath."

"I don't want that," I said. "I don't want to take your place."

"You won't have a choice," she informed me. "It's the expectations. When my father-in-law dies, Spencer will be the Duke of Wellesley and you will be the Duchess and that's that."

"But why do you have to...?"

"Because once you become one of us, there's no turning back. No remarriage. No divorce. No second chances. Remember that." She patted my arm, leaving me with the weight of her words, as she returned to her guests.

I don't know how long I stood there, but for the first time in weeks, I felt a familiar panic pressing down on me, suffocating me until I didn't think I could breathe. I was drowning, pushed below the water's surface, unable to reach air. I stumbled in the direction I had come from, ignoring concerned comments from the staff as I rushed past them. I let myself out a door onto a large balcony that overlooked the gardens. As soon as I stepped outside, I gulped the night air. Tipping my head back, I breathed deeply until the anxiety began to slowly ebb away.

"Beautiful night," a caustic voice broke the silence.

I opened my eyes to find Holden. It was strange how easily I could tell him apart from Spencer now. Whatever had changed between them, had changed for me as well. I just couldn't put my fingers on it. I swayed on my feet a little, still recovering from the sudden attack.

"Are you okay?" He sounded genuinely concerned. I took an unsteady step forward and his arm shot out to catch me. "Whoa, there."

I gripped the balcony's stone railing, pulling away from his touch.

"So you're ignoring me, too," he said bitterly.

"I'm not ignoring you." I shook my head, feeling tired from all the questions and the people. "I just don't think you should touch me."

I didn't bother to mince words, because I needed Holden to know where I stood. I'd chosen Spencer. He could punish me for it all he wanted, but it wouldn't change that fact.

"I belong with your brother." It felt right to say it. Good even. I ignored the tiny voice inside my head reminding me that I was a placeholder. For the moment and for whatever time I had left, it was the truth.

"You belong *to* my brother," he corrected me. "Think of

what he made you do and tell me you're more than a toy to him."

"That was done of my own free will." My heart started to hammer in my chest. Holden wasn't going to let this go. Somewhere inside me, in a place I tried to ignore, elation thrilled through me.

He smirked, his eyes focused on some shadow in the distance. "That's the thing about lies. Sometimes they get mixed up with the truth, don't they?"

"What are you getting at Holden?" I was tired of the subtle innuendos and flirtations. I didn't want to be part of their rivalry, and I refused to play their game.

"He won't be enough for you. He's jealous and controlling."

I flinched but held my ground. "You didn't seem to mind when he told me to get on my knees for you."

"Neither did you," he said pointedly. "Are you really going to claim you love him when I can feel what's happening between us?"

"Happened," I cut him off. "One time. We were drunk. It won't again."

Holden looked at me, wearing his brother's face. It was surprisingly soft even as an arrogant smile rolled across his mouth. "Who's lying now?"

"I'm marrying your brother." I took a step away and he grabbed my wrist. "Let me go, Holden."

"Never." In one swift movement, he caught my waist and dipped me backward.

I ignored the way his breath tickled my ear, the tempting scent of his cologne, the way my body tightened at the suggestion in his words. How could he be so like Spencer and so different? How could I want Spencer for being everything Holden wasn't? And want Holden for being Spencer's mirror opposite?

I pulled free of his arms, backing a few steps away, as we glared at one another.

"Kerrigan!" Spencer's voice sliced through the air, and I twisted to face my fiancé, who was watching us from the door. An unreadable expression on his face. "Are you ready to leave?"

"Yes," I called back. "I'm coming."

He nodded, still eying Holden with apprehension before he stepped back into the house. I hadn't imagined it. Something had changed between them, and I suspected it had to do with the five-carat diamond on my ring finger.

"Good night, Holden," I spoke as firmly as possible as I turned to go back inside—back to his brother.

"You aren't marrying my brother."

His words stopped me cold. I answered with an icy glare. If he thought he could win my heart away from Spencer, he was going to be disappointed. The more time I spent with Holden, the more layers I peeled back, the less I trusted him. "I am marrying your brother."

"No, you aren't, dirty girl." Holden leaned closer, lowering his voice so I was forced to hold my breath to hear him. "*Kerrigan Belmond is.*"

❦

CRUEL DYNASTY
Book Two in The Dynasties

I made a deal. One year of my life pretending to be a rich aristocrat in exchange for ten million pounds. Enough money to start over somewhere new. Enough money to disappear forever. It sounded simple, but being Kerrigan Belmond is more dangerous than I expected.

Because Kerrigan's world isn't as perfect behind closed doors as it is on paper. I didn't just sell one year of my life, I sold my virginity and soul to the cruel and manipulative Spencer Byrd. My body shouldn't tighten under his penetrating gaze. His touch shouldn't electrify me. I should say no to his dirty demands, especially when they involve his brother, Holden.

It should send me running from the Byrds. Instead, I keep playing their twisted game, knowing pleasure is the prize. Plus, I need Holden to spill the secret Spencer's keeping, especially since he might know the truth behind Kerrigan's absence. But if he does, that means he knows the truth about me, too.

And the longer I pretend to be Kerrigan, the harder it is to remember the fortune, the fame, and the brothers aren't mine--and that if I lose, I lose everything.

Available July 27, 2021 from Estate Publishing

ACKNOWLEDGMENTS

It takes a village to write a book, and I so blessed to have a supportive team and family.

Thank you to my agent, Louise Fury, for being a force of nature and to my foreign teams for going above and beyond.

Thank you to my team on the ground. Shelby, what would I do without you? Let's never find out. Natasha, I'll forever be grateful for our accidental meeting. Thank you for everything you do to keep me on track and sane.

Thank you to the team at Grey's Promotion for being on top of everything and providing another stellar release.

Thank you to my author friends for providing inspiration, especially during these strange times.

Thank you to my readers, especially my ARC Team! And thanks to Geneva Lee's Loves and all the incredible women who help me keep it fun and sexy in there!

Thanks to Elise for being team London Dynasty from

minute one. Some people have a sister. Some people have a best friend. I get both rolled into one.

Thank you to my family for putting up with deadlines and word lag. I could not do this without your constant understanding and support.

And as always, thank you to Josh for having all the layers I could ever want to peel back. I'm so grateful to build this life with you. You are my greatest adventure.

ABOUT THE AUTHOR

GENEVA LEE is the *New York Times*, *USA Today*, and internationally bestselling author of over a dozen novels, including the Royals Saga which has sold two million copies worldwide. She lives in Poulsbo Washington with her husband and three children, and she co-owns Away With Words Bookshop with her sister.

Connect with her online at:
www.GenevaLee.com

Or on social media at:

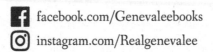

facebook.com/Genevaleebooks

instagram.com/Realgenevalee

YOUR 15-MONTH
COMPLETE AND INDIV

CANCER
June 21 - July 20

1988
SUPER HOROSCOPE

ARROW BOOKS LIMITED
62-65 Chandos Place
London WC2N 4NW

CONTENTS

NOTE TO THE CUSP-BORN iii
HISTORY AND USES OF ASTROLOGY 1
HOW TO USE THESE PREDICTIONS 20
THE MOON 21
MOON TABLES, 1988
   Time Conversions 28
   Moon Tables...................................... 29
   Planting Guide, 1988.............................. 33
   Fishing Guide, 1988............................... 34
   Influence Over Daily Affairs 34
   Influence Over Health and Plants 35
THE SIGNS OF THE ZODIAC
   Dominant Characteristics........................... 37
   Key Words 62
   The Elements and the Qualities..................... 63
   How to Approximate Your Rising Sign 71
THE PLANETS OF THE SOLAR SYSTEM............. 76
FAMOUS PERSONALITIES 86
CANCER: 1988
   Character Analysis 89
   Love and Marriage 96
   Yearly Forecast 125
   Daily Forecast 130
   October, November, December, 1987 229

THE PUBLISHERS REGRET THAT THEY CANNOT ANSWER INDIVIDUAL LETTERS REQUESTING PERSONAL HOROSCOPE INFORMATION.

FIRST PUBLISHED IN GREAT BRITAIN BY ARROW BOOKS 1987
© GROSSET & DUNLAP, INC., 1974, 1978, 1979, 1980, 1981, 1982
© CHARTER COMMUNICATIONS, INC., 1983, 1984, 1985
COPYRIGHT © 1986, 1987 THE BERKLEY PUBLISHING GROUP

PRINTED IN GREAT BRITAIN BY
GUERNSEY PRESS CO. LTD
GUERNSEY C.I.
ISBN 0 09 948820 5

NOTE TO THE CUSP-BORN

First find the year of your birth, and then find the sign under which you were born according to your day of birth. Thus, you can determine if you are a true Cancer (or Gemini or Leo), according to the variations of the dates of the Zodiac. (See also page 7.)

Are you *really* a Cancer? If your birthday falls during the fourth week of June, at the beginning of Cancer, will you still retain the traits of Gemini, the sign of the Zodiac before Cancer? And what if you were born late in July—are you more Leo than Cancer? Many people born at the edge, or cusp, of a sign have difficulty determining exactly what sign they are. If you are one of these people, here's how you can figure it out, once and for all.

Consult the following table. It will tell you the precise days on which the Sun entered and left your sign for the year of your birth. If you were born at the beginning or end of Cancer, yours is a lifetime reflecting a process of subtle transformation. Your life on Earth will symbolize a significant change in consciousness, for you are either about to enter a whole new way of living or are leaving one behind.

If you were born during the fourth week of June, you may want to read the Gemini book as well as Cancer. Because Gemini holds the keys to the more hidden sides of your personality; many of your dilemmas and uncertainties about the world and people around you, your secret wishes, and your potential for cosmic unfoldment.

Although you feel you have a lot to say, you will often withdraw and remain silent. Sometimes, the more you say the more confused a situation can get. Talking can drain you, and you are vulnerable to gossip. You feel secure surrounded by initimates you can trust, but sometimes the neighbors—even your own relatives—seem to be talking behind your back and you sense a vague plot in the air.

You symbolize the birth of feeling, the silent but rich condition of a fertilized seed growing full with life. The family is always an issue. At best you are a "feeling" type whose power of sensing things remains a force behind everything you think and do.

iii

If you were born the fourth week of July, you may want to read the horoscope book for Leo as well as Cancer, for Leo could be your greatest asset. You need a warm embrace, the comfort and safety of being cared for, protected, fed. You need strong ties to the past, to the family. Attachments are natural for you. You want to be your own person, yet you often find ties and attachments prohibiting you from the rebirth you are anticipating. You may find it hard to separate yourself from dependencies without being drawn backward again and again.

You symbolize the fullness of growth, the condition of being *nearly* ripe, the new life about to emerge from the shadows into the sunshine.

DATES SUN ENTERS CANCER (LEAVES GEMINI)

June 21 every year from 1900 to 2000, except for the following:

June 20:	June 22:		
1988	1902	1915	1931
92	03	18	35
96	06	19	39
	07	22	43
	10	23	47
	11	26	51
	14	27	55

DATES SUN LEAVES CANCER (ENTERS LEO)

July 23 every year from 1900 to 2000, except for the following:

July 22:				
1928	1953	1968	1981	1992
32	56	69	84	93
36	57	72	85	94
40	60	73	86	96
44	61	76	88	97
48	64	77	89	98
52	65	80	90	

HISTORY AND USES
OF ASTROLOGY

Does astrology have a place in the fast-moving, ultra-scientific world we live in today? Can it be justified in a sophisticated society whose outriders are already preparing to step off the moon into the deep space of the planets themselves? Or is it just a hangover of ancient superstition, a psychological dummy for neurotics and dreamers of every historical age?

These are the kind of questions that any inquiring person can be expected to ask when they approach a subject like astrology which goes beyond, but never excludes, the materialistic side of life.

The simple, single answer is that astrology works. It works for tens of millions of people in the western world alone. In the United States there are 10 million followers and in Europe, an estimated 25 million. America has more than 4000 practicing astrologers, Europe nearly three times as many. Even down-under Australia has its hundreds of thousands of adherents. The importance of such vast numbers of people from diverse backgrounds and cultures is recognized by the world's biggest newspapers and magazines who probably devote more of their space to this subject in a year than to any other. In the eastern countries, astrology has enormous followings, again, because it has been proved to work. In countries like India, brides and grooms for centuries have been chosen on the basis of astrological compatibility. The low divorce rate there, despite today's heavy westernizing influence, is attributed largely to this practice.

In the western world, astrology today is more vital than ever before; more practicable because it needs a sophisticated society like ours to understand and develop its contribution to the full; more valid because science itself is confirming the precepts of astrological knowledge with every new exciting step. The ordinary person who daily applies astrology intelligently does not have to wonder whether it is true nor believe in it blindly. He can see it working for himself. And, if he can use it—and this book is designed to help the reader to do just that—he can make living a far richer experience, and become a more developed personality and a better person.

Astrology is the science of relationships. It is not just a study of planetary influences on man and his environment. It is the study of man himself.

We are at the center of our personal universe, of all our rela-

1

tionships. And our happiness or sadness depends on how we act, how we relate to the people and things that surround us. The emotions that we generate have a distinct affect—for better or worse—on the world around us. Our friends and our enemies will confirm this. Just look in the mirror the next time you are angry. In other words, each of us is a kind of sun or planet or star and our influence on our personal universe, whether loving, helpful or destructive, varies with our changing moods, expressed through our individual character.

And to an extent that includes the entire galaxy, this is true of the planetary bodies. Their radiations affect each other, including the earth and all the things on it. And in comparatively recent years, giant constellations called "quasars" have been discovered. These exist far beyond the night stars that we can observe, and science says these quasars are emitting radiating influences more powerful and different than ever recorded on earth. Their effect on man from an astrological point of view is under deep study. Compared with these inter-stellar forces, our personal "radiations" are negligible on the planetary scale. But ours are just as potent in the way they affect our moods, and our ability to control them. To this extent they determine much of the happiness and satisfaction in our lives. For instance, if we were bound and gagged and had to hold some strong emotion within us without being able to move, we would soon start to feel very uncomfortable. We are obviously pretty powerful radiators inside, in our own way. But usually, we are able to throw off our emotion in some sort of action—we have a good cry, walk it off, or tell someone our troubles—before it can build up too far and make us physically ill. Astrology helps us to understand the universal forces working on us, and through this understanding, we can become more properly adjusted to our surroundings and find ourselves coping where others may flounder.

Closely related to our emotions is the "other side" of our personal universe, our physical welfare. Our body, of course, is largely influenced by things around us over which we have very little control. The phone rings, we hear it. The train runs late. We snag our stocking or cut our face shaving. Our body is under a constant bombardment of events that influence our lives to varying degrees.

The question that arises from all this is, what makes each of us act so that we have to involve other people and keep the ball of activity and evolution rolling? This is the question that both science and astrology are involved with. The scientists have attacked it from different angles: anthropology, the study of human evolution as body, mind and response to environment; anatomy, the study of bodily structure; psychology, the science of the human mind; and so on. These studies have produced very impressive classifications and valuable information, but because the approach to the problem is fragmented, so is the result. They remain "branches" of science. Science generally studies effects. It keeps turning up wonderful answers but no lasting solutions. Astrology, on the other hand approaches the question from the broader viewpoint. Astrology began its inquiry with the totality of human experience and saw it as an effect. It then looked to find the cause, or at least the prime movers, and during thousands of years of observation of man and his *universal* environment, came up with the extraordinary principle of planetary influence—or astrology, which, from the Greek, means the science of the stars.

Modern science, as we shall see, has confirmed much of astrology's foundations—most of it unintentionally, some of it reluctantly, but still, indisputably.

It is not difficult to imagine that there must be a connection between outer space and the earth. Even today, scientists are not too sure how our earth was created, but it is generally agreed that it is only a tiny part of the universe. And as a part of the universe, people on earth see and feel the influence of heavenly bodies in almost every aspect of our existence. There is no doubt that the sun has the greatest influence on life on this planet. Without it there would be no life, for without it there would be no warmth, no division into day and night, no cycles of time or season at all. This is clear and easy to see. The influence of the moon, on the other hand, is more subtle, though no less definite.

There are many ways in which the influence of the moon manifests itself here on earth, both on human and animal life. It is a well-known fact, for instance, that the large movements of water on our planet—that is the ebb and flow of the tides—are caused by the moon's gravitational pull. Since this is so, it follows that these water movements do not occur only in the oceans, but that all bodies of water are affected, even down to the tiniest puddle.

The human body, too, which consists of about 70 percent water, falls within the scope of this lunar influence. For example the menstrual cycle of most women corresponds to the lunar month; the period of pregnancy in humans is 273 days, or equal to nine lunar months. Similarly, many illnesses reach a crisis at the change of the moon, and statistics in many countries have shown that the crime rate is highest at the time of the full moon. Even human sexual desire has been associated with the phases of the moon. But, it is in the movement of the tides that we get the clearest demonstration of planetary influence, and the irresistible correspondence between the so-called metaphysical and the physical.

Tide tables are prepared years in advance by calculating the future positions of the moon. Science has known for a long time that the moon is the main cause of tidal action. But only in the last few years has it begun to realize the possible extent of this influence on mankind. To begin with, the ocean tides do not rise and fall as we might imagine from our personal observations of them. The moon as it orbits around the earth, sets up a circular wave of attraction which pulls the oceans of the world after it, broadly in an east to west direction. This influence is like a phantom wave crest, a loop of power stretching from pole to pole which passes over and around the earth like an invisible shadow. It travels with equal effect across the land masses and, as scientists were recently amazed to observe, caused oysters placed in the dark in the middle of the United States where there is no sea, to open their shells to receive the non-existent tide. If the land-locked oysters react to this invisible signal, what effect does it have on us who not so long ago in evolutionary time, came out of the sea and still have its salt in our blood and sweat?

Less well known is the fact that the moon is also the primary force behind the circulation of blood in human beings and animals, and the movement of sap in trees and plants. Agriculturists have established that the moon has a distinct influence on crops, which explains why for centuries people have planted according to moon cycles. The habits of many animals, too, are directed by the movement of the moon. Migratory birds, for instance, depart only at or near the time of the full moon. Just as certain fish, eels in particular, move only in accordance with certain phases of the moon.

Know Thyself—Why?

In today's fast-changing world, everyone still longs to know what the future holds. It is the one thing that everyone has in common: rich and poor, famous and infamous, all are deeply concerned about tomorrow.

But the key to the future, as every historian knows, lies in the past. This is as true of individual people as it is of nations. You cannot understand your future without first understanding your past, which is simply another way of saying that you must first of all know yourself.

The motto "know thyself" seems obvious enough nowadays, but it was originally put forward as the foundation of wisdom by the ancient Greek philosophers. It was then adopted by the "mystery religions" of the ancient Middle East, Greece and Rome, and is still used in all genuine schools of mind training or mystical discipline, both in those of the East, based on yoga, and those of the West. So it is universally accepted now, and has been through the ages.

But how do you go about discovering what sort of person you are? The first step is usually classification into some sort of system of types. Astrology did this long before the birth of Christ. Psychology has also done it. So has modern medicine, in its way.

One system classifies men according to the source of the impulses they respond to most readily: the muscles, leading to direct bodily action; the digestive organs, resulting in emotion, or the brain and nerves. Another such system says that character is determined by the endocrine glands, and gives us labels like "pituitary," "thyroid" and "hyperthyroid" types. These different systems are neither contradictory nor mutually exclusive. In fact, they are very often different ways of saying the same thing.

Very popular and useful classifications were devised by Dr. C. G. Jung, the eminent disciple of Freud. Jung observed among the different faculties of the mind, four which have a predominant influence on character. These four faculties exist in all of us without exception, but not in perfect balance. So when we say, for instance, that a man is a "thinking type," it means that in any situation he tries to be rational. It follows that emotion, which some say is the opposite of thinking, will be his weakest function. This type can be sensible and reasonable, or calculating and unsympathetic. The emotional type, on the other hand, can often be recognized by exaggerated language—everything is either marvelous or terrible—and in extreme cases they even invent dramas and quarrels out of nothing just to make life more interesting.

The other two faculties are intuition and physical sensation. The sensation type does not only care for food and drink, nice clothes and furniture; he is also interested in all forms of physical experience. Many scientists are sensation types as are athletes and nature-lovers. Like sensation, intuition is a form of perception and we all possess it. But it works through that part of the mind which is not under conscious control—consequently it sees meanings and connections which are not obvious to thought or emotion. Inventors and original thinkers are always intuitive, but so, too, are superstitious people who see meanings where none exist.

Thus, sensation tells us what is going on in the world, feeling (that is, emotion) tells us how important it is to ourselves, thinking enables us to interpret it and work out what we should do about it, and intuition tells us what it means to ourselves and others. All four faculties are essential, and all are present in every one of us. But some people are guided chiefly by one, others by another.

Besides these four types, Jung observed a division into extrovert and introvert, which cuts across them. By and large, the introvert is one who finds truth inside himself rather than outside. He is not, therefore, ideally suited to a religion or a political party which tells him what to believe. Original thinkers are almost necessarily introverts. The extrovert, on the other hand, finds truth coming to him from outside. He believes in experts and authorities, and wants to think that nature and the laws of nature really exists, that they are what they appear to be and not just generalities made by men.

A disadvantage of all these systems of classification, is that one cannot tell very easily where to place oneself. Some people are reluctant to admit that they act to please their emotions. So they deceive themselves for years by trying to belong to whichever type they think is the "best." Of course, there is no best; each has its faults and each has its good points.

The advantage of the signs of the Zodiac is that they simplify classification. Not only that, but your date of birth is personal—it is unarguably yours. What better way to know yourself than by going back as far as possible to the very moment of your birth? And this is precisely what your horoscope is all about.

What Is a Horoscope?

If you had been able to take a picture of the heavens at the moment of your birth, that photograph would be your horoscope. Lacking such a snapshot, it is still possible to recreate the picture—and this is at the basis of the astrologer's art. In other words, your horoscope is a representation of the skies with the planets in the exact positions they occupied at the time you were born.

This information, of course, is not enough for the astrologer. He has to have a background of significance to put the photograph on. You will get the idea if you imagine two balls—one inside the other. The inner one is transparent. In the center of both is the astrologer, able to look up, down and around in all directions. The outer sphere is the Zodiac which is divided into twelve approximately equal segments, like the segments of an orange. The inner ball is our photograph. It is transparent except for the images of the planets. Looking out from the center, the astrologer sees the planets in various segments of the Zodiac. These twelve segments are known as the signs or houses.

The position of the planets when each of us is born is always different. So the photograph is always different. But the Zodiac and its signs are fixed.

Now, where in all this are you, the subject of the horoscope?

You, or your character, is largely determined by the sign the sun is in. So that is where the astrologer looks first in your horoscope.

There are twelve signs in the Zodiac and the sun spends approximately one month in each. As the sun's motion is almost perfectly regular, the astrologers have been able to fix the dates governing each sign. There are not many people who do not know which sign of the Zodiac they were born under or who have not been amazed at some time or other at the accuracy of the description of their own character. Here are the twelve signs, the ancient zodiacal symbol, and their dates for the year 1988.*

ARIES	Ram	March 20–April 19
TAURUS	Bull	April 19–May 20
GEMINI	Twins	May 20–June 20
CANCER	Crab	June 20–July 22
LEO	Lion	July 22–August 22
VIRGO	Virgin	August 22–September 22
LIBRA	Scales	September 22–October 23
SCORPIO	Scorpion	October 23–November 21
SAGITTARIUS	Archer	November 21–December 21
CAPRICORN	Sea-Goat	December 21–January 20
AQUARIUS	Water-Bearer	January 20–February 19
PISCES	Fish	February 19–March 20

The time of birth—apart from the date—is important in advanced astrology because the planets travel at such great speed that the patterns they form change from minute to minute. For this reason, each person's horoscope is his and his alone. Further on we will see that the practicing astrologer has ways of determining and reading these minute time changes which dictate the finger character differences in us all.

However, it is still possible to draw significant conclusions and make meaningful predictions based simply on the sign of the Zodiac a person is born under. In a horoscope, the signs do not necessarily correspond with the divisions of the houses. It could be that a house begins half way across a sign. It is the interpretation of such combinations of different influences that distinguishes the professional astrologer from the student and the follower.

However, to gain a workable understanding of astrology, it is not necessary to go into great detail. In fact, the beginner is likely to find himself confused if he attempts to absorb too much too quickly. It should be remembered that this is a science and to become proficient at it, and especially to grasp the tremendous scope of possibilities in man and his affairs and direct them into a worthwhile reading, takes a great deal of study and experience.

*These dates are fluid and change with the motion of the Earth from year to year.

If you do intend to pursue it seriously you will have to learn to figure the exact moment of birth against the degrees of longitude and latitude of the planets at that precise time. This involves adapting local time to Greenwich Mean Time (G.M.T.), reference to tables of houses to establish the Ascendant, as well as making calculations from Ephemeris—the tables of the planets' positions.

After reading this introduction, try drawing up a rough horoscope to get the "feel" of reading some elementary characteristics and natal influences.

Draw a circle with twelve equal segments. Write in counterclockwise the names of the signs—Aries, Taurus, Gemini etc.—one for each segment. Look up an ephemeris for the year of the person's birth and note down the sign each planet was in on the birthday. Do not worry about the number of degrees (although if a planet is on the edge of a sign its position obviously should be considered). Write the name of the planet in the segment/sign on your chart. Write the number 1 in the sign where the sun is. This is the first house. Number the rest of the houses, counterclockwise till you finish at 12. Now you can investigate the probable basic expectation of experience of the person concerned. This is done first of all by seeing what planet or planets is/are in what sign and house. (See also page 72.)

The 12 houses control these functions:

1st.	Individuality, body appearance, general outlook on life	(Personality house)
2nd.	Finance, business	(Money house)
3rd.	Relatives, education, correspondence	(Relatives house)
4th.	Family, neighbors	(Home house)
5th.	Pleasure, children, attempts, entertainment	(Pleasure house)
6th.	Health, employees	(Health house)
7th.	Marriage, partnerships	(Marriage house)
8th.	Death, secret deals, difficulties	(Death house)
9th.	Travel, intellectual affairs	(Travel house)
10th.	Ambition, social standing	(Business and Honor house)
11th.	Friendship, social life, luck	(Friends house)
12th.	Troubles, illness, loss	(Trouble house)

The characteristics of the planets modify the influence of the Sun according to their natures and strengths.

Sun: Source of life. Basic temperament according to sun sign. The will.
Moon: Superficial nature. Moods. Changeable. Adaptive. Mother.
Mercury: Communication. Intellect. Reasoning power. Curiosity. Short travels.
Venus: Love. Delight. Art. Beautiful possessions.
Mars: Energy. Initiative. War. Anger. Destruction. Impulse.
Jupiter: Good. Generous. Expansive. Opportunities. Protection.
Saturn: Jupiter's opposite. Contraction. Servant. Delay. Hardwork. Cold. Privation. Research. Lasting rewards after long struggle.
Uranus: Fashion. Electricity. Revolution. Sudden changes. Modern science.
Neptune: Sensationalism. Mass emotion. Devastation. Delusion.
Pluto: Creates and destroys. Lust for power. Strong obsessions.

Superimpose the characteristics of the planets on the functions of the house in which they appear. Express the result through the character of the birth (sun) sign, and you will get the basic idea of how astrology works.

Of course, many other considerations have been taken into account in producing the carefully worked out predictions in this book: The aspects of the planets to each other; their strength according to position and sign; whether they are in a house of exaltation or decline; whether they are natural enemies or not; whether a planet occupies his own sign; the position of a planet in relation to its own house or sign; whether the planet is male, female or neuter; whether the sign is a fire, earth, water or air sign. These are only a few of the colors on the astrologer's pallet which he must mix with the inspiration of the artist and the accuracy of the mathematician.

The Problem of Love

Love, of course, is never a problem. The problem lies in recognizing the difference between infatuation, emotion, sex and, sometimes, the downright deceit of the other person. Mankind, with its record of broken marriages, despair and disillusionment, is obviously not very good at making these distinctions.

Can astrology help?

Yes. In the same way that advance knowledge can usually help in any human situation. And there is probably no situation as human, as poignant, as pathetic and universal, as the failure of man's love.

Love, of course, is not just between man and woman. It involves love of children, parents, home and so on. But the big problems usually involve the choice of partner.

Astrology has established degrees of compatibility that exist between people born under the various signs of the Zodiac. Because people are individuals, there are numerous variations and modifications and the astrologer, when approached on mate and marriage matters makes allowances for them. But the fact remains that some groups of people are suited for each other and some are not and astrology has expressed this in terms of characteristics which all can study and use as a personal guide.

No matter how much enjoyment and pleasure we find in the different aspects of each other's character, if it is not an overall compatibility, the chances of our finding fulfillment or enduring happiness in each other are pretty hopeless. And astrology can help us to find someone compatible.

History of Astrology

The origins of astrology have been lost far back in history, but we do know that reference is made to it as far back as the first written records of the human race. It is not hard to see why. Even in primitive times, people must have looked for an explanation for the various happenings in their lives. They must have wanted to know why people were different from one to another. And in their search they turned to the regular movements of the sun, moon and stars to see if they could provide an answer.

It is interesting to note that as soon as man learned to use his tools in any type of design, or his mind in any kind of calculation, he turned his attention to the heavens. Ancient cave dwellings reveal dim crescents and circles representative of the sun and moon, rulers of day and night. Mesopotamia and the civilization of Chaldea, in itself the foundation of those of Babylonia and Assyria, show a complete picture of astronomical observation and well-developed astrological interpretation.

Humanity has a natural instinct for order. The study of anthropology reveals that primitive people—even as far back as prehistoric times—were striving to achieve a certain order in their lives. They tried to organize the apparent chaos of the universe. They had the desire to attach meaning to things. This demand for order has persisted throughout the history of man. So that observing the regularity of the heavenly bodies made it logical that primitive peoples should turn heavenwards in their search for an understanding of the world in which they found themselves so random and alone.

And they did find a significance in the movements of the stars. Shepherds tending their flocks, for instance, observed that when the cluster of stars now known as the constellation Aries was in sight, it was the time of fertility and they associated it with the Ram. And they noticed that the growth of plants and plant life corresponded with different phases of the moon, so that certain times were favorable for the planting of crops, and other times were not. In this way, there grew up a tradition of seasons and causes connected with the passage of the sun through the twelve signs of the Zodiac.

Astrology was valued so highly that the king was kept informed of the daily and monthly changes in the heavenly bodies, and the results of astrological studies regarding events of the future. Head astrologers were clearly men of great rank and position, and the office was said to be a hereditary one.

Omens were taken, not only from eclipses and conjunctions of the moon or sun with one of the planets, but also from storms and earthquakes. In the eastern civilizations, particularly, the reverence inspired by astrology appears to have remained unbroken since the very earliest days. In ancient China, astrology, astronomy and religion went hand in hand. The astrologer, who was also an astronomer, was part of the official government service and had his own corner in the Imperial Palace. The duties of the Imperial astrologer, whose office was one of the most important in the land, were clearly defined, as this extract from early records shows:

"This exalted gentleman must concern himself with the stars in the heavens, keeping a record of the changes and movements of the Planets, the Sun and the Moon, in order to examine the movements of the terrestial world with the object of prognosticating good and bad fortune. He divides the territories of the nine regions of the empire in accordance with their dependence on particular celestial bodies. All the fiefs and principalities are connected with the stars and from this their prosperity or misfortune should be ascertained. He makes prognostications according to the twelve years of the Jupiter cycle of good and evil of the terrestial world. From the colors of the five kinds of clouds, he determines the coming of floods or droughts, abundance or famine. From the twelve winds, he draws conclusions about the state of harmony of heaven and earth, and takes note of good and bad signs that result from their accord or disaccord. In general, he concerns himself with five kinds of phenomena so as to warn the Emperor to come to the aid of the government and to allow for variations in the ceremonies according to their circumstances."

The Chinese were also keen observers of the fixed stars, giving them such unusual names as Ghost Vehicle, Sun of Imperial Concubine, Imperial Prince, Pivot of Heaven, Twinkling Brilliance or Weaving Girl. But, great astrologers though they may have been, the Chinese lacked one aspect of mathematics that the Greeks applied to astrology—deductive geometry. Deductive geometry was the basis of much classical astrology in and after the time of the Greeks, and this explains the different methods of prognostication used in the East and West.

Down through the ages the astrologer's art has depended, not so much on the uncovering of new facts, though this is important, as on the interpretation of the facts already known. This is the essence of his skill. Obviously one cannot always tell how people will react (and this underlines the very important difference between astrology and predestination which will be discussed later on) but one can be prepared, be forewarned, to know what to expect.

But why should the signs of the zodiac have any effect at all on the formation of human character? It is easy to see why people thought they did, and even now we constantly use astrological expressions in our everyday speech. The thoughts of "lucky star," "ill-fated," "star-crossed," "mooning around," are interwoven into the very structure of our language.

In the same way that the earth has been created by influences from outside, there remains an indisputable togetherness in the working of the universe. The world, after all, is a coherent structure, for if it were not, it would be quite without order and we would never know what to expect. A dog could turn into an apple, or an elephant sprout wings and fly at any moment without so much as a by your leave. But nature, as we know, functions according to laws, not whims, and the laws of nature are certainly not subject to capricious exceptions.

This means that no part of the universe is ever arbitrarily cut off from any other part. Everything is therefore to some extent linked with everything else. The moon draws an imperceptible tide on every puddle; tiny and trivial events can be effected by outside forces (such as the fall of a feather by the faintest puff of wind). And so it is fair to think that the local events at any moment reflect to a very small extent the evolution of the world as a whole.

From this principle follows the possibility of divination, and also knowledge of events at a distance, provided one's mind were always as perfectly undisturbed, as ideally smooth, as a mirror or unruffled lake. Provided, in other words, that one did not confuse the picture with hopes, guesses, and expectations. When people try to foretell the future by cards or crystal ball gazing they find it much easier to confuse the picture with expectations than to reflect it clearly.

But the present does contain a good deal of the future to which it leads—not all, but a good deal. The diver halfway between bridge and water is going to make a splash; the train whizzing towards the station will pass through it unless interfered with; the burglar breaking a pane of glass has exposed himself to the possibility of a prison sentence. Yet this is not a doctrine of determinism, as was emphasized earlier. Clearly, there are forces already at work in the present, and any one of them could alter the situation in some way. Equally, a change of decision could alter the whole situation as well. So the future depends, not on an irresistible force, but on a small act of free will.

An individual's age, physique, and position on the earth's surface are remote consequences of his birth. Birth counts as the original cause for all that happens subsequently. The horoscope, in this case, means "this person represents the further evolution of the state of the universe pictured in this chart." Such a chart can apply equally to man or woman, dog, ship or even limited company.

If the evolution of an idea, or of a person, is to be understood as a totality, it must continue to evolve from its own beginnings, which is to say, in the terms in which it began. The brown-eyed person will be faithful to brown eyes all his life; the traitor is being faithful to some complex of ideas which has long been evolving in him; and the person born at sunset will always express, as he evolves, the psychological implications or analogies of the moment when the sun sinks out of sight.

This is the doctrine that an idea must continue to evolve in terms of its origin. It is a completely non-materialist doctrine, though it never fails to apply to material objects. And it implies, too, that the individual will continue to evolve in terms of his moment of origin, and therefore possibly of the sign of the Zodiac rising on the eastern horizon at his birth. It also implies that the signs of the Zodiac themselves will evolve in the collective mind of the human race in the same terms that they were first devised and not in the terms in which modern astrologers consciously think they ought to work.

For the human race, like every other kind of animal, has a collective mind, as Professor Jung discovered in his investigation of dreams. If no such collective mind existed, no infant could ever learn anything, for communication would be impossible. Furthermore, it is absurd to suggest that the conscious mind could be older than the "unconscious," for an infant's nervous system functions correctly before it has discovered the difference between "myself" and "something else" or discovered what eyes and hands are for. Indeed, the involuntary muscles function correctly even before birth, and will never be under conscious control. They are part of what we call the "unconscious" which is not really "unconscious" at all. To the contrary, it is totally aware of itself and everything else; it is merely that part of the mind that cannot be controlled by conscious effort.

And human experience, though it varies in detail with every individual, is basically the same for each one of us, consisting of sky and earth, day and night, waking and sleeping, man and woman, birth and death. So there is bound to be in the mind of the human race a very large number of inescapable ideas, which are called our natural archetypes.

There are also, however, artificial or cultural archetypes which are not universal or applicable to everyone, but are nevertheless inescapable within the limits of a given culture. Examples of these are the cross in Christianity, and the notion of "escape from the wheel of rebirth" in India. There was a time when these ideas did not exist. And there was a time, too, when the scheme of the Zodiac did not exist. One would not expect the Zodiac to have any influence on remote and primitive peoples, for example, who have never heard of it. If the Zodiac is only an archetype, their horoscopes probably would not work and it would not matter which sign they were born under.

But where the Zodiac is known, and the idea of it has become worked into the collective mind, then there it could well appear to have an influence, even if it has no physical existence. For ideas do not have a physical existence, anyway. No physical basis has yet been discovered for the telepathy that controls an anthill; young swallows migrate before, not after, their parents; and the weaver-bird builds its intricate nest without being taught. Materialists suppose, but cannot prove, that "instinct" (as it is called, for no one knows how it works) is controlled by nucleic acid in the chromosomes. This is not a genuine explanation, though, for it only pushes the mystery one stage further back.

Does this mean, then, that the human race, in whose civilization the idea of the twelve signs of the Zodiac has long been embedded, is divided into only twelve types? Can we honestly believe that it is really as simple as that? If so, there must be pretty wide ranges of variation within each type. And if, to explain the variation, we call in heredity and environment, experiences in early childhood, the thyroid and other glands, and also the four functions of the mind mentioned at the beginning of this introduction, and extroversion and introversion, then one begins to wonder if the original classification was worth making at all. No sensible person believes that his favorite system explains everything. But even so, he will not find it much use at all if it does not even save him the trouble of bothering with the others.

Under the Jungian system, everyone has not only a dominant or principal function, but also a secondary or subsidiary one, so that the four can be arranged in order of potency. In the intuitive type, sensation is always the most inefficient function, but the second most inefficient function can be either thinking (which tends to make original thinkers such as Jung himself) or else feeling (which tends to make artistic people). Therefore, allowing for introversion and extroversion, there are at least four kinds of intuitive types, and sixteen types in all. Furthermore, one can see how the sixteen types merge into each other, so that there are no unrealistic or unconvincingly rigid divisions.

In the same way, if we were to put every person under only one sign of the Zodiac, the system becomes too rigid and unlike life. Besides, it was never intended to be used like that. It may be convenient to have only twelve types, but we know that in practice there is every possible gradation between aggressiveness and timidity, or between conscientiousness and laziness. How, then, do we account for this?

The Tyrant and the Saint

Just as the thinking type of man is also influenced to some extent by sensation and intuition, but not very much by emotion, so a person born under Leo can be influenced to some extent by one or two (but not more) of the other signs. For instance, famous persons born under the sign of Gemini include Henry VIII, whom nothing and no-one could have induced to abdicate, and Edward VIII, who did just that. Obviously, then, the sign Gemini does not fully explain the complete character of either of them.

Again, under the opposite sign, Sagittarius, were both Stalin, who was totally consumed with the notion of power, and Charles V, who freely gave up an empire because he preferred to go into a monastery. And we find under Scorpio, many uncompromising characters such as Luther, de Gaulle, Indira Gandhi and Montgomery, but also Petain, a successful commander whose name later became synonymous with collaboration.

A single sign is therefore obviously inadequate to explain the differences between people; it can only explain resemblances, such as the combativeness of the Scorpio group, or the far-reaching devotion of Charles V and Stalin to their respective ideals—the Christian heaven and the Communist utopia.

But very few people are born under one sign only. As well as the month of birth, as was mentioned earlier, the day matters, and, even more, the hour, which ought, if possible, to be noted to the nearest minute. Without this, it is impossible to have an actual horoscope, for the word horoscope means literally, "a consideration of the hour."

The month of birth tells you only which sign of the Zodiac was occupied by the sun. The day and hour tell you what sign was occupied by the moon. And the minute tells you which sign was rising on the eastern horizon. This is called the Ascendant, and it is supposed to be the most important thing in the whole horoscope.

If you were born at midnight, the sun is then in an important position, although invisible. But at one o'clock in the morning the sun is not important, so the moment of birth will not matter much. The important thing then will be the Ascendant, and possibly one or two of the planets. At a given day and hour, say, dawn on January 1st, or 9:00 p.m. on the longest day, the Ascendant will always be the same at any given place. But the moon and planets alter from day to day, at different speeds and have to be looked up in an astronomical table.

The sun is said to signify one's heart, that is to say, one's deepest desires and inmost nature. This is quite different from the moon, which, as we have seen, signifies one's superficial way of behaving. When the ancient Romans referred to the Emperor Augustus as a Capricornian, they meant that he had the moon in Capricorn; they did not pay much attention to the sun, although he was born at sunrise. Or, to take another example, a modern astrologer would call Disraeli a Scorpion because he had Scorpio rising, but most people would call him Sagittarian because he had the sun there. The Romans would have called him Leo because his moon was in Leo.

The sun, as has already been pointed out, is important if one is born near sunrise, sunset, noon or midnight, but is otherwise not reckoned as the principal influence. So if one does not seem to fit one's birth month, it is always worthwhile reading the other signs, for one may have been born at a time when any of them were rising or occupied by the moon. It also seems to be the case that the influence of the sun develops as life goes on, so that the month of birth is easier to guess in people over the age of forty. The young are supposed to be influenced mainly by their Ascendant which characterizes the body and physical personality as a whole.

It should be clearly understood that it is nonsense to assume that all people born at a certain time will exhibit the same characteristics, or that they will even behave in the same manner. It is quite obvious that, from the very moment of its birth, a child is subject to the effects of its environment, and that this in turn will influence its character and heritage to a decisive extent. Also to be taken into account are education and economic conditions, which play a very important part in the formation of one's character as well.

However, it is clearly established that people born under one sign of the Zodiac do have certain basic traits in their character which are different from those born under other signs. It is obvious to every thinking person that certain events produce different reactions in various people. For instance, if a man slips on a banana skin and falls heavily on the pavement, one passer-by may laugh and find this extremely amusing, while another may just walk on, thinking: "What a fool falling down like that. He should look where he is going." A third might also walk away saying to himself: "It's none of my business—I'm glad it wasn't me." A fourth might walk past and think: "I'm sorry for that man, but I haven't the time to be bothered with helping him." And a fifth might stop to help the fallen man to his feet, comfort him and take him home. Here is just one event which could produce entirely different reactions in different people. And, obviously, there are many more. One that comes to mind immediately is the violently opposed views to events such as wars, industrial strikes, and so on. The fact that people have different attitudes to the same event is simply another way of saying that they have different characters. And this is not something that can be put down to background, for people of the same race, religion, or class, very often express quite different reactions to happenings or events. Similarly, it is often the case that members of the same family, where there is clearly uniform background of economic and social standing, education, race and religion, often argue bitterly among themselves over political and social issues.

People have, in general, certain character traits and qualities which, according to their environment, develop in either a positive or a negative manner. Therefore, selfishness (inherent selfishness, that is) might emerge as unselfishness; kindness and consideration as cruelty and lack of consideration towards others. In the same way, a naturally constructive person, may, through frustration, become destructive, and so on. The latent characteristics with which people are born can, therefore, through environment and good or bad training, become something that would appear to be its opposite, and so give the lie to the astrologer's description of their character. But this is not the case. The true character is still there, but it is buried deep beneath these external superficialities.

Careful study of the character traits of different signs can be immeasurable help, and can render beneficial service to the intelligent person. Undoubtedly, the reader will already have discovered that, while he is able to get on very well with some people, he just "cannot stand" others. The causes sometimes seem inexplicable. At times there is intense dislike, at other times immediate sympathy. And there is, too, the phenomenon of love at first sight, which is also apparently inexplicable. People appear to be either sympathetic or unsympathetic towards each other for no apparent reason.

Now if we look at this in the light of the Zodiac, we find that people born under different signs are either compatible or incompatible with each other. In other words, there are good and bad interrelating factors among the various signs. This does not, of course, mean that humanity can be divided into groups of hostile camps. It would be quite wrong to be hostile or indifferent toward people who happen to be born under an incompatible sign. There is no reason why everybody should not, or cannot, learn to control and adjust their feelings and actions, especially after they are aware of the positive qualities of other people by studying their character analyses, among other things.

Every person born under a certain sign has both positive and negative qualities, which are developed more or less according to his free will. Nobody is entirely good or entirely bad, and it is up to each one of us to learn to control himself on the one hand, and at the same time to endeavor to learn about himself and others.

It cannot be repeated often enough that, though the intrinsic nature of man and his basic character traits are born in him, nevertheless it is his own free will that determines whether he will make really good use of his talents and abilities—whether, in other words, he will overcome his vices or allow them to rule him. Most of us are born with at least a streak of laziness, irritability, or some other fault in our nature, and it is up to each one of us to see that we exert sufficient willpower to control our failings so that they do not harm ourselves or others.

Astrology can reveal our inclinations and tendencies. Our weaknesses should not be viewed as shortcomings that are impossible to change. The horoscope of a man may show him to have criminal leanings, for instance, but this does not mean he will definitely become a criminal.

The ordinary man usually finds it difficult to know himself. He is often bewildered. Astrology can frequently tell him more about himself than the different schools of psychology are able to do. Knowing his failings and shortcomings, he will do his best to overcome them, and make himself a better and more useful member of society and a helpmate to his family and friends. It can also save him a great deal of unhappiness and remorse.

And yet it may seem absurd that an ancient philosophy, something that is known as a "pseudo-science," could be a prop to the men and women of the twentieth century. But below the materialistic surface of modern life, there are hidden streams of feeling and thought. Symbology is reappearing as a study worthy of the scholar; the psychosomatic factor in illness has passed from the writings of the crank to those of the specialist; spiritual healing in all its forms is no longer a pious hope but an accepted phenomenon. And it is into this context that we consider astrology, in the sense that it is an analysis of human types.

Astrology and medicine had a long journey together, and only parted company a couple of centuries ago. There still remain in medical language such astrological terms as "saturnine," "choleric," and "mercurial," used in the diagnosis of physical tendencies. The herbalist, for long the handyman of the medical profession, has been dominated by astrology since the days of the Greeks. Certain herbs traditionally respond to certain planetary influences, and diseases must therefore be treated to ensure harmony between the medicine and the disease.

No one expects the most eccentric of modern doctors to go back to the practices of his predecessors. We have come a long way since the time when phases of the moon were studied in illness. Those days were a medical nightmare, with epidemics that were beyond control, and an explanation of the Black Death sought in conjunction with the planets. Nowadays, astrological diagnosis of disease has literally no parallel in modern life. And yet, age-old symbols of types and of the vulnerability of, say, the Saturnian to chronic diseases or the choleric to apoplexy and blood pressure and so on, are still applicable.

But the stars are expected to foretell and not only to diagnose. The astrological forecaster has a counterpart on a highly conventional level in the shape of the weather prophet, racing tipster and stock market forecaster, to name just three examples. All in their own way are aiming at the same result. They attempt to look a little further into the pattern of life and also try to determine future patterns accurately.

Astrological forecasting has been remarkably accurate, but often it is wide of the mark. The brave man who cares to predict world events takes dangerous chances. Individual forecasting is less clear cut; it can be a help or a disillusionment. Then welcome to the nagging question: if it is possible to foreknow, is it right to foretell? A complex point of ethics on which it is hard to pronounce judgment. The doctor faces the same dilemma if he finds that symptoms of a mortal disease are present in his patient and that he can only prognosticate a steady decline. How much to tell an individual in a crisis is a problem that has perplexed many distinguished scholars. Honest and conscientious astrologers in this modern world, where so many people are seeking guidance, face the same problem.

The ancient cults, the symbols of old religions, are eclipsed for the moment. They may return with their old force within a decade or two. But at present the outlook is dark. Human beings badly need assurance, as they did in the past, that all is not chaos. Somewhere, somehow, there is a pattern that must be worked out. As to the why and wherefore, the astrologer is not expected to give judgment. He is just someone who, by dint of talent and training, can gaze into the future.

Five hundred years ago it was customary to call in a learned man who was an astrologer who was probably also a doctor and a philosopher. By his knowledge of astrology, his study of planetary influences, he felt himself qualified to guide those in distress. The world has moved forward at a fantastic rate since then, and in this twentieth century speed has been the keyword everywhere. Tensions have increased, the spur of ambition has been applied indiscriminately. People are uncertain of themselves. At first sight it seems fantastic in the light of modern thinking that they turn to the most ancient of all studies, and get someone to calculate a horoscope for them. But is it *really* so fantastic if you take a second look? For astrology is concerned with tomorrow, with survival. And in a world such as ours, those two things are the keywords of the time in which we live.

HOW TO USE
THESE PREDICTIONS

A person reading the predictions in this book should understand that they are produced from the daily position of the planets for a group of people and are not, of course, individually specialized. To get the full benefit of them he should relate the predictions to his own character and circumstances, co-ordinate them, and draw his own conclusions from them.

If he is a serious observer of his own life he should find a definite pattern emerge that will be a helpful and reliable guide.

The point is that we always retain our free will. The stars indicate certain directional tendencies but we are not compelled to follow. We can do or not do, and wisdom must make the choice.

We all have our good and bad days. Sometimes they extend into cycles of weeks. It is therefore advisable to study daily predictions in a span ranging from the day before to several days ahead; also to re-read the monthly predictions for similar cycles.

Daily predictions should be taken very generally. The word "difficult" does not necessarily indicate a whole day of obstruction or inconvenience. It is a warning to you to be cautious. Your caution will often see you around the difficulty before you are involved. This is the correct use of astrology.

In another section, detailed information is given about the influence of the moon as it passes through the various signs of the Zodiac. It includes instructions on how to use the Moon Tables. This information should be used in conjunction with the daily forecasts to give a fuller picture of the astrological trends.

THE MOON

Moon is the nearest planet to the earth. It exerts more observable influence on us from day to day than any other planet. The effect is very personal, very intimate, and if we are not aware of how it works it can make us quite unstable in our ideas. And the annoying thing is that at these times we often see our own instability but can do nothing about it. A knowledge of what can be expected may help considerably. We can then be prepared to stand strong against the moon's negative influences and use its positive ones to help us to get ahead. Who has not heard of going with the tide?

Moon reflects, has no light of its own. It reflects the sun—the life giver—in the form of vital movement. Moon controls the tides, the blood rhythm, the movement of sap in trees and plants. Its nature is inconstancy and change so it signifies our moods, our superficial behavior—walking, talking and especially thinking. Being a true reflector of other forces, moon is cold, watery like the surface of a still lake, brilliant and scintillating at times, but easily ruffled and disturbed by the winds of change.

The moon takes 28½ days to circle the earth and the Zodiac. It spends just over 2¼ days in each sign. During that time it reflects the qualities, energies and characteristics of the sign and, to a degree, the planet which rules the sign. While the moon in its transit occupies a sign incompatible with our own birth sign, we can expect to feel a vague uneasiness, perhaps a touch of irritableness. We should not be discouraged nor let the feeling get us down, or, worse still, allow ourselves to take the discomfort out on others. Try to remember that the moon has to change signs within 55 hours and, provided you are not physically ill, your mood will probably change with it. It is amazing how frequently depression lifts with the shift in the moon's position. And, of course, when the moon is transiting a sign compatible or sympathetic to yours you will probably feel some sort of stimulation or just plain happy to be alive.

In the horoscope, the moon is such a powerful indicator that competent astrologers often use the sign it occupied at birth as the birth sign of the person. This is done particularly when the sun is on the cusp, or edge, of two signs. Most experienced astrologers, however, coordinate both sun and moon signs by reading and confirming from one to the other and secure a far more accurate and personalized analysis.

For these reasons, the moon tables which follow this section (see pages 28–35) are of great importance to the individual. They show the days and the exact times the moon will enter each sign of the Zodiac for the year. Remember, you have to adjust the indicated times to local time. The corrections, already calculated for most of the main cities, are at the beginning of the tables. What follows now is a guide to the influences that will be reflected to the earth by the moon while it transits each of the twelve signs. The influence is at its peak about 26 hours after the moon enters a sign.

MOON IN ARIES

This is a time for action, for reaching out beyond the usual self-imposed limitations and faint-hearted cautions. If you have plans in your head or on your desk, put them into practice. New ventures, applications, new jobs, new starts of any kind—all have a good chance of success. This is the period when original and dynamic impulses are being reflected onto the earth. The energies are extremely vital and favor the pursuit of pleasure and adventure in practically every form. Sick people should feel an improvement. Those who are well will probably find themselves exuding confidence and optimism. People fond of physical exercise should find their bodies growing with tone and well-being. Boldness, strength, determination should characterize most of your activities with a readiness to face up to old challenges. Yesterday's problems may seem petty and exaggerated—so deal with them. Strike out alone. Self-reliance will attract others to you. This is a good time for making friends. Business and marriage partners are more likely to be impressed with the man and woman of action. Opposition will be overcome or thrown aside with much less effort than usual. CAUTION: Be dominant but not domineering.

MOON IN TAURUS

The spontaneous, action-packed person of yesterday gives way to the cautious, diligent, hardworking "thinker." In this period ideas will probably be concentrated on ways of improving finances. A great deal of time may be spent figuring out and going over schemes and plans. It is the right time to be careful with detail. People will find themselves working longer than usual at their desks. Or devoting more time to serious thought about the future. A strong desire to put order into business and financial arrangements may cause extra work. Loved ones may complain of being neglected and may fail to appreciate that your efforts are for their ultimate benefit. Your desire for system may extend to criticism of arrangements in the home and lead to minor upsets. Health may be affected through overwork. Try to secure a reasonable amount of rest and relaxation, although the tendency will be to "keep going" despite good advice. Work done conscientiously in this period should result in a solid contribution to your future security. CAUTION: Try not to be as serious with people as the work you are engaged in.

MOON IN GEMINI

The humdrum of routine and too much work should suddenly end. You are likely to find yourself in an expansive, quicksilver world of change and self-expression. Urges to write, to paint, to experience the freedom of some sort of artistic outpouring, may be very strong. Take full advantage of them. You may find yourself finishing something you began and put aside long ago. Or embarking on something new which could easily be prompted by a chance meeting, a new acquaintance, or even an advertisement. There may be a yearning for a change of scenery, the feeling to visit another country (not too far away), or at least to get away for a few days. This may result in short, quick journeys. Or, if you are planning a single visit, there may be some unexpected changes or detours on the way. Familiar activities will seem to give little satisfaction unless they contain a fresh element of excitement or expectation. The inclination will be towards untried pursuits, particularly those that allow you to express your inner nature. The accent is on new faces, new places. CAUTION: Do not be too quick to commit yourself emotionally.

MOON IN CANCER

Feelings of uncertainty and vague insecurity are likely to cause problems while the moon is in Cancer. Thoughts may turn frequently to the warmth of the home and the comfort of loved ones. Nostalgic impulses could cause you to bring out old photographs and letters and reflect on the days when your life seemed to be much more rewarding and less demanding. The love and understanding of parents and family may be important, and, if it is not forthcoming you may have to fight against a bit of self-pity. The cordiality of friends and the thought of good times with them that are sure to be repeated will help to restore you to a happier frame of mind. The feeling to be alone may follow minor setbacks or rebuffs at this time, but solitude is unlikely to help. Better to get on the telephone or visit someone. This period often causes peculiar dreams and up-surges of imaginative thinking which can be very helpful to authors of occult and mystical works. Preoccupation with the more person-al world of simple human needs should overshadow any material strivings. CAUTION: Do not spend too much time thinking—seek the company of loved ones or close friends.

MOON IN LEO

New horizons of exciting and rather extravagant activity open up. This is the time for exhilarating entertainment, glamorous and lavish parties, and expensive shopping sprees. Any merrymaking that relies upon your generosity as a host has every chance of being a spectacular success. You should find yourself right in the center of the fun, either as the life of the party or simply as a person whom happy people like to be with. Romance thrives in this heady at-mosphere and friendships are likely to explode unexpectedly into serious attachments. Children and younger people should be at-tracted to you and you may find yourself organizing a picnic or a visit to a fun-fair, the cinema or the seaside. The sunny company and vitality of youthful companions should help you to find some unsuspected energy. In career, you could find an opening for pro-motion or advancement. This should be the time to make a direct approach. The period favors those engaged in original research. CAUTION: Bask in popularity but not in flattery.

MOON IN VIRGO

Off comes the party cap and out steps the busy, practical worker. He wants to get his personal affairs straight, to rearrange them, if necessary, for more efficiency, so he will have more time for more work. He clears up his correspondence, pays outstanding bills, makes numerous phone calls. He is likely to make inquiries, or sign up for some new insurance and put money into gilt-edged invest-ment. Thoughts probably revolve around the need for future secur-ity—to tie up loose ends and clear the decks. There may be a ten-dency to be "finicky," to interfere in the routine of others, particu-larly friends and family members. The motive may be a genuine desire to help with suggestions for updating or streamlining their affairs, but these will probably not be welcomed. Sympathy may be felt for less fortunate sections of the community and a flurry of some sort of voluntary service is likely. This may be accompanied by strong feelings of responsibility on several fronts and health may suffer from extra efforts made. CAUTION: Everyone may not want your help or advice.

MOON IN LIBRA

These are days of harmony and agreement and you should find yourself at peace with most others. Relationships tend to be smooth and sweet-flowing. Friends may become closer and bonds deepen in mutual understanding. Hopes will be shared. Progress by coopera- tion could be the secret of success in every sphere. In business, es- tablished partnerships may flourish and new ones get off to a good start. Acquaintances could discover similar interests that lead to congenial discussions and rewarding exchanges of some sort. Love, as a unifying force, reaches its optimum. Marriage partners should find accord. Those who wed at this time face the prospect of a hap- py union. Cooperation and tolerance are felt to be stronger than dissension and impatience. The argumentative are not quite so loud in their bellowings, nor as inflexible in their attitudes. In the home, there should be a greater recognition of the other point of view and a readiness to put the wishes of the group before selfish insistence. This is a favorable time to join an art group. CAUTION: Do not be too independent—let others help you if they want to.

MOON IN SCORPIO

Driving impulses to make money and to economize are likely to cause upsets all round. No area of expenditure is likely to be spared the axe, including the household budget. This is a time when the desire to cut down on extravagance can become near fanatical. Care must be exercised to try to keep the aim in reasonable perspective. Others may not feel the same urgent need to save and may retaliate. There is a danger that possessions of sentimental value will be sold to realize cash for investment. Buying and selling of stock for quick profit is also likely. The attention may turn to having a good clean up round the home and at the office. Neglected jobs could suddenly be done with great bursts of energy. The desire for solitude may intervene. Self-searching thoughts could disturb. The sense of in- visible and mysterious energies at work could cause some excitabili- ty. The reassurance of loves ones may help. CAUTION: Be kind to the people you love.

MOON IN SAGITTARIUS

These are days when you are likely to be stirred and elevated by discussions and reflections of a religious and philosophical nature. Ideas of far-away places may cause unusual response and excite- ment. A decision may be made to visit someone overseas, perhaps a person whose influence was important to your earlier character development. There could be a strong resolution to get away from present intellectual patterns, to learn new subjects and to meet more interesting people. The superficial may be rejected in all its forms. An impatience with old ideas and unimaginative contacts could lead to a change of companions and interests. There may be an upsurge of religious feeling and metaphysical inquiry. Even a new insight into the significance of astrology and other occult studies is likely under the curious stimulus of the moon in Sagittarius. Physically, you may express this need for fundamental change by spending more time outdoors: sports, gardening or going for long walks. CAUTION: Try to channel any restlessness into worthwhile study.

MOON IN CAPRICORN

Life in these hours may seem to pivot around the importance of gaining prestige and honor in the career, as well as maintaining a spotless reputation. Ambitious urges may be excessive and could be accompanied by quite acquisitive drives for money. Effort should be directed along strictly ethical lines where there is no possibility of reproach or scandal. All endeavors are likely to be characterized by great earnestness, and an air of authority and purpose which should impress those who are looking for leadership or reliability. The desire to conform to accepted standards may extend to sharp criticism of family members. Frivolity and unconventional actions are unlikely to amuse while the moon is in Capricorn. Moderation and seriousness are the orders of the day. Achievement and recognition in this period could come through community work or organizing for the benefit of some amateur group. CAUTION: Dignity and esteem are not always self-awarded.

MOON IN AQUARIUS

Moon in Aquarius is in the second last sign of the Zodiac where ideas can become disturbingly fine and subtle. The result is often a mental "no-man's land" where imagination cannot be trusted with the same certitude as other times. The dangers for the individual are the extremes of optimism and pessimism. Unless the imgination is held in check, situations are likely to be misread, and rosy conclusions drawn where they do not exist. Consequences for the unwary can be costly in career and business. Best to think twice and not speak or act until you think again. Pessimism can be a cruel self-inflicted penalty for delusion at this time. Between the two extremes are strange areas of self-deception which, for example, can make the selfish person think he is actually being generous. Eerie dreams which resemble the reality and even seem to continue into the waking state are also possible. CAUTION: Look for the fact and not just for the image in your mind.

MOON IN PISCES

Everything seems to come to the surface now. Memory may be crystal clear, throwing up long-forgotten information which could be valuable in the career or business. Flashes of clairvoyance and intuition are possible along with sudden realizations of one's own nature, which may be used for self-improvement. A talent, never before suspected, may be discovered. Qualities not evident before in friends and marriage partners are likely to be noticed. As this is a period in which the truth seems to emerge, the discovery of false characteristics is likely to lead to disenchantment or a shift in attachments. However, where qualities are realized it should lead to happiness and deeper feeling. Surprise solutions could bob up for old problems. There may be a public announcement of the solving of a crime or mystery. People with secrets may find someone has "guessed" correctly. The secrets of the soul or the inner self also tend to reveal themselves. Religious and philosophical groups may make some interesting discoveries. CAUTION: Not a time for activities that depend on secrecy.

MOON TABLES

TIME CORRECTIONS FOR GREENWICH MOON TABLES

London, Glasgow, Dublin, Dakar	Same time
Vienna, Prague, Rome, Kinshasa, Frankfurt, Stockholm, Brussels, Amsterdam, Warsaw, Zurich	Add 1 hour
Bucharest, Istanbul, Beirut, Cairo, Johannesburg, Athens, Cape Town, Helsinki, Tel Aviv	Add 2 hours
Dhahran, Baghdad, Moscow, Leningrad, Nairobi, Addis Ababa, Zanzibar	Add 3 hours
Delhi, Calcutta, Bombay, Colombo	Add 5½ hours
Rangoon	Add 6½ hours
Saigon, Bangkok, Chungking	Add 7 hours
Canton, Manila, Hong Kong, Shanghai, Peking	Add 8 hours
Tokyo, Pusan, Seoul, Vladivostok, Yokohama	Add 9 hours
Sydney, Melbourne, Guam, Port Moresby	Add 10 hours
Azores, Reykjavik	Deduct 1 hour
Rio de Janeiro, Montevideo, Buenos Aires, Sao Paulo, Recife	Deduct 3 hours
LaPaz, San Juan, Santiago, Bermuda, Caracas, Halifax	Deduct 4 hours
New York, Washington, Boston, Detroit, Lima, Havana, Miami, Bogota	Deduct 5 hours
Mexico, Chicago, New Orleans, Houston	Deduct 6 hours
San Francisco, Seattle, Los Angeles, Hollywood, Ketchikan, Juneau	Deduct 8 hours
Honolulu, Fairbanks, Anchorage, Papeete	Deduct 10 hours

1988 MOON TABLES—GREENWICH TIME

JANUARY		FEBRUARY		MARCH	
Day Moon Enters		**Day Moon Enters**		**Day Moon Enters**	
1. Gemini		1. Leo	6:31 pm	1. Leo	
2. Gemini		2. Leo		2. Virgo	1:26 pm
3. Cancer	0:30 am	3. Leo		3. Virgo	
4. Cancer		4. Virgo	7:10 am	4. Virgo	
5. Leo	Noon	5. Virgo		5. Libra	1:29 am
6. Leo		6. Libra	7:27 pm	6. Libra	
7. Leo		7. Libra		7. Scorpio	0:35 pm
8. Virgo	0:37 am	8. Libra		8. Scorpio	
9. Virgo		9. Scorpio	6:38 am	9. Sagitt.	8:59 pm
10. Libra	1:12 pm	10. Scorpio		10. Sagitt.	
11. Libra		11. Sagitt.	2:19 pm	11. Sagitt.	
12. Scorpio	11:21 pm	12. Sagitt.		12. Capric.	2:35 am
13. Scorpio		13. Capric.	6:20 pm	13. Capric.	
14. Scorpio		14. Capric.		14. Aquar.	5:06 am
15. Sagitt.	5:28 am	15. Aquar.	7:22 pm	15. Aquar.	
16. Sagitt.		16. Aquar.		16. Pisces	5:30 am
17. Capric.	8:20 am	17. Pisces	6:43 pm	17. Pisces	
18. Capric.		18. Pisces		18. Aries	5:30 am
19. Aquar.	8:08 am	19. Aries	6:39 pm	19. Aries	
20. Aquar.		20. Aries		20. Taurus	6:56 am
21. Pisces	7:58 am	21. Taurus	8:56 pm	21. Taurus	
22. Pisces		22. Taurus		22. Gemini	10:58 am
23. Aries	8:32 am	23. Taurus		23. Gemini	
24. Aries		24. Gemini	2:42 am	24. Cancer	7:36 pm
25. Taurus	0:54 pm	25. Gemini		25. Cancer	
26. Taurus		26. Cancer	0:36 pm	26. Cancer	
27. Gemini	7:53 pm	27. Cancer		27. Leo	7:23 am
28. Gemini		28. Cancer		28. Leo	
29. Gemini		29. Leo	0:50 am	29. Virgo	8:13 pm
30. Cancer	6:39 am			30. Virgo	
31. Cancer				31. Virgo	

Summer time to be considered where applicable.

1988 MOON TABLES—GREENWICH TIME

APRIL		MAY		JUNE	
Day Moon Enters		**Day Moon Enters**		**Day Moon Enters**	
1. Libra	8:12 am	1. Scorpio	1:24 am	1. Capric.	8:51 pm
2. Libra		2. Scorpio		2. Capric.	
3. Scorpio	6:28 pm	3. Sagitt.	8:40 am	3. Aquar.	11:48 pm
4. Scorpio		4. Sagitt.		4. Aquar.	
5. Scorpio		5. Capric.	1:55 pm	5. Aquar.	
6. Sagitt.	2:28 am	6. Capric.		6. Pisces	2:16 am
7. Sagitt.		7. Aquar.	6:08 pm	7. Pisces	
8. Capric.	8:38 am	8. Aquar.		8. Aries	5:16 am
9. Capric.		9. Pisces	8:50 pm	9. Aries	
10. Aquar.	0:41 pm	10. Pisces		10. Taurus	9:12 am
11. Aquar.		11. Aries	11:20 pm	11. Taurus	
12. Pisces	2:46 pm	12. Aries		12. Gemini	2:22 pm
13. Pisces		13. Aries		13. Gemini	
14. Aries	3:39 pm	14. Taurus	2:22 am	14. Cancer	9:42 pm
15. Aries		15. Taurus		15. Cancer	
16. Taurus	5:26 pm	16. Gemini	6:24 am	16. Cancer	
17. Taurus		17. Gemini		17. Leo	7:10 am
18. Gemini	8:48 pm	18. Cancer	0:46 pm	18. Leo	
19. Gemini		19. Cancer		19. Virgo	7:04 pm
20. Gemini		20. Leo	10:54 pm	20. Virgo	
21. Cancer	4:04 am	21. Leo		21. Virgo	
22. Cancer		22. Leo		22. Libra	7:59 am
23. Leo	2:51 pm	23. Virgo	11:12 am	23. Libra	
24. Leo		24. Virgo		24. Scorpio	6:59 pm
25. Leo		25. Libra	11:55 pm	25. Scorpio	
26. Virgo	3:44 am	26. Libra		26. Scorpio	
27. Virgo		27. Libra		27. Sagitt.	2:21 am
28. Libra	3:55 pm	28. Scorpio	10:03 am	28. Sagitt.	
29. Libra		29. Scorpio		29. Capric.	6:06 am
30. Libra		30. Sagitt.	4:44 pm	30. Capric.	
		31. Sagitt.			

Summer time to be considered where applicable.

1988 MOON TABLES—GREENWICH TIME

JULY	AUGUST	SEPTEMBER
Day Moon Enters	Day Moon Enters	Day Moon Enters
1. Aquar. 7:38 am	1. Aries 5:48 pm	1. Taurus
2. Aquar.	2. Aries	2. Gemini 8:08 am
3. Pisces 8:52 am	3. Taurus 8:12 pm	3. Gemini
4. Pisces	4. Taurus	4. Cancer 3:50 pm
5. Aries 10:41 am	5. Taurus	5. Cancer
6. Aries	6. Gemini 1:34 am	6. Cancer
7. Taurus 2:31 pm	7. Gemini	7. Leo 2:32 am
8. Taurus	8. Cancer 10:07 am	8. Leo
9. Gemini 8:17 pm	9. Cancer	9. Virgo 3:02 pm
10. Gemini	10. Leo 8:57 pm	10. Virgo
11. Gemini	11. Leo	11. Virgo
12. Cancer 4:29 am	12. Leo	12. Libra 3:32 am
13. Cancer	13. Virgo 8:37 am	13. Libra
14. Leo 2:25 pm	14. Virgo	14. Scorpio 3:25 pm
15. Leo	15. Libra 9:26 pm	15. Scorpio
16. Leo	16. Libra	16. Scorpio
17. Virgo 2:24 am	17. Libra	17. Sagitt. 2:01 am
18. Virgo	18. Scorpio 9:37 am	18. Sagitt.
19. Libra 3:04 pm	19. Scorpio	19. Capric. 9:40 am
20. Libra	20. Sagitt. 7:49 pm	20. Capric.
21. Libra	21. Sagitt.	21. Aquar. 2:09 pm
22. Scorpio 3:01 am	22. Sagitt.	22. Aquar.
23. Scorpio	23. Capric. 1:45 am	23. Pisces 2:45 pm
24. Sagitt. Noon	24. Capric.	24. Pisces
25. Sagitt.	25. Aquar. 4:20 am	25. Aries 2:33 pm
26. Capric. 4:15 pm	26. Aquar.	26. Aries
27. Capric.	27. Pisces 4:14 am	27. Taurus 2:30 pm
28. Aquar. 5:58 pm	28. Pisces	28. Taurus
29. Aquar.	29. Aries 3:45 am	29. Gemini 5:01 pm
30. Pisces 5:45 pm	30. Aries	30. Gemini
31. Pisces	31. Taurus 4:30 am	

Summer time to be considered where applicable.

1988 MOON TABLES—GREENWICH TIME

OCTOBER	NOVEMBER	DECEMBER
Day Moon Enters	**Day Moon Enters**	**Day Moon Enters**
1. Cancer 10:43 pm	1. Leo	1. Virgo
2. Cancer	2. Leo	2. Virgo
3. Cancer	3. Virgo 4:25 am	3. Libra 1:13 am
4. Leo 9:00 am	4. Virgo	4. Libra
5. Leo	5. Libra 5:15 pm	5. Scorpio 0:47 pm
6. Virgo 9:22 pm	6. Libra	6. Scorpio
7. Virgo	7. Libra	7. Sagitt. 10:10 pm
8. Virgo	8. Scorpio 4:39 am	8. Sagitt.
9. Libra 10:00 am	9. Scorpio	9. Sagitt.
10. Libra	10. Sagitt. 1:53 pm	10. Capric. 4:14 am
11. Scorpio 9:34 pm	11. Sagitt.	11. Capric.
12. Scorpio	12. Capric. 9:23 pm	12. Aquar. 9:04 am
13. Scorpio	13. Capric.	13. Aquar.
14. Sagitt. 7:35 am	14. Capric.	14. Pisces 0:10 pm
15. Sagitt.	15. Aquar. 2:46 am	15. Pisces
16. Capric. 3:38 pm	16. Aquar.	16. Aries 2:53 pm
17. Capric.	17. Pisces 6:37 am	17. Aries
18. Aquar. 9:07 pm	18. Pisces	18. Taurus 5:50 pm
19. Aquar.	19. Aries 8:50 am	19. Taurus
20. Pisces 11:56 pm	20. Aries	20. Gemini 9:48 pm
21. Pisces	21. Taurus 10:41 am	21. Gemini
22. Pisces	22. Taurus	22. Gemini
23. Aries 0:49 am	23. Gemini 1:13 pm	23. Cancer 2:42 am
24. Aries	24. Gemini	24. Cancer
25. Taurus 1:22 am	25. Cancer 5:36 pm	25. Leo 10:08 am
26. Taurus	26. Cancer	26. Leo
27. Gemini 3:07 am	27. Cancer	27. Virgo 8:36 pm
28. Gemini	28. Leo 1:04 am	28. Virgo
29. Cancer 7:42 am	29. Leo	29. Virgo
30. Cancer	30. Virgo 0:12 pm	30. Libra 8:58 am
31. Leo 4:25 pm		31. Libra

Summer time to be considered where applicable.

1988 PHASES OF THE MOON—GREENWICH TIME

New Moon	First Quarter	Full Moon	Last Quarter
(1987)	(1987)	Jan. 4	Jan. 12
Jan. 19	Jan. 25	Feb. 2	Feb. 10
Feb. 17	Feb. 24	Mar. 3	Mar. 11
Mar. 18	Mar. 25	Apr. 1	Apr. 9
Apr. 16	Apr. 23	May 1	May 9
May 15	May 23	May 31	June 7
June 14	June 22	June 29	July 6
July 13	July 22	July 29	Aug. 4
Aug. 12	Aug. 20	Aug. 27	Sep. 3
Sep. 11	Sep. 19	Sep. 25	Oct. 2
Oct. 10	Oct. 18	Oct. 25	Nov. 1
Nov. 9	Nov. 16	Nov. 23	Dec. 1
Dec. 9	Dec. 16	Dec. 23	Dec. 31

1988 PLANTING GUIDE

	Aboveground Crops	Root Crops	Pruning	Weeds Pests
January	3-21-22-26-30-31	4-11-12-13-14-17-18	4-13-14	6-7-8-9-15-16
February	18-22-23-27-28	7-8-9-10-14	9-10	3-4-5-12-16
March	20-21-25-26	5-6-7-8-12-13-16-17	8-16-17	4-10-11-14-15
April	1-17-21-22-29-30	2-3-4-5-8-9-13	4-5-13	6-7-11-15
May	1-19-20-26-27-28-29	2-6-10-11-14-15	2-10-11	3-4-8-12-13
June	15-16-22-23-24-25-26	2-3-6-7-10-11-30	6-7	4-5-8-9-13
July	20-21-22-23-27	3-4-8-12-13-31	3-4-12-13-31	1-2-6-10-11-29
August	16-17-18-19-23-24	4-5-9-28-31	9-28	2-6-7-11-29-30
September	12-13-14-15-16-19-20-24	1-5-6-28	5-6	2-3-7-8-9-10-26-30
October	11-12-13-17-21-22	2-3-9-25-26-29-30	2-3-29-30	1-4-5-6-7-27-28
November	13-14-17-18-21-22	6-7-8-26-27	8-26-27	1-2-3-4-24-28-29-30
December	10-11-15-19	3-4-5-6-7-23-24-30-31	6-7-23-24	1-2-8-26-27-28-29

1988 FISHING GUIDE

	Good	Best
January	1-2-5-6-7-19-25	3-4-12-30-31
February	1-2-3-4-5-17-24-29	10
March	1-2-3-4-11-18-30-31	5-6-25
April	16-23-28	1-2-3-4-5-9-29-30
May	3-4-9-23-30-31	1-2-15-28-29
June	1-14-27-28	2-3-7-22-26-29-30
July	1-2-6-26-28-29-30	13-22-27-31
August	1-12-20-25-26-29-30	4-24-27-28
September	3-11-22-23-25-26-27	19-24-28
October	18-23-24-27-28	2-10-22-25-26
November	1-16-20-21-23-24-25	9-22-26
December	1-9-16-20-21-22-25-26	23-24-31

MOON'S INFLUENCE OVER DAILY AFFAIRS

The Moon makes a complete transit of the Zodiac every 27 days 7 hours and 43 minutes. In making this transit the Moon forms different aspects with the planets and consequently has favorable or unfavorable bearings on affairs and events for persons according to the sign of the Zodiac under which they were born.

Whereas the Sun exclusively represents fire, the Moon rules water. The action of the Moon may be described as fluctuating, variable, absorbent and receptive. It is well known that the attraction to the Moon in combination with the movement of the Earth is responsible for the tides. The Moon has a similar effect on men. A clever navigator will make use of the tides to bring his ship to the intended destination. You also can reach your "destination" better by making use of your tides.

When the Moon is in conjunction with the Sun it is called a New Moon; when the Moon and Sun are in opposition it is called a Full Moon. From New Moon to Full Moon, first and second quarter—which takes about two weeks—the Moon is increasing or waxing. From Full Moon to New Moon, third and fourth quarter, the Moon is said to be decreasing or waning. The Moon Table indicates the New Moon and Full Moon and the quarters.

ACTIVITY	MOON IN
Business	
buying and selling	Sagittarius, Aries, Gemini, Virgo
new, requiring public support	1st and 2nd quarter
meant to be kept quiet	3rd and 4th quarter
Investigation	3rd and 4th quarter
Signing documents	1st & 2nd quarter, Cancer, Scorpio, Pisces
Advertising	2nd quarter, Sagittarius
Journeys and trips	1st & 2nd quarter, Gemini, Virgo
Renting offices, etc.	Taurus, Leo, Scorpio, Aquarius
Painting of house/apartment	3rd & 4th quarter, Taurus, Scorpio, Aquarius
Decorating	Gemini, Libra, Aquarius
Buying clothes and accessories	Taurus, Virgo
Beauty salon or barber shop visit	1st & 2nd quarter, Taurus, Leo, Libra, Scorpio, Aquarius
Weddings	1st & 2nd quarter

MOON'S INFLUENCE OVER YOUR HEALTH

ARIES   Head, brain, face, upper jaw
TAURUS   Throat, neck, lower jaw
GEMINI   Hands, arms, lungs, shoulders, nervous system
CANCER   Esophagus, stomach, breasts, womb, liver
LEO   Heart, spine
VIRGO   Intestines, liver
LIBRA   Kidneys, lower back
SCORPIO   Sex and eliminative organs
SAGITTARIUS   Hips, thighs, liver
CAPRICORN   Skin, bones, beeth, knees
AQUARIUS   Circulatory system, lower legs
PISCES   Feet, tone of being

Try to avoid work being done on that part of the body when the Moon is in the sign governing that part.

MOON'S INFLUENCE OVER PLANTS

Centuries ago it was established that seeds planted when the Moon is in certain signs and phases called "fruitful" will produce more than seeds planted when the Moon is in a Barren sign.

FRUITFUL SIGNS	*BARREN SIGNS*	*DRY SIGNS*
Taurus	Aries	Aries
Cancer	Gemini	Gemini
Libra	Leo	Sagittarius
Scorpio	Virgo	Aquarius
Capricorn	Sagittarius	
Pisces	Aquarius	

ACTIVITY	MOON IN
Mow lawn, trim plans	Fruitful sign, 1st & 2nd quarter
Plant flowers	Fruitful sign, 2nd quarter; best in Cancer and Libra
Prune	Fruitful sign, 3rd & 4th quarter
Destroy pests; spray	Barren sign, 4th quarter
Harvest potatoes, root crops	Dry sign, 3rd & 4th quarter; Taurus, Leo, and Aquarius

THE SIGNS: DOMINANT CHARACTERISTICS

March 21–April 20

The Positive Side of Aries

The Arien has many positive points to his character. People born under this first sign of the Zodiac are often quite strong and enthusiastic. On the whole, they are forward-looking people who are not easily discouraged by temporary setbacks. They know what they want out of life and they go out after it. Their personalities are strong. Others are usually quite impressed by the Arien's way of doing things. Quite often they are sources of inspiration for others traveling the same route. Aries men and women have a special zest for life that is often contagious; for others, they are often the example of how life should be lived.

The Aries person usually has a quick and active mind. He is imaginative and inventive. He enjoys keeping busy and active. He generally gets along well with all kinds of people. He is interested in mankind, as a whole. He likes to be challenged. Some would say he thrives on opposition, for it is when he is set against that he often does his best. Getting over or around obstacles is a challenge he generally enjoys. All in all, the Arien is quite positive and young-thinking. He likes to keep abreast of new things that are happening in the world. Ariens are often fond of speed. They like things to be done quickly and this sometimes aggravates their slower colleagues and associates.

The Aries man or woman always seems to remain young. Their whole approach to life is youthful and optimistic. They never say die, no matter what the odds. They may have an occasional setback, but it is not long before they are back on their feet again.

The Negative Side of Aries

Everybody has his less positive qualities—and Aries is no exception. Sometimes the Aries man or woman is not very tactful in communicating with others; in his hurry to get things done he is apt to

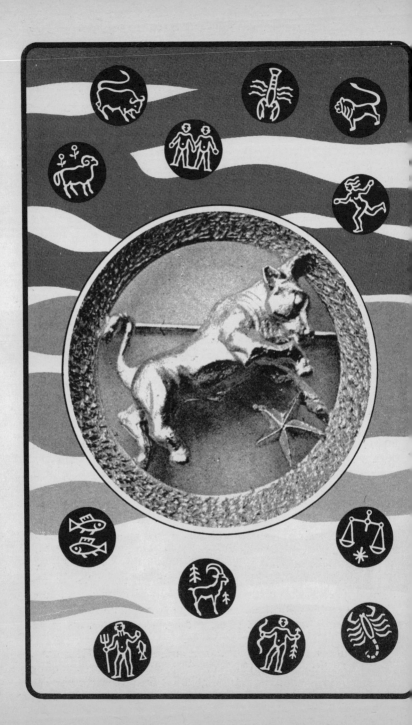

be a little callous or inconsiderate. Sensitive people are likely to find him somewhat sharp-tongued in some situations. Often in his eagerness to achieve his aims, he misses the mark altogether. At times the Arien is too impulsive. He can occasionally be stubborn and refuse to listen to reason. If things do not move quickly enough to suit the Aries man or woman, he or she is apt to become rather nervous or irritable. The uncultivated Arien is not unfamiliar with moments of doubt and fear. He is capable of being destructive if he does not get his way. He can overcome some of his emotional problems by steadily trying to express himself as he really is, but this requires effort.

April 21–May 20

The Positive Side of Taurus

The Taurus person is known for his ability to concentrate and for his tenacity. These are perhaps his strongest qualities. The Taurus man or woman generally has very little trouble in getting along with others; it's his nature to be helpful toward people in need. He can always be depended on by his friends, especially those in trouble.

The Taurean generally achieves what he wants through his ability to persevere. He never leaves anything unfinished but works on something until it has been completed. People can usually take him at his word; he is honest and forthright in most of his dealings. The Taurus person has a good chance to make a success of his life because of his many positive qualities. The Taurean who aims high seldom falls short of his mark. He learns well by experience. He is thorough and does not believe in short-cuts of any kind. The Taurean's thoroughness pays off in the end, for through his deliberateness he learns how to rely on himself and what he has learned. The Taurus person tries to get along with others, as a rule. He is not overly critical and likes people to be themselves. He is a tolerant person and enjoys peace and harmony—especially in his home life.

The Taurean is usually cautious in all that he does. He is not a person who believes in taking unnecessary risks. Before adopting any one line of action, he will weigh all of the pros and cons. The

Taurus person is steadfast. Once his mind is made up it seldom changes. The person born under this sign usually is a good family person—reliable and loving.

The Negative Side of Taurus

Sometimes the Taurus man or woman is a bit too stubborn. He won't listen to other points of view if his mind is set on something. To others, this can be quite annoying. The Taurean also does not like to be told what to do. He becomes rather angry if others think him not too bright. He does not like to be told he is wrong, even when he is. He dislikes being contradicted.

Some people who are born under this sign are very suspicious of others—even of those persons close to them. They find it difficult to trust people fully. They are often afraid of being deceived or taken advantage of. The Taurean often finds it difficult to forget or forgive. His love of material things sometimes makes him rather avaricious and petty.

May 21–June 20

The Positive Side of Gemini

The person born under this sign of the Heavenly Twins is usually quite bright and quick-witted. Some of them are capable of doing many different things. The Gemini person very often has many different interests. He keeps an open mind and is always anxious to learn new things.

The Geminian is often an analytical person. He is a person who enjoys making use of his intellect. He is governed more by his mind than by his emotions. He is a person who is not confined to one view; he can often understand both sides to a problem or question. He knows how to reason; how to make rapid decisions if need be.

He is an adaptable person and can make himself at home almost anywhere. There are all kinds of situations he can adapt to. He is a person who seldom doubts himself; he is sure of his talents and his

ability to think and reason. The Geminian is generally most satisfied when he is in a situation where he can make use of his intellect. Never short of imagination, he often has strong talents for invention. He is rather a modern person when it comes to life; the Geminian almost always moves along with the times—perhaps that is why he remains so youthful throughout most of his life.

Literature and art appeal to the person born under this sign. Creativity in almost any form will interest and intrigue the Gemini man or woman.

The Geminian is often quite charming. A good talker, he often is the center of attraction at any gathering. People find it easy to like a person born under this sign because he can appear easygoing and usually has a good sense of humor.

The Negative Side of Gemini

Sometimes the Gemini person tries to do too many things at one time—and as a result, winds up finishing nothing. Some Geminians are easily distracted and find it rather difficult to concentrate on one thing for too long a time. Sometimes they give in to trifling fancies and find it rather boring to become too serious about any one thing. Some of them are never dependable, no matter what they promise.

Although the Gemini man or woman often appears to be well-versed on many subjects, this is sometimes just a veneer. His knowledge may be only superficial, but because he speaks so well he gives people the impression of erudition. Some Geminians are sharp-tongued and inconsiderate; they think only of themselves and their own pleasure.

June 21–July 20

The Positive Side of Cancer

The Cancerians's most positive point is his understanding nature. On the whole, he is a loving and sympathetic person. He would never go out of his way to hurt anyone. The Cancer man or woman

is often very kind and tender; they give what they can to others. They hate to see others suffering and will do what they can to help someone in less fortunate circumstances than themselves. They are often very concerned about the world. Their interest in people generally goes beyond that of just their own families and close friends; they have a deep sense of brotherhood and respect humanitarian values. The Cancerian means what he says, as a rule; he is honest about his feelings.

The Cancer man or woman is a person who knows the art of patience. When something seems difficult, he is willing to wait until the situation becomes manageable again. He is a person who knows how to bide his time. The Cancerian knows how to concentrate on one thing at a time. When he has made his mind up he generally sticks with what he does, seeing it through to the end.

The Cancerian is a person who loves his home. He enjoys being surrounded by familiar things and the people he loves. Of all the signs, Cancer is the most maternal. Even the men born under this sign often have a motherly or protective quality about them. They like to take care of people in their family—to see that they are well loved and well provided for. They are usually loyal and faithful. Family ties mean a lot to the Cancer man or woman. Parents and in-laws are respected and loved. The Cancerian has a strong sense of tradition. He is very sensitive to the moods of others.

The Negative Side of Cancer

Sometimes the Cancerian finds it rather hard to face life. It becomes too much for him. He can be a little timid and retiring, when things don't go too well. When unfortunate things happen, he is apt to just shrug and say, "Whatever will be will be." He can be fatalistic to a fault. The uncultivated Cancerian is a bit lazy. He doesn't have very much ambition. Anything that seems a bit difficult he'll gladly leave to others. He may be lacking in initiative. Too sensitive, when he feels he's been injured, he'll crawl back into his shell and nurse his imaginary wounds. The Cancer woman often is given to crying when the smallest thing goes wrong.

Some Cancerians find it difficult to enjoy themselves in environments outside their homes. They make heavy demands on others, and need to be constantly reassured that they are loved.

July 21–August 21

The Positive Side of Leo

Often Leos make good leaders. They seem to be good organizers and administrators. Usually they are quite popular with others. Whatever group it is that he belongs to, the Leo man is almost sure to be or become the leader.

The Leo person is generous most of the time. It is his best characteristic. He or she likes to give gifts and presents. In making others happy, the Leo person becomes happy himself. He likes to splurge when spending money on others. In some instances it may seem that the Leo's generosity knows no boundaries. A hospitable person, the Leo man or woman is very fond of welcoming people to his house and entertaining them. He is never short of company.

The Leo person has plenty of energy and drive. He enjoys working toward some specific goal. When he applies himself correctly, he gets what he wants most often. The Leo person is almost never unsure of himself. He has plenty of confidence and aplomb. He is a person who is direct in almost everything he does. He has a quick mind and can make a decision in a very short time.

He usually sets a good example for others because of his ambitious manner and positive ways. He knows how to stick to something once he's started. Although the Leo person may be good at making a joke, he is not superficial or glib. He is a loving person, kind and thoughtful.

There is generally nothing small or petty about the Leo man or woman. He does what he can for those who are deserving. He is a person others can rely upon at all times. He means what he says. An honest person, generally speaking, he is a friend that others value.

The Negative Side of Leo

Leo, however, does have his faults. At times, he can be just a bit too arrogant. He thinks that no one deserves a leadership position except him. Only he is capable of doing things well. His opinion of himself is often much too high. Because of his conceit, he is sometimes rather unpopular with a good many people. Some Leos are too materialistic; they can only think in terms of money and profit.

Some Leos enjoy lording it over others—at home or at their place of business. What is more, they feel they have the right to. Egocentric to an impossible degree, this sort of Leo cares little about how others think or feel. He can be rude and cutting.

August 22–September 22

The Positive Side of Virgo

The person born under the sign of Virgo is generally a busy person. He knows how to arrange and organize things. He is a good planner. Above all, he is practical and is not afraid of hard work.

The person born under this sign, Virgo, knows how to attain what he desires. He sticks with something until it is finished. He never shirks his duties, and can always be depended upon. The Virgo person can be thoroughly trusted at all times.

The man or woman born under this sign tries to do everything to perfection. He doesn't believe in doing anything half-way. He always aims for the top. He is the sort of a person who is constantly striving to better himself—not because he wants more money or glory, but because it gives him a feeling of accomplishment.

The Virgo man or woman is a very observant person. He is sensitive to how others feel, and can see things below the surface of a situation. He usually puts this talent to constructive use.

It is not difficult for the Virgoan to be open and earnest. He believes in putting his cards on the table. He is never secretive or under-handed. He's as good as his word. The Virgo person is generally plain-spoken and down-to-earth. He has no trouble in expressing himself.

The Virgo person likes to keep up to date on new developments in his particular field. Well-informed, generally, he sometimes has a keen interest in the arts or literature. What he knows, he knows well. His ability to use his critical faculties is well-developed and sometimes startles others because of its accuracy.

The Virgoan adheres to a moderate way of life; he avoids excesses. He is a responsible person and enjoys being of service.

The Negative Side of Virgo

Sometimes a Virgo person is too critical. He thinks that only he can do something the way it should be done. Whatever anyone else does is inferior. He can be rather annoying in the way he quibbles over insignificant details. In telling others how things should be done, he can be rather tactless and mean.

Some Virgos seem rather emotionless and cool. They feel emo-

tional involvement is beneath them. They are sometimes too tidy, too neat. With money they can be rather miserly. Some try to force their opinions and ideas on others.

September 23–October 22

The Positive Side of Libra

Librans love harmony. It is one of their most outstanding character traits. They are interested in achieving balance; they admire beauty and grace in things as well as in people. Generally speaking, they are kind and considerate people. Librans are usually very sympathetic. They go out of their way not to hurt another person's feelings. They are outgoing and do what they can to help those in need.

People born under the sign of Libra almost always make good friends. They are loyal and amiable. They enjoy the company of others. Many of them are rather moderate in their views; they believe in keeping an open mind, however, and weighing both sides of an issue fairly before making a decision.

Alert and often intelligent, the Libran, always fair-minded, tries to put himself in the position of the other person. They are against injustice; quite often they take up for the underdog. In most of their social dealings, they try to be tactful and kind. They dislike discord and bickering, and most Libras strive for peace and harmony in all their relationships.

The Libra man or woman has a keen sense of beauty. They appreciate handsome furnishings and clothes. Many of them are artistically inclined. Their taste is usually impeccable. They know how to use color. Their homes are almost always attractively arranged and inviting. They enjoy entertaining people and see to it that their guests always feel at home and welcome.

The Libran gets along with almost everyone. He is well-liked and socially much in demand.

The Negative Side of Libra

Some people born under this sign tend to be rather insincere. So eager are they to achieve harmony in all relationships that they will even go so far as to lie. Many of them are escapists. They find facing

the truth an ordeal and prefer living in a world of make-believe.

In a serious argument, some Librans give in rather easily even when they know they are right. Arguing, even about something they believe in, is too unsettling for some of them.

Librans sometimes care too much for material things. They enjoy possessions and luxuries. Some are vain and tend to be jealous.

October 23–November 22

The Positive Side of Scorpio

The Scorpio man or woman generally knows what he or she wants out of life. He is a determined person. He sees something through to the end. The Scorpion is quite sincere, and seldom says anything he doesn't mean. When he sets a goal for himself he tries to go about achieving it in a very direct way.

The Scorpion is brave and courageous. They are not afraid of hard work. Obstacles do not frighten them. They forge ahead until they achieve what they set out for. The Scorpio man or woman has a strong will.

Although the Scorpion may seem rather fixed and determined, inside he is often quite tender and loving. He can care very much for others. He believes in sincerity in all relationships. His feelings about someone tend to last; they are profound and not superficial.

The Scorpio person is someone who adheres to his principles no matter what happens. He will not be deterred from a path he believes to be right.

Because of his many positive strengths, the Scorpion can often achieve happiness for himself and for those that he loves.

He is a constructive person by nature. He often has a deep understanding of people and of life, in general. He is perceptive and unafraid. Obstacles often seem to spur him on. He is a positive person who enjoys winning. He has many strengths and resources; challenge of any sort often brings out the best in him.

The Negative Side of Scorpio

The Scorpio person is sometimes hypersensitive. Often he imagines injury when there is none. He feels that others do not bother to

recognize him for his true worth. Sometimes he is given to excessive boasting in order to compensate for what he feels is neglect

The Scorpio person can be rather proud and arrogant. They can be rather sly when they put their minds to it and they enjoy outwitting persons or institutions noted for their cleverness.

Their tactics for getting what they want are sometimes devious and ruthless. They don't care too much about what others may think. If they feel others have done them an injustice, they will do their best to seek revenge. The Scorpion often has a sudden, violent temper; and this person's interest in sex is sometimes quite unbalanced or excessive.

November 23–December 20

The Positive Side of Sagittarius

People born under this sign are often honest and forthright. Their approach to life is earnest and open. The Sagittarian is often quite adult in his way of seeing things. They are broadminded and tolerant people. When dealing with others the person born under the sign of Sagittarius is almost always open and forthright. He doesn't believe in deceit or pretension. His standards are high. People who associate with the Sagittarian, generally admire and respect him.

The Sagittarian trusts others easily and expects them to trust him. He is never suspicious or envious and almost always thinks well of others. People always enjoy his company because he is so friendly and easy-going. The Sagittarius man or woman is often good-humored. He can always be depended upon by his friends, family, and co-workers.

The person born under this sign of the Zodiac likes a good joke every now and then; he is keen on fun and this makes him very popular with others.

A lively person, he enjoys sports and outdoor life. The Sagittarian is fond of animals. Intelligent and interesting, he can begin an animated conversation with ease. He likes exchanging ideas and discussing various views.

He is not selfish or proud. If someone proposes an idea or plan that is better than his, he will immediately adopt it. Imaginative yet practical, he knows how to put ideas into practice.

He enjoys sport and game, and it doesn't matter if he wins or loses. He is a forgiving person, and never sulks over something that has not worked out in his favor.

He is seldom critical, and is almost always generous.

The Negative Side of Sagittarius

Some Sagittarians are restless. They take foolish risks and seldom learn from the mistakes they make. They don't have heads for money and are often mismanaging their finances. Some of them devote much of their time to gambling.

Some are too outspoken and tactless, always putting their feet in their mouths. They hurt others carelessly by being honest at the wrong time. Sometimes they make promises which they don't keep. They don't stick close enough to their plans and go from one failure to another. They are undisciplined and waste a lot of energy.

December 21–January 19

The Positive Side of Capricorn

The person born under the sign of Capricorn is usually very stable and patient. He sticks to whatever tasks he has and sees them through. He can always be relied upon and he is not averse to work.

An honest person, the Capricornian is generally serious about whatever he does. He does not take his duties lightly. He is a practical person and believes in keeping his feet on the ground.

Quite often the person born under this sign is ambitious and knows how to get what he wants out of life. He forges ahead and never gives up his goal. When he is determined about something, he almost always wins. He is a good worker—a hard worker. Although things may not come easy to him, he will not complain, but continue working until his chores are finished.

He is usually good at business matters and knows the value of money. He is not a spendthrift and knows how to put something away for a rainy day; he dislikes waste and unnecessary loss.

The Capricornian knows how to make use of his self-control. He

can apply himself to almost anything once he puts his mind to it. His ability to concentrate sometimes astounds others. He is diligent and does well when involved in detail work.

The Capricorn man or woman is charitable, generally speaking, and will do what is possible to help others less fortunate. As a friend, he is loyal and trustworthy. He never shirks his duties or responsibilities. He is self-reliant and never expects too much of the other fellow. He does what he can on his own. If someone does him a good turn, then he will do his best to return the favor.

The Negative Side of Capricorn

Like everyone, the Capricornian, too, has his faults. At times, he can be over-critical of others. He expects others to live up to his own high standards. He thinks highly of himself and tends to look down on others.

His interest in material things may be exaggerated. The Capricorn man or woman thinks too much about getting on in the world and having something to show for it. He may even be a little greedy.

He sometimes thinks he knows what's best for everyone. He is too bossy. He is always trying to organize and correct others. He may be a little narrow in his thinking.

January 20–February 18

The Positive Side of Aquarius

The Aquarius man or woman is usually very honest and forthright. These are his two greatest qualities. His standards for himself are generally very high. He can always be relied upon by others. His word is his bond.

The Aquarian is perhaps the most tolerant of all the Zodiac personalities. He respects other people's beliefs and feels that everyone is entitled to his own approach to life.

He would never do anything to injure another's feelings. He is never unkind or cruel. Always considerate of others, the Aquarian is always willing to help a person in need. He feels a very strong tie between himself and all the other members of mankind.

The person born under this sign is almost always an individualist. He does not believe in teaming up with the masses, but prefers going his own way. His ideas about life and mankind are often quite advanced. There is a saying to the effect that the average Aquarian is fifty years ahead of his time.

He is broadminded. The problems of the world concern him greatly. He is interested in helping others no matter what part of the globe they live in. He is truly a humanitarian sort. He likes to be of service to others.

Giving, considerate, and without prejudice, Aquarians have no trouble getting along with others.

The Negative Side of Aquarius

The Aquarian may be too much of a dreamer. He makes plans but seldom carries them out. He is rather unrealistic. His imagination has a tendency to run away with him. Because many of his plans are impractical, he is always in some sort of a dither.

Others may not approve of him at all times because of his unconventional behavior. He may be a bit eccentric. Sometimes he is so busy with his own thoughts, that he loses touch with the realities of existence.

Some Aquarians feel they are more clever and intelligent than others. They seldom admit to their own faults, even when they are quite apparent. Some become rather fanatic in their views. Their criticism of others is sometimes destructive and negative.

February 19–March 20

The Positive Side of Pisces

The Piscean can often understand the problems of others quite easily. He has a sympathetic nature. Kindly, he is often dedicated in the way he goes about helping others. The sick and the troubled often turn to him for advice and assistance.

He is very broadminded and does not criticize others for their faults. He knows how to accept people for what they are. On the whole, he is a trustworthy and earnest person. He is loyal to his

friends and will do what he can to help them in time of need. Generous and good-natured, he is a lover of peace; he is often willing to help others solve their differences. People who have taken a wrong turn in life often interest him and he will do what he can to persuade them to rehabilitate themselves.

He has a strong intuitive sense and most of the time he knows how to make it work for him; the Piscean is unusually perceptive and often knows what is bothering someone before that person, himself, is aware of it. The Pisces man or woman is an idealistic person, basically, and is interested in making the world a better place in which to live. The Piscean believes that everyone should help each other. He is willing to do more than his share in order to achieve cooperation with others.

The person born under this sign often is talented in music or art. He is a receptive person; he is able to take the ups and downs of life with philosophic calm.

The Negative Side of Pisces

Some Pisceans are often depressed; their outlook on life is rather glum. They may feel that they have been given a bad deal in life and that others are always taking unfair advantage of them. The Piscean sometimes feel that the world is a cold and cruel place. He is easily discouraged. He may even withdraw from the harshness of reality into a secret shell of his own where he dreams and idles away a good deal of his time.

The Piscean can be rather lazy. He lets things happen without giving the least bit of resistance. He drifts along, whether on the high road or on the low. He is rather short on willpower.

Some Pisces people seek escape through drugs or alcohol. When temptation comes along they find it hard to resist. In matters of sex, they can be rather permissive.

THE SIGNS AND
THEIR KEY WORDS

		POSITIVE	NEGATIVE
ARIES	self	courage, initiative, pioneer instinct	brash rudeness, selfish impetuosity
TAURUS	money	endurance, loyalty, wealth	obstinacy, gluttony
GEMINI	mind	versatility	capriciousness, unreliability
CANCER	family	sympathy, homing instinct	clannishness, childishness
LEO	children	love, authority, integrity	egotism, force
VIRGO	work	purity, industry, analysis	fault-finding, cynicism
LIBRA	marriage	harmony, justice	vacillation, superficiality
SCORPIO	sex	survival, regeneration	vengeance, discord
SAGITTARIUS	travel	optimism, higher learning	lawlessness
CAPRICORN	career	depth	narrowness, gloom
AQUARIUS	friends	human fellowship, genius	perverse unpredictability
PISCES	confine- ment	spiritual love, universality	diffusion, escapism

THE ELEMENTS AND QUALITIES OF THE SIGNS

ELEMENT	SIGN	QUALITY	SIGN
FIRE...............	ARIES LEO SAGITTARIUS	CARDINAL.........	ARIES LIBRA CANCER CAPRICORN
EARTH.............	TAURUS VIRGO CAPRICORN	FIXED...............	TAURUS LEO SCORPIO AQUARIUS
AIR..................	GEMINI LIBRA AQUARIUS		
WATER.............	CANCER SCORPIO PISCES	MUTABLE.........	GEMINI VIRGO SAGITTARIUS PISCES

Every sign has both an element and a quality associated with it. The element indicates the basic makeup of the sign, and the quality describes the kind of activity associated with each.

Signs can be grouped together according to their *element* and *quality*. Signs of the same element share many basic traits in common. They tend to form stable configurations and ultimately harmonious relationships. Signs of the same quality are often less harmonious, but they share many dynamic potentials for growth as well as profound fulfillment.

THE FIRE SIGNS

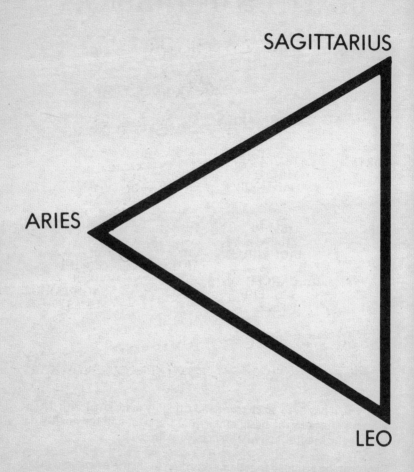

SAGITTARIUS

ARIES

LEO

This is the fire group. On the whole these are emotional, volatile types, quick to anger, quick to forgive. They are adventurous, powerful people and act as a source of inspiration for everyone. They spark into action with immediate exuberant impulses. They are intelligent, self-involved, creative and idealistic. They all share a certain vibrancy and glow that outwardly reflects an inner flame and passion for living.

THE EARTH SIGNS

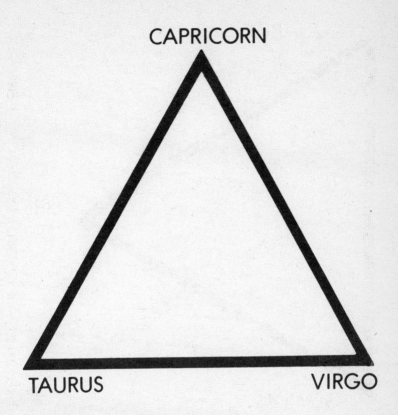

CAPRICORN

TAURUS   VIRGO

This is the earth group. They are in constant touch with the material world and tend to be conservative. Although they are all capable of spartan self-discipline, they are earthy, sensual people who are stimulated by the tangible, elegant and luxurious. The thread of their lives is always practical, but they do fantasize and are often attracted to dark, mysterious, emotional people. They are like great cliffs overhanging the sea, forever married to the ocean but always resisting erosion from the dark, emotional forces that thunder at their feet.

THE AIR SIGNS

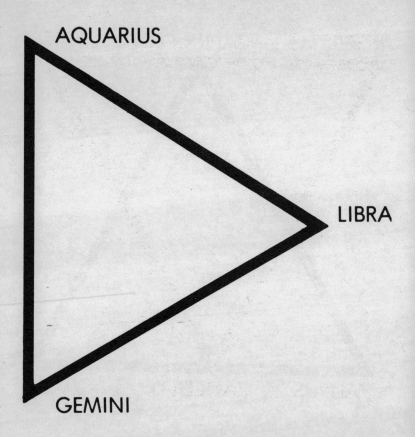

AQUARIUS

LIBRA

GEMINI

This is the air group. They are light, mental creatures desirous of contact, communication and relationship. They are involved with people and the forming of ties on many levels. Original thinkers, they are the bearers of human news. Their language is their sense of word, color, style and beauty. They provide an atmosphere suitable and pleasant for living. They add change and versatility to the scene, and it is through them that we can explore new territory of human intelligence and experience.

THE WATER SIGNS

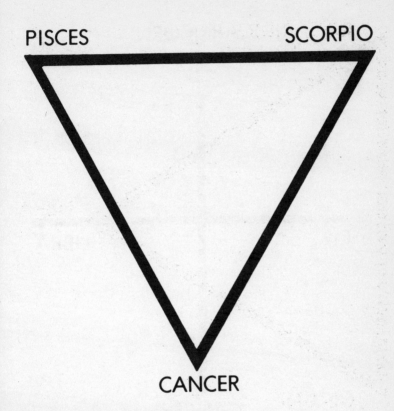

PISCES   SCORPIO

CANCER

This is the water group. Through the water people, we are all joined together on emotional, non-verbal levels. They are silent, mysterious types whose magic hypnotizes even the most determined realist. They have uncanny perceptions about people and are as rich as the oceans when it comes to feeling, emotion or imagination. They are sensitive, mystical creatures with memories that go back beyond time. Through water, life is sustained. These people have the potential for the depths of darkness or the heights of mysticism and art.

THE CARDINAL SIGNS

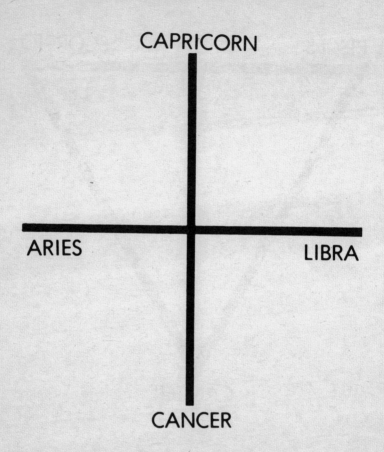

Put together, this is a clear-cut picture of dynamism, activity, tremendous stress and remarkable achievement. These people know the meaning of great change since their lives are often characterized by significant crises and major successes. This combination is like a simultaneous storm of summer, fall, winter and spring. The danger is chaotic diffusion of energy; the potential is irrepressible growth and victory.

THE FIXED SIGNS

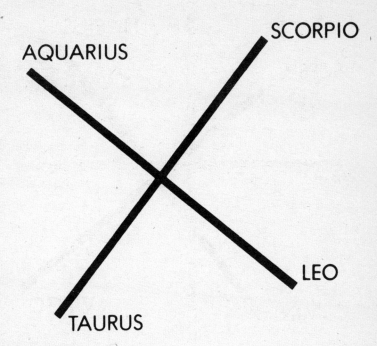

Fixed signs are always establishing themselves in a given place or area of experience. Like explorers who arrive and plant a flag, these people claim a position from which they do not enjoy being deposed. They are staunch, stalwart, upright, trusty, honorable people, although their obstinacy is well-known. Their contribution is fixity, and they are the angels who support our visible world.

THE MUTABLE SIGNS

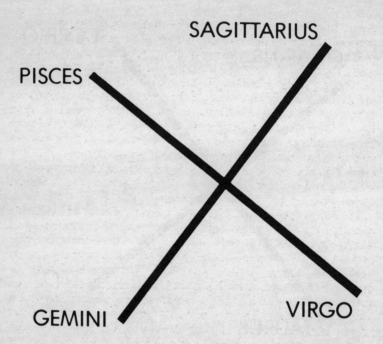

Mutable people are versatile, sensitive, intelligent, nervous and deeply curious about life. They are the translators of all energy. They often carry out or complete tasks initiated by others. Combinations of these signs have highly developed minds; they are imaginative and jumpy and think and talk a lot. At worst their lives are a Tower of Babel. At best they are adaptable and ready creatures who can assimilate one kind of experience and enjoy it while anticipating coming changes.

HOW TO APPROXIMATE YOUR RISING SIGN

Apart from the month and day of birth, the exact *time* of birth is another vital factor in the determination of an accurate horoscope. Not only do the planets move with great speed, but one must know how far the Earth has turned during the day. That way you can determine exactly where the planets are located with respect to the precise birthplace of an individual. This makes *your* horoscope *your* horoscope. In addition to these factors, another grid is laid upon that of the Zodiac and the planets: the houses. After all three have been considered, specific planetary relationships can be measured and analyzed in accordance with certain ordered procedures. It is the skillful translation of all this complex astrological language that a serious astrologer strives for in his attempt at coherent astrological synthesis. Keep this in mind.

The horoscope sets up a kind of framework around which the life of an individual grows like wild ivy, this way and that, weaving its way around the trellis of the natal positions of the planets. The year of birth tells us the positions of the distant, slow-moving planets like Jupiter, Saturn, Uranus and Pluto. The month of birth indicates the Sun sign, or birth sign as it is commonly called, as well as indicating the positions of the rapidly moving planets like Venus, Mercury and Mars. The day of birth locates the position of our Moon, and the moment of birth determines the houses through what is called the Ascendant, or Rising Sign.

As the Earth rotates on its axis once every 24 hours, each one of the twelve signs of the Zodiac appears to be "rising" on the horizon, with a new one appearing about every two hours. Actually it is the turning of the Earth that exposes each sign to view, but you will remember that in much of our astrological work we are discussing "apparent" motion. This *Rising Sign* marks the Ascendant and it colors the whole orientation of a horoscope. It indicates the sign governing the first house of the chart, and will thus determine which signs will govern all the other houses. The idea is a bit complicated at first, and we needn't dwell on complications in this introduction, but if you can imagine two color wheels with twelve divisions superimposed upon each other, one moving slowly and the other remaining still, you will have some idea of how the signs keep shifting the "color" of the houses as the Rising Sign continues to change every two hours.

The important point is that the birth chart, or horoscope, actually does define specific factors of a person's makeup. It contains a picture of being, much the way the nucleus of a tiny cell contains the potential for an entire elephant, or a packet of seeds contains a rosebush. If there were no order or continuity to the world, we could plant roses and get elephants. This same order that gives continuous flow to our lives often annoys people if it threatens to determine too much of their lives. We must grow from what we were planted, and there's no reason why we can't do that magnificently. It's all there in the horoscope. Where there is limitation, there is breakthrough; where there is crisis, there is transformation. Accurate analysis of a horoscope can help you find these points of breakthrough and transformation, and it requires knowledge of subtleties and distinctions that demand skillful judgment in order to solve even the simplest kind of personal question.

It is still quite possible, however, to draw some conclusions based upon the sign occupied by the Sun alone. In fact, if you're just being introduced to this vast subject, you're better off keeping it simple. Otherwise it seems like an impossible jumble, much like trying to read a novel in a foreign language without knowing the basic vocabulary. As with anything else, you can progress in your appreciation and understanding of astrology in direct proportion to your interest. To become really good at it requires study, experience, patience and above all—and maybe simplest of all—a fundamental understanding of what is actually going on right up there in the sky over your head. It is a vital living process you can observe, contemplate and ultimately understand. You can start by observing sunrise, or sunset, or even the full Moon.

In fact you can do a simple experiment after reading this introduction. You can erect a rough chart by following the simple procedure below:

1. Draw a circle with twelve equal segments.

2. Starting at what would be the nine o'clock position on a clock, number the segments, or houses, from 1 to 12 in a *counterclockwise direction*.

3. Label house number 1 in the following way: 4 A.M.-6 A.M.

4. In a counterclockwise direction, label the rest of the houses: 2 A.M.-4 A.M., MIDNIGHT-2 A.M., 10 P.M-MIDNIGHT, 8 P.M.-10 P.M., 6 P.M.-8 P.M., 4 P.M.-6 P.M., 2 P.M.-4 P.M., NOON-2 P.M., 10 A.M.-NOON, 8 A.M.-10 A.M., and 6 A.M.-8 A.M.

5. Now find out what time you were born and place the sun in the appropriate house.

6. Label the edge of that house with your Sun sign. You now have a description of your basic character and your fundamental drives. You can also see in what areas of life on Earth you will be most likely to focus your constant energy and center your activity.

7. If you are really feeling ambitious, label the rest of the houses with the signs, starting with your Sun sign, in order, still in a *counterclockwise direction*. When you get to Pisces, start over with Aries and keep going until you reach the house behind the Sun.

8. Look to house number 1. The sign that you have now labeled and attached to house number 1 is your Rising sign. It will color your self-image, outlook, physical constitution, early life and whole orientation to life. Of course this is a mere approximation, since there are many complicated calculations that must be made with respect to adjustments for birth time, but if you read descriptions of the sign preceding and the sign following the one you have calculated in the above manner, you may be able to identify yourself better. In any case, when you get through labeling all the houses, your drawing should look something like this:

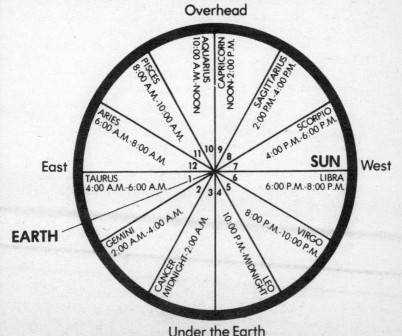

Basic chart illustrating the position of the Sun in Scorpio, with the Ascendant Taurus as the Rising Sign.

This individual was born at 5:15 P.M. on October 31 in New York City. The Sun is in Scorpio and is found in the 7th house. The Rising sign, or the sign governing house number 1, is Taurus, so this person is a blend of Scorpio and Taurus.

Any further calculation would necessitate that you look in an ephemeris, or table of planetary motion, for the positions of the rest of the planets for your particular birth year. But we will take the time to define briefly all the known planets of our Solar System and the Sun to acquaint you with some more of the astrological vocabulary that you will be meeting again and again. (See page 21 for a full explanation of the Moon in all the Signs.)

THE PLANETS AND SIGNS THEY RULE

The signs of the Zodiac are linked to the planets in the following way. Each sign is governed or ruled by one or more planets. No matter where the planets are located in the sky at any given moment, they still rule their respective signs, and when they travel through the signs they rule, they have special dignity and their effects are stronger.

Following is a list of the planets and the signs they rule. After looking at the list, go back over the definitions of the planets and see if you can determine how the planet ruling *your* Sun sign has affected your life.

SIGNS	RULING PLANETS
Aries	Mars, Pluto
Taurus	Venus
Gemini	Mercury
Cancer	Moon
Leo	Sun
Virgo	Mercury
Libra	Venus
Scorpio	Mars, Pluto
Sagittarius	Jupiter
Capricorn	Saturn
Aquarius	Saturn, Uranus
Pisces	Jupiter, Neptune

THE PLANETS
OF THE
SOLAR SYSTEM

Here are the planets of the Solar System. They all travel around the Sun at different speeds and different distances. Taken with the Sun, they all distribute individual intelligence and ability throughout the entire chart.

The planets modify the influence of the Sun in a chart according to their own particular natures, strengths and positions. Their positions must be calculated for each year and day, and their function and expression in a horoscope will change as they move from one area of the Zodiac to another.

Following, you will find brief statements of their pure meanings.

THE SUN

SUN

This is the center of existence. Around this flaming sphere all the planets revolve in endless orbits. Our star is constantly sending out its beams of light and energy without which no life on Earth would be possible. In astrology it symbolizes everything we are trying to become, the center around which all of our activity in life will always revolve. It is the symbol of our basic nature and describes the natural and constant thread that runs through everything that we do from birth to death on this planet.

To early astrologers, the sun seemed to be another planet because it crossed the heavens every day, just like the rest of the bodies in the sky.

It is the only star near enough to be seen well—it is, in fact, a dwarf star. Approximately 860,000 miles in diameter, it is about ten times as wide as the giant planet Jupiter. The next nearest star is nearly 300,000 times as far away, and if the Sun were located as far away as most of the bright stars, it would be too faint to be seen without a telescope.

Everything in the horoscope ultimately revolves around this singular body. Although other forces may be prominent in the charts of some individuals, still the Sun is the total nucleus of being and symbolizes the complete potential of every human being alive. It is vitality and the life force. Your whole essence comes from the position of the Sun.

You are always trying to express the Sun according to its position by house and sign. Possibility for all development is found in the Sun, and it marks the fundamental character of your personal radiations all around you.

It is the symbol of strength, vigor, wisdom, dignity, ardor and generosity, and the ability for a person to function as a mature individual. It is also a creative force in society. It is consciousness of the gift of life.

The underdeveloped solar nature is arrogant, pushy, undependable and proud, and is constantly using force.

MERCURY

Mercury is the planet closest to the Sun. It races around our star, gathering information and translating it to the rest of the system. Mercury represents your capacity to understand the desires of your own will and to translate those desires into action.

In other words it is the planet of Mind and the power of communication. Through Mercury we develop an ability to think, write, speak and observe—to become aware of the world around us. It colors our attitudes and vision of the world, as well as our capacity to communicate our inner responses to the outside world. Some people who have serious disabilities in their power of verbal communication have often wrongly been described as people lacking intelligence.

Although this planet (and its position in the horoscope) indicates your power to communicate your thoughts and perceptions to the world, intelligence is something deeper. Intelligence is distributed throughout all the planets. It is the relationship of the planets to each other that truly describes what we call intelligence. Mercury rules speaking, language, mathematics, draft and design, students, messengers, young people. offices, teachers and any pursuits where the mind of man has wings.

VENUS

Venus is beauty. It symbolizes the harmony and radiance of a rare
and elusive quality: beauty itself. It is refinement and delicacy,
softness and charm. In astrology it indicates grace, balance and the
aesthetic sense. Where Venus is we see beauty, a gentle drawing in
of energy and the need for satisfaction and completion. It is a special touch that finishes off rough edges. It is sensitivity, and affection, and it is always the place for that other elusive phenomenon:
love. Venus describes our sense of what is beautiful and loving.
Poorly developed, it is vulgar, tasteless and self-indulgent. But its
ideal is the flame of spiritual love—Aphrodite, goddess of love, and
the sweetness and power of personal beauty.

MARS

This is raw, crude energy. The planet next to Earth but outward from the Sun is a fiery red sphere that charges through the horoscope with force and fury. It represents the way you reach out for new adventure and new experience. It is energy and drive, initiative, courage and daring. The power to start something and see it through. It can be thoughtless, cruel and wild, angry and hostile, causing cuts, burns, scalds and wounds. It can stab its way through a chart, or it can be the symbol of healthy spirited adventure, well-channeled constructive power to begin and keep up the drive. If you have trouble starting things, if you lack the get-up-and-go to start the ball rolling, if you lack aggressiveness and self-confidence, chances are there's another planet influencing your Mars. Mars rules soldiers, butchers, surgeons, salesmen—any field that requires daring, bold skill, operational technique or self-promotion.

JUPITER

This is the largest planet of the Solar System. Scientists have recently learned that Jupiter reflects more light than it receives from the Sun. In a sense it is like a star itself. In astrology it rules good luck and good cheer, health, wealth, optimism, happiness, success and joy. It is the symbol of opportunity and always opens the way for new possibilities in your life. It rules exuberance, enthusiasm, wisdom, knowledge, generosity and all forms of expansion in general. It rules actors, statesmen, clerics, professional people, religion, publishing and the distribution of many people over large areas.

Sometimes Jupiter makes you think you deserve everything, and you become sloppy, wasteful, careless and rude, prodigal and lawless, in the illusion that nothing can ever go wrong. Then there is the danger of over-confidence, exaggeration, undependability and over-indulgence.

Jupiter is the minimization of limitation and the emphasis on spirituality and potential. It is the thirst for knowledge and higher learning.

SATURN

Saturn circles our system in dark splendor with its mysterious rings, forcing us to be awakened to whatever we have neglected in the past. It will present real puzzles and problems to be solved, causing delays, obstacles and hindrances. By doing so, Saturn stirs our own sensitivity to those areas where we are laziest.

Here we must patiently develop *method,* and only through painstaking effort can our ends be achieved. It brings order to a horoscope and imposes reason just where we are feeling least reasonable. By creating limitations and boundary, Saturn shows the consequences of being human and demands that we accept the changing cycles inevitable in human life. Saturn rules time, old age and sobriety. It can bring depression, gloom, jealousy and greed, or serious acceptance of responsibilities out of which success will develop. With Saturn there is nothing to do but face facts. It rules laborers, stones, granite, rocks and crystals of all kinds.

The Outer Planets

The following three are the outer planets. They liberate human beings from cultural conditioning, and in that sense are the law breakers. In early times it was thought that Saturn was the last planet of the system—the outer limit beyond which we could never go. The discovery of the next three planets ushered in new phases of human history, revolution and technology.

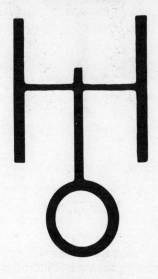

URANUS

Uranus rules unexpected change, upheaval, revolution. It is the symbol of total independence and asserts the freedom of an individual from all restriction and restraint. It is a breakthrough planet and indicates talent, originality and genius in a horoscope. It usually causes last-minute reversals and changes of plan, unwanted separations, accidents, catastrophes and eccentric behavior. It can add irrational rebelliousness and perverse bohemianism to a personality or a streak of unaffected brilliance in science and art. It rules technology, aviation and all forms of electrical and electronic advancement. It governs great leaps forward and topsy-turvy situations, and *always* turns things around at the last minute. Its effects are difficult to ever really predict, since it rules sudden last-minute decisions and events that come like lightning out of the blue.

NEPTUNE

Neptune dissolves existing reality the way the sea erodes the cliffs beside it. Its effects are subtle like the ringing of a buoy's bell in the fog. It suggests a reality higher than definition can usually describe. It awakens a sense of higher responsibility often causing guilt, worry, anxieties or delusions. Neptune is associated with all forms of escape and can make things seem a certain way so convincingly that you are absolutely sure of something that eventually turns out to be quite different.

It is the planet of illusion and therefore governs the invisible realms that lie beyond our ordinary minds, beyond our simple factual ability to prove what is "real." Treachery, deceit, disillusionment and disappointment are linked to Neptune. It describes a vague reality that promises eternity and the divine, yet in a manner so complex that we cannot really fathom it at all. At its worst Neptune is a cheap intoxicant; at its best it is the poetry, music and inspiration of the higher planes of spiritual love. It has dominion over movies, photographs and much of the arts.

PLUTO

Pluto lies at the outpost of our system and therefore rules finality in a horoscope—the final closing of chapters in your life, the passing of major milestones and points of development from which there is no return. It is a final wipeout, a closeout, an evacuation. It is a distant, subtle but powerful catalyst in all transformations that occur. It creates, destroys, then recreates. Sometimes Pluto starts its influence with a minor event or insignificant incident that might even go unnoticed. Slowly but surely, little by little, everything changes, until at last there has been a total transformation in the area of your life where Pluto has been operating. It rules mass thinking and the trends that society first rejects, then adopts and finally outgrows.

Pluto rules the dead and the underworld—all the powerful forces of creation and destruction that go on all the time beneath, around and above us. It can bring a lust for power with strong obsessions.

It is the planet that rules the metamorphoses of the caterpillar into a butterfly, for it symbolizes the capacity to change totally and forever a person's life style, way of thought and behavior.

FAMOUS PERSONALITIES

ARIES: Hans Christian Andersen, Pearl Bailey, Marlon Brando, Wernher Von Braun, Charlie Chaplin, Joan Crawford, Da Vinci, Bette Davis, Doris Day, W. C. Fields, Alec Guinness, Adolf Hitler, Billie Holiday, Thomas Jefferson, Nikita Khrushchev, Elton John, Arturo Toscanini, J. P. Morgan, Paul Robeson, Gloria Steinem, Lowell Thomas, Vincent van Gogh, Tennessee Williams

TAURUS: Fred Astaire, Charlotte Brontë, Carol Burnett, Irving Berlin, Bing Crosby, Salvador Dali, Tchaikovsky, Queen Elizabeth II, Duke Ellington, Ella Fitzgerald, Henry Fonda, Sigmund Freud, Orson Welles, Joe Louis, Lenin, Karl Marx, Golda Meir, Eva Peron, Bertrand Russell, Shakespeare, Kate Smith, Benjamin Spock, Barbra Streisand, Shirley Temple, Harry Truman

GEMINI: Mikhail Baryshnikov, Boy George, Igor Stravinsky, Carlos Chavez, Walt Whitman, Bob Dylan, Ralph Waldo Emerson, Judy Garland, Paul Gauguin, Allen Ginsberg, Benny Goodman, Bob Hope, Burl Ives, John F. Kennedy, Peggy Lee, Marilyn Monroe, Joe Namath, Cole Porter, Laurence Olivier, Harriet Beecher Stowe, Queen Victoria, John Wayne, Frank Lloyd Wright

CANCER: "Dear Abby," David Brinkley, Yul Brynner, Pearl Buck, Marc Chagall, Jack Dempsey, Mildred (Babe) Zaharias, Mary Baker Eddy, Henry VIII, John Glenn, Ernest Hemingway, Lena Horne, Oscar Hammerstein, Helen Keller, Ann Landers, George Orwell, Nancy Reagan, Rembrandt, Richard Rodgers, Ginger Rogers, Rubens, Jean-Paul Sartre, O. J. Simpson

LEO: Neil Armstrong, Russell Baker, James Baldwin, Emily Brontë, Wilt Chamberlain, Julia Child, Cecil B. De Mille, Ogden Nash, Amelia Earhart, Edna Ferber, Arthur Goldberg, Dag Hammarskjöld, Alfred Hitchcock, Mick Jagger, George Meany, George Bernard Shaw, Napoleon, Jacqueline Onassis, Henry Ford, Francis Scott Key, Andy Warhol, Mae West, Orville Wright

VIRGO: Ingrid Bergman, Warren Burger, Maurice Chevalier, Agatha Christie, Sean Connery, Lafayette, Peter Falk, Greta Garbo, Althea Gibson, Arthur Godfrey, Goethe, Buddy Hackett, Michael Jackson, Lyndon Johnson, D. H. Lawrence, Sophia Loren, Grandma Moses, Arnold Palmer, Queen Elizabeth I, Walter Reuther, Peter Sellers, Lily Tomlin, George Wallace

LIBRA: Brigitte Bardot, Art Buchwald, Truman Capote, Dwight D. Eisenhower, William Faulkner, F. Scott Fitzgerald, Gandhi, George Gershwin, Micky Mantle, Helen Hayes, Vladimir Horowitz, Doris Lessing, Martina Navratalova, Eugene O'Neill, Luciano Pavarotti, Emily Post, Eleanor Roosevelt, Bruce Springsteen, Margaret Thatcher, Gore Vidal, Barbara Walters, Oscar Wilde

SCORPIO: Vivien Leigh, Richard Burton, Art Carney, Johnny Carson, Billy Graham, Grace Kelly, Walter Cronkite, Marie Curie, Charles de Gaulle, Linda Evans, Indira Gandhi, Theodore Roosevelt, Rock Hudson, Katherine Hepburn, Robert F. Kennedy, Billie Jean King, Martin Luther, Georgia O'Keeffe, Pablo Picasso, Jonas Salk, Alan Shepard, Robert Louis Stevenson

SAGITTARIUS: Jane Austen, Louisa May Alcott, Woody Allen, Beethoven, Willy Brandt, Mary Martin, William F. Buckley, Maria Callas, Winston Churchill, Noel Coward, Emily Dickinson, Walt Disney, Benjamin Disraeli, James Doolittle, Kirk Douglas, Chet Huntley, Jane Fonda, Chris Evert Lloyd, Margaret Mead, Charles Schulz, John Milton, Frank Sinatra, Steven Spielberg

CAPRICORN: Muhammad Ali, Isaac Asimov, Pablo Casals, Dizzy Dean, Marlene Dietrich, James Farmer, Ava Gardner, Barry Goldwater, Cary Grant, J. Edgar Hoover, Howard Hughes, Joan of Arc, Gypsy Rose Lee, Martin Luther King, Jr., Rudyard Kipling, Mao Tse-tung, Richard Nixon, Gamal Nasser, Louis Pasteur, Albert Schweitzer, Stalin, Benjamin Franklin, Elvis Presley

AQUARIUS: Marian Anderson, Susan B. Anthony, Jack Benny, Charles Darwin, Charles Dickens, Thomas Edison, John Barrymore, Clark Gable, Jascha Heifetz, Abraham Lincoln, John McEnroe, Yehudi Menuhin, Mozart, Jack Nicklaus, Ronald Reagan, Jackie Robinson, Norman Rockwell, Franklin D. Roosevelt, Gertrude Stein, Charles Lindbergh, Margaret Truman

PISCES: Edward Albee, Harry Belafonte, Alexander Graham Bell, Frank Borman, Chopin, Adelle Davis, Albert Einstein, Jackie Gleason, Winslow Homer, Edward M. Kennedy, Victor Hugo, Mike Mansfield, Michelangelo, Edna St. Vincent Millay, Liza Minelli, John Steinbeck, Linus Pauling, Ravel, Diana Ross, William Shirer, Elizabeth Taylor, George Washington

CANCER

CHARACTER ANALYSIS

The Cancerian is generally speaking a rather sensitive person. He is quite often a generous person by nature, and he is willing to help almost anyone in need. He is emotional and often feels sorry for persons less fortunate than he. He could never refuse to answer someone's call for help. It is because of his sympathetic nature that others take advantage of him now and again.

In spite of his willingness to help others, the Cancer man or woman may seem difficult to approach by people not well acquainted with his character. On the whole, he seems rather subdued and reserved. Others may feel there is a wall between them and the Cancerian while this may not be the case at all. The person born under this sign is careful not to let others hurt him; he has learned through hard experience that protection of some sort is necessary in order to get along in life. The person who wins his confidence and is able to get beyond this barrier will find him a warm and loving person.

With his family and close friends, he is a very faithful and dependable person. In his quiet way, he can be affectionate and loving. He is generally not one given to demonstrative behavior. He can be fond of someone without telling them so a dozen times a day. With people he is close to, the Cancerian is bound to be more open about his own need for affection, and he enjoys being made over by his loved ones. He likes to feel wanted and protected.

When he has made up his mind about something, he sticks to it, and is generally a very constant person. He knows how to hold his ground. He never wavers. People who don't know him may think him weak and easily managed, because he is so quiet and modest, but this is far from true. He can take a lot of punishment for an idea or a cause he believes in. For the Cancerian, right is right. In order to protect himself, the person born under this sign will sometimes put up a pose as someone bossy and domineering. Sometimes he is successful in fooling others with his brash front. People who have known him for a while, however, are seldom taken in.

Many people born under this sign are rather shy and seemingly lacking confidence. They know their own minds, though, even if they do not seem to. He responds to kindness and encouragement. He will be himself with people he trusts. A good person can bring out the best in this person. Disagreeable or unfeeling people can send him scurrying back into his shell. He is a person who does not appreciate sharp criticism. Some people born under this sign are worriers. They are very concerned about what others may think of them. This may bother them so much that they develop a deep feeling of inferiority. Sometimes this reaches the point where he is so unsure of himself in some matters that he allows himself to be influenced by someone who has a stronger personality. The Cancerian is sometimes afraid that people will talk behind his back if he doesn't comply to their wishes. However, this does not stop him from doing what he feels is right. The cultivated Cancerian learns to think for himself and has no fear of disapproval.

The Cancer man or woman is most himself at home. The person born under this sign is a real lover of domesticity. He likes a place where he can relax and feel properly sheltered. Cancerians like things to stay as they are; they are not fond of changes of any sort. They are not very adaptable people. When visiting others or going to unfamiliar places, they are not likely to feel very comfortable. They are not the most talkative people at a party. In the comfort of their own homes, however, they blossom and bloom.

The Cancer man or woman sticks by the rules, whatever the game. He is not a person who would ever think of going against an established grain. He is conventional and moderate in almost all things. In a way he likes the old-fashioned things; however, in spite of this, he is interested in new things and does what he can to keep up with the times. In a way, he has two sides to his character. He is seldom forgetful. He has a memory like an elephant and can pick out any detail from the past with no trouble at all. He often reflects on things that have happened. He prefers the past to the future, which sometimes fills him with a feeling of apprehension.

This fourth sign of the Zodiac is a motherly one. Even the Cancer man has something maternal about him. He is usually kind and considerate; ready to help and protect. Others are drawn to them because of these gentle qualities. People in trouble often turn to him for advice and sympathy. People find him easy to confide in.

The Cancer person in general is a very forgiving person. He almost never holds a grudge. Still, it would not be wise to anger him. Treat him fairly and he will treat you the same. He does not appreciate people who lose patience with him. The Cancerian is usually proud of his mind and does not like to be considered unintelligent. Even if others feel that he is somewhat slow in some areas, he would rather not have this opinion expressed in his presence. He's not a person to be played with; he can tell when someone is treating him like a fool.

Quite often people born under this sign are musically inclined. Some of them have a deep interest in religious matters. They are apt to be interested in mystical matters, as well. Although they are fascinated by these things, they may be somewhat afraid of being overwhelmed if they go into them too deeply. In spite of this feeling of apprehension, they try to satisfy their curiosity in these matters.

Health

For the person born under the sign of Cancer, the stomach is his weak point. Chances are that the Cancerian is very susceptible most of the time to infectious diseases. Sometimes his health is affected by nervousness. He can be quite a worrier; even little things eat at him from time to time and this is apt to lower his resistance to infectious illnesses. He is often upset by small matters.

The Cancerian as a child is sometimes rather sickly and weak. His physique during this period of growth can be described in most cases as fragile. Some develop into physically strong adults, others may have the remnants of childhood ailments with them for a good part of their adult lives. They are rather frightened of being sick. Illness is a word they would rather not mention. Pain is also a thing they fear.

They are given to quick-changing moods at times and this often has an effect on their overall health. Worry or depression can have a subliminal effect on their general health. Usually their illnesses are not as serious as they imagine them to be. They sometimes find it easy to feel sorry for themselves.

On the whole, the Cancer man or woman is a quiet person. He is not one to brag or push his weight around. However, let it not be thought that he lacks the force that others have. He can be quite purposeful and energetic when the situation calls for it. However, when it comes to tooting their own horn, they can be somewhat shy and reticent. They may lack the get-up-and-go that others have when it comes to pushing their personal interests ahead.

Some Cancerians are quite aware of the fact that they are not what one would call sturdy in physique or temperament, and often they go through life rather painfully trying to cover up the weak side of their nature.

The man or woman born under the sign of Cancer is not apt to be very vigorous or active. As a rule, they are not too fond of physical exercise, and they have a weakness for rich and heavy foods. As a result, in later life they could end up overweight. Some Cancerians have trouble with their kidneys and intestines. Others digest their food poorly. The wise Cancer man or woman, however, adheres to a strict and well-balanced diet with plenty of fresh fruit and vegetables. Moreover, they see to it that they properly exercise their bodies daily. The Cancer man or woman who learns to cut down on rich foods and worry, often lives to a ripe old age.

Occupation

The Cancer person generally has no trouble at all establishing himself in the business world. He has all those qualities that generally make one a success professionally. He is careful with his equipment as well as his money. He is patient and he knows how to persevere. Any job where he has a chance to use his mind instead of his body is usually a job in which he has no trouble succeeding. He can work well with people—especially persons situated in dire straits. Welfare work is the kind of occupation in which he usually excels. He can really be quite a driving person if his job calls for it. The Cancerian is surprisingly resourceful. In spite of his retiring disposition, he is capable of accomplishing some very difficult tasks.

The Cancerian can put on an aggressive front, and in some cases it can carry him far. Quite often he is able to develop leadership qualities and make good use of them. He generally knows how to direct his energy so that he never becomes immediately exhausted. He'll work away at a difficult chore gradually; seldomly approaching anything head on. By working at something obliquely he often finds advantages along the way that are not apparent to others. In spite of his cautious approach, the Cancerian is often taxed by work that is too demanding of his energy. He may put up a good front of being strong and courageous while actually he is at the end of his emotional rope. Risks sometimes frighten the person born under this sign. It is often this fear which exhausts him. The possible dangers in the world of business set him to worrying.

The Cancerian does not boast about what he is going to do; he just quietly goes ahead and does it. Quite often he accomplishes more than others in this quiet way.

The person born under this sign enjoys helping others. By nature, he is quite a sympathetic individual. He does not like to see others suffer or do without. He is willing to make sacrifices for someone he trusts and cares for. The Cancerian, as was mentioned before, has a maternal streak in him, which is perhaps why he works so well with children. People born under the fourth sign of the Zodiac often make excellent teachers. They understand young people well and do what they can to help them grow up properly.

Cancerians also are fairly intuitive. In business or financial matters, they often make an important strike by playing a strong hunch. In some cases they are able to rely almost entirely on their feelings rather than on reason.

Water attracts the Cancer person. Often they have connections with the sea through their professions. The Cancerian housewife may find herself working with various liquids quite successfully while at home. Trade and commerce often appeal to the person born under this sign.

The average Cancerian has many choices open to him as far as a career is concerned. There are many things that he can do well once he puts his mind to it. In the arts he is quite likely to do well. The Cancer man or woman has a way with beauty, harmony, and creativity. Basically, he is a very capable person in many things; it depends on which of his talents he wants to develop to a professional point. He has a rich imagination and sometimes can make use of it in the area of painting, music, or sculpture.

When working for someone else, the Cancerian can always be depended upon. He makes a loyal and conscientious employee.

It is important for the Cancerian that he select a job that is well suited to his talents and temperament. Although he may feel that earning money is important, the Cancerian eventually comes to the point where he realizes that it is even more important to enjoy the work he is doing. He should have a position which allows him to explore the recesses of his personality and to develop. When placed in the wrong job, the Cancer man or woman is apt to spend a good deal of time wishing he were somewhere else.

Cancerians know the value of money. They are not the sort of people who go throwing money about recklessly. The Cancer person is honest and expects others to be the same. He is quite modest in most things and deplores extravagance and unnecessary display. There are many rich Cancerians. They have a genius for making money and for investing or saving it. Security is important to the person born under this sign. He'll always see to it that he has something put away for that inevitable rainy day. He is also a hard worker and is willing to put in long hours for the money it brings him. Financial success is usually the result of his own perseverance and industry. Through his own need for security, it is often easy for the Cancerian to sympathize with those of like dispositions. He is a helpful person. If he sees someone trying to do his best to get ahead—and still not succeeding—he is quite apt to put aside his own interests temporarily to help the other man. Sometimes the Cancerian worries over money even when he has it. He can never be too secure. It would be better for him to learn how to relax and not to let his worries undermine his health. Financial matters often cause him considerable concern—even when it is not necessary.

Home and Family

People born under this sign are usually great home-lovers. They are very domestic by nature; home for them spells security. The Cancerian is a family person. He respects those who are related to him. He feels a great responsibility toward all the members of his family. There is usually a very strong tie between the Cancer person and his mother that lasts through his whole life. Something a Cancerian will not tolerate is for someone to speak ill of a member of his family. This for him is a painful and deep insult. He has a great respect for his family and family traditions. Quite often the person under this sign is well-acquainted with his family tree. If he happens to have a relative who has been quite successful in life, he is quite proud of the fact. Once he is home for the weekend, he generally stays there. He does not particularly care for moving about. He is a born stay-at-home, in most cases.

The Cancerian is sentimental about old things and habits. He is apt to have many things stored away from years ago. Something that was dear to his parents will probably be dear to him as well.

Some Cancerians do travel about from time to time. But no matter what their destination, they are always glad to be back where they feel they belong.

The home of a person born under this sign is usually quite comfortable and tastefully furnished. The Cancerian is a bit of a romantic and usually this is reflected in the way his house is arranged.

The Cancer child is always attached to his home and family. He may not care to go out and play with other children very much but enjoys it when his friends come to his house.

The maternal nature of the Cancer person comes out when he gives a party. He is a very attentive host and worries over a guest like a mother hen—anxious to see that they are comfortable and lack nothing. He does his best to make others happy and at home, and he is admired and loved for that. People who visit Cancerians are usually deeply impressed by their out-going ways. The Cancer hostess prepares unusual and delicious snacks for her visitors. She is very concerned about them and likes to see to it that they are well-fed while visiting her.

Homebodies that they are, Cancerians generally do what they can to make their home a comfortable and interesting place for themselves as well as for others. They feel very flattered when a visitor pays them a compliment on their home.

Children play a very important part in the lives of people born under this sign. They like to fuss over their offspring and give them the things they feel that they need. They generally like to have large families. They like to see to it that their children are well-provided for and that they have the chances in life that their parents never had. The best mother of the Zodiac is usually someone born under the sign of Cancer. They have a strong protective nature. They usually have a strong sense of duty, and when their children are in difficulty they do everything they can to set matters right. Children, needless to say, are fond of their Cancerian parent, and do what they can to make the parent-child relationship a harmonious one.

Social Relationships

The Cancer person may seem rather retiring and quiet and this gives people the impression that he is not too warm or sympathetic. However, the person born under this sign is very sensitive and loving. His ability to understand and sympathize with others is great. He likes to have close friends—people who love and understand him as well as he tries to love and understand them. He wants to be well-liked—to be noticed by people who he feels should like him. If he does not get the attention and affection he feels he is entitled to, he is apt to become a little sullen and difficult to deal with.

The Cancer man or woman has strong powers of intuition and he can generally sense when he has met a person who is likely to turn into a good friend. The Cancerian suffers greatly if ever he should lose a friend. To him friendships are sacred. Sometimes the Cancerian sets his friends on too high a pedestal; he is apt to feel quite crest-fallen when he discovers that they have feet of clay. He is often romantic in his approach to friendship and is likely to seek people out for sentimental reasons rather than for practical ones.

The Cancerian is a very sensitive person and sometimes this contributes to making a friendship unsatisfactory. He sometimes makes the wrong interpretation of a remark that is made by a friend or acquaintance. He imagines something injurious behind a very innocent remark. He sometimes feels that people who profess to be his friends laugh at him cruelly behind his back. He has to be constantly reassured of a friend's sincerity, especially in the beginning of a relationship. If he wants to have the wide circle of friends he desires, the Cancerian must learn to curb these persecution fantasies.

LOVE AND MARRIAGE

The Cancer man or woman has to have love in his life, otherwise his existence is a dull and humdrum affair. When he loves someone, the Cancerian will do everything in his power to make her happy. He is not afraid to make sacrifices in order to make an important relationship work. To his loved one he is likely to seem uncertain and moody. The Cancer person is usually very influenced by the impression he has of his lover. He may even be content to let his romance partner have her own way in the relationship. He may not make many demands but be willing to follow those of his loved one. At times he may feel that he is not really loved, and draw away somewhat from the relationship. Sometimes it takes a lot of coaxing before he can be won over to the fact that he is indeed loved for himself alone.

The Cancerian is often possessive about people as well as material objects. This often makes the relationship difficult to accept for his partner.

His standards are sometimes impossibly high and because of this he is rather difficult to please. The Cancer man or woman is interested in finding someone with whom he can spend the rest of his life. He or she is not interested in any fly-by-night romance.

Romance and the Cancer Woman

The Cancer woman is usually a very warm and loving person. Her feelings run deep. She is sincere in her approach to love. Still and all, she is rather sensitive when in love and her lover may find her difficult to understand at times. The Cancer woman is quite given to crying and when she has been wronged or imagines she has, she is capable of weeping buckets. It may be quite a while before she comes out of her shell again.

Marriage is a union quite suited to the Cancer woman's temperament. She longs for permanence in a relationship and is not fond of flings or meaningless romantic adventures. Her emotions are usually very deep. She desires a man who is protective and affectionate; someone who can help and guide her through life.

She may be too possessive with her husband and this may cause discord. The demands she is likely to make on her family may be overbearing at times. She often likes to be reassured that she is loved and appreciated.

She makes a devoted and loving wife and mother who will do everything to keep her family life harmonious and affectionate.

Romance and the Cancer Man

Quite often the Cancer man is the reserved type. He may be difficult for some women to understand. Generally speaking, he is a very loving person; but sometimes he has difficulty in letting this appear so. He is a bit afraid of being rejected or hurt, so he is liable to keep his true feelings hidden until he feels that the intended object of his affection is capable of taking him seriously.

Quite often he looks for a woman who has the same qualities as his mother. He is more easily attracted to a woman who has old-fashioned traits than to a modern woman. He likes a woman who is a good cook; someone who does not mind household chores and a quiet life.

When deeply in love, the Cancer man does everything in his power to hold the woman of his choice. He is very warm and affectionate and may be rather extravagant from time to time in entertaining the woman he loves.

Marriage is something in which the Cancer man is seriously interested. He wants to settle down with a warm and loving wife—someone who will mother him to some extent. He makes a good father. He is fond of large families. His love of his children may be too possessive.

Woman—Man

CANCER WOMAN
ARIES MAN

Although it's possible that you could find happiness with a man born under the sign of the Ram, it's uncertain as to how long that happiness would last.

An Arien who has made his mark in the world and is somewhat steadfast in his outlooks and attitudes could be quite a catch for you. On the other hand, men under this sign are often swift-footed and quick-minded; their industrious mannerisms may fail to impress you, especially if you feel that much of their get-up-and-go often leads nowhere.

When it comes to a fine romance, you want someone with a nice, broad shoulder to lean on. You are likely to find a relationship with someone who doesn't like to stay put for too long somewhat upsetting.

The Arien may have a little trouble in understanding you, too . . . at least, in the beginning of the relationship. He may find you a bit too shy and moody. Ariens tend to speak their minds; he's liable to criticize you at the drop of a hat.

You may find a man born under this sign too demanding. He may give you the impression that he expects you to be at his beck-and-call. You have a barrelful of patience at your disposal and he may try every last bit of it. He is apt not to be as thorough as you are in everything that he does. In order to achieve success or a goal quickly, he is liable to overlook small but important details—and regret it when it is far too late.

Being married to an Arien does not mean that you'll have a secure and safe life as far as finances are concerned. Not all Ariens are rash with cash, but they lack that sound head you have for putting away something for that inevitable rainy day. He'll do his best, however, to see that you're adequately provided for—even though his efforts may leave something to be desired as far as you're concerned.

With an Aires man for a mate, you'll find yourself constantly among people. Ariens generally have many friends—and you may not heartily approve of them all. People born under this sign are more interested in "Interesting" people than they are in influential ones. Although there is liable to be a family squabble from time to time, you are stable enough to take it all in your stride. Your love of permanence and a harmonious homelife will help you to take the bitter with the sweet.

Aries men love children. They make wonderful fathers. Kids take to them like ducks to water. Their quick minds and behavior appeal to the young.

CANCER WOMAN
TAURUS MAN

Some Taurus men are strong and silent. They do all they can to protect and provide for the women they love. The Taurus man will never let you down. He's steady, sturdy, and reliable. He's pretty honest and practical, too. He says what he means and means what he says. He never indulges in deceit and will always put his cards on the table.

The Tauren is a very affectionate man. Being loved, appreciated, and understood is very important for his well-being. Like you, he is also looking for peace, harmony, and security in his life. If you both work toward these goals together, you'll find that they are easily attained.

If you should marry a Taurus man, you can be sure that the wolf will never darken your door. They are notoriously good providers and do everything they can to make their families comfortable and happy.

He'll appreciate the way you have of making a home warm and inviting. Slippers and pipe, and the evening papers are essential ingredients in making your Taurus husband happy at the end of the workday. Although he may be a big lug of a guy, you'll find he's pretty fond of gentleness and soft things. If you puff up his pillow and tuck him in at night, he won't complain. He'll eat it up and ask for more.

You probably won't complain about his friends. The Taurean tends to seek out friends who are successful or prominent. You admire people, too, who work hard and achieve what they set out for. It helps to reassure your way of life and the way you look at things.

Like you, the Taurus man doesn't care too much for change. He's a stay-at-home of the first degree. Chances are that the house you move into after you're married will be the house you'll live in for the rest of your life.

You'll find that the man born under this sign is easy to get along with. It's unlikely that you'll have many quarrels or arguments.

Although he'll be gentle and tender with you, your Taurus man is far from being a sensitive type. He's a man's man. Chances are he loves sports like fishing and football. He can be earthy as well as down-to-earth.

Taureans love their children very much but do everything they can not to spoil them. They believe in children staying in their places. They make excellent disciplinarians. Your children will be polite and respectful. They may find their Taurus father a little gruff, but as they grow older they'll learn to understand him.

CANCER WOMAN
GEMINI MAN

Gemini men, in spite of their charm and dashing manner, may make your skin crawl. They may seem to lack the sort of common sense you set so much store in. Their tendency to start something, then—out of boredom—never finish it, may do nothing more than exasperate you.

You may be inclined to interpret a Geminian's jumping around from here to there as childish if not downright neurotic. A man born under this sign will seldom stay put and if you should take it upon yourself to try and make him sit still, he's liable to resent it strongly.

On the other hand, the Gemini man is liable to think you're an old slowpoke—someone far too interested in security and material things. He's attracted to things that sparkle and dazzle; you, with your practical way of looking at things, are likely to seem a little dull and uninteresting to this gadabout. If your're looking for a life of security and permanence—and what Cancerian isn't—then you'd better look elsewhere for your Mr. Right.

Chances are you'll be taken in by his charming ways and facile wit—few women can resist Gemini-magic—but after you've seen through his live-for-today, gossamer facade, you'll most likely be very happy to turn your attention to someone more stable—even if he is not as interesting. You want a man who is there when you need him. You need someone on whom you can fully rely. Keeping track of a Gemini's movements will make you dizzy. Still, you are a patient woman, most of the time, and you are able to put up with something contrary if you feel that in the end it will prove well worth the effort.

A successful and serious Gemini could make you a very happy woman, perhaps, if you gave him half a chance. Although you may think that he has holes in his head, the Gemini man generally has a good brain and can make good use of it when he wants. Some Geminians who have learned the importance of being consequent have risen to great heights, professionally. President Kennedy was a Gemini as was Thomas Mann and William Butler Yeats. Once you can convince yourself that not all people born under the sign of the Twins are witless grasshoppers, you'll find you've come a long way in trying to understand them.

Life with a Gemini man can be more fun than a barrel of clowns. You'll never have a chance to experience a dull moment. He lacks your sense when it comes to money, however. You should see to it that you handle the budgeting and bookkeeping.

In ways, he's like a child himself; perhaps that is why he can get along so well with the younger generation.

CANCER WOMAN
CANCER MAN

You'll find the man born under the same sign as you easy to get along with. You're both sensitive and sensible people; you'll see eye-to-eye on most things. He'll share your interest in security and practicality.

Cancer men are always hard workers. They are very interested in making successes of themselves in business and socially. Like you, he's a conservative person who has a great deal of respect for tradition. He's a man you can depend on come rain or come shine. He'll never shirk his responsibilities as provider and will always see to it that you never want.

The Cancer man is not the type that rushes headlong into romance. Neither are you, for that matter. Courtship between the two of you will be a sensible and thorough affair. It may take months before you even get to that holding-hands stage of romance. One thing you can be sure of: he'll always treat you like a lady. He'll have great respect and consideration for your feelings. Only when he is sure that you approve of him as someone to love, will he reveal the warmer side of his nature. His coolness, like yours, is just a front. Beneath it lies a very affectionate heart.

Although he may seem restless or moody at times, on the whole the Cancer man is a very considerate and kind person. His standards are extremely high. He is looking for a girl who can measure up to his ideals . . . a girl like you.

Marriage means a lot to the Cancer male. He's very interested in settling down with someone who has the same attitudes and outlooks as he has. He's a man who loves being at home. He'll be a faithful husband. Cancerians never pussyfoot around after they've made their marriage vows. They do not take their marriage responsibilities lightly. They see to it that everything in this relationship is just the way it should be. Between the two of you, your home will be well managed; bills will be paid on time, there will be adequate insurance on everything of value, and there will be money in the bank. When retirement time rolls around, you both should be very well off.

The Cancer man has a great respect for family. You'll most likely be seeing a lot of his mother during your marriage, just as he'll probably be seeing a lot of yours. He'll do his best to get along with your relatives; he'll treat them with the kindness and concern you think they deserve. He'll expect you to be just as considerate with his relatives.

The Cancerian makes a very good father. He's very patient and understanding, especially when the children are young and dependent.

CANCER WOMAN
LEO MAN

To know a man born under the sign of the Lion is not necessarily to love him—even though the temptation may be great. When he fixes most girls with his leonine double-whammy, it causes their hearts to pitter-pat and their minds to cloud over.

But with you, the sensible Cancerian, it takes more than a regal strut and a roar to win you over. There is no denying that Leo has a way with women—even practical Cancerians—and that once he's swept a girl off her feet, it may be hard for her to scramble upright again. Still, you are no pushover for romantic charm when you feel there may be no security behind it.

He'll wine you and dine you in the fanciest places. He'll croon to you under the moon and shower you with diamonds if he can get a hold of them. Still, it would be wise to find out just how long that shower is going to last before consenting to be his wife.

Lions in love are hard to ignore, let alone brush off. Once mesmerized by this romantic powerhouse, you will most likely find yourself doing things you never dreamed of. Leos can be like vain pussycats when involved romantically. They like to be cuddled and curried, tickled under the chin and told how wonderful they are. This may not be your cup of tea, exactly, still when you're romantically dealing with a man born under the sign of Leo, you'll find yourself doing all kinds of things to make him purr.

Although he may be big and magnanimous while trying to win you, he'll let out a blood-curdling roar if he thinks he's not getting the tender love and care he feels is his due. If you keep him well supplied with affection, you can be sure his eyes will never stray and his heart will never wander.

Leo men often tend to be authoritarian—they are born to lord it over others in one way or another, it seems. If he is the top banana of his firm, he'll most likely do everything he can to stay on top. If he's not number one, he's most likely working on it and will be sitting on the throne before long. You'll have more security than you can use if he is in a position to support you in the manner to which he feels you should be accustomed. He's apt to be too lavish, though—at least, by your standards.

You'll always have plenty of friends when you have a Leo for a mate. He's a natural born friend-maker and entertainer. He loves to kick up his heels at a party.

As fathers, Leos tend to spoil their children no end.

CANCER WOMAN
VIRGO MAN

The Virgo man is often a quiet, respectable type who sets great store in conservative behavior and level-headedness. He'll admire you for your practicality and tenacity—perhaps even more than for your good looks. The Virgo man is seldom bowled over by glamour pusses. When looking for someone to love, he always turns to a serious, reliable girl.

He'll be far from a Valentino while dating. In fact, you may wind up making all the passes. Once he gets his motor running, however, he can be a warm and wonderful fellow—to the right girl.

The Virgo man is gradual about love. Chances are your romance with him will start out looking like an ordinary friendship. Once he's sure that you are no fly-by-night flirt and have no plans of taking him for a ride, he'll open up and rain sunshine all over your heart.

The Virgo man takes his time about romance. It may be many years before he seriously considers settling down. Virgos are often middle-age when they make their first marriage vows. They hold out as long as they can for that girl who perfectly measures up to their ideals.

He may not have many names in his little black book; in fact, he may not even have a little black book. He's not interested in playing the field; leave that to the more flamboyant signs. The Virgo man is so particular that he may remain romantically inactive for a long period of time. The girl he chooses has to be perfect or it's no go.

With your sure-fire perseverance, you'll most likely be able to make him listen to reason, as far as romance is concerned; before long, you'll find him returning your love. He's no block of ice and will respond to what he considers to be the right feminine flame.

Once your love-life with Virgo starts to bubble, don't give it a chance to die down. The Virgo man will never give a woman a second chance at winning his heart. If there should ever be a falling-out between you: forget about picking up the pieces. By him, it's one strike and you're out.

Once married, he'll stay that way—even if it hurts. He's too conscientious to back out of a legal deal of any sort. He'll always be faithful and considerate. He's as neat as a pin and will expect you to be the same.

If you marry a Virgo man, keep your kids spic-and-span, at least by the time he gets home from work. He likes children to be clean and polite.

CANCER WOMAN
LIBRA MAN

Cancerians are apt to find men born under the sign of Libra too wrapped up in their own private dreams to be romantically interesting. He's a difficult man to bring back down to earth, at times. Although he may be very careful about weighing both sides of an argument, he may never really come to a reasonable decision about anything. Decisons, large and small, are capable of giving a Libran the willies. Don't ask him why. He probably doesn't know, himself.

You are looking for permanence and constancy in a love relationship; you may find him a puzzlement. One moment he comes on hard and strong with declarations of his love; the next moment you find he's left you like yesterday's mashed potatoes. It does no good to wonder "what went wrong." Chances are: nothing, really. It's just one of Libra's strange ways.

On the other hand, you'll probably admire his way with harmony and beauty. If you're all decked out in your fanciest gown, you'll receive a ready compliment and one that's really deserved. Librans don't pass out compliments to all and sundry. If something strikes him as distasteful, he'll remain silent. He's tactful.

He may not seem as ambitious as you would like your lover or husband to be. Where you have a great interest in getting ahead, the Libran is often content just to drift along. It is not that he is lazy or shiftless; material gain generally means little to him. He is more interested in aesthetic matters. If he is in love with you, however, he'll do everything in his power to make you happy.

You may have to give him a good nudge now and again to get him to recognize the light of reality. On the whole, he'll enjoy the company of his artistic dreams when you're not around. If you love your Libran, don't be too harsh or impatient with him. Try to understand him.

Librans are peace-loving people. They hate any kind of confrontation that might lead to an argument. Some of them will do almost anything to keep the peace—even tell a little lie.

If you find yourself involved with a man born under this sign, either temporarily or permanently, you'd better take over the task of managing his money. It's for his own good. Money will never interest a Libran as much as it should; he often has a tendency to be generous when he shouldn't be.

Don't let him see the materialistic side of your nature too often. It's liable to frighten him off.

He makes a gentle and understanding father. He's careful not to spoil children.

CANCER WOMAN
SCORPIO MAN

Some people have a hard time understanding the man born under the sign of Scorpio; few, however, are able to resist his fiery charm. When angered, he can act like an overturned wasps' nest; his sting can leave an almost permanent mark.. If you find yourself interested in a man born under this sign, you'd better learn how to keep on his good side.

The Scorpio man can be quite blunt when he chooses; at times, he'll seem like a brute to you. He's touchy—more so than you—and it is liable to get on your nerves after a while. When you feel like you can't take it anymore, you'd better tiptoe away from the scene rather than chance an explosive confrontation. He's capable of giving you a sounding-out that will make you pack your bags and go back to Mother—for good.

If he finds fault with you, he'll let vou know. He's liable to misinterpret your patience and think it a sign of indifference. Still and all, you are the kind of woman who can adapt to almost any sort of relationship or circumstance if you put your heart and mind to it.

Scorpio men are all quite perceptive and intelligent. In some respects, they know how to use their brains more effectively than most. They believe in winning in whatever they do; second-place holds no interest for them. In business, they usually achieve the position they want through drive and use of intellect.

Your interest in home-life is not likely to be shared by him. No matter how comfortable you've managed to make the house, it will have very little influence on him with regards to making him aware of his family responsibilities. He does not like to be tied down, generally, and would rather be out on the battlefield of life, belting away for what he feels is a just and worthy cause. Don't try to keep the homefires burning too brightly while you wait for him to come home from work—you may just run out of firewood.

The Scorpio man is passionate in all things—including love. Most women are easily attracted to him—and the Cancer woman is no exception . . . that is, at least before she knows what she might be getting into. Those who allow themselves to be swept off their feet by a Scorpio man, shortly find that they're dealing with a carton of romantic fireworks. The Scorpio man is passionate with a capital P, make no mistake about that.

Scorpio men are straight to the point. They can be as sharp as a razor blade and just as cutting. Always manage to stay out of his line of fire; if you don't, it could cost you your love-life.

Scorpio men like large families. They love children but they do not always live up to the role of father.

CANCER WOMAN
SAGITTARIUS MAN

Sagittarius men are not easy to catch. They get cold feet whenever visions of the altar enter the romance. You'll most likely be attracted to the Sagittarian because of his sun-shiny nature. He's lots of laughs and easy to get along with, but as soon as the relationship begins to take on a serious hue, you may feel yourself a little let-down.

Sagittarians are full of bounce; perhaps too much bounce to suit you. They are often hard to pin down; they dislike staying put. If he ever has a chance to be on-the-move, he'll latch on to it without so much as a how-do-you-do. Sagittarians are quick people —both in mind and spirit. If ever they do make mistakes, it's because of their zip; they leap before they look.

If you offer him good advice, he's liable not to follow it. Sagittarians like to rely on their own wits and ways whenever possible.

His up-and-at-'em manner about most things is likely to drive you up the wall at times. And your cautious, deliberate manner is likely to make him cluck his tongue occasionally. "Get the lead out of your shoes," he's liable to tease when you're accompanying him on a stroll or jogging through the park with him on a Sunday morning. He can't abide a slowpoke.

At times you'll find him too much like a kid—too breezy. Don't mistake his youthful zest for premature senility. Sagittarians are equipped with first-class brain power and know how to use it well. They are often full of good ideas and drive. Generally, they are very broad-minded people and very much concerned with fair play and equality.

In the romance department, he's quite capable of loving you whole-heartedly while treating you like a good buddy. His hail-fellow-well-met manner in the arena of love is likely to scare off a dainty damsel. However, a woman who knows that his heart is in the right place, won't mind it too much if, once in a while, he slaps her (lightly) on the back instead of giving her a gentle embrace.

He's not very much of a homebody. He's got ants in his pants and enjoys being on-the-move. Humdrum routine—especially at home—bores him silly. At the drop of a hat, he may ask you to whip off your apron and dine out for a change. He's a past-master in the instant-surprise department. He'll love keeping you guessing. His friendly, candid nature will win him many friends. He'll expect his friends to be yours, and vice-versa.

Sagittarians make good fathers when the children become older; with little shavers, they feel all thumbs.

CANCER WOMAN
CAPRICORN MAN

The Capricorn man is quite often not the romantic kind of lover that attracts most women. Still, with his reserve and calm, he is capable of giving his heart completely once he has found the right girl. The Cancer woman who is thorough and deliberate can appreciate these same qualities in the average Capricorn man. He is slow and sure about most things—love included.

He doesn't believe in flirting and would never lead a heart on a merry chase just for the game of it. If you win his trust, he'll give you his heart on a platter. Quite often, it is the woman who has to take the lead when romance is in the air. As long as he knows you're making the advances in earnest, he won't mind—in fact, he'll probably be grateful. Don't get to thinking he's all cold fish; he isn't. While some Capricorns are indeed quite capable of expressing passion, others often have difficulty in trying to display affection. He should have no trouble in this area, however, once he has found a patient and understanding girl.

The Capricorn man is very interested in getting ahead. He's quite ambitious and usually knows how to apply himself well to whatever task he undertakes. He's far from being a spendthrift. Like you, he knows how to handle money with extreme care. You, with your knack for putting pennies away for that rainy day, should have no difficulty in understanding his way with money. The Capricorn man thinks in terms of future security. He saves to make sure that he and his wife have something to fall back on when they reach retirement age. There's nothing wrong with that; in fact, it's a plus quality.

The Capricorn man will want to handle household matters efficiently. Most Cancerians have no trouble in doing this. If he should check up on you from time to time, don't let it irritate you. Once you assure him that you can handle this area to his liking, he'll leave it all up to you.

Although he's a hard man to catch when it comes to marriage, once he's made that serious step, he's quite likely to become possessive. Capricorns need to know that they have the support of their women in whatever they do, every step of the way.

The Capricorn man likes to be liked. He may seem like a dull, reserved person but underneath it all, he's often got an adventurous nature that has never had the chance to express itself. He may be a real dare-devil in his heart of hearts. The right woman, the affectionate, adoring woman, can bring out that hidden zest in his nature.

Although he may not understand his children fully, he'll be a loving and dutiful father.

CANCER WOMAN
AQUARIUS MAN

You are liable to find the Aquarious man the most broadminded man you have ever met; on the other hand, you are also liable to find him the most impractical. Oftentimes, he's more of a dreamer than a doer. If you don't mind putting up with a man whose heart and mind are as wide as the Missouri but whose head is almost always up in the clouds, then start dating that Aquarian who has somehow captured your fancy. Maybe you, with your good sense, can bring him back down to earth when he gets too starry-eyed.

He's no dumb-bell; make no mistake about that. He can be busy making some very complicated and idealistic plans when he's got that out-to-lunch look in his eyes. But more than likely, he'll never execute them. After he's shared one or two of his progressive ideas with you, you are liable to ask yourself "Who is this nut?" But don't go jumping to conclusions. There's a saying that Aquarians are a half-century ahead of everybody else in the thinking department.

If you decide to say "yes" to his "will you marry me", you'll find out how right his zany whims are on or about your 50th anniversary. Maybe the waiting will be worth it. Could be that you have an Einstein on your hands—and heart.

Life with an Aquarian won't be one of total despair if you can learn to temper his airiness with your down-to-earth practicality. He won't gripe if you do. The Aquarius man always maintains an open mind; he'll entertain the ideas and opinions of everybody. He may not agree with all of them.

Don't go tearing your hair out when you find that it's almost impossible to hold a normal conversation with your Aquarius friend at times. He's capable of answering your how-are-you-feeling with a run-down on the price of Arizona sugar beets. Always try to keep in mind: he means well.

His broadmindedness doesn't stop when it comes to you and your personal freedom. You won't have to give up any of your hobbies or projects after you're married; in fact, he'll encourage you to continue your interests.

He'll be a kind and generous husband. He'll never quibble over petty things. Keep track of the money you both spend. He can't. Money burns a hole in his pocket.

You'll have plenty of chances to put your legendary patience to good use during your relationship with an Aquarian. At times, you may feel like tossing in the towel, but you'll never call it quits.

He's a good family man. He understands children as much as he loves them.

CANCER WOMAN
PISCES MAN

The Pisces man is perhaps the man you've been looking all over for, high and low; the man you almost thought didn't exist.

The Pisces man is very sensitive and very romantic. Still, he is a reasonable person. He may wish on the moon, yet he's got enough good sense to know that it isn't made of green cheese.

He'll be very considerate of your every wish and whim. He will do his best to be a very compatible mate. The Pisces man is great for showering the object of his affection with all kinds of little gifts and tokens of his affection. He's just the right mixture of dreamer and realist that pleases most women.

When it comes to earning bread and butter, the strong Pisces man will do all right in the world. Quite often they are capable of rising to very high positions. Some do very well as writers or psychiatrists. He'll be as patient and understanding with you as you are with him.

One thing a Pisces man dislikes is pettiness. Anyone who delights in running another into the ground is almost immediately crossed off his list of possible mates. If you have any small grievances with any of your girl friends, don't tell him about them. He couldn't care less about them and will be quite disappointed in you if you do.

If you fall in love with a weak Pisces man, don't give up your job at the office before you get married. Better still: hang onto it until a good while after the honeymoon; you may need it.

A funny thing about the man born under this sign is that he can be content almost anywhere. This is perhaps because he is quite inner-directed and places little value on some exterior things.

In a shack or a palace, the Pisces man is capable of making the best of all possible adjustments. He won't kick up a fuss if the roof leaks or if the fence is in sad need of repair. He's got more important things on his mind, he'll tell you. Still and all, the Pisces man is not lazy or aimless. It's important to understand that material gain is never a direct goal for him.

Pisces men have a way with the sick and troubled. He'll offer his shoulder to anyone in the mood for a good cry. He can listen to one hard luck story after another without seeming to tire. Quite often he knows what is bothering someone before that person, himself, realizes what it is. It's almost intuitive with Pisceans, it seems.

As a lover, he'll be attentive and faithful. Children are often delighted with Pisces men. As fathers, they are never strict, always permissive.

Man—Woman

CANCER MAN
ARIES WOMAN

The Aires woman may be a little too bossy and busy for you. Generally speaking, Ariens are ambitious creatures. They can become a little impatient with people who are more thorough and deliberate than they are—especially if they feel such people are taking too much time. The Aries woman is a fast worker. Sometimes she's so fast she forgets to look where she's going. When she stumbles or falls, it would be nice if you were there to grab her. Ariens are proud women. They don't like to be told "I told you so" when they err. Tongue-wagging can turn them into blocks of ice. Don't begin to think that the Aires woman frequently gets tripped up in her plans. Quite often they are capable of taking aim and hitting the bull's-eye. You'll be flabbergasted at times by their accuracy as well as by their ambition. On the other hand, because of your interest in being sure and safe, you're apt to spot a flaw in your Arien's plans before she does.

You are somewhat slower than the Arien in attaining what you have your sights set on. Still, you don't make any mistakes along the way; you're almost always well-prepared.

The Aries woman is rather sensitive at times. She likes to be handled with gentleness and respect. Let her know that you love her for her brains as well as for her good looks. Never give her cause to become jealous. When your Aires date sees green, you'd better forget about sharing a rosy future together. Handle her with tender love and care and she's yours.

The Aires woman can be giving if she feels her partner is deserving. She is no iceberg; she responds to the proper flame. She needs a man she can look up to and feel proud of. If the shoe fits, put it on. If not, better put your sneakers back on and quietly tiptoe out of her sight. She can cause you plenty of heart ache if you've made up your mind about her but she hasn't made up hers about you. Aires women are very demanding at times. Some of them are high-strung; they can be difficult if they feel their independence is being hampered.

The cultivated Aires woman makes a wonderful homemaker and hostess. You'll find she's very clever in decorating and color-use. Your house will be tastefully furnished; she'll see to it that it radiates harmony. Friends and acquaintances will love your Aries wife. She knows how to make everyone feel at home and welcome.

Although the Aries woman may not be keen on burdening responsibilities, she is fond of children and the joy they bring.

CANCER MAN
TAURUS WOMAN

A Taurus woman could perhaps understand you better than most women. She is a very considerate and loving kind of person. She is methodical and thorough in whatever she does. She knows how to take her time in doing things; she is anxious to avoid mistakes. Like you, she is a careful person. She never skips over things that may seem unimportant; she goes over everything with a fine-tooth comb.

Home is very important to the Taurus woman. She is an excellent homemaker. Although your home may not be a palace, it will become, under her care, a comfortable and happy abode. She'll love it when friends drop by for the evening. She is a good cook and enjoys feeding people well. No one will ever go away from your house with an empty stomach.

The Taurus woman is serious about love and affection. When she has taken a tumble for someone, she'll stay by him—for good, if possible. She will try to be practical in romance, to some extent. When she sets her cap for a man, she keeps after him until he's won her. Generally, the Taurus woman is a passionate lover, even though she may appear otherwise at first glance. She is on the look-out for someone who can return her affection fully. Taureans are sometimes given to fits of jealousy and possessiveness. They expect fair play in the area of marriage; when it doesn't come about, they can be bitingly sarcastic and mean.

The Taurus woman is generally an easy-going person. She's

fond of keeping peace. She won't argue unless she has to. She'll do her best to keep a love relationship on even keel.

Marriage is generally a one-time thing for Taureans. Once they've made the serious step, they seldom try to back out of it. Marriage is for keeps. They are fond of love and warmth. With the right man, they turn out to be ideal wives.

The Taurus woman will respect you for your steady ways; she'll have confidence in your common sense.

Taurus women seldom put up with nonsense from their children. They are not so much strict as concerned. They like their children to be well-behaved and dutiful. Nothing pleases a Taurus mother more than a compliment from a neighbor or teacher about her child's behavior. Although children may inwardly resent the iron hand of a Taurus woman, in later life they are often quite thankful that they were brought up in such an orderly and conscientious way.

CANCER MAN
GEMINI WOMAN

The Gemini woman may be too much of a flirt ever to take your heart too seriously. Then again, it depends on what kind of mood she's in. Gemini women can change from hot to cold quicker than a cat can wink its eye. Chances are her fluctuations will tire you after a time, and you'll pick up your heart—if it's not already broken into small pieces—and go elsewhere. Women born under the sign of the Twins have the talent of being able to change their moods and attitudes as frequently as they change their party dresses.

Sometimes, Gemini girls like to whoop it up. Some of them are good-time girls who love burning the candle to the wick. You'll always see them at parties and gatherings, surrounded by men of all types, laughing gaily or kicking up their heels at every opportunity. Wallflowers, they're not. The next day you may bump into the same girl at the neighborhood library and you'll hardly recognize her for her "sensible" attire. She'll probably have five or six books under her arm—on five or six different subjects. In fact, she may even work there. If you think you've met the twin sister of Dr. Jekyll and Mr. Hyde, you're most likely right.

You'll probably find her a dazzling and fascinating creature—for a time, at any rate. Most men do. But when it comes to being serious about love you may find that that sparkling Eve leaves quite a bit to be desired. It's not that she has anything against being serious, it's just that she might find it difficult trying to be serious with you.

At one moment, she'll be capable of praising you for your steadfast and patient ways; the next moment she'll tell you in a cutting way that you're an impossible stick in the mud.

Don't even begin to fathom the depths of her mercurial soul—it's full of false bottoms. She'll resent close investigation anyway, and will make you rue the day you ever took it into your head to try to learn more about her than she feels is necessary. Better keep the relationship fancy free and full of fun until she gives you the go-ahead sign. Take as much of her as she is willing to give; don't ask for more. If she does take a serious interest in you, then she'll come across with the goods.

There will come a time when the Gemini girl will realize that she can't spend her entire life at the ball and that the security and warmth you offer is just what she needs to be a happy, fulfilled woman.

She'll be easy-going with her children. She'll probably spoil them silly.

CANCER MAN
CANCER WOMAN

The girl born under Cancer needs to be protected from the cold cruel world. She'll love you for your gentle and kind manner; you are the kind of man who can make her feel safe and secure.

You won't have to pull any he-man or heroic stunts to win her heart; she's not interested in things like that. She's more likely to be impressed by your sure, steady ways—the way you have of putting your arm around her and making her feel that she's the only girl in the world. When she's feeling glum and tears begin to well up in her eyes, you'll know how to calm her fears, no matter how silly some of them may seem.

The girl born under this sign—like you—is inclined to have her ups and downs. Perhaps you can both learn to smooth out the roughed-up spots in each other's life. She'll most likely worship the ground you walk on or place you on a very high pedestal. Don't disappoint her if you can help it. She'll never disappoint you. The Cancer woman is the sort who will take great pleasure in devoting the rest of her natural life to you. She'll darn your socks, mend your overalls, scrub floors, wash windows, shop, cook, and do anything short of murder in order to please you and to let you know that she loves you. Sounds like that legendary good old-fashioned girl, doesn't it? Contrary to popular belief, there are still a good number of them around and the majority of them are Cancerians.

Treat your Cancer mate fairly and she'll treat you like a king.

There is one ohing you should be warned about: never be unkind to your mother-in-law. It will be the only golden rule your Cancerian wife will probably expect you to live up to. Mother is something pretty special for her. You should have no trouble in understanding this, for your mother has a special place in your heart, too. It's always that way with people born under this sign. They have great respect and love for family-ties. It might be a good idea for you both to get to know each other's relatives before tying the marriage knot, because after the wedding bells have rung, you'll be seeing a lot of them.

Of all the signs in the Zodiac, the woman born under Cancer is the most maternal. In caring for and bringing up children, she knows just how to combine tenderness and discipline. A child couldn't ask for a better mother. Cancer women are sympathetic, affectionate, and patient with children. Both of you will make excellent parents—especially when the children are young; when they grow older you'll most likely be reluctant to let them go out into the world.

CANCER MAN
LEO WOMAN

The Leo woman can make most men roar like lions. If any woman in the Zodiac has that indefinable something that can make men lose their heads and find their hearts, it's the Leo woman.

She's got more than a fair share of charm and glamour and she knows how to make the most of her assets, especially when she's in the company of the opposite sex. Jealous men either lose their cool or their sanity when trying to woo a woman born under the sign of the Lion. She likes to kick up her heels quite often and doesn't care who knows it. She often makes heads turn and toungues wag. You don't necessarily have to believe any of what you hear—it's most likely just jealous gossip or wishful thinking. Needless to say, other women in her vicinity turn green with envy and will try anything short of shoving her into the nearest lake in order to put her out of commission.

Although this vamp makes the blood rush to your head and makes you momentarily forget all the things you thought were important and necessary in your life, you may feel differently when you come back down to earth and the stars are out of your eyes. You may feel that although this vivacious creature can make you feel pretty wonderful, she just isn't the kind of girl you planned to bring home to Mother. Not that your mother might disapprove of your choice—but *you might* after the shoes and rice are a thing of the past. Although the Leo woman may do her best to be a good wife for you, chances are she'll fall short of your idea of what a good wife should be.

If you're planning on not going as far as the altar with that Leo woman who has you flipping your lid, you'd better be financially equipped for some very expensive dating. Be prepared to shower her with expensive gifts and to take her dining and dancing to the smartest spots in town. Promise her the moon if you're in a position to go that far. Luxury and glamour are two things that are bound to lower a Leo's resistance. She's got expensive tastes and you'd better cater to them if you expect to get to first base with this femme.

If you've got an important business deal to clinch and you have doubts as to whether you can swing it or not, bring your Leo girl along to the business luncheon. Chances are that with her on your arm, you'll be able to win any business battle with both hands tied. She won't have to say or do anything—just be there at your side. The grouchiest oil magnate can be transformed into a gushing, obediant schoolboy if there's a charming Leo woman in the room.

Leo mothers are blind to the faults of their children. They make very loving and affectionate mothers and tend to spoil their offspring.

CANCER MAN
VIRGO WOMAN

The Virgo woman is pretty particular about choosing her men friends. She's not interested in just going out with anybody; she has her own idea of what a boyfriend or prospective husband should be—and it's quite possible that that image has something of you in it. Generally speaking, she's a quiet girl. She doesn't believe that nonsense has any place in a love affair. She's serious about love and she'll expect you to be. She's looking for a man who has both feet on the ground—someone who can take care of himself as well as her. She knows the value of money and how to get the most out of a dollar. She's far from being a spendthrift. Throwing money around turns her stomach—even when it isn't her money.

She'll most likely be very shy about romancing. Even the simple act of holding hands may make her turn crimson—at least, on the first couple of dates. You'll have to make all the advances—which is as it should be—and you'll have to be careful not to make any wrong moves. She's capable of showing anyone who oversteps the boundaries of common decency the door. It may even take quite a long time before she'll accept that goodnight kiss it the front gate. Don't give up. You are perhaps the kind of man ho can bring out the warm woman in her. There is love and tenderness underneath Virgo's seemingly frigid facade. It will take a patient and understanding man to bring it out into the open. She may have the idea that sex is something very naughty, if not unnecessary. The right man could make her put this old-fashioned idea in the trunk up in the attic along with her great grandmother's woolen nighties.

She is a very sensitive girl. You can help her overcome this by treating her with gentleness and affection.

When a Virgo has accepted you as a lover or mate, she won't stint in giving her love in return. With her, it's all or nothing at all. You'll be surprised at the transformation your earnest attention can bring about in this quiet kind of woman. When in love, Virgos only listen to their hearts, not to what the neighbors say.

Virgo women are honest about love once they've come to grips with it. They don't appreciate hypocrisy—particularly in this area of life. They will always be true to their hearts—even if it means tossing you over for a new love. But if you convince her that you are earnest about your interest in her, she'll reciprocate your love and affection and never leave you. Do her wrong once, however, and you can be sure she'll call the whole thing off.

Virgo mothers are tender and loving. They know what's good for their children and will always take great pains in bringing them up correctly.

CANCER MAN
LIBRA WOMAN

The song goes: It's a woman's prerogative to change her mind. The lyricist must have had the Libra woman in his thoughts when he jotted this ditty out. Her changeability, in spite of its undeniable charm (sometimes), could actually drive even a man of your patience up the wall. She's capable of smothering you with love and kisses one day and on the next, avoid you like the plague. If you think you're a man of steel nerves then perhaps you can tolerate her sometimey-ness without suffering too much. However, if you own up to the fact that you're a mere mortal who can only take so much, then you'd better fasten your attention on a girl who's somewhat more constant.

But don't get the wrong idea—a love affair with a Libran is not all bad. In fact, it can have an awful lot of plusses to it. Libra women are soft, very feminine, and warm. She doesn't have to vamp all over the place in order to gain a man's attention. Her delicate presence is enough to warm the cockles of any man's heart. One smile and you're like a piece of putty in the palm of her hand.

She can be fluffy and affectionate—things you like in a girl. On the other hand, her indecision about which dress to wear, what to cook for dinner, or whether or not to redo the rumpusroom could make you tear your hair out. What will perhaps be more exasperating is her flat denial to the accusation that she cannot make even the simplest decision. The trouble is that she wants to be fair or just in all matters; she'll spend hours weighing both sides of an argument or situation. Don't make her rush into a decision; that would only irritate her.

The Libra woman likes to be surrounded by beautiful things. Money is no object when beauty is concerned. There will always be plenty of flowers in her apartment. She'd rather die than do without daisies and such. She'll know how to arrange them tastefully, too. Women under this sign are fond of beautiful clothes and furnishings. They will run up bills without batting an eye—if given the chance.

Once she's cottoned to you, the Libra woman will do everything in her power to make you happy. She'll wait on you hand and foot when you're sick, bring you breakfast in bed on Sundays, and even read you the funny papers if you're too sleepy to open your eyes. She'll be very thoughtful and devoted. If anyone dares suggest you're not the grandest man in the world, your Libra wife will give that person a good sounding-out.

Librans work wonders with children. Gentle persuasion and affection are all she uses in bringing them up. It works.

CANCER MAN
SCORPIO WOMAN

When the Scorpio woman chooses to be sweet, she's apt to give the impression that butter wouldn't melt in her mouth . . . but, of course, it would. When her temper flies, so will everything else that isn't bolted down. She can be as hot as a *tamale* or as cool as a cucumber when she wants. Whatever mood she's in, you can be sure it's for real. She doesn't believe in poses or hypocrisy.

The Scorpio woman is often seductive and sultry. Her femme fatale charm can pierce through the hardest of hearts like a laser ray. She doesn't have to look like Mata Hari (many of them resemble the tomboy next door) but once you've looked into those tantalizing eyes, you're a goner.

The Scorpio woman can be a whirlwind of passion. Life with a girl born under this sign will not be all smiles and smooth-sailing. If you think you can handle a woman who can purr like a pussycat when handled correctly but spit bullets once her fur is ruffled, then try your luck. Your stable and steady nature will most likely have a calming effect on her. You're the kind of man she can trust and rely on. But never cross her—even on the smallest thing; if you do, you'd better tell Fido to make room for you in the dog-house—you'll be his guest for the next couple of days.

Generally, the Scorpio woman will keep family battles within the walls of your home. When company visits, she's apt to give the impression that married life with you is one big joy-ride. It's just her way of expressing her loyalty to you—at least, in front of others. She believes that family matters are and should stay private. She certainly will see to it that others have a high opinion of you both. She'll be right behind you in whatever it is you want to do. Although she's an individualist, after she has married she'll put her own interests aside for those of the man she loves. With a woman like this behind you, you can't help but go far. She'll never try to take over your role as boss of the family. She'll give you all the support you need in order to fulfill that role. She won't complain if the going gets rough. She knows how to take the bitter with the sweet. She is a courageous woman. She's as anxious as you are to find that place in the sun for you both. She's as determined a person as you are.

Although she may love her children, she may not be very affectionate toward them. She'll make a devoted mother, though. She'll be anxious to see them develop their talents. She'll teach the children to be courageous and steadfast.

CANCER MAN
SAGITTARIUS WOMAN

The Sagittarius woman is hard to keep track of: first she's here, then she's there. She's a woman with a severe case of itchy feet. She's got to keep on the move.

People generally like her because of her hail-fellow-well-met manner and her breezy charm. She is constantly good-natured and almost never cross. She is the kind of girl you're likely to strike up a palsy-walsy relationship with; you might not be interested in letting it go any farther. She probably won't sulk if you leave it on a friendly basis, either. Treat her like a kid-sister and she'll eat it up like candy.

She'll probably be attracted to you because of your restful, self-assured manner. She'll need a friend like you to help her over the rough spots in her life; she'll most likely turn to you for advice frequently.

There is nothing malicious about a girl born under this sign. She is full of bounce and good cheer. Her sunshiny dispositon can be relied upon even on the rainiest of days. No matter what she says or does, you'll always know that she means well. Sagittarians are sometimes short on tact. Some of them say anything that comes into their pretty little heads, no matter what the occasion. Sometimes the words that tumble out of their mouths seem downright cutting and cruel; they mean well but often everything they say comes out wrong. She's quite capable of losing her friends—and perhaps even yours—through a careless slip of the lip. Always remember that she is full of good intentions. Stick with her if you like her and try to help her mend her ways.

She's not a girl that you'd most likely be interested in marrying, but she'll certainly be lots of fun to pal around with. Quite often, Sagittarius women are outdoor types. They're crazy about things like fishing, camping, and mountain climbing. They love the wide open spaces. They are fond of all kinds of animals. Make no mistake about it: this busy little lady is no slouch. She's full of pep and vigor.

She's great company most of the time; she's more fun than a three-ring circus when she's in the right company. You'll like her for her candid and direct manner. On the whole, Sagittarians are very kind and sympathetic women.

If you do wind up marrying this girl-next-door type, you'd better see to it that you take care of all financial matters. Sagittarians often let money run through their fingers like sand.

As a mother, she'll smother her children with love and give them all of the freedom they think they need.

CANCER MAN
CAPRICORN WOMAN

The Capricorn woman may not be the most romantic woman of the Zodiac, but she's far from frigid when she meets the right man. She believes in true love; she doesn't appreciate getting involved in flings. To her, they're just a waste of time. She's looking for a man who means "business"—in life as well as in love. Although she can be very affectionate with her boyfriend or mate, she tends to let her head govern her heart. That is not to say that she is a cool, calculating cucumber. On the contrary, she just feels she can be more honest about love if she consults her brains first. She wants to size-up the situation first before throwing her heart in the ring. She wants to make sure it won't get stepped on.

The Capricorn woman is faithful, dependable, and systematic in just about everything that she undertakes. She is quite concerned with security and sees to it that every penny she spends is spent wisely. She is very economical about using her time, too. She does not believe in whittling away her energy on a scheme that is bound not to pay off.

Ambitious themselves, they are quite often attracted to ambitious men—men who are interested in getting somewhere in life. If a man of this sort wins her heart, she'll stick by him and do all she can to help him get to the top.

The Capricorn woman is almost always diplomatic. She makes an excellent hostess. She can be very influential when your business acquaintances come to dinner.

The Capricorn woman is likely to be very concerned, if not downright proud, about her family tree. Relatives are pretty important to her, particularly if they're socially prominent. Never say a cross word about her family members. That can really go against her grain and she'll punish you by not talking for days.

She's generally thorough in whatever she does: cooking, housekeeping, entertaining. Capricorn women are well-mannered and gracious, no matter what their backgrounds. They seem to have it in their natures to always behave properly.

If you should marry a woman born under this sign, you need never worry about her going on a wild shopping spree. They understand the value of money better than most women. If you turn over your paycheck to her at the end of the week, you can be sure that a good hunk of it will go into the bank and that all the bills will be paid on time.

With children, the Capricorn mother is both loving and correct. She'll see to it that they're polite and respectful.

CANCER MAN
AQUARIUS WOMAN

The woman born under the sign of the Water Bearer can be pretty odd and eccentric at times. Some say that this is the source of her mysterious charm. You're liable to think she's just a plain screwball; you may be 50 percent right.

Aquarius women often have their heads full of dreams and stars in their eyes. By nature, they are often unconventional; they have their own ideas about how the world should be run. Sometimes their ideas may seem pretty weird—chances are they're just a little bit too progressive. There is a saying that runs "The way the Aquarian thinks, so will the world in fifty years."

If you find yourself falling in love with a woman born under this sign, you'd better fasten your safety belt. It may take some time before you know what she's like and even then, you may have nothing to go on but a string of vague hunches.

She can be like a rainbow: full of dazzling colors. She's like no other girl you've ever known. There is something about her that is definitely charming—yet elusive, you'll never be able to put your finger on it. She seems to radiate adventure and optimism without even trying. She'll most likely be the most tolerant and open-minded woman you've ever encountered.

If you find that she's too much mystery and charm for you to handle—and being a Cancerian, chances are you might—just talk it out with her and say that you think it would be better if you called it quits. She'll most likely give you a peck on the cheek and say "Okay, but let's still be friends." Aquarius women are like that. Perhaps you'll both find it easier to get along in a friendship than in a romance.

It is not difficult for her to remain buddy-buddy with an ex-lover. For many Aquarians, the line between friendship and romance is a pretty fuzzy one.

She's not a jealous person and while you're romancing her, she won't expect you to be, either. You'll find her a pretty free spirit most of the time. Just when you think you know her inside-out, you'll discover that you don't really know her at all. She's a very sympathetic and warm person; she is often helpful to those in need of assistance and advice.

She'll seldom be suspicious even when she has every right to be. If the man she loves makes a little slip, she's liable to forget it.

She makes a fine mother. Her positive and big-hearted qualities are easily transmitted to her offspring.

CANCER MAN
PISCES WOMAN

The Pisces woman places great value on love and romance. She's gentle, kind, and romantic. Perhaps she's that girl you've been dreaming about all these years. Like you, she has very high ideals, she will only give her heart to a man who she feels can live up to her expectations.

She'll never try to wear the pants in the family. She's a staunch believer in the man being the head of the house. Quite often, Pisces women are soft and cuddly. They have a feminine, domestic charm that can win the heart of just about any man.

Generally, there's a lot more to her than just her pretty face and womanly ways. There's a brain ticking behind that gentle facade. You may not become aware of it—that is, until you've married her. It's no cause for alarm, however; she'll most likely never use it against you. But if she feels you're botching up your married life through careless behavior or if she feels you could be earning more money than you do, she'll tell you about it. But any wife would, really. She will never try to usurp your position as head and bread winner of the family. She'll admire you for your ambition and drive. If anyone says anything against you in her presence, she'll probably break out into tears. Pisces women are usually very sensitive. Their reaction to adversity or frustration is often just a plain good old fashioned cry. They can weep buckets when inclined.

She'll have an extra-special dinner waiting for you when you call up and tell her that you've just landed a new and important contract. Don't bother to go into the details at the dinner table, though; she probably doesn't have much of a head for business matters. She's only too glad to leave those matters up to you.

She's a wizard in decorating a house. She's fond of soft and beautiful things. She's a good housekeeper. She'll always see to it that you have plenty of socks and underwear in the top drawer of your dresser.

Treat her with tenderness and your relationship will be an enjoyable one. Pisces women are generally fond of sweets and flowers. Never forget birthdays, anniversaries, and the like. She won't.

Your talent for patience and gentleness can pay off in your relationship with a Pisces woman. Chances are she'll never make you sorry you placed that band of gold on her finger.

There's a strong bond between a Pisces mother and her children. She'll try to give them all the things she never had as a child. Chances are she'll spoil them a little.

CANCER

CANCER

YEARLY FORECAST: 1988

Forecast for 1988 Concerning Business and
Financial Matters, Job Prospects,
Travel, Health, Romance and Marriage
for Those Born with the Sun
in the Zodiacal Sign of Cancer.
June 21-July 20

As ever, you can look forward to a year when change and adjust-
ment to circumstances will be all-important. Your sign ruler, the
Moon, gives you the essential ability to accept the tides of life and
take advantage of the positive developments that arise continually.
Teamwork and cooperative endeavors will prove to be both
stimulating and rewarding. This could be a year when you make
firm decisions on business and marital issues. Once you are quite
clear about where you stand in relation to others, you will feel
strong enough to accept any challenge or cement any long-
standing tie. You appear to have considerable freedom to make
progress in social ways. Cooperation with people in general can
give much satisfaction and enable you to reach some social or humanitarian goal to which you have long aspired. Added responsibility and expanding business may make it essential that you increase your workload or take on staff to cope with extra work. As
cooperative effort is so important this year, you will possibly stand
or fall on your ability to come to terms with the people you employ
or work with. Equally important will be the effort you yourself are
prepared to put into any venture you undertake.

A variety of interests may attract your attention so you are
likely to be involved with a number of specialists, or people in
various trades, to satisfy your desires. A positive attitude to future
planning can boost business profits. In personal finances you
should be prepared to make your own judgments rather than rely
too much on the advice you may receive from so-called friends.
Your ability to feel what is going on is well-known and this adds to
your business acumen. You will find it advisable to resist the temp-

tation to speculate if you value your financial security, a vital feature that means so much to you.

Good performance at work depends on you health. You will be subject to the usual ups and downs. This year, as in recent years, you will experience highs and lows. But you should feel that the extremes will soon begin to disappear and that a more settled phase lies ahead. Take note of any sudden changes in your health. An early warning can save you later difficulty. Extra work may tax your strength, so the added help of colleagues or partners will be one form of support you will appreciate. Do not be afraid to share your health problems or seek advice if you need it. There are likely to be occasions when you have to meet a crisis or rise to some pressure at the drop of a hat.

Traveling may have to be unplanned and could cause you inconvenience. In the long run, you will benefit, but at the time you may feel put out. It is only right that you should keep on your toes. There is so much of importance going on that you must consider any opportunity will be fleeting. So look after the bread-and-butter issues of work and health.

Romantic matters could come to a head for many. As partnership may be a matter of some concern or consideration, this could be a year when you make the great decision and accept the dual role of marriage. You are likely to come to a firm decision. If you are not taking on a partner for life, you may well concentrate your attention in one direction prior to making the final move in a year or so. Things that last and are dependable mean a great deal this year. In a negative sense you may feel you are being exploited or are at the beck and call of all and sundry. This feeling should not be fostered long if you are to make full use of the experience that can come your way. It will give you an understanding of your own capacity and ability that you have not fully appreciated till now.

Until the end of the first week in March your business prospects can be blooming. Take any opportunity to increase your reputation and develop your business interests. Your business qualities are well known, so you should be right on the ball for any chance to advance with the best. Between March 8 and July 21, and again during December, you should find the financial side of business is most interesting. Profits can increase. You may have to take on added staff to manage extra business that has begun to bring in a profit. During the period between July 22 and November 29, it may pay you to operate further away from the public eye, do more private transactions or prepare for further advance. Opportunity is fleeting, so you should take advantage of these different pressures at the appropriate time if you are to make essential progress. Your tact and charm are well understood in business circles, so in the last-named period you should be able to achieve a lot of meaningful progress. Look to the future also between October 23 and 31. You may be fully extended and this could make you ambitious for more. Be on your guard against exploitation by those with whom you associate closely. You can make or mar a business project and the ball is firmly in your court. Training of others to help in your work may slow you down, but the extra effort should prove worthwhile. Slipshod management may let you down and there could be some possibility of seeking legal decisions to straighten out problems. There could be staff changes and a constant watch should be kept to maintain standards of production. You may be blessed with some exceptionally gifted staff, while others could be troublemakers. Between March 20 and April 18 is the most favorable time for dealing with influential people in the business world. Between August 22 and September 21 should be good for a publicity drive and this is when you should seek to advertise at home and overseas.

Up to about March 7 you should be able to earn good money in your everyday occupation. If you are self-employed you should improve your reputation as a reliable performer and build up your clientele. Until February 13, and between June 10 and November 11, you may find the going is hard. Your health may suffer or you could be working long hours to keep pace with developments. Extra expense can be incurred for health reasons or for some other purpose. Keep things in perspective and do not give up. But coach yourself or those who assist you, and be prepared to give and take in order to give satisfaction all around. You may need to resort to the courts to resolve some issue, but it should be worthwhile. Between February 14 and June 9 can be a heavy period when changes bring problems. Do not worry. Be practical and all will be straightened out. Your financial situation can be affected by marriage. You must be quite sure you are in a sound financial position before taking the plunge and should have no false ideas that wedding bells will give you an open checkbook. Accept the appropriate limitations of your personal needs and be prepared to share your resources with that one, whether in business or love, who agrees to become your partner. Do not risk your money on the advice of friends between March 8 and July 21 and again during December. You can do some wise saving between July 22 and November 29. Keep it under your hat. Between January 20 and February 18 to look after insurance, family savings and pension rights. Taxation problems can be worked out, also.

Treat your health with care and respect. You have a lot on your mind and will cope best only if you look after yourself. It may be appropriate to undergo some form of treatment between January 1 and February 14, and again between May 27 and December 1 which will do you good. Unorthodox methods may solve some problems. Do not be surprised if beneficial results come from healing methods not normally practiced. Emotional problems can be upsetting. Look after these and your nervous condition. Seek attention early and you will be all right. Between May 22 and July 12 you can push yourself too far and this can happen again between October 23 and 31. If you find you need expert advice, it could pay you to have a checkup between November 22 and December 20.

Traveling can give you some headaches. Between July 22 and the end of November, you could have too much on your agenda to cope and may make mistakes or just forget. Double-check all travel arrangements. Between May 22 and July 12, and also between October 23 and the end of that month, you may have to undertake unscheduled business trips. It would be wise to have a bag packed in readiness. The best period to travel seems to be between February 19 and March 19. This is a quiet time of year and you may be able to fit a well-earned vacation abroad in with your business situation. Local or home-based travel would seem to fit in best between August 22 and September 21.

Pressures of work may be wearing. You have experienced this for a year or more now and may be glad if there is some easement. You may change jobs at the drop of a hat or may find you have a great opportunity to take a promotion elsewhere. If you are just restless, try to avoid making a hasty move that will diminish your security. It could be unwise to drop tools in a temper tantrum and put your career in jeopardy. Some might get an opportunity to take their lost job back, but you cannot always expect employers to be so understanding. Until February 13, and between June 10 and November 11, you may take on more responsible work or be put in charge of some operation. There should be the appropriate financial reward and, for some, this will mean promotion. It will pay you to persevere to the bitter end because you are coming to a point where true values are important. Recognition of this is important. Sickness or other absence of management or employer could put you in a position of trust which you should not waste or abuse. Before February 14, and between May 27 and December 1, are good periods for seeking specialist employment. You should not be afraid to make a break and seek new pastures if you wish to try something different.

Romance can demand special consideration and much understanding. This is no year to toy with your fancies. Look at the overall picture and be prepared to share with the right person. Many may feel inhibited. For them more time is needed. You may be indecisive with good cause. Between March 6 and April 2 a friendship could bloom into a deeper liaison. Between May 17 and July 4 you could have your doubts. Between August 6 and September 6 you could be strongly emotional and feel this is the right time and the right partner. For many there will be a straightforward decision to make and positive action to seal the bargain. Though you may know the meaning of support and complete sharing, you are not likely to make any move that will precipitate an early acceptance of marriage. Take your time and you can make the biggest decision of your life and, as legend has it, live happily ever after.

DAILY FORECAST
January–December 1988
JANUARY

1. FRIDAY. Happy. The year gets off to quite a favorable start for you people born under the sign of Cancer. This is a good day for staying well away from the public eye. Jobs that do not require the cooperation or assistance of others will be preferable. Secrecy can be especially useful in both career and private affairs. Get your financial affairs into better order. After all your recent spending you should take account of the state of your bank balance. You will doubtless have to build up your reserves to a more reasonable and acceptable level. Romance is starred for the unattached. Try to widen your social circle in order to meet more people.

2. SATURDAY. Disquieting. Try to keep calm above all. Do not work yourself up into a nervous state. Cancer-born people who are not feeling too well should avoid overexertion. You may be feeling both physically and mentally drained after all of your recent celebrating. It would appear that the time has come to slow down the tempo of your life somewhat. You should aim to take things at a more leisurely pace than heretofore. Extra chores or tasks that are foisted on you by others may need to be put off or refused altogether. After all, why should you do other people's dirty work? Routine desk jobs will require greater attention to detail than is usually the case.

3. SUNDAY. Deceptive. The chances are you will be feeling restless. Nervous energy is likely to be high. It will be difficult for you to understand the thinking processes of other members of your family. Your partner or loved one will be acting in a mystifying way. You will most certainly find this mood and odd manner most frustrating. It would be best to go on facts, and facts alone. Do not listen to rumormongers. Spend at least some time in your own company planning business moves. You hope to make these in the future and it would not be a bad idea to get plans formulated. It should also be favorable for creative and artistic endeavors that do not require outside help.

4. MONDAY. Upsetting. You do not seem to be able to settle down into any sort of a routine pattern at your place of employment. There is a risk today of starting new business ventures off on the wrong basis. It may well be that you are trying to rush things too much. More attention to detail and overall planning is required. Go over contracts and other similar binding documents that you are required to execute with a fine-tooth comb. You may find that people with whom you have to deal today are casual and unreliable. Discussions with partners can lead to misunderstandings. Spell out what you mean clearly. Then there will be no risk of people saying they did not know what you were talking about.

5. TUESDAY. Quiet. Make this a day for gathering your thoughts together. You should slow your work down to a pace that you find manageable. Do not allow colleagues to put the pressure on you. They may try to twist your arm to act before you are ready to make your decision. Sensitivity to public needs and opinions can bring you financial gains. You should be very much in tune with what is required on the open market if you are a traveling salesperson. If you make full use of your usual tenacity and shrewdness in money matters, you may be able to make even routine affairs more profitable. Go over business-related paperwork very thoroughly. Check all accounts to make sure they are in order.

6. WEDNESDAY. Demanding. Pressure may be placed upon you to become involved in speculative moves. This is not the right day for taking any chances with your reserves. Do not allow forceful people to try to put pressure on you. They will attempt to persuade you to agree to their schemes for making money through gambling. It will not be easy for you to say no. But you will kick yourself later if you let anyone talk you into investments that you do not really believe in. Later on, you will have to be more tactful and subtle when dealing with all joint financial matters. Meantime, try to be in touch with others more experienced in business matters than you. At the same time, enjoy some leisure time away from work.

7. THURSDAY. Changeable. Extra exertion may have to be put into routine affairs that you want to clear up. You will have to push yourself quite hard if you are going to keep abreast of the

heavy schedule that you have set for yourself. You will also have
to take a firmer stand with loved ones. You cannot permit them to
burden you with personal problems while you are at the office or
factory. Your obvious determination to succeed, despite the odds,
will not go unnoticed by superiors. There will undoubtedly be bonus payments and increases in salary in the offing. Romance can
be happier and more fortunate in this new year. It will be especially so for those readers who have recently recovered from a
rather torrid love affair.

8. FRIDAY. Good.   This looks as if it will be the most exciting
day of this year for you so far. At last you will have the opportunity to push ahead with some exciting business plans. You had
been hoping and planning to put them into operation before
Christmas. Influential people will be approachable and they will be
more than willing to listen to what you have to say. Teamwork is
starred. You will find that there are extremely good vibrations between you and your co-workers at your place of employment. At
home, too, partners and loved ones will be genuinely willing to fall
in with the plans and the wishes of the Crab. Try your best to
maintain this harmony for as long as possible.

9. SATURDAY. Good.   Looking back over the past few days,
you should be fairly well pleased with the way the year has opened
up for you. Perhaps there have been one or two rough times, but
you ought to expect that. And you can be justly proud at the way
you have kept your cool. You made the right decisions when the
pressure was really placed on you. Casual acquaintances or new
contacts may be able to provide the Cancer person with useful introductions to influential people. This is an exciting day for social
interaction. Perhaps you will have the opportunity to meet people
from different walks of life. Be sure to take your loved one on your
outings. Conditions at home are as important as at work.

10. SUNDAY. Important.   All in all, it will be a pleasant and
relaxing day. Women readers should be able to get ahead with
tasks that have been postponed for one reason or another. This is
one of those Sundays when you can get your affairs in order. That
will assure that you are able to start the working week with a clean
sheet. Discuss current issues frankly and openly with other members of your family. You should be able to say what is on your
mind without fear of giving offense. Opportunities may arise for
furthering current real estate transactions. The day should be good
for completing written work. You can also take time out from necessary work to catch up on your reading.

11. MONDAY. Mixed. Thoughts may turn to the past quite a lot. You will be going down memory lane. Perhaps a friend who you have not seen for ages will get in touch with you. You will be delighted to encounter people with whom you once had a lot in common. But they seemed to have drifted out of your life in recent years, for one reason or another. This can be a somewhat nostalgic day. Things seen or heard are likely to plunge you back into your own past. But you must not allow yourself to be distracted from the type of work that you know you have to complete on schedule. This applies especially to routine desk jobs, dull though they may be. But the sooner you deal with them, the sooner you'll finish.

12. TUESDAY. Good. It will be an important day from the personal point of view. Some critical changes would appear to be taking part in your life about now. This is a starred day for setting up housekeeping with a loved one. Take the plunge and try to make a go of a new relationship if you have been living on your own for a long time. You will enjoy sharing things, not only material things but interests as well. Inventive ideas will help the Cancer worker to finish off routine jobs ahead of schedule. It will be favorable for starting a new romantic relationship with a person much older or younger than you are. You should try to get out and socialize as much as possible. It will ensure your meeting a broad range of people.

13. WEDNESDAY. Useful. Problems are likely to arise for the Cancer parent. This will be especially true for readers with children who have reached what is termed the awkward age. Teenagers will not want to listen to reason. Even if you try to be tolerant and sympathetic you will still feel that you are not getting through. Speculative ventures may require extra caution and restraint. Do not take any chances with reserves that you have so painstakingly built up. Those of you who like to play cards for money could inadvisably throw caution to the winds. That is because you get so carried away by the excitement of the game! This is unwise, and it could wreak havoc with finances.

14. THURSDAY. Good. Do what you can to be of assistance to friends who may have been having a rough time of it. Remember how you were not left high and dry when you were going through a difficult time. It is not as likely to be financial as much as moral support that will be required of you today. Influential people will undoubtedly give you the official go-ahead for jobs that require teamwork. It should be good for discussing the progress of children with their teachers. Legal decisions that are made today will probably be settled in your favor. Romance will be exciting. Sudden developments will sweep you off your feet in the area of your love life!

15. FRIDAY. Sensitive. This is not a day when you should overdo so you would be wise to take it easy. You seem to have been pushing yourself very hard recently. There are, no doubt, many matters that you want to wind up before you take a weekend break. You must not think that you can achieve the impossible, however. You will be more susceptible to mental and physical strain that usual. Minor ailments that have not bothered you for ages may recur if you do not take note of the warning signs. Tools and machinery need handling with more care than usual. Follow all safety instructions to the letter. If you decide to take shortcuts, you could suffer serious injury.

16. SATURDAY. Mixed. Some good luck may help you to get out of an extremely awkward situation. It seems that good fortune will be smiling in your direction. Some mistakes that you may have made in routine work could be spotted by an associate. It could happen just before your work gets submitted to the boss for his O.K. You will thus have good reason to be grateful to your colleague today. New offers of employment should be considered as they could turn out to be very worthwhile. Later in the day you may feel run-down and drained. It might be best not to take on too much this evening. You may prefer attending small gatherings rather than large social affairs.

17. SUNDAY. Deceptive. It will not be as easy to relax today as you would have liked. Perhaps you have been straining yourself a bit so that nervous tension will be at a high level in you. Partners and loved ones may be demanding and overly sensitive. They may not realize that you are suffering from emotional tension yourself. Try to get more rest today. Do not take on any jobs that would put you under a great deal of physical strain. The intentions of people may need some sounding out if you are to avoid the risk of deception. People and situations may not be quite what they seem. But the day is favorable for travel in the company of romantic partners. Somehow, your vibes might communicate the wrong signals.

18. MONDAY. Variable. Watch your temper first thing. You might not be in too good a mood upon waking. If you are late for the office or factory, do not blame others. You are the one guilty of oversleeping. It looks as if you will spend quite a lot of time today attempting to catch up with your schedule. You won't have much opportunity to take it easy. You must try to find out exactly where you stand in relation to colleagues and business associates. A conflict of interests could lead to loss of money and reputation. It may be necessary to issue some kind of ultimatum to keep others in line. It could take the form of overtime penalties or loss of special privileges.

19. TUESDAY. Variable. All readers should try to get ahead with their mundane chores early on this week. As the days by go you are likely to find that other situations will arise that will demand all of your time and attention. These could stop you from attending to your day-to-day duties. Do what you can to clear away obstacles that have been preventing you from making greater gains in partnership ventures. Perhaps a frank talk with other interested participants may help you to clear the air. Extra exertion put into routine jobs can bring you excellent bonus payments. These may come just at the time when you could do with some extra cash. If this does materialize, try not to spend it at all once.

20. WEDNESDAY. Good. This should be an excellent midweek day. You will feel more confident than usual. This is a super period for Cancers who are scheduled for auditions or interviews for jobs. People who are involved in the world of show business may get the feeling that their career is taking off. They are being brought to the attention of people who matter in this world of theater at last. The day will be favorable for doing some background research in connection with routine business transactions. Professional people will be helpful with the advice that they have to offer. Tax rebates may come in and help to swell mutual resources. If the sum is large, investigate high-interest funds.

21. THURSDAY. Sensitive. You should be feeling a lot more optimistic about what the future holds for you and yours now. The feeling derives from the events of the previous few days. Loved ones will also be equally cheerful. It should be possible to reach an agreement as to the best way to put more cash to one side. Savings that you make now can be plowed into investments that earn you good interest. Self-improvement and study efforts will progress without too many hitches. You are not likely to be interrupted if you have to work alone. But it is important that you avoid uttering harsh words in a moment of passion. People's feelings are easily hurt. Furthermore, you cannot retract what has been spoken.

22. FRIDAY. Variable. Plans for the future can be drawn up. You should be thinking and planning ahead. Readers who earn their livings through self-employment in any of its many forms should try to make more use of any good contacts they have. Do not take quite such a live-for-the-moment attitude. This is a good day for travel and for doing business with people who are at a distance or come from a distance. Even wishful thinking may have its proper place in your life. Cancer people have it in their power to make what they want to happen come true. Later in the day there are likely to be moments of depression and self-doubt. Try to think about all the work you have done that turned out well.

23. SATURDAY. Sensitive. Sports people among you should take things easily. If you are involved in a dangerous outdoor activity, you should be even more aware of the danger of accidents. This is not a time when you can afford to take any silly risks. Influential people can be of assistance to the Crab in both their career as well as in public affairs. Social introductions that are arranged for you could be extremely helpful. Readers who have only recently started work with a new company should be feeling pretty happy with the way things have gone so far. Legal matters will require careful attention. Try hard to finish work deadlines so you can rest up and relax with a clear conscience tomorrow.

24. SUNDAY. Lucky. All in all this will be a happy and relatively carefree day. There is not likely to be any great friction between you and other members of the household. Luck may come to Cancer people through career or business affairs. Other people may surprise you with their kindness and their generosity. It should be favorable for reading books and pamphlets that can be helpful to running financial affairs in connection with your partner. You may pick up useful tips on economizing. Outings should leave the Cancer woman in a cheerful and optimistic mood. Children can add much to the spontaneous fun of family groups. Their outlook on life can add new perspectives.

25. MONDAY. Mixed. It might be a little difficult for you to get back into the swing of things today. You should not attempt to expand as fast as you have been doing recently in business affairs. Finances require careful handling and conserving. Do not push more capital into ventures that have not, as yet, shown a profit. The advice of people in authority may not be wholly reliable. Do not follow others if you would end up being the one who took the blame for the decisions that they had made. But bright or imaginative ideas of colleagues may help reduce unnecessary overheads and increase real earnings. Romance would seem to have a pretty good chance of blossoming.

26. TUESDAY. Productive. Do not allow yourself to be swayed by friends when it comes to investing capital. Listen to the advice of professional people like your bank manager and your accountant. Even if the profits from their schemes are not quite as high, at least they should be fairly secure. You may find routine jobs a bit of a drag, but you should try to carry them out with diligence. You do not want to do anything to upset your boss who seems to have been pretty fair with you of late. Speaking to large groups of people may fail to win their support or their goodwill. A secret wish or dream may move nearer to fulfillment. Do not confide in anyone or the secret may be one no more.

27. WEDNESDAY. Difficult. The morning is an inauspicious time for the signing of any contracts or documents related to money. Avoid committing yourself to large financial expenditures. This is going to be a difficult day to balance the books. Do not try to get any new projects started. You appear to have your hands fairly full now with what is already under way. Cancer-born people will live to rue the day if they take on any new commitments at this delicate stage. Partnership affairs are best kept confidential. Do not pay too much attention to rumor or gossip that is being spread about a close friend. It is not likely to be based on fact.

28. THURSDAY. Mixed. The first month of the year is coming to an end. You should try to take advantage of any lulls today to bring your affairs for this period up to date. There may even be one or two thank-you letters left that you should have written. People may have sent you Christmas presents from distant places. Do not lose touch with old friends. Even if you do not get an opportunity to see as much of them as you used to, you can write. It should be good for getting influential people on a more informal level. Cancers may be able to catch them with their defenses down, and favors granted could well be the happy result. Try to socialize as much as possible and make good contacts.

29. FRIDAY. Uncertain. Concentrate on details connected with background affairs. This is a lucky day for Cancers who are able to operate from a position behind the scenes. See what you can arrange at secret meetings. Plans for the future can be organized. You should be able to find ways to cut out unnecessary waste and expenditure. Favors may be granted or money received from anonymous benefactors. But as the day progresses, there may be some dispiriting developments. Health needs protecting. Wrap yourself up at the first sign of a chill or a cold. Drivers must be more careful as road conditions could be hazardous.

30. SATURDAY. Deceptive. Cancer-born people need to be clearer in their own minds about their true wishes and priorities. Perhaps you have been deluding yourself. Do not get involved in any new close personal relationship. It would only complicate your life more than you could imagine. Do not do anything that would hurt loved ones. There is a risk of self-deception. You could easily be taken in by glamorous people or deceptive situations. Charitable and compassionate urges are likely to be strong. But the Crab may have neither the means nor the ability to be of any real assistance. Compassion and kind words are often better than nothing.

31. SUNDAY. Changeable. The month ends and the new week begins. But you will have quite a few important matters to straighten out before you can make any new starts. It is vital that you do not allow your personal life to become too complicated. Otherwise it will start to affect your career performance. This is a favorable day for travel. You certainly won't be too happy if you are stuck in one place all the time. Visit a loved one whom you have not seen for ages. You do not have to stay long, but they would certainly appreciate a chance to get caught up on news from you. Reading and academic pursuits can bring great pleasure. Appointments or commitments made last week should not be forgotten, even if they are a bit inconvenient.

FEBRUARY

1. MONDAY. Disquieting. There are likely to be problems that you had not anticipated would crop up today. You might not be able to get to your place of employment on time. Problems of loved ones that you thought you had solved successfully may require your immediate attention. But personal plans can be furthered for readers who do not have to attend regular places of employment. Pet schemes that you have been keeping to yourself can now be implemented. Influential people will be less concerned about Cancer people's well-being than they pretend. Keep this in mind if you have any reason to need their help with a business venture. They may pull out the rug from under you.

2. TUESDAY. Disturbing. A telephone call or a message that you receive could send you into a flap. Money that you sent off some time ago may not have arrived as it should have. Deliveries of important goods and produce could have been delayed. This is one of those aggravating days when you will find you have to round up associates or others whom you have paid to do a service. You will have difficulty in controlling your temper with people who you consider to be incompetent. The temptation to invest money in untried schemes can be especially great. Cancer people should place more faith in their own shrewdness and financial astuteness. Their assessment of a proposed investment can be as good as another's.

3. WEDNESDAY. Fair. You do not appear to have gotten off to a very good start so far this month. Problems that you have had to cope with from the past may have been the reason. They could have hindered you from making the progress that you had been hoping for. Still and all, there is no good moaning about the past. This is one of those days when you should shrug your shoulders and turn to new schemes. If your old ones seem to be faltering, don't waste more time on them. Routine business, or career and public transactions can be made more lucrative. It could possibly be done without any direct action on the part of the Cancer person. Short trips and outings may be unnecessarily expensive.

4. THURSDAY. Good. It looks as if this will be the best day of the month so far. You will find it easier to cope with your regular duties. You will have the opportunity to win the support of an important person. Simply show whoever it is that you are reliable and hard-working. Cancers who have anything to do with advertising or public relations should get out and about. They must try to meet people who can be useful and helpful. It will also be an important day for contacting casual acquaintances because they may be able to provide valuable information. In addition, it should be good for more involvement in community and neighborhood affairs. There is almost always great need for support from individuals who are genuinely interested.

5. FRIDAY. Disturbing. Cancer-born people may feel like hiding away in their shells today. You will have problems when it comes to communication. It will not be easy to express yourself. This is one of those days when your character is likely to be tested to the fullest. You will not have a great deal of energy at your disposal. This will be a tiring day in many ways. You will find that any sort of routine work that you have to attend to will be particularly draining. Don't run around more than is absolutely necessary. Try to conserve your energy. Cancer drivers need to be even more careful than usual when they are behind the wheel. Speeding can lead to accidents.

6. SATURDAY. Disturbing. You do not seem to have gotten off to the start that you had been hoping for this month. More haste would certainly mean less speed today, despite all efforts. There is no good trying to rush in order to catch up with your chores. You had better look critically at the jobs that you still have to attend to. Then decide which ones should be given priority. You will require a definite plan of action if you hope to succeed. You cannot allow things to drift. Nothing should be left to chance where money is concerned. Short trips and errands can prove to be ineffective. Letters or telephone calls to romantic partners can be misinterpreted, giving rise to ill-feelings.

7. SUNDAY. Deceptive. You may be looking back over the week that has just come to a close with dismay. You are wondering where you made a mistake. You must not blame yourself totally for all of the problems that cropped up. These occurred in your personal as well as in your public life. Try to be more logical and less emotional. It would be a good idea to stay away from people who have a depressing influence over you on occasions. Family and household members may be devious and indirect. Suspicions of dishonesty among such people may turn out to be fully justified. There is a risk of deception that is hard to dispel. Homes may need to be tidied up and some extra cleaning done.

8. MONDAY. Variable. An early start is required. You must get your priorities right. Get yourself involved in jobs where deadlines have to be met. Do all that you can to make the right impression on influential people. They could turn out to be very important to your future career plans. You will have to be more direct in your approach to your job. Don't sit on the fence. Once you have decided what you want out of life, you must let no one and nothing stand in your way. It should be a favorable climate for property and joint financial agreements. Relatives can be helpful to domestic and career affairs. But romance can cause quarrels. This will be a sensitive area of your life so try to be patient and understanding.

9. TUESDAY. Disquieting. It may be that you are in need of more rest. The chances are you have been living off nervous energy for all too long. Readers who have the opportunity to work in solitude should be able to make some quite good progress. This is a better day for relying on yourself than on others. Nevertheless, less exertion put into teamwork endeavors may provide consistently good results. It should be a favorable period for devoting more time to hobbies. Be sure that you fill in your leisure hours in a meaningful way. Romance contains the risk of temporary or even permanent separation and estrangements. Try to avoid possible confrontations. Any other action is preferable to that.

10. WEDNESDAY. Variable. Romance appears to be very much on your mind. Many of your hopes and dreams in connection with your love life appear to be in shatters after the events of the past few days. The strange thing for Cancers is that they are likely to be feeling relief now that a relationship has at least been straightened out. You cannot have been feeling happy about much that has been taking place in your personal life over the past few weeks. Matters are now likely to be brought to a head. Be yourself and speak your mind. Bankers and other influential people can be contrary and unhelpful. It may be good for gathering information that would not readily come to hand. If you are familiar with good, reliable sources, see what you can ascertain.

11. THURSDAY. Good. The Crab should be feeling much happier about the future now. It looks as if the breaks are about to go your way at last. Influential people whom you have been trying to track down for some time will become available. Appointments for meetings can be made that should turn out to be most constructive. You might be able to raise cash to back a project. It is one that you have been keen to get off the ground for some time. Today contains excellent opportunities for mixing work and pleasure. New romantic attractions can be formed through routine employment affairs. There will be greater interest shown in you by members of the opposite sex. If you feel attracted to someone, show your feelings clearly.

12. FRIDAY. Variable. Don't make too many demands on your boss. This is not the right day for asking for time off to attend to personal matters. Nor is it wise to expect any other special favor, for that matter. The atmosphere at your place of employment will be extremely sensitive. Be careful what you say to people who are not known for their sense of humor. Also absent is their ability to take a joke against themselves. But good work carried out in the past can, at last, bring the much awaited promotions or appointments. Nothing should be done to ruffle employers. Unconventional actions would be best avoided. All in all, it is a day recommended for sticking to the straight and narrow.

13. SATURDAY. Variable. This will not be a particularly important ending to the week. It looks as if a good deal of your time will be spent rounding off routine affairs. Loved ones will be helpful and will show more understanding than usual. You will probably not be able to give quite as much time to your personal affairs as you usually try to do on Saturdays. You might have to make some unexpected short trip. But this is not likely to take you very long or interfere with your plans. Regular jobs may contain some radical new developments, or indications of such in the near future. Influential people can be energetically helpful. Take advantage of any offers you may get.

14. SUNDAY. Good. This should be a terrific start to the week. Aches, pains, and any other minor ailments that have been troubling you will be much easier to deal with. Some light exercise and more attention to your diet would not go amiss. Make sure that you are getting all of the vitamins that your mind and your body require. This will be a favorable time for giving loved ones a special treat. Extra effort should be made to entertain them. Cheer them up if they have been getting a little depressed of late. Later on, Cancer people should have some free spare time to devote to their own hobbies and creative endeavors. Don't overlook your need to be creative and to get away from the daily grind.

15. MONDAY. Variable. Don't allow yourself to become too pessimistic if you do not achieve all of your aims and ambitions today. You may be aiming a little too high. Try to persuade influential people to grant you small favors. But wait to propose your larger projects until the atmosphere is wholly conducive. There is a risk for people born under the sign of the Crab of committing perjury without even realizing it. The consequences can be severe. Business colleagues may be unreliable, and let Cancer-born people down. It might be good for dealing with large companies or corporations. Be wary in your approach and ready to retreat if the atmosphere does not seem receptive.

16. TUESDAY. Fair. The day will be favorable for readers who are in a line of business which requires them to deal with property or money matters on behalf of others. You will find that you have the opportunity to make more use of your natural talents in your line of work. Influential people are likely to be very pleased with your efforts. You might get an increase in salary or a bonus payment. But loved ones may deplete marital funds through spending on luxury articles. They are also capable of being extravagant generally. It should be good for shopping expeditions and for stocking up on basic necessities. Be on the lookout for special bargains that can save you money.

17. WEDNESDAY. Fair. Don't allow yourself to get too down-in-the-mouth. Although you may not have made a lot of progress with important career matters so far this year, nothing appears to have gone dramatically wrong either. Just keep on plugging away. The best way to impress your boss is to show that you have tons of determination and enthusiasm. It's a good day for making new business investments. Older professional people may be able to direct some good tips your way. Cancer employees may receive opportunities for more favorable and lucrative employment. In-laws can be helpful. You will get on better with relatives with whom you have not always seen eye-to-eye.

18. THURSDAY. Good. A first-class day would appear to lie ahead for you. As long as you do not take too many chances with your career all will be well. Loved ones will be backing you to the hilt. You may have serious doubts or uncertainties about the best way to turn. If so, it would be a good idea to discuss such matters with your mate or partner. People who have your best interests at heart will not let you down. It will be favorable for all creative and artistic ventures, as well as study and academic endeavors. People who are at a distance, or have come from one, can be particularly helpful. Do not be backward in accepting their advice and then acting upon it.

19. FRIDAY. Variable. Don't push yourself too hard today. In your eagerness to consolidate gains that you have recently made you might be biting off more than you can chew. Self-improvement endeavors, in particular, may contain a risk of mental or physical overstrain. Cancer-born people should not try to make their progress too rapid. Business colleagues will not be very helpful. They may even interfere with routine transactions. They could do this by introducing unnecessary changes into regular procedures. But influential people will be on hand to offer sound advice. What is more, they could give you outright assistance.

20. SATURDAY. Good. The week comes to an end on a high note. You will have an excellent opportunity to clinch a deal that you have been working on painstakingly for the greater part of the last six days. You will have better chances to influence people who are in a position to offer you financial backing. It will be an excellent period for attending important social functions where you will have an opportunity to mix business with pleasure. It will pay you to use more adaptability and flexibility in the running of routine and business affairs. It should be favorable for taking loved ones on any outings or trips that you are invited to. Partnership financial problems will be easier to solve than has been true.

21. SUNDAY. Good. Coupled with what took place yesterday, this should turn out to be one of your most contented weekends ever! It will surely be true of those you have spent so far this year.

Cancer parents should have the opportunity to get closer to loved ones. It will be possible for you to share important experiences with members of the younger generation. They naturally mean a great deal to you and you will welcome the chance. Good names can be made even better and reputations improved. This can occur without any overt effort on the part of Cancer people themselves. Extra overtime can be put into furthering routine work affairs. These can play an important role in your overall scheme.

22. MONDAY. Variable. You may be feeling a little tired and worn out today. It is understandable after what appears to have been a pretty hectic weekend. This is a favorable day for more involvement on your part in humanitarian or alttuistic projects. Add to those all schemes that are aimed at making the world a better place in which to live. You will be happier if you can spend more time on what means a lot to you. It will help compensate for dealing with regular routine affairs that are surely bread-and-butter-jobs. Friendship activities can interfere with romance. The financial advice of friends could prove to be disastrous and should not be followed. Don't take risks that you cannot afford.

23. TUESDAY. Disturbing. Emotions may be bubbling very near to the surface. You will be unusually vulnerable to criticism, even if it is offered in an effort to help rather than hinder. Problems of a personal nature must not be allowed to affect your work performance. Don't try to attend to routine affairs in fits and starts. Steady effort is the answer to bringing Cancers nearer to the realization of secret hopes and dreams. But it is best not to look for immediately tangible results as this will only lead to disappointment. Accidents or injuries incurred by loved ones may incapacitate them for awhile. This could prove a heavy burden for you if you have to take a hand in their care.

24. WEDNESDAY. Variable. A fairly run-of-the-mill midweek day will arrive. You are not likely to be asked to put yourself out in any particularly annoying way. But Cancer men and women should be rather skeptical about the propositions that are made by influential people. Distant government or custom officials may be difficult to get in touch with. This will probably cause frustration or impatience. Later in the day will be the most favorable time for carrying out all secret transactions. It will also be best for attempting to sign confidential agreements. Even so, you may find that others who had previously agreed are now balking. This could cease further delays and disagreements.

25. THURSDAY. Good. After a topsy-turvy few days, you should discover that you are back on the right track. Thinking will be a good deal more straightforward where financial matters are concerned. Go over old problems. You may come up with some interesting and novel solutions that had not crossed your mind before. You should be able to give more time to accounts and to routine matters. You might not otherwise get such an opportunity to concentrate on these areas and get caught up before you take a weekend break. It will be a good time for secret and clandestine romantic affairs. Try to get away from familiar haunts and gain new perspectives.

26. FRIDAY. Variable. Cancer-born people will probably not be in a particularly good position today. Winning the goodwill and support of others will not come about easily, perhaps not at all. This is not the best of days to try to have any special favors granted. The more that you can rely on yourself the better it will be. Don't attempt to get new creative projects off the ground. There are likely to be better opportunities tomorrow for doing that. On the other hand you should not put up with unfair emotional demands made on you by others. Be yourself and live according to your own standards and beliefs. It you try to adapt yours to suit another, you will fail miserably.

27. SATURDAY. Good. This should be a favorable day for all forms of self-expression. Do not stifle your natural talents. You should give more time to artistic jobs. The creative urge in you is likely to be particularly strong today. Loved ones will be easier to get along with and will be very much on your wavelength. Cancers must not allow themselves to become the underdogs during the coming few weeks. Stand up for what you believe to be right. No matter what kind of pressures are placed upon you, do what you know is right. If you make your views and interests known to others in unmistakable terms today, it will help you avoid clashes in the future. Others will respect your opinions.

28. SUNDAY. Disquieting. This may be a rather difficult day for you. There are quite likely to be a number of new pressures placed upon you. They may be aimed at limiting your authority and frustrating you. Dear ones, especially older relatives, may be expecting the Cancer-born person to spend more time in their company. If you have to attend very formal occasions, you must be much more careful than usual. You must not get a reputation for irresponsible behavior or excessive disregard for convention. Doing what you want, and trying to get your own way, could be dangerous. You must ensure that you are not endangering your own long-term interests at the same time. Don't wage personal quarrels or vendettas.

29. MONDAY. Variable. Influential people such as employers and superiors are likely to take a greater interest in the personal futures of Cancer men and women. You will find that your boss is more sympathetic to your problems at home. You might find it reassuring that people who you only know on a professional level feel concern for your happiness and your well-being. You may feel that you can confide some of your personal feelings in someone who obviously wants you to be happy. Government and public officials will be more lenient over points of law. It is possible that they may even bend the rules slightly. Later in the day warns against any form of speculation or gambling.

MARCH

1. TUESDAY. Good. You should be feeling a good deal more confident about yourself this first day of the month. You will have much more energy than usual. This will make you keen to grab any chances that come your way to increase your income. Means of getting out of your present economic problems are likely to present themselves. In all likelihood, these will entail your taking on additional workloads. But your are not likely to mind this because you will be keen to protect the welfare of your loved ones and yourself. Other people may have a tendency to be thrifty one moment and extravagant the next. This could create financial problems which will need straightening out.

2. WEDNESDAY. Good. Today should be favorable for furthering your moneymaking endeavors. This could result through employment or some other means. The best time for giving more attention to family matters will come later on in the day. Give your beloved a special treat if you have been paying quite a lot of attention to outside affairs of late. Shrewdness can be an invaluable asset. You should keep your wits about you today. There could be unexpected opportunities to add to your income through some form of speculation. Negotiations that have been dragging on for some time can be settled in your favor in a spectacular way. Knowing a person's character will be helpful in deciding what move you should make next. Be aware of his or her reaction.

3. THURSDAY. Disquieting. Provide yourself with more protection against minor ailments. At the first sign of a chill or a cough you should take steps to reinforce your physical defenses. It might be a good idea to pay a visit to your doctor if you feel you have a slight fever. It is a more favorable day for mental work than it is for dealing with heavy-duty jobs. These would definitely take a lot out of you physically. Writing projects that force you to make more use of your imagination can be taken a stage further. Cancer people can be especially accurate in their assessment of public opinion. This gives you a big advantage over so-called rivals when making important decisions involving the public.

4. FRIDAY. Disquieting. Influential people will not be as helpful as you might have hoped. This is not a very good day for winning financial backing from people in authority. You will be disappointed if you were hoping to get an artistic project off the ground. You cannot do so without the help of other people's money. The more you realize that you should rely on yourself the better it will be. Loans that have been offered to you will have too many strings attached to make them lucrative. Domestic pressure on you will also be increased. Your loved ones expect you to give more time to their needs and desires. This will create a situation both awkward and difficult for you. Use great tact to keep peace.

5. SATURDAY. Deceptive. After getting off to a flying start this month, you are likely to be feeling somewhat disappointed by now. You find that you have not made all the progress you had been hoping for. This is quite likely to be due more to the unreliability of others than to any failure on your part. Cancer people may find themselves suddenly confronted with unexpected jobs to handle. Influential people may change workloads around at the last moment. It would be advisable to take no one and nothing for granted today. Mistakes that you make may require you to do finished work all over again. This is such an obvious waste of time that you should be sure not to let it happen to you.

6. SUNDAY. Good. Don't overdramatize family problems. This is an important day for discussions with loved ones about finances. But it is essential to build up mutual trust. To do so, you must maintain a more realistic sense of proportion. It will be a favorable day for buying and selling antiques. It should also be good for seeing older relatives. If you have not paid a visit to your parents recently, you should try to find time today to visit with them and exchange news. This can be an exciting day for romance. Social activities can lead to new attractions being formed. Get out and about as much as possible. Try to meet as many people as you can in social surroundings.

7. MONDAY. Variable. Domestic problems may be more pressing than you realize. Do not ignore the demands of loved ones. There will be serious arguments if you do not pull your weight on the domestic front. Don't make jokes on subjects that might be rather sensitive for your mate or partner. Words spoken in jest could easily be taken the wrong way. You may even have to put career affairs to one side for the time being. It might take more time and thought to deal with the situation at home than you had realized. New and original ideas can lend fresh inspiration to creative and artistic enterprises. Romance can bring about practical benefits, but is not likely to be particularly exciting.

8. TUESDAY. Fair. Conserve your energy. Do not push yourself too hard. You may be trying to achieve too much too quickly. The Cancer native should try to conserve his or her energy. Physical and mental responses may be noticeably slower than usual. As the day goes on you will find it becomes increasingly difficult for you to maintain a fast pace. Perhaps it would be a good idea to delegate some of your lesser responsibilities so that you can concentrate on priorities. Try to put some time to one side for complete rest and relaxation. It will be favorable for attempts to obtain extra leave from superiors. However, keep your request within reasonable bounds so as not to cause resentment.

9. WEDNESDAY. Quiet. This rather slow-moving day is likely to be just what the doctor ordered. You will have an opportunity to catch up with your backlog of work, both business and personal. People will not be as pushy as usual. Go over accounts. Try to work out a budget that will enable you to put more of your take-home pay to one side. This will not be a particularly active period from the point of view of getting new projects launched. Cancer people may decide to fill in their spare time with some exercise. You may involve yourself in a sporting activity which helps to tone your muscles. This is an important factor in maintaining good health and should not be neglected.

10. THURSDAY. Quiet. This could turn out to be a rather boring day. You must not allow restless impulses to permit you to gamble or to fritter your cash away in unnecessary spending. Do all that you can to keep extravagance on a tight rein. You should find that you have more freedom of choice in deciding how you wish to spend your time. It will be best to concentrate on routine work and occupational activities. Use any spare time that you have to catch up on your backlogs. If you have recently started a diet to lose weight, you are going to have to be strict with yourself. The temptations to break it will be great. Make up your mind right at the start to stick to the regimen faithfully.

11. FRIDAY. Fair. Cancer-born people will be fairly astute. If anyone tries to put a fast one over on you, it is quite likely to backfire on the doer. You will not have too much trouble in judging people's characters. Partnership finances should be given special attention. Discuss outstanding points with colleagues or loved ones. Do what you can to help dispel dangerous illusions that others may be harboring. It should be a favorable day for dealing with the legal side of speculative matters. Get official contracts drawn up so that you are covered where and when it counts. The evening can bring you some special surprises. Romance is likely to be in the air. This will be a good time for an affair.

12. SATURDAY. Deceptive. Watch your step today. You seem to be in a generous sort of a mood. Do not part with cash too easily. Do not lend money to associates who live by their wits. It would be advisable for you not to get involved in any form of speculation. There is a risk of some confusion, and even deception, in legal affairs. Make sure that you are represented by people who should know what they are talking about when it comes to straightening out contracts. But the day can be happy for romance and socializing. Visiting mutual friends together with loved ones would be a particularly good idea. Make plans for some kind of entertainment later on. You might want to party with friends.

13. SUNDAY. Good. This will turn out to be an extremely important day. You will be able to take a breather. There will be good opportunities to look at career problems with a more dispassionate eye. Loved ones will not be as pushy as they are sometimes. You will be able to fill in your leisure time as you see fit. Nor will you have to give in so much to the will of others. Close acquaintances may provide the Crab with useful introductions to people in positions of authority. They will, in all probability, be experts in their field. You may be able to obtain some useful advice without having to pay for it. But do not give the impression that you are interested only in picking their brains.

14. MONDAY. Disquieting. You will not be in the mood to deal with routine affairs today. You would much prefer to have the opportunity to attend to jobs that give free rein to your artistic talents. However, this is one of those tricky periods. You will not have quite so much choice as you would like over your work situation. Influential people will be fairly adamant about what course you follow. Partnership and matrimonial finances can give rise to disputes. However, there is almost nothing that subtlety and tact will not smooth over. But the key lies in the ability of both people being willing to concede points.

15. TUESDAY. Good. It looks as though you are in for a favorable period. Make sure that you do all within your power to cash in on the excellent opportunities that will present themselves to you. These will undoubtedly help you to make progress in your private as well as in your public life. There is not apt to be any conflict between domestic affairs and your work. It should be a good day for attempts to get older people at your place of employment to fall in with your ideas for modernization. You should be able to streamline the way you handle routine chores. Friendships may turn into romances. But don't rush into a hasty partnership that might prove disastrous.

16. WEDNESDAY. Good. Partners and loved ones will be instrumental in bringing about the realization of secret hopes and dreams. This is quite likely to be an inspirational day from many angles. Some news that comes through first thing will probably give your confidence a boost. Business or marital partners are apt to be accurate in their predications and almost prophetic. Their intuitions are more likely than not to be sound. Loved ones can be of particular assistance to Cancer people in their self-improvement and study endeavors. This is a good time for buying articles made or prepared in distant places. But you should seek the out-of-the-way shops that specialize in foreign imports.

17. THURSDAY. Fair. Don't allow the narrow-mindedness of other people to get you down. Rise above petty, emotional, and minor differences and make a resolution not to be affected by them in the future. You will have to take more responsibility for the decisions that you make. Do not allow people to boss you around. It is about time that you stood up for your rights. Cancer men and women may have more control over their futures than they realize. Positive thinking and actions are essential for you. Otherwise, you are not going to prove to superiors that your desire for promotion should be taken seriously. Romantic partners can be something of a handful. You may have to talk very firmly.

18. FRIDAY. Deceptive. Don't allow yourself to be swayed by glib-talking people. You must not get involved in any schemes in which you would be expected to put up a great deal of the capital. Get-rich-quick projects are not likely to bring you in the profits that are undoubtedly being promised. Keep your thinking practical and rooted in reality. Daydreaming would only leave you wide open to exploitation and deception. Efforts at consolidating partnership and teamwork endeavors will help to boost profits from cooperative business dealings. Try to wind up all your outstanding accounts at work before the weekend. You should try to get some rest and relaxation then.

19. SATURDAY. Quiet. You will be grateful that you can take things a little easier on this last day of the week. It looks as if you will have quite a lot of routine matters to attend to in any case. Come to grips with desk jobs and pay any outstanding bills. Do what you can to ensure that you will have maximum time to enjoy your leisure all day tomorrow. All in all, this will be an undemanding period. This will allow Cancer people to enjoy more freedom for implementing their own ideas and following their own whims. But it is important to pay more attention to public opinion and convention in this world. The impression made on others can ultimately affect whether or not personal desires are attained.

20. SUNDAY. Fair. The morning period is a pleasant time for get-togethers with friends. They may have recently arrived in the country or will shortly be leaving to work abroad. In many ways, this will be a rather emotional period. You may be saying goodbye to an old pal whom you have known for many years. It is hard to say when you will be seeing this friend again so there will probably be a lump in your throat. Discussions about the future with loved ones will be fruitful. This will be especially true if you are trying to find ways to solve financial problems. Later on in the day you are likely to be disappointed in romance. This could stem from a recent clash with your special date.

21. MONDAY. Variable. More attention should be paid to your physical condition. You need to get yourself in better shape. Otherwise, you will not be able to maintain a high output at your place of employment. Paying attention to health problems is a sound investment. It could save you a lot of money. Do not try to cram too much activity into your working hours. This can be a fruitful day as long as you get your priorities right. This is a favorable period for putting more energy into joint cooperative ventures. Cancer people will receive more than adequate returns for the exertion they put in. It should be good for tackling legal problems head-on. Whatever is wrong should be corrected.

22. TUESDAY. Variable. Maintain a low profile today. This is not one of those days when the Cancer native should attempt to grab the limelight. But it is an excellent day for partnership affairs. Let people who you are in business with do most of the talking. It would seem that your most important job today would be to ferret around in the background. Look for facts that would serve to back up your argument. It will be good for contacting people who wield influence and power. Valuable business cooperation can be obtained. But don't take too much for granted. Influential people can tend to hold Cancer people to legal obligations at the cost of severe penalties if they overstep the mark.

23. WEDNESDAY. Excellent. It should be one of the best days that you have experienced this month, if not this year. This is a very important day for your career. Do all that you can to make a success of employment affairs. Approach influential people who have given you backing in the past. You can afford to be just a little more pushy. It looks as if a secret dream or ambition can move a step nearer to fruition. You will find it easier to see eye-to-eye with people in authority. This is also a favorable day for spending some of your leisure time in solitude. You will find it easier to work out problems that have been aggravating you on your own in quiet meditation.

24. THURSDAY. Variable. Cancer-born people are advised to tread very carefully when attending to all marital and partnership affairs. Your opposite number is likely to be in a sensitive mood. Do not ask your nearest and dearest to make sacrifices that you might not be willing to consider making yourself. Perhaps you have been a little too extravagant of late and should consider drawing in your horns. A foot wrong on the domestic front could lead to quarrels and even walkouts. Friends will be generous and timely with the assistance that they offer. But influential people are unlikely to show any interest in your personal problems. Turn to close family and relatives if matters do not improve.

25. FRIDAY. Deceptive. Keep your opinions to yourself. You could easily get into arguments with people who know a little more about the subject under discussion than you do. You could even lose your temper because you feel that someone is making a fool of you. Actually, it is really only your own ignorance that is showing you up. You will learn more by keeping your mouth shut and listening to what other people have to say. Cancer people who dabble in intrigue and behind-the-scenes maneuvering may find it is they themselves who are being deceived. Don't try to be so clever that you end up outsmarting yourself. This can happen so quickly that your head will spin.

26. SATURDAY. Variable. The problems that you have to face today are likely to be personal. Current partnership or romantic situations may tie Cancer-born people down. You could find that you spend rather more time dealing with domestic issues than you had hoped. You might not be able to accept all of the social invitations that are offered to you. There will be resentment felt which could severely strain close relationships. You may feel that unnecessary restraints are being put upon you. Spouses may become jealous of the amount of time you spend with friends. It will be a happier day for casual than for serious relationships.

27. SUNDAY. Variable. Spending must be kept in check. You appear to be in one of those moods today when you could easily throw caution to the winds. You must bear the future in mind. There will be one or two hefty bills coming up at the end of the first quarter of the year. You must make provision for these as there will be no grace period. There is a risk of self-indulgence that could cause more than mere financial suffering! Even though it is a Sunday, it is possible to come to some important business arrangements with people in authority. It will be more favorable for romance than for marital affairs. You may recently have met someone special, so put aside some time for getting better acquainted.

28. MONDAY. Quiet. There is not likely to be a great deal of action during the day. In fact, during the morning period you could find yourself hard pushed to find enough jobs that will keep you meaningfully occupied. This is one of those days when you will not feel in a particularly pushy mood. It would be easy for you to spend this day doing virtually nothing. But Cancer people should not waste opportunities for attending to practicalities, especially those of a financial nature. Go over accounts. There are plenty of desk jobs that you can turn your hand to with good effect. Routine affairs can be made more lucrative through economizing here and there. The same amount of money can be made to go further.

29. TUESDAY. Good. This is sure to an enjoyable day. Problems that have been worrying you for some time will be easier to straighten out. You should be able to track down important people with whom you wish to have serious talks. They have proved to be irritatingly elusive of late. The day is favorable for getting out and about. You will find that there is plenty to keep you enjoyably occupied away from your home base. A change of company can have a surprisingly good effect on the Crab! Casual acquaintances will have the ability to boost your confidence. Unexpected marriage proposals can be received. These will tend to make former uncertain people come to a decision.

30. WEDNESDAY. Variable. Relatives and neighbors will be especially understanding and sympathetic. Cancer people may find their true friends where they least expect to. People who live in your community will be willing to help you. They will stand in for you and take care of your family and your domestic duties in emergencies. Important appointments may force you to remain away from your home base. It will be a favorable time for taking loved ones on outings. Try to get close to children. Cancer parents should make more of an effort to bridge the generation gap. Influential people could withdraw their support without any good reason being given.

31. THURSDAY. Variable. Communicating with people at or from a distance can lead to misunderstandings. What is worse, they will be hard to resolve. You must be careful that you do not jump to the wrong conclusions. You may misunderstand what someone says over the telephone or in a letter he or she writes to you. It would be wise to save your judgment of the motives until you can have a chat with this person on a one-to-one basis, in person. Life may become so confused that important advance planning becomes virtually impossible. It will be favorable for travel undertaken in the company of partners or loved ones. Casual romantic involvements should work out better than expected.

APRIL

1. FRIDAY. Disturbing. You may find that additional responsibilities are forced upon you when you least want them.

Influential people may require you to step in for associates who are on vacation or are sick. It may well have been that you were hoping for more spare time to attend to home and family affairs. Loved ones will be overly demanding. Your mate or partner may feel that you are not pulling your weight at home. Property transactions may be subject to annoying and continuous delays. Attempts to bring outstanding affairs to a close may be spoiled by the incompetence of others. You may have to find someone else to work with so you can get rid of this irritating situation.

2. SATURDAY. Disturbing. You do not appear to have gotten off to a very good start for the month ahead. In fact, it seems that you are bogging down on these first two days. The bottleneck was caused by problems that you should have straightened out before last month came to a close. Problems connected with your working life, as well as with your home life, will be difficult to resolve. It would not be a good idea to mix business with pleasure. Cancer career people may be forced to refuse favorable business offers and opportunities. The reasons will be tied to domestic duties and other obligations. This is not a particularly good day for carrying out home entertaining.

3. SUNDAY. Variable. This will be an important day for routine matters. Although you may have to push yourself quite hard, this is the right time to attend to desk jobs and other paperwork. You have been putting off this chore too long. Pay up outstanding bills that you should have settled last month. Go over your personal accounts carefully. Try to get all of your financial affairs into better order. Some attention to income tax matters would not go amiss. Confrontations and arguments with loved ones would appear to be unavoidable. It is an important day for Cancer-born people to stand up for their rights. They must let people close to them know exactly where they stand.

4. MONDAY. Variable. This is not a good day to gamble. The Crab is well advised not to commit himself to speculative activities. Stick to regular ways of earning your livelihood. Do not allow yourself to be influenced by associates who have wild ideas. Keep a check on the impulsive side of your nature. Don't get involved in any deals that you may wish to withdraw from in the cold light of day. Deep feelings of anger or resentment may come to the surface between lovers. These will have to be dealt with at once if current involvements are to have any future. The day should be favorable for artistic and creative endeavors. These must not be allowed to interfere with your regular duties, however.

5. TUESDAY. Variable. It would appear that you have not been able to make a very stimulating start. Many of your original ideas that you had hoped to put into action have stalled. It may be that there was a lukewarm response by the people from whom you had hoped to get financial backing. More care is needed in the handling of routine business transactions. It would be best not to commit yourself too far into the future. Don't pick up your pen to sign any agreements without careful review first. It is essential to ensure that there are no available loopholes for others who might decide to break their word. Later in the day can be exciting and happy for romance.

6. WEDNESDAY. Quiet. This will be a slow-moving and fairly run-of-the-mill day, on the whole. You probably will not be able to get any new profit-making transactions off the ground, however. But you will discover that this is an important day for putting your affairs into better order. You will be pleased to have more time to attend to small jobs. And you will have time to bring correspondence under control. You will be able to determine for yourself the pace at which you handle routine matters. Concentrate on what would appear to others to be relatively trivial affairs. This will at least help you to make your life run more smoothly. It will also allow you to devote full attention to business affairs.

7. THURSDAY. Quiet. This should be another easygoing day for you. In all likelihood, you will be particularly grateful for it. You will have plenty of time to attend to any little jobs that have been piling up. This is the right day to have in-depth discussions with members of your family to try to find ways to put more cash to one side. You and your mate or partner are likely to find that you are on an acceptable wavelength. This has not been the case for some time past. Pay more attention to matters connected with your health. Some Cancer-born people may be feeling somewhat below par. They should consider special dieting programs.

8. FRIDAY. Deceptive. Teamwork and partnership commitments can impose extra restrictions upon you. There may be jobs that you were hoping to handle alone today. The main problem is that you will not have the opportunities to operate in solitude that you were hoping for. Close associates are likely to get on your nerves. The health problems of loved ones may be the cause of some anxiety for you. But friends who live nearby will be especially helpful. The people who live in your locality will be prepared to run errands for you. Some will offer to stand in for you if you are not able to deal with matters of great urgency yourself.

9. SATURDAY. Disturbing. You could easily misjudge the motives of others. People with whom you have to do business should be given the opportunity to explain their ideas fully. You seem to be in an impetuous mood. It makes you unwilling to listen to younger associates who may have some excellent ideas for change and progress. But, to be fair, you must give them half a chance to propose them. The Crab may have trouble meeting the demands of those who wield influence and authority. A basic difference in viewpoints may seem to be irreconcilable. But clashes with the authorities should be avoided, if this is at all possible. Be more conciliatory and less opinionated.

10. SUNDAY. Variable. Try to steer clear of legal problems and complications. You are probably worried about many matters connected with your career. But you must give yourself a break and try to put these worries aside today. Devote some portion of the day to yourself. This will enable you to get the rest and the relaxation that your mind and your body require for keeping healthy. Partnership financial affairs will be rather sensitive. It would be in your best interests to try to work out a budget in which all of the family can participate. It will be favorable for clandestine romantic affairs. Be on guard against letting your secret out by mistake. It could lead to trouble.

11. MONDAY. Important. Push yourself much harder than usual. You will be able to make a good impression on the authorities. Now is the time to try to promote your original ideas for increasing profits. You must get them accepted by people who are in a position to back you. Do not bother with subordinates. Go right to the top management. This is a propitious day for travel. Trips to meet important people in other towns or cities are likely to work out successfully for you. The day will also be favorable for attending to matters connected with insurance and taxation. And it will be good for discussions with bankers and other people who can pull strings in the financial world.

12. TUESDAY. Good. This should be an excellent follow-up day. You can afford to be more pushy. Associates will show a greater willingness to follow any lead that you give. Now is the time to do what you can to obtain the professional advice of experts in connection with legal problems. The solutions may be surprisingly simple. After all the worry and anxiety you appear to have been going through, you find you were doing so in vain. Friends who live at a distance may put in an unexpected, but most welcome, appearance. You may be reunited with a person whom you have not seen for ages. Any entertainment plans that you get involved in this evening are likely to work out most successfully.

13. WEDNESDAY. Quiet. You must not allow feelings of frustration to get the better of you. This will be a slow-moving day when you should pay a good deal more attention to detail. There will be a temporary lifting of financial pressure. You should find it easier to concentrate for longer periods on desk jobs. You have to handle these on your own and in your own way. Cancer people should try to rise above their immediate circumstances. They must look at things from a broader and more all-inclusive perspective. This is a good day for future planning. It should be favorable for all attempts at self-betterment and broadening horizons.

14. THURSDAY. Variable. You Cancer business and career people may not realize that the time to remain sitting on the fence is past. But attempts to commit yourselves to action may be thwarted. It might be best to operate from a position in the background. Certainly the fewer people who know what you are aiming to achieve, the better will be your chances for success. Partners and colleagues can be unpredictable. Their actions may be the cause of some anxiety for the Crab. Later in the day is good for dealing with troublemakers at your place of employment. But act now before you lose control.

15. FRIDAY. Good. If you go with your intuition, it will not play you false. This is probably the best day of the year for acting on hunches. It should be favorable for attempts at furthering routine business and public affairs. And transactions that are already in the pipeline can be made more lucrative. But the Crab is advised not to look for quick results. Some degree of blind faith may be necessary for the time being. Homelife is not likely to pose any new problems for you. Later in the day will be good for the signing of important agreements or contracts. Try to finish up as much of the week's work as you can today. It will give you a better chance of enjoying the weekend.

16. SATURDAY. Good. This will be a happy ending to the week. You should be feeling a good deal more confident about what the future holds for you. Your relationships with people who hold positions of influence and power should be very much improved. You should have had the opportunity to show off your talents in the latter half of the week that is about to come to a close. It should be favorable for beginning or planning for the start of a new cycle of business activities. You will be able to improve your reputation in your chosen field of endeavor. Friendship, as well as social activities will be starred. Enjoy yourself today.

17. SUNDAY. Disquieting. Restlessness is likely to overtake you on this weekend. It would seem that you are creating quite a few problems for yourself. Try to seek out the company of people who are easygoing and relaxing. You will not like it if any pressure is placed upon you. Friends and close acquaintances may prove to be more of a burden than an asset. Social commitments may interfere with your romantic plans. Do not accept invitations that would require you to do a great deal of traveling. You will be happier if you stick to familiar surroundings. Cancer-born parents should pay more attention to the desires of their children. They may feel that they are being left out in the cold, otherwise.

18. MONDAY. Disquieting. Odd jobs that you did not get around to tackling over the weekend can be completed with a minimum of disruption to your schedule. This is a favorable day for paying more attention to the detailed ins and outs of business affairs. Cancer people will be in a more logical frame of mind which should be a big help. Your judgment of the best way to tackle financial problems could be right on target and meet with the approval of other interested parties. Careful planning can help you to reduce overheads and increase profits in real terms. Spare time can be spent pleasantly in the company of close friends and associates.

19. TUESDAY. Good. Cancers may find it particularly easy to sway people by appealing to their emotions. Your charm and your ability to weigh up situations very quickly will stand you in good stead today. Go with your intuition because it will not play you false. Once you have decided on a definite course of action you should stick to your guns. You are more than likely to be proved right in the long run. You will probably be feeling in better health than has been the case for some time past. Your powers of observation should be used to the full. Influential people are certain to favor you. New contracts can be won if you play your cards right.

20. WEDNESDAY. Good. You will be feeling much more confident about the future today. Lucrative contracts are likely to be dangled before you. This is also an excellent day for attending to any jobs that can be handled in solitude. This will apply especially if you work from within the confines of your own four walls. You may be in a more reflective and meditative mood. Today should be favorable for secret trysting and romances. Compassionate urges are likely to be stronger than ever. You will find it easier to see aspects of your day-to-day living which you may fail to notice as a rule. Meetings with influential people can produce important results for the future.

21. THURSDAY. Variable. This is a favorable day for secret business transactions. Cancer-born men and women appear to be going through a lucky stretch at the moment. Secret hopes and wishes are likely to move a step nearer to realization. New business ventures that you have recently embarked upon are likely to begin to show a profit now. Partners may not now be so confused within themselves as had been the case. It will be easier to get agreements with other members of the family on the best way to tackle day-to-day domestic problems. Practical assistance from your mate or partner is sure to be forthcoming. The evening favors a search for pleasurable pursuits.

22. FRIDAY. Good. The chances are, this has been a highly successful week right from the start. This Friday sees you in a very happy position. You are going to be able to put the finishing touches to a deal that you have been moving carefully toward closing over the last two or three days. Try to tie influential people down to a definite course of action. Contracts should be signed. It would not appear to be a good idea to hold out for better terms. That which is being offered now is not likely to be improved upon in the near future. Lack of overt enthusiasm on the parts of associates does not mean that they are not interested in the personal schemes of Cancer people.

23. SATURDAY. Disturbing. People are likely to let you down today. This will be a difficult period for getting all of your plans off the ground. An important relationship may not be working out as you had hoped. This is not a day for going chasing after someone who appears to have cooled in his or her feelings toward you. You may be forced to part ways with influential people over important financial issues. People may be trying to get you to agree to terms that you consider to be most unfair. If you feel you are being exploited, it is important for you to keep your dignity and your integrity intact. Do not stoop to their level to fight back.

24. SUNDAY. Variable. Gambling urges need to be kept under control. There is always a risk of Cancer-born people pushing their luck too far. Do not take any risks with the money that you have had to struggle hard to put to one side. Friends can be infuriatingly careless with the property of other people, Cancers included. Romance may put you to considerable expense. Even then, it might not work out according to your hopes. Disagreements can lead to arguments over joint spending and marital funds. Thinking can be original and inspired when attending to artistic hobbies. Later in the day is more favorable for love and all other matters of the heart.

25. MONDAY. Fair. It is important that you keep a very tight rein on the financial situation. Be firm with extravagant loved ones. They probably want to splurge indiscriminately on clothes or unnecessary luxury household articles. Some scrutiny will also be required at your place of employment. Cancer employers must make sure that waste is cut back. Keep an eye on younger members of your work force. Be constantly on the lookout for ways to make extra savings. Discussions on the subject of business finances will leave you feeling more confident and cheerful. Youngsters may require some disciplining. Much depends on their ages and their companions.

26. TUESDAY. Variable. Casual acquaintances who you have known for some time could turn into close friends. You might find yourself involved in in-depth conversation with a person with whom you have only exchanged pleasantries, to date. It should be good for getting on more friendly terms with your boss. This would also be true for any other influential people who could help you to get on in your career. Business and pleasure will mix together rather well. But thinking can be faulty where taxation is concerned. It is important not to jump to conclusions. Seek professional advice where it may be necessary or even just helpful.

27. WEDNESDAY. Variable. Short trips can be especially effective today. In addition, the mail and the telephone can also produce good results. But you may find that it is important for you to see one or two business associates face to face. Money could be the subject to be discussed. It may be possible to increase your earnings. This is a good day for the writers and artists among you. It should be good for Cancers who earn their livings by working on a commission basis. It will be favorable for mental endeavors. You should not have quite so much difficulty as you have been encountering of late in attending to desk jobs.

28. THURSDAY. Disquieting. Cancer-born people will have to make a special effort today; that is, if they want to preserve their much loved desire for peace and security. People may call in on you uninvited. It will be difficult to refuse friends admission to your home when they are standing on your doorstep. Your privacy will be easily invaded. Unexplained developments on the property market may require the postponement of some lucrative real estate transactions that you were hoping to wind up. Profits are likely to be less than you expected from affairs connected with the land and its products.

29. FRIDAY. Deceptive. This will be an extremely sensitive day. It would be all too easy for you to jump to the wrong conclusions. Give associates, especially younger associates, better opportunities to air their views. You could learn quite a lot from younger colleagues. But you should listen in full to their ideas for streamlining output. Family and household members can create unnecessary confusion by not being willing to tell the truth. You may wonder what games your nearest and dearest are playing. The more that you can rely on yourself within your own four walls, the better it will be. This will be especially true where money matters are concerned. There is a risk of deception in buying or selling valuable antiques.

30. SATURDAY. Good. The week and the month come to an end with you feeling full of optimism and bounce. Some speculative scheme that you made an investment in some time ago may now pay off at last. It looks as if you should be able to balance the books. It will be easier for you to settle outstanding bills that may have been weighing rather heavily on your mind. The morning will be an especially happy time. Small incidents can bring back happy childhood memories. The search for pleasure can be rewarded in unexpected ways. Chance meetings can lead to new romantic attractions. Brief vacations will bring you pleasure. You will enjoy not only a change of scenery, but also of your routine and of faces.

MAY

1. SUNDAY. Disturbing. A somewhat worrying start to the week and the month would appear to be in store for the Crab. This will be a difficult day for planning ahead. It is not going to be an easy matter to get loved ones to agree with any plans that you come up with for making additional savings. Children will be a source of problems and trouble for the Cancer parent. You will have special reason to be disturbed by youngsters who are of school age. Pleasure plans are likely to run into opposition from your mate or partner. Don't go along with the entertainment plans of friends. What they are likely to suggest in the way of having a good time could lead you into a good deal of trouble.

2. MONDAY. Fair. You will be somewhat relieved that the weekend is over. Put much more effort into matters connected with your career. By dogged determination you may be able to win the support of people who are in a position to offer you financial backing. Make sure that loved ones do not bother you with matters connected with your personal life while you are at the office or doing other work. Business financial negotiations with people at a distance may prove to be rather unproductive. Cancer-born people must avoid being forced into compromise solutions. These would undoubtedly cause regrets later. Romantic plans or entertainment may have to be postponed.

3. TUESDAY. Quiet. This is not a good day for speculation or gambling. In fact, you would be wise not to take any risks at all with your hard-earned savings. Stick to routine matters as much as you possibly can. This may not be a particularly stimulating day either. But you will be able to get on top of any chores that are left over from the month just past. It will be a good day for furthering occupational affairs. Superiors will be impressed by your ability to stick to the task at hand. Not only that, but you also see it through to a satisfactory conclusion. Steady and persistent effort will be more effective than short bursts or intense activity.

4. WEDNESDAY. Good. Don't overstrain yourself unnecessarily. You can save yourself quite a lot of trouble this midweek day. Do this by sitting down first thing and working out a schedule that is manageable. For those of you holding positions of superiority, it will be favorable for straightening out labor problems. This is an important day for finding out what makes people tick. Dig beneath the surface. Try to discover the underlying reasons why colleagues react as they do. Research and deliberate investigation are likely to produce first-class results. Closer analysis of current business transactions can reveal ways of increasing profitability.

5. THURSDAY. Disquieting. You may not be feeling up to par physically. Perhaps you should embark on a new diet or some sort of exercises course. It is important that you treat your mate or partner with greater sensitivity. Cancer men and women need to tread much more carefully in matrimonial and partnership affairs. A wrong word or unjust criticism could easily rub your opposite number the wrong way. Spouses and associates can demand freedom and security at the same time. Such conflicting demands make the Crab unsure of how to meet them. The outcome of legal proceedings in which you may be involved cannot be predicted with any certainty.

6. FRIDAY. Good.   This will probably be the best day of the month so far. Much of your old confidence and drive will be returning now. This is also an important period for the house-proud Cancer. You will enjoy puttering around your home. There will be a chance to straighten domestic problems that you have had to put to one side lately. These were caused by external pressures. Your relationship with your beloved will be very much improved. Joint decisions connected with domestic affairs will be a good deal easier to make. The morning is a starred period for all cooperative endeavors. Later in the day, social contacts may provide valuable introductions to influential people.

7. SATURDAY. Good.   Today will bring a happy ending to the week. You may have had good reason to be concerned when this month and this week got under way. But many of your earlier problems are likely to be forgotten in the elation that you are feeling now. Business and pleasure can be mixed in a most satisfactory way. It should be favorable for all attempts at providing economic security for yourself and for your dependents. Today is good for handling matters connected with pension and retirement schemes. Cancer people, whose job it is to handle property or money on behalf of others, can make such transactions more profitable.

8. SUNDAY. Disturbing.   You may have to be rather stricter with offspring than you really like to be. You will be disappointed with those youngsters who seem to you to be lacking in self-discipline. There could well be flare-ups within the home. But you will still feel that it is necessary for you to speak your piece. In fact, you may well feel that it is your duty to do so. Pleasure plans may well have to be canceled or postponed because of the lack of available cash. Creative endeavors will be frustrating and may not provide you with the results that you had been hoping for. Friends may be imperious and selfish in unexpected ways.

9. MONDAY. Good.   Count on a super start to the working week. After a rather nightmarish Sunday, you will be pleased that you have this unexpected boon. Take the opportunity to throw yourself into your career wholeheartedly. Influential people will admire your inventiveness and will encourage you to go further.

You will be pleased that there will not be very many restrictions placed upon you. Your imaginative ideas will be augmented by the advice you receive. It will come from people with power and professional expertise. You will be able to obtain a good deal by employing subtlety and charm. It should be favorable for confidential financial dealings. This can be an exciting day for Cancers.

10. TUESDAY. Fair. Some disturbing news may be received first thing. But you must not resort to panic measures. Check all the facts for yourself to make sure they are correct before you take any action. That could wrongly change the direction that you are going in. It would be best to meet professional people face-to-face. Trying to obtain advice from them over the telephone or through writing letters is not advisable. Cancer people may have to show a greater willingness to break their ties connected with the past. Openness to change can be an invitation to greater fulfillment. This could be a favorable time for finalizing vacation plans.

11. WEDNESDAY. Disturbing. This will be somewhat of a disturbing day. You will find it very difficult to settle down and concentrate on the job in hand. You may find that you are hard-pushed to attend to the simplest of routine tasks. It might even be necessary to put in overtime without much chance of earning extra money. There are likely to be quite a few interruptions to your schedule. Perhaps you will have to attend to personal affairs during office or factory hours. Loved ones and romantic companions can have a negative influence. They might even try to put a damper on the aspirations of the Crab. Physical separation from dear ones can cause longing and sadness.

12. THURSDAY. Deceptive. Be very careful that you do not jump to the wrong conclusions today. Cancer people are likely to be overemotional and sensitive. Do not bread off a long-standing romantic involvement. It would be a mistake just because of the fact you could be temporarily unsure of your feelings. Give emotional wounds more time to heal. Your judgment can be detrimentally impaired. This could have a possible adverse effect upon your professional reputation. Business competitors may even resort to deception or double-dealing in order to score points over you. But the day is favorable for confidential negotiations with trusted people. Try to concentrate on this positive aspect.

13. FRIDAY. Good. There is no need to feel superstitious about this particular Friday! In fact, this is likely to be a somewhat lucky day for people born under the sign of Cancer. You should be able to make good progress in areas where you have come to a dead stop of late. This is a favorable time for taking the initiative in business and career affairs. It should also be good for attempts to obtain contracts from large firms. Those of you who are attempting to drum up business should be particularly successful. Loved ones will be wielding their influence in peculiar ways. This will actually work to your advantage.

14. SATURDAY. Fair. Organizing and participating actively in charity events should prove satisfying and worthwhile. You will have the opportunity to be of assistance to people who are far less fortunate than yourself. You ought to be able to handle matters connected with your regular job first thing. That will ensure leaving yourself to your own devices for the remainder of the day. Cancer-born people can play an especially important part in humanitarian and altruistic ventures. Imaginative projects and bright ideas may help to boost business profits. But such profits will only be on a small scale.

15. SUNDAY. Variable. Friends and acquaintances are likely to be putting pressure on you to act according to their whims and fancies. It is important that you do not allow close associates to dictate terms to you today. It is also important that on your day of rest you do your own thing. You will want to get more rest this weekend day. Relax and unwind frayed nerves. You will not get much satisfaction from making long journeys just to seek pleasure and entertainment. Keep your spending within reasonable limits. Cancers must not allow themselves to be taken advantage of or exploited in any way. Just stand your ground.

16. MONDAY. Quiet. Joint finances are likely to be under review. You may be able to straighten out sensitive monetary problems. These erupted between you and your spouse or partner over the weekend. This will be a good day for having important discussions about the future. Members of your family will be more likely to see reason and less likely to lose their tempers. Attend to minor matters. You can clear the decks so that it will be possible to make new starts later in the week. Spare time should be used for meditation and contemplation. More privacy and seclusion will help you to clear your mind of trivial matters.

17. TUESDAY. Variable. The more that you can operate from a position in the background, the more it is likely to be to your advantage. You will be able to learn from the mistakes made by impetuous colleagues. For some reason, they seem to be only too willing to put themselves on the firing line. Loved ones will offer you good advice about the best way to handle career matters. It would be a good time for secret discussions with older relatives. Cancer people are likely to reach a closer understanding with them. Chewing over new ideas before you act upon them is a wise policy. But watch your step with superiors. They may be overly domineering. Their pride could be injured if they feel rejected.

18. WEDNESDAY. Variable. This appears to be something of a marking-time period. Some of you may be finishing off jobs and waiting for instructions from people in authority as to when to make new starts. Perhaps you will have the opportunity to spend more time dealing with personal issues. Whatever you do today, it is important that you keep yourself meaningfully occupied. Spending for pleasure must be kept to a minimum. A tactful and tasteful gesture can win the hearts of loved ones. Old flames may reappear in the lives of Cancer men and women. But attempts to further personal schemes are not likely to meet with cooperation.

19. THURSDAY. Good. The breakthrough that you have been waiting for is likely to come your way today. You can move forward smoothly and efficiently. People in whom you have confidence will encourage you to go further. Secret hopes and wishes in connection with your personal life and your career can be taken a stage further. You will have much more driving force at your disposal. Good luck may come to you in a roundabout way. It could possibly be the result of activities of your friends and acquaintances. New business financial opportunities that present themselves to you deserve more attention than you may have thought. They are quite likely to prove themselves worthwhile.

20. FRIDAY. Good. Another first-class day for people born under the sign of Cancer has arrived. People in positions of authority will be far more approachable. Influential associates may make moves on their own initiative to improve your financial situation. Any extra cash that comes in should be plowed into savings funds. Important contacts that you have in high places would be best approached on an informal basis. It should be appropriate for contacting people who hold the strings and wield the real authority behind the scenes. Taking out a club membership or joining a society is recommended. Fund-raising tasks will boost your morale.

21. SATURDAY. Disquieting. This is a problematical day. You may not be able to carry out the plans that you had made. It would be a good idea not to make definite decisions. People in positions of power may be wavering and changing their minds, and this could affect your own activities. Cancer people must try to cut back on their spending. You will be more disposed than usual to excess and extravagance in money matters. Your usual common sense in such affairs is likely to desert you. Expenditure could easily outweigh income unless you are prepared to tread a good deal more cautiously. Romance may be marred by anxieties.

22. SUNDAY. Good.   A restful day would appear to be in store for you. This does not mean to say that you will be in for a boring or monotonous Sunday; far from it. Secret errands and confidential trips can bring financial gain. Any meetings you may have with influential people might produce backing for your artistic endeavors. You may be able to achieve a secret dream, or at any rate, move a good deal closer to its fulfillment. New romantic attractions will be more easily formed. They may result in especially compatible partnerships. If you feel great attraction for some special person, be sure to take some initiative.

23. MONDAY. Variable.   Self-improvement and study endeavors look very favorable. This is a good period for readers who are able to work on their own. Those Cancers who do not have to move very far from familiar surroundings should be especially delighted. Later in the day you will find it is better for getting out and about. Meeting people who can be of assistance is a worthwhile project in itself. And you are not likely to have to make any long trips in order to achieve this. Neighbors can be helpful in lots of little ways. The day should be favorable for entering into new partnership agreements. Cancers will consider these as insurance.

24. TUESDAY. Excellent.   This can be a very important day for making decisions. You will decide what course of action you should take in a particular area of your life. Heretofore, you have been dithering, unable to choose. It will be easier for you to make important decisions about the future. This will be true because of the wholehearted support that you get from influential people. Casual acquaintances or contacts can be especially kind and helpful. Advertising drives and publicity compaigns may produce very good results. They could easily lead to an immediate increase in profits. Cancers enjoy helping others less fortunate than they are.

25. WEDNESDAY. Disturbing.   Do not try to speed through work that requires special attention to detail. Superiors will be putting more emphasis on the results that you achieve than you might imagine. You must try to find ways to direct more imagination toward tasks that have become commonplace and mundane. If you take a couldn't-care-less attitude, you could easily find yourself out of a job. Do not act in an impulsive manner either. Take time to consider all aspects of any problem. Do not listen to so-called friends who live by their wits. Cancer workers must make an extra effort to keep their minds on the job in hand.

26. THURSDAY. Deceptive. Don't allow yourself to be duped into buying things from door-to-door salespeople. If they do not have I.D.s and carry definite guarantees you could be gypped. Or you could easily fall for the confidence trick. It would be easy to be tricked into buying things that look more valuable than they turn out to be. You will have to show more care with what you sign. Do not enter into any long-term contracts or obligations without seeking the advice of influential people. Attempts to bring outstanding affairs to a satisfactory conclusion can be thwarted by incompetence and inefficiency on the part of others. So-called hunches and intuitions are likely to be proved false.

27. FRIDAY. Variable. This is a good day for visiting parents and for reestablishing past ties. Do not lose touch with people who once meant a great deal to you. Trips are likely to work out better than you would have anticipated. Friends will be helpful. Some good advice is likely to be forthcoming from colleagues who are older and more experienced than you are. Do not go rushing into making new investments without giving the matter a good deal more thought and consideration. Thinking is likely to be strongly nostalgic. Memories will bring you happiness. But present-day romantic relationships will be going through a period of strain.

28. SATURDAY. Good. A new love affair could well begin on this last day of the week. Someone whom you have known quite well for a long period of time may suddenly appear in quite a different light to you. Long-term relationships will be going through something of an upheaval. Although you might find this state of affairs rather emotionally upsetting, things are likely to work out for the best in the long run. You may be getting involved with a person a good deal older or younger than you are. It will be favorable for distant travel especially if you do so for holidays or vacations. The day should be good for all artistic and creative endeavors. Provide pleasure and entertainment for others.

29. SUNDAY. Disquieting. Friends and acquaintances may make untimely appearances. These could interfere with your plans for pleasure and romance. Readers who have recently taken new lovers will not be very delighted to see close associates today. You may not have wanted to introduce your new boy or girlfriend to your special circle at this early date. You may find it rather embarrassing to have to be dealing with people who come from very different areas of your life. Gambling urges will have to be kept under control. The results are likely to be disastrous if you go in for speculation. Children can behave thoughtlessly and do themselves harm. They need constant supervision and guidance.

30. MONDAY. Disquieting. This will be a difficult period for concentrating on your work. You seem to have a number of personal problems on your mind for which there is no ready-made solution. Influential people will not be very helpful or understanding. For those of you who have no steady employment at the moment the future may look rather depressing. However, you must continue to be optimistic and look on the brighter side of things. It is not going to be easy to keep your emotions in check. The best period of the day will be the early-morning period. If you have a number of routine matters that you wish to get rid of, that will be the time to act.

31. TUESDAY. Disturbing. Influential people, such as employers and superiors, will be unhelpful and uncooperative. This is not the right day to apply for a salary increase. Nor would it be wise to talk about some improvement in your present status. Even if you have been planning to bring this subject up at the end of this current month, do not do so. The atmosphere is not right for discussing your future with your boss. People in positions of power may seem to have little interest in your future well-being. But ill feelings and resentment will get you nowhere. There is no knowing what strains those who have authority over you may be undergoing themselves at this particular time.

JUNE

1. WEDNESDAY. Disturbing. One of the most worrisome problems for you today will be your lack of energy. It will be difficult for you to concentrate for very long spells on the tasks that have been assigned to you. This will be a testing period when it comes to handling routine affairs. You do not want to do anything that would upset your boss. Partners and colleagues will be behaving erratically. They may possibly make major moves without consulting you. Be alive to the danger of accidents. Electrical and other machinery may be left around where it could cause injury. Too much running around may be to no avail. It will also be mentally and physically tiring. Get to bed at a reasonable hour.

2. THURSDAY. Deceptive. Be more honest with yourself. Go over the financial situation. You may find that you have been overspending. Do not blame other members of the family for the sorry state of your finances. If you have not been making any cutbacks yourself, what do you expect? You cannot demand that others make sacrifices unless you are prepared to show the way yourself. There is more room for self-deception in the lives of the Cancer native. Do not allow so-called friends to influence the way you handle your reserves. Wishful thinking may blind you to the faults of others which is bound to cause disappointment sometimes.

3. FRIDAY. Quiet. This will be just the sort of day that you require to gather your senses before the weekend. There will also be an opportunity to get finished with odd jobs. You should have tidied these up before May came to a close. It will be a helpful day for attending to legal matters. Get your accounts in order. Meetings with accountants will go off better than you had imagined. You may find that you can claim more against income tax expenses than you thought you would be able to. Publicity matters can be dealt with. Cancers who have to deal with members of the press should discover that they are able to do so tactfully. Any spare time that you have on your hands should be given over to assisting partners or other loved ones.

4. SATURDAY. Fair. Joint financial matters will be rather sensitive. There would seem to be even greater urgency in making cutbacks in unnecessary expenditures. Go over any budgets that have recently been drawn up. With the help of other loved ones you will surely find areas where costs can be drastically reduced. If others who are involved continue to be extravagant, it may be necessary for you to take some firm action to stop funds from being further depleted. You might not get as much pleasure as you hoped from attending parties and other gatherings. Don't travel too far out of familiar territory seeking pleasure.

5. SUNDAY. Good. It should be possible to have things go your own way today, by and large. Use the subtle approach to win around loved ones who may have been opposing your plans for having a good time. It should not be necessary to spend a great deal of money. There are ways to get the very best that the day has to offer. Any spare time you may have on your hands can be put to good use. Become involved with your hobbies again. They serve to bring you satisfaction and take your mind off problems of the work-a-day week. It's a favorable day for secret trysting and clandestine love affairs. Romance looks as if it will go all-out for those readers who have recently found themselves new partners.

6. MONDAY. Fair.   Once you have gotten over the Monday morning blues feeling,this will be quite a successful day. You will have to drive yourself on in the early morning period, however. At first, you will probably find it fairly difficult to accept the orders you are given by superiors. But it would be unwise to argue with the voice of authority at this point. No matter how much in the right you may think that you are, just remember you are not the boss. Forward-looking Cancers can be accurate in their predictions. This automatically makes it a good day for future planning. Professional experts will help to clear up any legal confusion which may have arisen recently.

7. TUESDAY. Variable.   There will be opportunities for making progress today. But you must grab them pretty quickly as they are not likely to offer themselves to you a second time. It should be a good day for business expansion schemes. Cancer bosses would be wise to listen to the new ideas that are suggested by younger members of the firm. The forward-looking and original approach is what is needed today. Those of you who are thinking in terms of expanding present business arrangements may be able to set up new branches in distant places. You should get help in choosing sites and availability of workers. Acquiring specialist skills through training programs can boost business profits.

8. WEDNESDAY. Deceptive.   Cancer people will have to be more realistic in conducting their business, career, and public affairs. You want to be a little more careful about whom you trust. Some of the new information that is passed on to you should be checked out. Make sure that it is correct and not accepted blindly. People whom you thought you could trust may not be acting with your best interests at heart. Reputations must not be endangered by leaving documents that have been put in your trust lying about where all can see them. There may be certain difficulties to overcome within the home. Cancer parents may be worried about youngsters mixing with people of dubious backgrounds.

9. THURSDAY. Good. Some exciting news is likely to reach you through the mail or over the telephone today. You may be told that you are the person who has been accepted for a new and exciting job. Or it could be that you are paid for a part-time job that you completed some time ago. There is just one thing that you have to be careful of and that is giving in to extravagant impulses. You must be sure that you put a fair portion of any extra cash that comes in to one side. Behind-the-scenes maneuvering can be helpful for furthering career and business activities. Influential people in the background may show a greater willingness to give you a helping hand. It will be favorable for romantic involvements.

10. FRIDAY. Variable. Compassionate and charitable urges are likely to be stronger than ever. You will have the opportunity to lend a helping hand to someone for whom you feel very much sympathy. It will be a pleasure to you to give some definite assistance to a friend. This person has been going through a very difficult period of late. Your mate or partner will be helpful too. He or she will show a greater understanding of what you are trying to achieve on behalf of others. Cancer people may realize the advantage of joining forces and combining their efforts with like-minded people. Group activities can conflict with romance.

11. SATURDAY. Good. All the pointers are that you have an excellent weekend in store for you. It is important, however, not to make decisions too fast about how your leisure time should best be spent. This is especially applicable to this Saturday. You are likely to have one or two offers to attend social gatherings. Do not accept two invitations for the same time or get yourself in the bad books of any of your friends by letting them down. This will be a cheerful and happy period for you and yours. Close friends may give Cancer men and women plenty of cause for being optimistic about the future. It should be an excellent day for readers who have to address large groups of people.

12. SUNDAY. Good. Coupled with what took place yesterday, you will be well pleased with the way things shape up for you and your nearest and dearest. Although this is a Sunday, there may well be possibilities of encountering colleagues with whom you can do a bit of business. Social occasions could lead to useful new contacts being made. You can then get in touch with these people in the days ahead during office or other business hours. People or events behind the scenes may be operating strongly in favor of Cancer men and women. Charm and flattery are more than likely to achieve their aim. This will be true even though the results may not be immediately visible.

13. MONDAY. Disturbing. One of the main problems for you today is that you may feel let down by others. The more you can rely on yourself, the better it will be. Even forward-looking Cancer people are likely to find themselves inhibited or tied down by their own pasts. You will have certain duties and obligations to fulfill that you could well do without. It may be necessary to spend some time with older relatives. But your feeling is that you would much rather be attending to career matters. It will be particularly difficult to break with well-established habits. The actions of people at a distance will be enough to arouse suspicion in you.

14. TUESDAY. Variable. Travel is not likely to produce very good results. Make sure that appointments you made before the weekend are still in effect before you start out on your appointed journeys. This is a good day for buying gifts and other surprises for dear ones. You may be able to make up a fight with a romantic partner by arranging a special surprise for him or her this evening. Cancer-born people need to pay particular attention to timing. Impatience to get new schemes off the ground could produce results opposite to those intended. A couple of days' wait could change the situation drastically. Routine work affairs might entail your taking on extra responsibilities.

15. WEDNESDAY. Deceptive. This day will not be as straightforward as it may first appear to be. There will be a number of problems that you will not be immediately aware of. One golden rule you would be wise to remember at all times will apply. It is to be totally honest and forthright in all of your business dealings. People will realize it if you attempt to put a fast one over on them. There is a danger of misplacing love or loyalties. Cancers' intuitive discernment can desert them. Go on facts and facts alone this midweek day. People may require excessive sacrifices or compromises on the part of Cancer men or women.

16. THURSDAY. Good. This should be a much better day in many respects. You might at last be able to make a start with an important project. It is one that you have had to postpone, for one reason or another, far too many times. You will feel more in charge of yourself and your own destiny now. This is an excellent period for submitting your original business ideas for acceptance by influential people. In many ways, this could be the day that you have been waiting for. Personal plans can be activated with the minimum amount of opposition. Ideas for new opportunities can be received from friends and these should be given attention.

17. FRIDAY. Disquieting. Perhaps this will be a somewhat anti-climactic day. Although nothing in particular is likely to go wrong, you may have been expecting to wind up one or two important business agreements. You would doubtless then see an immediate profit for your efforts. The important thing about today is not to push too hard too quickly. Influential people will not be rushed into signing important and long-lasting contracts. Slow down the tempo of your life. Try to straighten out important accounts and paperwork. Write any letters that you wish people to receive before or immediately after the weekend. This may be the right time for implementing some definite budgeting and savings plans.

18. SATURDAY. Good. It would appear that you will end the week feeling a lot more confident than you did when it began. You may not have achieved all of your dreams and ambitions. But even so, you should have gone a long way toward making some important starts. This is a favorable time for secret financial transactions. Money can be made quickly and without too much fuss or bother. Cancer men and women will have a way of winning loved ones over to their way of thinking more successfully than usual. This is especially true where money and other practical matters are concerned. It will be a good day for buying special gifts for romantic companions. It will be the little things that count for most today.

19. SUNDAY. Good. This will be a pleasant and easygoing Sunday. You should be able to pretty well please yourself as to how you spend your leisure time. Loved ones will be concerned with your well-being and happiness. Influential people may be prepared to meet you on a purely informal basis. This would be an important day to have superiors over to your house. In that way, you can get to know them a great deal better. You should have no reason to feel insecure about your future career prospects. It would seem that you will be branching out in a new and exciting direction fairly soon. Enjoy a get-together with friends.

20. MONDAY. Variable. Romantic affairs are likely to cause disagreements and even arguments. You will find that it would be best to keep your business affairs and your personal life entirely separate. Keep them as far removed, one from the other, as you possibly can. Do not allow your mate or partner to get in touch with you at your place of business. If it is sometimes absolutely essential, make the contact brief. It is important that you prove to superiors how keen you are to make a big success of projects that are currently under way. It should be a favorable day for mental endeavors, especially the kind that require you to use your imagination. It will also be good for all creative and artistic work.

21. TUESDAY. Variable. Today is favorable for signing business agreements. Readers who have recently been offered new contracts should accept them. It would not seem to be a good idea to hold out any longer. If you were hoping that more favorable terms would be offered, this is not likely to be the case. It would be in your best interests to become more of a realist. With the present hard, economic times, you must do all that you can to protect the future for you and yours. Try to put more cash aside if you are hoping to take a more exotic vacation than usual this year. Putting in more overtime to increase your income is a good way. Words need to be chosen with more care.

22. WEDNESDAY. Deceptive. Cancer people should try to be a lot more careful when adding the finishing touches to their work. Be sure that you follow to the letter the guidelines set for you by your boss. You may think that you are doing people a favor by being inventive. This, however, is not the way it will be viewed at all. You may also feel that your natural talents are being stifled. The only way you can find any sort of creative release is to give over more time to hobbies. You can work on these in your own way and in your own time. Other family and household members can be devious and even dishonest. Everything they say need not necessarily be believed. You will have to establish mutual trust.

23. THURSDAY. Good. Today, some of the opportunities you had been hoping for during the earlier part of the week, may suddenly become available. You are well prepared for handling these. It is essential that you get off to an early start. You will find that there are quite a lot of routine matters to attend to. Business meetings and writing letters are among these. You will have to handle these before you can come to grips with the exciting ways of earning extra money. Success, and moments of real happiness in the past, can act as a great inspiration to Cancer men and women. The day will be favorable for bringing outstanding affairs to a close. You will then be prepared for a new cycle of activity.

24. FRIDAY. Good. It should be another excellent day. You will be able to use your natural talents to the full. This, in itself, will enable you to let off steam. People will show a greater willingness to fall in with your original ideas. It's a good day for keeping your eyes open for bargains. You may be able to pick up antiques or similar objets-d'art at very reasonable prices. Events will conspire to help the Cancer worker, provided he or she puts in the initial effort. It should be favorable for making changes within the home. Come to grips with painting and redecorating jobs in your spare time. Once you start, the rest will be easy.

25. SATURDAY. Disquieting. You will feel strangely unsettled today. Perhaps after your recent gains this will be something of an anti-climactic day. You will find that in the main you will be dealing with dull routine tasks. There may be quite a lot of letters to write or bills to be paid. More time will have to be spent keeping a closer check on the amount of cash that you have been spending. You might also find it necessary to have a word with loved ones who you feel have been living above their means. Cancer people may find that children are quite a handful. This applies equally to teachers and parents. Exuberance is due to the coming vacation.

26. SUNDAY. Variable. Romance may fail to supply the pleasure and enjoyment that you have probably been hoping for. Loved ones may not be willing to go along with your plans. Ideas that you had for going out and socializing may not meet with all-around approval. Those who are most important to you could have different ideas. You may feel frustrated and disappointed. Indeed, pleasure may be something of an elusive nature. The more you search for it, the further it seems to recede from you. Profound changes may be occurring within spouses and loved ones. Cancers are having a hard time understanding precisely what is happening. It may just be a low point for everyone, happening to coincide.

27. MONDAY. Disquieting. This is not likely to be a very worrisome day. But it would appear that you will have to wait on the actions of others. You would much rather be able to take the lead yourself. It might not be possible to initiate the kind of changes you were hoping to get under way at your place of employment. Those with whom you have to work alongside may appear lazy, as well as indifferent to your efforts. Earlier in the day, you would be wise to give more time to routine work. It will certainly not be possible to get new and exciting ventures launched. Cancer men and women may feel that they are missing out on something where romance is concerned.

28. TUESDAY. Disturbing. This will not be an easy day. Your nerves will be on edge. Perhaps your health will not be up to snuff. Go and see your doctor if you are run-down. Do not ignore minor ailments, thinking they will disappear of their own accord. This can tend to be a rather bleak and depressing week for Cancer people. The set-backs that you are suffering from currently are likely be only temporary. You, perhaps, are not apt to view it this way. You must try to be more optimistic about the future and not adopt a negative point of view. Tempers will be easily lost, but arguments must be avoided as much as possible.

29. WEDNESDAY. Disturbing. You will be rather pleased to see the end of this month just ahead. You may feel that the energy has drained away from you. You will be feeling that you cannot make any progress with current negotiations. Perhaps you have not received some money that was due to you. People will be rather slow in settling up with you for goods or services recently rendered. Influential people may give the go-ahead for personal schemes and ventures. Such new projects are likely to founder, however, due to lack of general support and publicity. You may find that you want to crawl into that Cancer shell of yours and get away from it all. But sooner or later, you will have to get back in the arena.

30. THURSDAY. Variable. The day will be good for putting more exertion into self-improvement efforts. Perhaps your lack of energy and vitality is in some way due to your diet and the state of your health. You must take better care of yourself. Friends can be particularly helpful in connection with distant affairs. They may be able to put you in touch with a particular professional person. You are seeking some special information that you may not have been able to come by through your own contacts. But influential people will continue to be unreliable. They may even make promises that they cannot keep. Depending on such help would be most unwise. You would be better advised to forget that kind of help and find some other source.

JULY

1. FRIDAY. Fair. The second half of the year will get off to a fairly good start. It would be a wise move for you to keep a closer eye on taxation and insurance affairs. You seem to have been doing too little in this area of late. Go over your accounts. Make sure that you have kept a proper record of all of your earnings. Be sure, too, that you have retained bills and receipts for goods that you may be able to claim against expenditures. Bankers are likely to refuse requests for loans to sponsor speculative ventures. But influential people will be helpful. They will give Cancers more scope and freedom for self-expression and originality. Even if no funds are available, their faith in you will raise your morale.

2. SATURDAY. Variable. There will be a good deal for you to do today. You will be concerned with a number of minor matters. These are connected with recent events and they could keep you busy with desk jobs for quite a large proportion of the day. See what you can do to further business ventures that are already in the pipeline. You may be able to enlist the support of an influential person. He or she might be able to supply you with information that you could not normally be able to come by. And this person may well feel it is not for them to help you directly. It will be a favorable time for signing contracts or agreements with people known in the past. It will help Cancers to know something of the nature and the character of their associates!

3. SUNDAY. Good. This will be a happy and exciting day. You should be able to more or less please yourself as to how you want to spend your spare time. There are likely to be opportunities coming your way to earn some handy money on the side. Friends may come up with some original ideas that will enable you to show off your natural talents. This is the right time for bringing more imagination and artistry into self-improvement endeavors. Cancer people may be more capable of producing creative works of art than they had imagined. It should be a good day for travel and for meeting certain people. You have not had the opportunity to have a chat with many of them.

4. MONDAY. Disturbing. It will be very difficult for you to concentrate today. Your mind will constantly be going over problems of a personal nature. Cancers who have to attend to desk jobs may find, to their subsequent dismay, that mistakes made now are not easy to rectify. Influential people will not be very helpful or sympathetic. Communicating with people at a great distance can lead to misunderstanding. Thinking could be confused so that important forward planning has to be postponed. Cancer-born people are unlikely to see eye-to-eye with their in-laws, but there is no point in making a big issue out of this as you would only upset your mate or partner if you were to do so.

5. TUESDAY. Deceptive. It would be wise to allow yourself more time to finish jobs than you may have thought you would need. Some jobs require special attention to detail, and therefore cannot be rushed. You must not hurry chores that could have an important influence on your promotional chances in the future. Cancer career or business people who try to get new projects off the ground may be disappointed. The lack of support that is forthcoming from people at the top will account for that. The performance of other people at your place of employment is also likely to be a source of disappointment to you. You had been hoping to get some sort of teamwork going with them. Confusion over legal affairs may leave you vulnerable to deception and exploitation.

6. WEDNESDAY. Variable. Influential people will be more helpful than normal today. If you have any problems with current work you should take them to your boss. Do not bottle up your feelings inside of you. It would be a good idea to get things off your chest. You may be able to find new methods you can employ. Attending to jobs that have become somewhat routine and commonplace has a tendency to lull one into complacency. It should be good day for pinning down people who are generally evasive. Try to get some straight answers to questions that you have been asking for a long time. You should find that your company is very much in demand socially. Do not ignore the chances to meet as many people as you can.

7. THURSDAY. Good. The chances are this will be the best day of the month that has dawned thus far. Much of your old vim and vigor will be returning. It looks as if the Crab will be scheming exciting new ways to add to their regular income. You will be pleased to find that you are now able to rely on a good deal more support from members of your family. This will be the reverse of what you appear to have been getting of late. An early start to the day would be a good idea. There are quite likely to be additional appointments that you have to cram into your waking hours at the last moment. Routine work and occupational activities can contain opportunities for furthering ambitious urges. But it will be entirely up to you as to how you use these.

8. FRIDAY. Good. People in positions of authority will be helpful. Your boss is likely to have words of encouragement for you that will be a booster for your confidence. A secret hope or wish that you have been harboring for some time is likely to move a step nearer to fruition. Friends may be able to supply you with some useful introductions. Accept any social invitations that arrive by mail or telephone. They may be instrumental in helping you to do yourself some good in your career. Continued efforts at implementing business expansion can easily be financed. There should be extra profits coming in from day-to-day transactions.

9. SATURDAY. Variable. If you want to make a success of this day, you are going to have to divide your time between business and home affairs more equally. Loved ones must not be made to feel neglected. Your mate or partner will take a fairly dim view of the situation if you do not show more interest in making a happier and more contented homelife. Social or group activities may provide Cancer people with a lucky break. You might be able to secure an introduction to an influential person. You have been wanting to meet someone in particular for some time. This is a favorable day for travel, even if you have not drawn up any plans beforehand. Just act on impulse and go somewhere you have never been. The change of pace should do you good.

10. SUNDAY. Variable. Make the most of this day. Otherwise, it can be a rather indecisive period if you simply allow yourself to drift. Romance will be playing an important role in your affairs. You seem to have reached the crossroads in a relationship that has been developing very swiftly of late. But the Cancer-born person is advised to wait and see before rushing into any new commitments. Listen to, even if you do not act on, the advice of older people where your private life is concerned. Cancers should get more rest. It could be that you are overestimating your physical resources or stamina. Getting run-down physically is not advisable. Not only will you feel badly but you will be prey to sickness.

11. MONDAY. Disturbing. Watch your temper today. You could easily jump to the wrong conclusions and lash out at someone with whom you have a very close relationship. Do not listen to gossips or rumormongers. The more that you can rely on yourself at work, the better it will be. This is not the best of days for attempts to promote team effort. Do not risk savings on speculative ventures that are suggested to you by others. Routine jobs and employment affairs will probably require you to keep a lower profile than usual. But attempts on the part of superiors to introduce new working methods or procedures can meet with some justified protest.

12. TUESDAY. Deceptive. Restlessness must be curbed. This is not the best of times to take any risks at work. Stick to tried and trusted methods. Do not take responsibility for decisions that would easily backfire on you if anything were to go wrong. Perhaps you are being too idealistic and expecting too much from other people. Refusal to see friends as they really are could cost you dearly in the long run. You are a generous person by nature. But sometimes, for your own protection, you need to keep a tighter control over this side of your psyche. Cancers who can afford it may decide that this is the day for treating themselves to something they have wanted for a long time.

13. WEDNESDAY. Good. There may well be an important breakthrough today. What takes place early in the day at your place of employment is likely to boost your optimism about the future. You should be feeling much more confident about your ability to handle a certain job. Not only is it interesting, but it also poses an exciting new challenge. It should be favorable for making new resolutions and for turning over a new leaf. Activities that require no support or cooperation from other people can be furthered. There will be fewer distractions or interruptions to slow down your progress. But the impetus for getting any major new projects off the ground is likely to be lacking.

14. THURSDAY. Good. More of your time must be given over to attempts to increase profits. Put as much cash as you can into lucrative savings schemes. It is vital that you think about the future more constructively in connection with the well-being of you and yours. Look into new business methods that you may be able to put into practice as a way to boost your earnings. Look at insurance policies and also at income tax affairs. Financial and business success are likely to go hand in hand. Taking a firmer stand with difficult people and trouble-makers can help to make transactions more lucrative. Show them, right from the start, that you cannot be pushed around.

15. FRIDAY. Good. This would appear to be the third in a cycle of good days. In fact, today could see the fruition of much of what you have been trying so hard to achieve for a good part of the week. A letter that arrives this morning could set your mind at rest. It tells about a tricky situation that has been nagging away at the back of your mind for weeks. Someone at a distance may make an offer to you that you feel you can now accept. Some immediate improvement in your finances would appear to be in the cards. Inside contacts and friends may help to get you interviews with important people. They will be willing to give a boost to your original ideas. This should be of invaluable assistance.

16. SATURDAY. Variable. This will be a reasonably easygoing day. You need to unwind. You may be feeling a bit down after all the activity that appears to have been going on over the last two or three days. Perseverance in routine matters is vital. There appear to be many little desk jobs that you really should try to clear up before you take a weekend break. Presumably you would not want to have these matters hanging over your head on Monday. Overtime may have to be figured on. But this would not be such a bad thing as it can win you substantial bonuses or even permanent pay raises. Treatment should be obtained without delay for any health problems that may have been bothering you. The longer you delay this, the more likely you are to suffer unnecessarily.

17. SUNDAY. Variable. Get a grip on yourself. Exercise more self-discipline. Do not listen to the ideas that friends may come up with for seeking pleasure or entertainment. This applies especially if they are expecting you to pay the bill. The day will be favorable for mental or artistic endeavors. You should try to make more of your natural talents. Why not take up hobbies or pastimes again? They used to bring you a lot of pleasure, but they have been sadly neglected of late. This should be a truly happy day for giving more attention to your mate or partner. In fact, the more that you are involved with family affairs, the better it is likely to be.

18. MONDAY. Variable. It might be a little difficult for you to get back into the swing of things today at your place of work or business. You may find that concentration is rather difficult after your weekend break. Attempts to get hold of or communicate with loved ones at a distance can lead to misunderstandings. Be careful what you say over the telephone. It could easily be open to misinterpretation. Casual acquaintances may be more reserved and less friendly than usual. But the thinking of Cancers can be especially astute. This should be particularly helpful to furthering speculative ventures. Don't allow business affairs to rob you and your loved ones of a summer vacation.

19. TUESDAY. Variable. It might be best for you to get out of familiar surroundings sometime today. As far as business is concerned, you will function better in new surroundings. Short trips are likely to prove to be the most successful. Make more of your natural talents. Do not be afraid to experiment. Cancers can be particularly fortunate in attempts to enlarge their circle of friends and acquaintances. Casual conversation or gossip will supply you with valuable tidbits of information. But domestic affairs could interfere with business meetings that you had hoped to arrange for later on in the day. This will prove irritating and awkward. A cancellation is aggravating.

20. WEDNESDAY. Variable. You must allow yourself more time to get through your work this midweek day. It would appear that you are attempting to rush certain important jobs. Do not do anything that could affect your remaining in the good graces of superiors. It would be foolish to throw into jeopardy a reputation that you have been painstakingly building up. See what you can do to bring more originality into routine affairs. It is important that you do not allow superiors to get away with the idea that you have gone stale and lost interest in your job. Remember that big bills will soon have to be paid. Try to bring about some innovative changes in what has become routine.

21. THURSDAY. Variable. You have a good day ahead for additional efforts to bring outstanding affairs to a satisfactory conclusion. You should be able to wind up jobs that have been hanging over your head for all too long. Now is the right time to bring any grievances you may have out into the open. Your boss will be more understanding and will show a greater willingness to see things from your point of view. Health problems can be alleviated by spending more of your spare time resting. In your leisure hours, you will find that home, and the comforts that it has to offer, is the best place for you. But it is important that you do not neglect occupational duties or commitments.

22. FRIDAY. Fair. You have a favorable day for creative and artistic ventures. Make more of your natural talents. You will find that there are valuable ways to earn money from being more creative in your spare time. But you must put your mind to it. It won't just happen. This is a day when Cancers who decide to have a bit of a gamble are likely to be more successful than usual. Speculators should be pleased with results, provided they can account accurately for shifts in public opinion. Children will need treating with more gentleness and feeling. Cancer parents should try to get closer to members of the younger generation.

23. SATURDAY. Good. The chances are good that you will awaken in a happy mood. From almost every angle this should be a satisfactory and successful day. You will be much cheered by some news that comes to you first thing. Friends will be helpful with personal problems. You may at last be able to see your way out of an emotional situation that has been bothering you for some time. Romance looks more promising for the single Cancer. It will be a happy time for social activities. You will be able to put the problems of the working week behind you. Casual acquaintances can develop into longer-lasting associations. This is also a favorable time for catching up on correspondence backlogs.

24. SUNDAY. Variable. It is more that likely that you will be feeling a bit down in the dumps. You will have to exercise greater self-discipline. This is one of those days when the weight-watchers among you could be tempted to break with diets. That will lead them to eat the kinds of foods that put on the pounds fast. You should try to develop more interest in other people and in events that take you away from the home. Do not allow yourself to get stuck in too much of a rut. There is an indication that some change in your daily routine is required. Pessimism about future work prospects is unlikely to be justified. This is particularly true where earnings are concerned. Change your life-style.

25. MONDAY. Quiet. This will be a nice and steady day in which to ease into the working week. There is not likely to be any special pressure placed upon you. Cancers who happen to be left alone to cope in the home will have the chance to tidy it up generally. They could also catch up with any odd chores that were left undone before the weekend. More attention can be paid to the needs and requirements of the very young. At the office or factory you should not have any problems in getting along with co-workers. Team effort will bring about good results. The day is unlikely to bring any exciting developments. That should please you.

26. TUESDAY. Disturbing. Money problems will be very much on your mind. On going over your accounts you may find that you are not quite so well off as you first thought. Perhaps there are some extra bills to pay that you had not taken into consideration. Arguments between you and loved ones could erupt over recent extravagances. It may be difficult for you to keep control over your emotions. Cancer people must try harder not to become overexcited. Greater effort will be needed to overcome instability and nervous tension. Think before you say anything that could hurt people who mean a great deal to you. Later in the day, arguments could become heated at your place of employment.

27. WEDNESDAY. Quiet. Take life at a somewhat slower pace. It is important that you pay more attention to learning the art of relaxation. Problems that you have been encountering recently will not be made any better by working yourself up into a snit. Listen to the advice that is given to you by older business associates. More than likely, it will be well worth heeding. The day is good for making any extra effort to understand the point of view of other members of your family. You and they may not have been seeing eye-to-eye of late. There is the possibility of compromise solutions being found that will be acceptable to all.

28. THURSDAY. Variable. It would be totally wrong for you to assume that everyone else understands or shares your point of view. Do not try to lay down the law at home. Take more of a live-and-let-live attitude. Cancer parents should not try to enforce their will on youngsters. Allow more give-and-take to enter into all of your personal relationships. Lengthy discussions may prove to be just a waste of time. You will probably fare better when dealing with matters at a distance. This looks like a promising day for Cancers who are trying to win new contracts. Evening will be a pleasant period if you are socializing. Try to introduce some new ideas for having a good time.

29. FRIDAY. Variable. Precise information, gleaned from private research, should give Cancer people the upper hand. This will pertain when it comes to discussing new business ventures and transactions. You should be able to get a jump on your competitors. The groundwork that you have been putting in on jobs that you knew would be cropping up will pay off well. It looks as if the special attention you have been paying to detail can be turned to profit. But public or government officials will not be very helpful with information relating to income tax or insurance matters. There is a possibility of your getting a pay raise or some sort of promotion. This will boost your morale.

30. SATURDAY. Variable. This is another day when there are likely to be rather mixed trends. You will lose on the swings and gain on the roundabouts. To put it another way, you win some, you lose some. Limited speculations will have a better chance of paying off than if you gamble wildly. Do not take any risks with cash that you have put to one side to pay specific bills. The morning period looks particularly promising for dealing with employment matters. New investment schemes will be particularly successful. But don't place too much reliance on people at or from a distance. They could let Cancers down at the last minute.

31. SUNDAY. Quiet. This will be a rather slow start on which to begin the week. And it will be an equally slow one to end the month on. However, you will be pleased that you have the chance to catch up with your letter writing and to go over your accounts. Pay off any small bills. Do not keep local traders waiting for cash that you owe them. This is a good day for putting things into a more realistic and broader perspective. Today can provide you with especially good opportunities for rising above emotional and practical difficulties. These tend to upset the Cancer's sense of proportion. It should be favorable later for any reading, study or academic pursuits. Self-improvement endeavors will be starred.

AUGUST

1. MONDAY. Variable. You will be in a more determined mood than ever on this first day of the new month. You are determined to succeed where you may feel you have failed during the last few weeks. This is a fairly important day for catching up with any backlog of work. It will also be good for answering business and personal letters. Cancers may be forced by circumstances beyond their control to be more serious and painstaking. Influential people are likely to ask more of you. It is vital that you show superiors that you are keen to gain early promotion. All planning for the future should be kept on more practical and straightforward levels. The financial advice of influential people should be taken with a pinch of salt.

2. TUESDAY. Variable. Don't rush through important chores. Although you are in a hurry to make progress in your career, more haste would definitely mean less speed. The morning will offer you good opportunities to make routine business calls and to drum up support in general. Cancers who earn their living as traveling salespeople may be able to win lucrative contracts. Someone at a distance, who is in a position of authority, will be especially helpful. Romantic affairs may give rise to suspicions in the Cancer man or woman. There could be fears of misplaced love. The health of your mate or partner could be a cause for some anxiety. Tension could have a lot to do with symptoms. Work together to reduce it.

3. WEDNESDAY. Deceptive. Don't take too much for granted on this midweek day. Influential people who promised to give you support before the end of July may be reneging now. The more that you can rely on yourself, the better you are likely to fare. Teamwork is not as promising as it may first have appeared to be. Make a concerted effort to come to grips with jobs that you have been putting off. Ambitious urges can be furthered. But that will be true only as long as you do not gamble or take any other silly risks with your money. Business competitors may turn out to be devious customers. They may try to entangle Cancers in deceptive situations.

4. THURSDAY. Disturbing. Speculation would be best postponed. Colleagues would seem to be trying to pressure you into backing some sort of risky enterprise. Keen as you may be to get hold of more cash, you must be very cautious about what you dip into your reserves for. Pay more attention to the advice of older, professional people. Listen to what those, who you know have your best interests at heart, have to say. Friends are likely to be in a depressed and depressing mood. The Crab may have considerable trouble in cheering them up and might not be able to do so. Business financial negotiations could lead you into trouble with the authorities. That is one reason for you to have legal advice.

5. FRIDAY. Quiet. This will be a relatively peaceful day. You will not have too many difficult situations to attend to. In fact, there will be some excellent opportunities to deal with routine jobs. You do not want to have these hanging over your head when you come to take a weekend break. Cancer-born people are likely to find themselves spending more time than usual in the company of friends and close acquaintances. Chores that you find rather boring can be dealt with effectively by joining forces with others. It is best not to waste time on pointless activities. If there is any possibility of furthering secret hopes and dreams, you want to devote your whole being to that purpose. Understand your priorities so that you don't short-change yourself.

6. SATURDAY. Good. You are likely to have more driving force at your disposal today than usual. There will be a sense of urgency about the way you tackle your jobs, which can only be for the good. You ought to be able to put on a spurt of energy and increase your output to a satisfactory level. Influential people will be pleased with your efforts. There could even be some talk about promotion or an increase in salary in the not too distant future. Later in the day, you will prefer to spend more time in privacy and seclusion. This can be a surprisingly effective approach when it comes to dealing with creative hobbies. It will be good for making confidential partnership financial arrangements.

7. SUNDAY. Variable. It is vital that you exercise more self-control and discipline. There will be lots of minor chores that you had planned to deal with on this day of rest. You must not allow yourself to be sidetracked by close acquaintances. There will be plenty of time to let your hair down and enjoy yourself after you have completed your duties. Secret errands or outings can bring financial gain. Cancers are keeping hidden from the people around them their real purpose. Relatives may make generous gestures. An older family member will be keen to come to your support in one way or another. However, this person wishes to remain anonymous. That suits you very well. You will certainly keep quiet.

8. MONDAY. The Crab will be especially fearful of making mistakes in his or her private life. This could have an overly inhibitive effect on your actions. The best way to overcome your problems today is by using more charm. You can easily win over influential people to support your personal plans. You may have to take time off from your regular job in order to attend to a family matter. Be sure that you get the permission of your boss first. Otherwise, you could get involved in something that could leave you open to criticism. Appeals to the emotions, rather than to people's logical reasoning, can produce good results. At the same time, there is the risk of deception.

9. TUESDAY. Good. This will probably be the best day of the month so far. With an upsurge or energy, as well as confidence, you will feel that you are ready to take on exciting new challenges. Nothing is likely to hold you back now. Influential people will like your style. As a result, they will show a greater willingness to support you with more than words. Routine occupational affairs will also be an area where you can earn more money. It will be either as bonuses or permanent pay raises. It should be good for discussing long-term business prospects with employers. It will also be favorable for the recovery of old debts. When people forget to repay a debt, don't hesitate to remind them.

10. WEDNESDAY. Quiet. There is unlikely to be anything of great importance taking place now. This is certainly not apt to worry you. There seems to be plenty to keep you meaningfully occupied. Seeking outside stimulation would simply be like looking for trouble. It will be a good day for catching up with paperwork. Attending to minor matters connected with personal resources and expenditure is also recommended. Get your accounts up to date. Be sure that you keep a clear record of all expenses that you are hoping to claim back from the Internal Revenue Service. More secrecy will be helpful to all your financial affairs. You should learn to trust your own judgment.

11. THURSDAY. Fair. Children and their affairs could involve you in additional expenditure. It may well be that there was some unexpected outgoing that you had not budgeted for. It may even be necessary to dip into your savings. This would be so you can meet bills that it would be unwise to delay paying for too long. The search for pleasure could turn out to be more costly than you realize. Do not get involved unwisely in any outings that friends may suggest. First, you must ascertain just how deeply you would have to dig into your pocket to cover costs. Extra exertion put into career and public ventures can produce substantial gains and profits. It will be good for shopping expeditions.

12. FRIDAY. Good. This could probably rival the best day of the month, so far. You will fare particularly well if you are applying for a new job. Your charm and your easygoing manner will go a long way to win people over to you. If they should have some sort of authority over you, it will be helpful. You should be feeling much more optimistic about what the future holds. Get new contracts signed and co-signed before you take a weekend break. New opportunities that are offered to you will be particularly worthy of consideration. They are more than likely to prove lucrative over a long period of time. It will be a good time for setting work and labor affairs on a more secure footing.

13. SATURDAY. Variable. You may be a little disappointed at your close associates' lack of enthusiasm over your proposals for making money. Friends will not be as keen to dip into their pockets as you may have hoped. It would be best to bide your time and not be too pushy. Little will be gained by adopting an aggressive approach. Do not attempt to get casual acquaintances to back you either. You should not place too much trust in people who are comparative or total strangers. It would be best not to reveal personal problems to neighbors or relatives. But the day is favorable for romance. Make some plans for socializing in the evening as early as possible.

14. SUNDAY. Disquieting. The chances are that you will be in a restless frame of mind. It would be easy for you to get caught up in the affairs of other people. Social invitations should not be accepted until you can find out exactly what would be involved in visiting the homes of other people. Friends may make suggestions that would cause you to dig very deeply into your pocket. It would also be wise to give people plenty of warning before you descend on them. Relatives may feel that it is an intrusion if you drop by without phoning first. People, as a whole, will tend to be uncommunicative and withdrawn. Why not make a short trip?

15. MONDAY. Disturbing. People will be very helpful. This is one day when you should rely on yourself more than ever. Promises of support that were made to you before the weekend are likely to be reneged upon. Trips or journeys may have to be postponed at the last moment. This could be due to illness or appointments having been canceled. It would be best not to make any long journeys until you have checked up and made absolutely sure that meetings are still on. Ill health could be another problem. You should take more care of your physical condition. Cancer men and women must try to control their emotions more.

16. TUESDAY. Deceptive. Continued care of your health is very important. Take the advice of your doctor. It may be necessary to slow down a bit. Keen as you are to make money, you must put your physical condition first. There is a risk of deception where it hurts the most: in the home. But Cancer people must try not to exaggerate the importance of small lies and deceptions. They should not blow them up into moral issues. This can be a time when both career and romantic affairs never get off the ground. You do not appear to be having a great deal of luck in your love life at this particular point. But a greater understanding with loved ones can be reached this evening.

17. WEDNESDAY. Good. At last there seems to be a silver lining to the clouds for you. There can be an important breakthrough taking place for the Cancer person today. You must be alive to the rare opportunity. You can improve your career prospects quite dramatically. Influential people will be easier to win over. Your charm will work wonders for you. It should be favorable for efforts to bring outstanding financial affairs to a satisfactory close. Some nagging money problem that has been giving you headaches and sleepless nights can be straightened out amicably. Your boss may now be willing to lend you financial aid. Your need is in connection with real estate affairs.

18. THURSDAY. Good. Perseverance in routine work activities will bring rewards. You will find it a lot easier to cope with jobs today that you had felt you simply could not face earlier in the week. Influential people may take the long-term interests of Cancer workers and employees into consideration. You should be feeling a lot more secure now. It's a good day for making reservations for late holidays if you have not already taken your vacation. Ambitious urges can be recognized by the people who matter most where future occupational prospects are concerned. The evening looks very promising for romantic meetings. You should try to plan ahead, however, if you want to go to a good restaurant.

19. FRIDAY. Variable. The more you try to rush things, the less you will probably achieve. Try to get more enjoyment from your job. Give free rein to creative impulses. Figure out the best way to win the praise of people who can have some definite voice in your future career prospects. One way would be to show off the inventive side of your nature. Do what you can to give a shot in the arm to routine chores. Cancer-born people may have the opportunity to combine work with pleasure. At any rate, routine employment activities should be less monotonous than usual. Loved ones will be easier to get along with. Your plans for outings this evening will be acceptable to your mate or partner.

20. SATURDAY. Disturbing. Gamblers or speculators had better watch their step. If they do not, they will probably find themselves on the wrong side of the law. Do not do anything that would set you in opposition to authority. Children can cause damage which will have to be paid out of the Cancer parents' own pocket. You will have cause to grumble about the way members of the younger generation conduct themselves today. You may have to be stricter than you really like to be. There could be arguments erupting in the home that drive you out to visit friends. Later in the day may require that you take some extra rest and relaxation.

21. SUNDAY. Variable. Quite a lot of your time this Sunday is likely to be spent tidying up odd jobs that should have been completed by the end of last week. You are handicapping yourself by having to work on old stuff. You should be making preparations for new starts that you will want to launch tomorrow. Cancer-born people should apply themselves today to their occupational or career prospects. They should then be able to make strides forward in their chosen field of endeavor. If you have recently started a diet as part of an exercise course, you may have some difficulty in maintaining the necessary discipline over yourself to keep it up. Words spoken in jest may be regretted later.

22. MONDAY. Variable. It is not going to be at all easy for you to stick to the schedule that you have set for yourself. The main reason for this is that most of the jobs that you have to handle will be routine and monotonous. Above all, you will be eager to take on exciting new challenges. Influential people will not be very helpful if you are keen to break new ground. You may be thinking seriously about changing your job. This would not be a good idea, however, until you have something definite to go to. Cancer workers may be called upon to undertake workloads that they could well do without. If they are clever, such disadvantages can be turned to their own benefit in the long run.

23. TUESDAY. Deceptive. More haste would definitely mean less speed today. Do not try to rush through desk jobs that require special attention to detail. You will only have to go over such work again without earning any extra money for it. Be sure that you give value for your pay at the office or factory. Your boss may be paying greater attention to your progress than you realize at this time. Legal or publicity affairs may not be as straightforward as you first supposed. You must take steps to avoid being deceived by glamorous people or circumstances. This is a favorable time for imaginative or artistic work. Romance may be tense, but it will also be exciting. You could be making a liaison more permanent.

24. WEDNESDAY. Good. There could be an exciting and stimulating day in store for you. This will be true from both the personal as will as the public point of view. You will enjoy any new challenges that are set for you. Influential people will show a greater understanding for what you are trying to achieve. It should be favorable for the signing of legal contracts or documents. It will be a good day for entering into new partnership associations. It should also be favorable for writing up reports for eventual publication. More traveling around, or extra phone calls can help gain additional and much-needed support and cooperation.

25. THURSDAY. Fair. The day will be excellent for dealing with matters that require you to handle them in private. Confidential business meetings should go off particularly well. Get together with large business firms and corporations. You may be able to land some lucrative deals. Some information that is passed on to you in secret can be stored away for use at a later date. Some behind-the-scenes maneuvering can be especially helpful for furthering partnership financial ventures. But the financial moves of partners can be overly speculative. Reserves have to be defended against unwise moves by others. This would be a favorable time for attempts to improve your reputation.

26. FRIDAY. Excellent. This will be one of the best days of the month, if not the whole year. You should make an early start with business and career matters. Be sure that you make the most of the excellent opportunities that are likely to come your way. You can afford to be a little more pushy with influential people. Your ideas are likely to be favorably accepted by those in positions of authority. Cancer-born people may win long-term contracts which will guarantee them work for some time to come. It's a good time for investments and savings. Extra earnings should be put into the bank rather than spent immediately. Romance will be happier and more settled than has been the case for some time past.

27. SATURDAY. Disquieting.   It looks as if you will be feeling a little depressed when you wake up this morning. It may be that a letter or telephone call that you receive does little to improve your mood. Perhaps you will discover that some social outing you had been looking forward to all week has been canceled at the last moment. You could well find yourself at a loose end. It might be best to give more time over to hobbies and artistic pursuits that you can handle on your own. That might be preferable to relying overly much on other people. Distant travel can involve complications. Government officials and customs-men may be unusually obstructive and deliberately unhelpful.

28. SUNDAY. Disturbing.   Be extremely careful of what you say to relatives and friends. What you might mean as a joke could easily be taken the wrong way and lead to serious differences of opinion. There could be walkouts unless you watch that tongue of yours and think before you utter a single remark. Cancer-born people also need to take extra precautions to guard their health. This will be especially true when traveling to distant places. Accidents or injuries would only create additional problems. Opportunities to make trips may have to be turned down due to work commitments and similar responsibilities. Concentrating on mental endeavors may turn out to be more difficult than you realized.

29. MONDAY. Variable.   Propositions that your receive from unexpected sources would be worth taking a stage further. Opportunities that come to you from people at a distance must not be passed up without a great deal of consideration. Do not act with haste this Monday. Take more time before you turn down contracts that could offer you security and stability for some time to come. People who reappear from the past could turn out to be very helpful. This help could come from assisting you with your business affairs. But routine transactions have to be dealt with more calmly and more impartially. This will be a happy day for romance as long as you do not try to rush loved ones.

30. TUESDAY. Fair. Romantic affairs could conflict with your work. This is not a good day for trying to mix business and pleasure. Try to impress on loved ones that you should not be disturbed at your place of employment unless the matter is absolutely essential. Cancer-born people can be overly gullible. Do not invest in get-rich-quick schemes that are proposed by people who you do not know at all well. People who you consider to be friends may, in fact, be working against your better interests. But the day is good for earning a reputation for reliability and honesty. Influential people, such as judges, are likely to make decisions that will favor you. You instill feelings that you are competent.

31. WEDNESDAY. Fair. You may be surprised at the attitude of a person who you have always secretly fancied. This person may show more than a passing interest in you. It looks as if some of your hopes and wishes that you have been keeping to yourself will move nearer to fruition. Bright ideas on the part of business colleagues would be worth investigating further. It might be possible to streamline jobs that have become boring and commonplace. Influential people may become intimate friends. This is a good day to ask superiors home to dinner or for some light refreshments. But there is a risk that social commitments will conflict with your romantic plans. You may somehow have mixed up the dates and now you are on the spot.

SEPTEMBER

1. THURSDAY. Good. Someone who you have known for a long time could begin to play an even more important role in your life. This will come as something of a surprise to you. You had undoubtedly thought that by this time your relationship was well established. This is an exciting day for romance. Friends can turn into lovers. Circumstances may throw you close to people in situations that are conducive to making love blossom. More flexibility, plus a willingness to adapt to new eventualities, can help to boost profits. This will be true even of routine business transactions. Becoming members of groups or societies can be a good way of promoting personal interests and aims.

2. FRIDAY. Variable.   Minor matters should be given priority now. Attend to jobs that you should have cleared out of the way before the close of last month. There will be more time to attend to letter writing, the payment of bills, and chores in general. Clear the decks so that you are ready to make the important moves that you have planned for this month. You should be thinking with the future very much in mind now. Discussions with family members can produce good results, especially if you are trying to get your loved ones to live within a new budget. Influential people will be difficult to track down. Even if they are not out of the country, or on vacation, they may take steps to remain out of reach.

3. SATURDAY. Good.   The month of September is still very young. But you should be well pleased with the progress that you have made over the first couple of days. Today should be no exception and the week comes to an end with you in fine shape. There are likely to be quite a few offers for Cancers who are involved in the arts in any way. Your specialist talents will be very much in demand. This is a helpful day for furthering personal plans and schemes. You will have a better chance of increasing your income by working on your own than if you have to rely on others. Superiors will admire the independent streak in your nature. It should be favorable for conducting negotiations in secrecy.

4. SUNDAY. Quiet.   This is a helpful day for catching up with people who you have not seen for some time. If there has been a family breakup fairly recently, you should do what you can to repair the damage. Show that you are big enough to say you are sorry. Travel will bring good results. You can spring a pleasant surprise on an older family member. Cancer people should have fewer inhibitions about making their views and opinions known. Even if it develops that others fail to agree with them, at least everyone will know where they stand. People can be slow to respond to requests for help, but this is not a day for showing impatience.

5. MONDAY. Variable.   The more time you are able to spend on the domestic front, attending to family issues, the better it will be. The Cancer parent will find that youngsters require a good deal of attention. This is a good period for trying to get to the basic cause of problems connected with offspring. This pertains especially to those children who have reached the awkward age. There will also be better opportunities for launching speculative ventures. Even so, it would be a good idea to keep investments small. There is a real danger of loss if you take silly risks with your reserves. In the big world of business, Cancer people may find that competitors are especially harsh and hostile; they may fear you.

6. TUESDAY. Good. It would be in your best interests to make your intentions clear from the start. Lay your cards on the table. Play it up front with people who have always been direct and honest with you. There will be nothing lost by speaking your mind. But it should also be pointed out that you should use great tact, plus the necessary discretion, in relation to more confidential matters. This is a time when you should make more use of your powers of intuition. Later in the day, you could find yourself feeling very emotional. Someone from the past may come back into your life. Charm and flattery can win you entry into closed and privileged circles. Try to plan on something special.

7. WEDNESDAY. Variable. There are likely to be opportunities to improve your financial situation. But you must employ more tact and diplomacy when you are trying to do so. When dealing with professional people you must do everything in your power to ensure that you have got your facts right. Do not try to pull the wool over the eyes of accountants and bank managers. People and events behind the scenes will be especially helpful to money-making operations. Make the most of any contacts that you have with people in positions of authority. Do not be afraid to ask favors of those who have your best interests at heart.

8. THURSDAY. Quiet. This will be a pleasant and easygoing day. You will be pleased that you have the chance to take a breather. The pace seems to have been pretty hot for you so far this month. You should do all that you can now to relax and unwind frayed nerves. Cancers will be grateful that this is not a particularly exciting or demanding day. There will be plenty to keep you meaningfully occupied both at home and at your place of regular employment. The day will give you the chance to further routine monetary transactions. It will also be good for attending to the details of smaller financial affairs. Cancer people should try not to let their possessions start possessing them.

9. FRIDAY. Disquieting. This is likely to be a somewhat more active day than normal. You will have more energy and driving force at your disposal. You may be keen to make new starts with exciting business plans. But the chances are you would appear to be jumping the gun if you approach influential people with your proposals now. Make sure that you get all of your facts right. Both mentally and physically you could find that you are using a good deal more energy than normal. You will have to have your wits about you. There could be quite a lot of traveling involved today which you find rather tiring. Cancers must avoid expending their energies in pointless daydreaming.

10. SATURDAY. Good. The early morning period will be good for shopping expeditions. You should be able to pick up quite a few bargains if the autumn sales are starting in your area. Don't forget, you will have to make an early start at the big department stores. You really want to get the best of the bargains that are available today. There is not likely to be any friction at home. Savings can be made with the cooperation of your mate or partner. It is an excellent time for creative endeavors, especially in the line of artistic writing. It should be a good opportunity for taking children on short outings, either to visit older relatives or friends. It will be favorable for writing letters to certain people.

11. SUNDAY. Disquieting. This will not be an easy day for getting along with other members of the family. Arguments are likely to erupt first thing. The main problem for you this Sunday would appear to concern your mate or partner. He or she will not agree with your plans for seeking pleasure and entertainment. That will be especially true if you do not include them in all the trips that you are contemplating. You will have to give more time to domestic issues if you are going to avoid a big breakup. It is essential that you pay greater attention to the precise words used in the expressions you choose. Careless statements can easily cause offense. Health problems may be exacerbated by too much running around.

12. MONDAY. Deceptive. Loved ones and romantic partners can be especially helpful where financial or property affairs are concerned. If you are having some difficulty in these areas of your life, it would be a good idea to talk these issues over frankly and openly. There are people who you know will do all they can to come to your assistance. Cancer people should remain more in the background at their place of employment. They will be in a far stronger position by doing so. This is definitely not the day when you should try to steal the limelight. You will learn more by making this a look, listen, and learn day. Family or household affairs contain the risk of deception later on.

13. TUESDAY. Good. This is an important day for getting back on the right track. You seem to have been emotionally disturbed over the last couple of days. But you should be able to put all that behind you now. Dame Fortune would appear to be smiling in your direction. There will not be any important family problems to cope with. That will enable you to give more of your time and your energy to your work. Do all that you can to further any real estate transactions that are already under way. Property matters can be speeded up without any damage being caused. Thoughts about the past can give Cancer people some bright ideas. This would be a good time for entertaining relatives at home.

14. WEDNESDAY. Quiet. Cancer people will be pleased that they have the opportunity to spend more time at home. There appear to be a lot of odd jobs piling up that you had intended to complete over the weekend. Other members of your family are not so likely to get under your feet. Hard-working Cancer natives deserve a rest. It looks as if the people for whom you are working will by sympathetic to any requests you make for attending to personal affairs. It might even be possible to get some time off during office or factory hours. There is little point in taking occupational responsibilities too seriously. Things will tend to look after themselves, provided the most essential matters are not neglected.

15. THURSDAY. Fair. Perhaps you will feel that you are being put under quite a lot of pressure today. You will certainly not react very favorably to that in your present mood. It seems that you are taking very much a live-and-let-live attitude to life at the moment. Arguments are likely to erupt if you feel that your spare time is being encroached upon. If this is the case, it is probably best to be honest about the matter without hurting anyone's feelings. If you try to bottle things up inside you, you will reach a breaking point. Routine business and public affairs may lead to the forming of new romantic attractions. Business dealings will be more profitable today than they have been all week.

16. FRIDAY. Good. This would appear to be a first-class day. You will be able to make important decisions much more readily. You and your partner will be able to reach agreement. This will be in areas where differences may have been souring your relationship to a certain extent. People will admire your honesty and your straightforward way of dealing with things. Influential people may be willing to sponsor Cancer men and women in their more speculative ventures. The day can also provide good opportunities for turning hobbies and creative enterprises into regular sources of income. The day will be good for obtaining extended vacation leave from superiors and employers.

17. SATURDAY. Variable. Efficiency can be impaired by the inability of Cancer workers to discipline their thinking. Allowing thoughts to wander into the past could make you unhappy and unproductive. You must try to live more in the moment. Influential people will expect some pretty quick thinking on your part. There will be opportunities to increase your earnings today, but they are not likely to be offered to you twice. See what you can do to cheer up an older relative who has been rather down in the dumps. Some of your spare time may have to be used visiting hospitals or shutins. Current romantic involvements can bring happiness.

18. SUNDAY. Disquieting. This is a good day for seeking different ways to improve your health. You may have been suffering from minor ailments that have not been responding to regular treatment. Perhaps it is time for you to try a new approach. Cancers who suffer from muscular aches and pains may find that Yoga is the answer. They must not become impatient and expect immediate results. Health tips picked up in discussion with others may prove to be especially useful. Ambitious Cancer people may be able to carry on their employment endeavors from home. Influential people may be considering imposing extra responsibilities and workloads.

19. MONDAY. Deceptive. You may be feeling a little unsettled today. Certainly it will not be easy for you to concentrate. And this is only the first day of the working week. Team effort will be difficult to put into operation. You received promises of support from your working colleagues before you took a weekend break. These are now likely to be reneged on today. Cancer people can be overly idealistic. This can lead to a false assessment of others. That, in turn, will leave you susceptible to deception. Influential people may also be difficult to fathom. People in positions of authority will be erratic and undependable. You could be feeling more depressed by day's end than you did this morning.

20. TUESDAY. Disturbing. It will be one of the trickiest days that you have had to cope with for many a week. Emotions will be very much on the surface. You might find yourself dwelling a good deal on the past. It is no good getting down in the dumps over situations that you are powerless to alter. Try to think of the future. Count your blessings. It might be a good idea to have a chat with an older relative or friend whose opinions and judgment you have always respected. But discussions with influential people at your place of employment can give rise to misunderstandings. Rather than creating greater mutual empathy, the talks have caused more uncertainty. It seems that this is not your day.

21. WEDNESDAY. Good.   Perhaps you will get up this morning with a greater sense of purpose. Whatever it is, you will have much more energy. The blues that seem to have been getting you down of late should have disappeared. Loved ones will be constructively helpful. This is the right time to try to put more cash to one side. See what you can do to cut down on your expenses without lowering your cost of living. The morning is a favorable time for attempts to make contact with influential people in connection with legal or partnership affairs. It should be a good time for resorting to more original and skillful means in attempts to further partnership financial ventures.

22. THURSDAY. Disquieting.   You would probably prefer to keep a low profile today. But it is very unlikely that you will find this possible to do. The main reason why you will feel that you must have your say is that you might be accused of prejudice if you hold your tongue. This is especially true in all financial affairs. Hasty and impetuous people will have to be reprimanded even if it is not in your best short-term interests to do so. Loved ones will fail to appreciate the ins and outs of insurance and taxation matters. This could create further financial problems in the near future. Get an early night. Your nerves will be on edge and you should take it easy during leisure hours.

23. FRIDAY. Disquieting.   Important new projects will not be met with the enthusiastic reception you had probably been hoping for. Business expansion schemes may fail to get off the ground. You will be rather disappointed with influential people. You may feel that you have been let down just when you were on the brink of an important breakthrough. However, it is no good crying over spilt milk. You will have to adopt a more positive attitude toward your job. Make an effort to judge the situation that you find yourself in more dispassionately. You will then have to admit that this is not the best of times to branch off in an entirely new direction. Later in the day tends to be more favorable for romance.

24. SATURDAY. Quiet.   Cancer-born people will be glad of the weekend break. You should be able to take life at a slower pace, and you will find this more than satisfactory. Loved ones will show more understanding and sympathy for the setbacks you may have encountered over the past few days. It is particularly important for the Crab to get priorities right. They must not allow themselves to be discouraged about the future. Planning should be kept not only realistic but also optimistic, despite the secret fears and worries you may be harboring. Communicating with distant people may provide useful knowledge. Evening could see you either bumping into or hearing from an old buddy.

25. SUNDAY. Variable. Perhaps it would be best to avoid putting real estate or property plans into action. This will be a difficult day for dealing with professional people or any government official whom you meet socially. It would be best to wait until regular office hours before you present your ideas for any changeover. Loved ones may not be the best people to pay attention to when it comes to advice on such matters. Family members could find themselves in trouble with the law today. This could send you into a bit of a flap and require you to take some prompt action. Good names can be endangered by the rash and thoughtless actions of others. This is a favorable day for doing charity work.

26. MONDAY. Good. Problems that you thought you would have some difficulty in handling will not be such a worry after all. Influential people may be willing to use the good contacts that they have to intercede on your behalf. This is an appropriate day for projecting a more favorable image to the public. Readers who have to make speeches, or attract the attention of large groups of people in some way, are not likely to feel so nervous or uptight. Politicians among you will feel more sure of yourselves when having to answer awkward questions. Business and career affairs are likely to experience a definite improvement. Loved ones can lend a helping hand in the running of routine and business activities.

27. TUESDAY. Variable. There is likely to be a sudden rush job for you to deal with this morning. You may even be required to drop everything at a moment's notice at your place of employment. You will be told to follow the dictates of someone who has authority over you. Career people would be wise to remain aloof from family disputes. Do not get involved in quarrels that are not of your making. Leave it to your nearest and dearest to sort out their own difficulties. If you offer your opinion now, you could find yourself committed to one side. Appeals that you make against-government, or against any official decisions, are unlikely to be granted. Your boss may be infuriatingly inconsiderate.

28. WEDNESDAY. Good. Cancer men and women may make steady progress toward the realization of secret hopes and dreams. This may not be visible immediately, however. Friends may prove to be particularly helpful in this specific area of your life. You will be pleased that you have the support and advice to lean on of people who have your best interests at heart. This will be a good time for catching influential people with their guard down. This also seems to be quite a positive day for asking for pay raises. Increase in salary or just a little extra time off to deal with personal issues may be all you need to assure peace of mind. The unusual approach can succeed in winning goodwill and cooperation.

29. THURSDAY. Good. Anything that you had started yesterday but not finished should be followed up. Artistic enterprises that you have been undertaking on your own for some time can be offered to influential people. There will be much better chances of receiving acceptance and approval. Good luck can come to the Crab through the medium of past acquaintances. Someone who you have not seen for some time may have been singing your praises to a person who wields a considerable amount of power. This may prove to be a special boon to your progress. Interviews for new jobs are likely to come off particularly well for you. Charity work can produce good results.

30. FRIDAY. Deceptive. It would be best to avoid the spotlight. The Cancer-born person would be well advised to keep a low profile. Listen to what other people have to say rather than taking any definite steps yourself. Be sure that you do not do anything that would involve you in scandal or other trouble. Those of you in the public eye should keep away from newsmen and gossip columnists. Influential people, such as employers, may make gross miscalculations of the work involved when setting deadlines for Cancer employees. Property transactions are likely to contain risks of deception. Unless it is absolutely essential to deal in real estate now, avoid it. Try to postpone any pending deals.

OCTOBER

1. SATURDAY. Variable. You are likely to find that you have one or two secret errands to carry out today. This will be an important day for financial transactions that you are able to negotiate under a cloud of secrecy. It would be best not to let close associates know what you are planning in the way of future business moves. Keep these to yourself for the time being until you have formulated them more clearly in your own mind. Today should be favorable for secret trysting. It should also be a good day for visiting the sick and infirm. They may be confined in hospital wards or even in their homes. You should take more care of your own physical well-being, too. You could become prey to an illness.

2. SUNDAY. Deceptive.   Cancer-born people may be disappointed at the feeble support they receive from their nearest and dearest. You will not get very much encouragement for your new ideas for changes. You were hoping to implement these around the home this free day. It might be best to attend to hobbies that you can deal with on your own, rather than turning to close friends or family for support. Marital affairs contain the risk of deception. Your mate or partner may have been spending rather more money on riotous living than you had realized. It will be difficult not to lose your temper with people who have not been entirely straight with you. When you deal fairly and squarely with others, you naturally expect the same.

3. MONDAY. Disquieting.   Don't sell yourself short on your work loads. You should allow more time for dealing with heavy, manual jobs. You will get yourself into a state if you try to hurry through chores that require meticulous handling. Although you are keen to add to your income, it would be silly to gloss over details. Do what you can to please your boss today. Influential people will be very helpful if you just try a little harder to satisfy them. Take orders from above and do not attempt to put your original ideas into action just yet. You will get behind schedule if you try to force the pace. Discussions with family or household members are most unlikely to be productive or constructive.

4. TUESDAY. Good.   This is probably going to be the best day of the month, so far. You will find that you are able to get ahead with plans that you have been keeping up your sleeve to date. Influential people will be much more constructive and helpful. Far more exertion should be put into routine affairs so that you can get them cleared out of the way early on. You will require more time to attend to hobbies and creative self-expression. People who operate away from the public eye will be more favorably inclined toward the efforts of the Crab. There will be a good opportunity for projects aimed at raising funds for charity. All in all, you can anticipate a cheerful and more fulfilling day.

5. WEDNESDAY. Quiet.   This will probably not be a particularly active or exciting day. But it will be a valuable period for taking stock of the situation that you currently find yourself in. Once you have that clear, you can decide what moves should be made in the future. You are not likely to be confused or bothered by people in authority. There will be good opportunities to catch up with your backlog of jobs. You had allowed these to pile up since before September came to a close. Go over your accounts and pay up on any bills that are still outstanding. Financial affairs, in general, must be handled with more attention to detail. Attempts to make things happen can lead to disappointment and financial loss.

6. THURSDAY. Good. You will be in a more relaxed mood today. It will be easier for you to see the way ahead. Financial decisions that you have to make will not seem so complicated. Cancer-born people will be able to find valuable ways to cut down on expenditures without lowering any of their living standards. Delay in financial and employment affairs could, in a funny sort of way, turn out to the advantage of Cancer people. You will have more time to make decisions that require caution and a lot of thinking through. Experience and sound common sense are invaluable in attempts to make routine occupational affairs more lucrative. Since you do not lack either, you should do well in that area.

7. FRIDAY. Good. You should find this to be an even better day than yesterday. You will have more determination to carry out your plans. Doubts and fears that you may have been harboring are likely to fade into the background. You and your mate or partner should be able to reconcile differences over money that may have been souring your relationship lately. Thinking can be inspired. This is a period when you should make much more use of your natural talents. Go with your intuition because it will not play you false. Cancer people will also tend to be more compassionate and charitable in their thoughts as well as in their actions. Children will appreciate being treated as grown-ups.

8. SATURDAY. Quiet. There is not much likelihood of a lot of activity taking place either at home or your place of employment. You will be rather pleased that the tempo has slowed down somewhat this Saturday. You will discover that you have any number of minor chores to attend to. Fortunately, they do not require you to rely overly much on others. There would appear to be some necessity for going over the books. Get your accounts straight. Discuss with your mate or partner ways in which expenses can be cut down before you get the weekly shopping done. This is an excellent time for furthering mental and creative endeavors. Devote time to hobbies which give you the most pleasure.

9. SUNDAY. Deceptive. Be very careful about who you confide in today. Sympathetic people may make you want to pour your heart out to them. The trouble is that the very people you might feel you want to discuss your personal problems with are the most likely to gossip or to speak out of turn. It would be best to keep your personal thoughts and feelings to yourself. Or you should restrict such discussions to parents, brothers, or sisters. Spouses and family members will take exception if you spend a lot of time attending to business or public affairs. You must try and make it up to your nearest and dearest if you have been spending a lot of time away from home of late.

10. MONDAY. Good. With more energy at your disposal you will be raring to go this first day of the working week. You should be able to interest superiors in backing your original and unusual ideas. The Cancer charm will work very much to your advantage this time around. You should push hard to get the results that you know you are capable of achieving. Get official letters dealt with early on. You will not be able to cope so well if you get bogged down with routine matters later in the day. It will be favorable for fundamental reassessment of domestic affairs. It is also a good day for frankness with parents and other family members. You should be able to persuade them to speak their minds freely.

11. TUESDAY. Good. Extra perseverance will allow Cancer people to finish work loads ahead of schedule. You should be able to get off to an early start. There will be certain jobs that you can come to grips with before you leave home to travel to your place of employment. Cancer-born people should have good reason to feel pleased with themselves. There is likely to be some good news received over the telephone or through the mail. Someone who is based overseas now may be able to do you a bit of good. This is a very important day for the Cancer business person. Readers who are involved in buying and selling should be able to increase profits. But they must act cautiously, nevertheless.

12. WEDNESDAY. Fair. More of your time should be spent with parents. Do not neglect other older relatives, either. Make sure that loved ones who spend a lot of time on their own are well provided for. Speculative ventures must not be allowed to get out of hand. Do not dip into reserves that are earmarked to pay income tax and other important bills to support gambling habits. It is important that you do not allow yourself to be easily led by close associates. They may try to tell you there are easy pickings to be had if you just follow their tips and their hunches. Public opinion may change unexpectedly. This could affect Cancer people who are involved in the world of show business and entertainment.

13. THURSDAY. Quiet. It would look as if you have been working yourself up into quite a state of tension over the past few days. Although it would seem you have made good progress in your job, you have paid a price, as well. Nerves are likely to be on edge. Perhaps you should slow down a bit. Do not allow yourself to be pushed around by people with powerful personalities. The decisions that you make today must have the comfort and well-being of your nearest and dearest very much at heart. This would be a good day for discussions with loved ones to find better ways to cut down on unnecessary expenditures. This is also the right time to start a new diet.

14. FRIDAY. Variable. perhaps you are expecting too much from this day. You should lower your sights. Readers who are in the world of show business, or are in the public eye in any other way, should not be too pushy. Those of you attending auditions must try harder to show off special talents without appearing over-confident or cocky. Careless thoughts or actions can endanger the health and the welfare of Cancer people. Routine occupational affairs can create some nervous tension and even anxiety. It is important to keep level-headed and efficient, as usual. It should be a good time for strengthening ties of affection. This should not pose any great problem. There are many ways one can do so.

15. SATURDAY. Good. The week will go out with more of a bang than a whimper. Cancer people should be highly delighted if they are able to get through with their work. They probably feared there might be a lot left over until after they had taken a weekend break. Loved ones will be more easygoing and affectionate. Your mate or partner will be more than willing to allow you to go your own way. Family members, generally, will be taking much more of a live-and-let-live attitude to life. Extra time and effort put into routine employment affairs will pay off. There will be good opportunities to influence your boss today. It will be favorable for obtaining the assistance of influential people.

16. SUNDAY. Disturbing. For some reason or another, you are likely to awaken in an extremely bad mood today. It will be hard for you to control your temper. Do not take it out on loved ones just because you are feeling at odds with the world. Try to keep control of your emotions. You may be dwelling in the past. It is no good getting down-in-the-dumps over situations that you are powerless to alter. Ill health may be another problem. Do not ignore minor ailments. If you do not take better care of yourself now, you could find that you are quite sick for a good deal of the week that is about to start. If you want to stay away from everyone today, just do so. You don't have to explain.

17. MONDAY. Variable.   This would be a good time to obtain legal assistance in connection with speculative ventures. You may have been given some information about a certain project that associates wish you would invest in. It would be a good idea to check the facts out with a professional person whom you have found to be reliable in the past. Spouses and partners will be especially helpful when it comes to dealing with the problems of children. Your opposite number will be willing to take on more than his or her fair share of domestic responsibility. You both understand that there is a good deal to cope with in connection with maintaining careers and a busy household.

18. TUESDAY. Variable.   You seem to be going very hard at it for the moment. You do not appear to have a moment to spare. The chances are that you will have to do quite a bit of traveling in your attempts to drum up support. One of the problems for the Cancer-born person today is the fact that government or its officials may withdraw sponsorship from an ongoing project or other cooperative ventures. But partnership resources can help in the launching of new business enterprises. You will be well pleased with the results of any trip that you make. You want to see someone who should be able to give you information that you would not be able to come by nearer to home. Try to put time aside each day for recreation or relaxation.

19. WEDNESDAY. Fair.   Correspondence should be brought up to date. This includes that especially relating to income tax and insurance matters. This is an important day for coming to grips with desk jobs. These may have been postponed or left to one side for some reason or another. Cancer-born people will feel better and will be in a much stronger position from knowing precisely where they stand. Children and youngsters will create something of a problem. You may have to spend quite a long time dealing with the emotional difficulties of members of the younger generation. Pleasure and entertainment plans could lead to some disappointment. You may have been expecting too much.

20. THURSDAY. Good.   This will probably be the best day of the month that you have experienced so far. It would appear that you have had to wait until this middle-of-the-month period to achieve your goals. It involves straightening out certain problems connected with your career and getting influential people won over. You will be feeling much more confident and sure of yourself now. Superiors will show greater interest in your original ideas and you will be encouraged to use your imagination. You may be urged to take your ideas a stage further. It will be favorable for concluding partnership transactions that seem to have become bogged down for one reason or another.

21. FRIDAY. Good.   Make hay while the sun shines. It may be an old maxim, but it still holds. You certainly appear to be in a very strong position. Cancers who are offered new jobs should be able to hold out for a salary they feel that they deserve. Those of you with specialist skills and talents will be able to pick and choose the position they wish to undertake. Loved ones will be helpful. There are not likely not be any important confrontations at home to slow you down in any real way. It will be a favorable day for all Cancers for all study and academic pursuits. It is especially true of those that require you to make special use of your imagination. This is a day for excellence and you should not waste a moment.

22. SATURDAY. Disturbing.   This is likely to be a frustrating day in many ways. It will not be easy to make any new starts. Influential people who you were hoping to track down are likely to be unavailable. The more you can rely on yourself, the better it will be for you. In-laws may place obstacles in the way of the Crab. Overexertion in any self-improvement endeavors could endanger your health. Pay more attention to minor aches and pains. Do not involve yourself in any strenuous physical exercise unless you are almost one hundred percent fit. Long journeys can be subject to unexpected delays and interruptions. This may have serious repercussions for you in the form of missed appointments or even of social affairs.

23. SUNDAY. Deceptive.   Do not get into extravagant habits. Keep your spending within reasonable limits. Try to ascertain just what it will cost you before you agree to go along with the plans for pleasure and entertainment of some of your friends. It would be best to stick to familiar surroundings and not to travel too far afield. It is also important that you give time over to attending to the desires and the needs of your close family. Youngsters may be in need of the moral support of their Cancer parent. Be sure that you do not do anything to shake the belief of a person who looks to you for guidance and advice. You have to spend time listening to them and trying to understand their problems. Otherwise, you will not be able to win their confidence and their implicit trust.

24. MONDAY. Variable. New ways of dealing with persons or labor problems are likely to come to light. Cancer bosses should be able to avoid industrial actions. They will have to talk frankly with the leader of the opposition to find out what the problems are. Only then can any sort of progress be made. Do not lose your temper if and when people make excessive demands on you. Use logic to defeat silly arguments. You should be able to increase efficiency and general output. But the support of influential people and government officials for new business ventures is unlikely to be forthcoming. If that is final, start looking for private groups to approach. Do not be defeated without a struggle.

25. TUESDAY. Variable. This is an auspicious day for becoming actively involved in schemes or organizations that help to make the world a better place to live in. The crusading spirit will be very much in evidence in you today. This is a useful period for drumming up support from people who have the influence and the power to assist you. Relations and friends will become more confiding. You should be able to discuss sensitive issues that you have been keeping bottled up inside of you. This is also an important day for readers who wish to express themselves artistically. Business financial affairs should not be endangered through participation in hazardous ventures. If you want to get involved, do so on your own.

26. WEDNESDAY. Good. This midweek day sees you full of vim and vigor. There will be excellent opportunities to impress people who are in a position to do you some good. Any journeys that you undertake to benefit your career are likely to work out even better than you would have anticipated. Single and unattached Cancer-born people can be fortunate when it comes to forming new relationships. You are likely to find that your company is much in demand by members of the opposite sex. It will be a good day for reaching a friendly agreement with people with whom you have been bickering over money recently. Make every effort to ensure that you and anyone else involved are agreed.

27. THURSDAY. Quiet. Get on top of all jobs that have been piling up throughout the month. Concentrate especially on those chores that you do not want to have hanging over your head when November gets underway. There are not likely to be any particularly difficult situations to cope with either at home or at your place of employment. You may have been contemplating doing something entirely different this Christmas. If so, it would be a good idea to book reservations well in advance. This will pertain especially if your plans incorporate going abroad. Remember that it is not very long now before the festive season will be getting into high gear. Spare time will allow the Crab some opportunities for introspection and soul-searching.

28. FRIDAY. Disturbing. Health may be a problem. You may simply be feeling drained of energy. It is not going to be easy for you to fulfill a heavy schedule. It would be a good idea to cut your workload to the bone. You must not put too much pressure on yourself, either mental or physical. Romantic partners will be jealous and resentful if you do not appear to be giving as much attention to them as usual. People will show little understanding of your desire to get away on your own. Casual romantic affairs may not contain a genuine enough mutual attraction to make the involvement either happy or enduring. Nervousness could lead to insomnia which, in turn, could lead to a run-down physical condition.

29. SATURDAY. Variable. The month and the week are about to come to an end. This will mean there are likely to be quite a few chores in and around the home that you will be eager to catch up with. There also seem to be a number of problems connected with your love life that you will be keen to straighten out. This is a time for making a clean and honest disclosure of things. Try to clear the air between you and your nearest-and-dearest. More time should also be given over to ways to put much more extra cash to one side. You will soon have to meet the heavier winter fuel bills that are going to be coming in within the next few weeks. Sporting activities can bring success and renown for those of you so inclined.

30. SUNDAY. Variable. Romance may contain some disagreements and arguments first thing. Perhaps you and your beloved cannot agree on the best way that leisure time should be spent today. Try not to lose your temper with people who mean a great deal to you. Be more willing to give way on minor issues. Personal plans and schemes may fail to work to your advantage. It would be best not to work out too tight a schedule for today. Family members may require you to do a good deal of running about on their behalf. But influential people will need to be more sympathetic to the individual needs and desires of the Crab. This could prove to be a great boon for you and a real feather in your cap.

31. MONDAY. Good. The month comes to an end on an inspired note. Many of the problems that have been nagging away at the back of your mind will be easier to solve. It should be a favorable period for putting more time and energy into forward planning. Your more ambitious schemes will give you the necessary incentive for further improving your performance. Influential people will be full of praise for any effort on your part to make the most of your natural skills and talents. It will be a good time for concluding financial deals and transactions. Loved ones can be a powerfully beneficial influence behind the scenes. Evening will be a time for jollity. Don't be left out of the fun. Organize a party yourself.

NOVEMBER

1. TUESDAY. Fair. Take one job at a time. There could be a tendency to rush today and this would be a pity. As many of you have learned, more haste would definitely mean less speed. Pay close attention to the advice that is given to you by influential people at your place of employment. Most superiors will not be ordering you around because they enjoy it. If they are telling you what to do, it will be in the interests of your own work performance and for the firm's good. It may be necessary to make a check on recent expenditures. More cash seems to have been going out than has been coming in of late. The pursuit of pleasure may not yield enjoyment equal to the expenses entailed.

2. WEDNESDAY. Good. This should be a very positive day. You should be full of vim and vigor. Make sure that you direct the driving force you seem to possess in a positive way. Do not allow yourself to be misled by friends. Influential people will be helpful. Good advice is more than likely to be passed on to you by people in authority. This is also a starred period for financial transactions. Profits can be increased. It should be a good day for buying and selling antiques and other valuable objects. It should also be favorable for travel in the company of friends and members of your household. Later on, there will be good opportunities for entertaining friends and neighbors.

3. THURSDAY. Variable. There could be some interference with your plans today. You may have to alter business arrangements in order to fit yours in with others. It would be best not to be too dogmatic. You will have to fall in with the schemes of your colleagues if you wish to make any progress at all. You may have to give rather more time to routine affairs than you anticipated. There is a danger of wrongly assessing the character of casual acquaintances. These people may be more unreliable than they seem. More care is needed in the signing of formal documents and contracts. Read the small print before you tie yourself down for years to come. Seek advice of professionals in the field.

4. FRIDAY. Disquieting.   Your health may not be up to snuff. Readers who have recently begun a keep-fit course may be feeling the strain. Do not push your body too far. Diets should not be too severe. You do not want to take any action that could adversely affect your work performance. If you are trying to lose weight, it would be better to do so in easy stages rather than resorting to crash-course methods. This is likely to be a fairly active day, both mentally and physically. Cancer natives would be wise to restrict their activities to what is really useful. Energy can be conserved by using the mail or the telephone rather than making trips in person.

5. SATURDAY. Variable.   There may be far more odd jobs to attend to than you had anticipated. You will not have quite as much time for social activity as you may have hoped. This will be especially true during the daytime period. It might be best to make an early start with your routine affairs. If you leave mundane tasks until later in the day, you will be hard pushed to find the necessary drive to carry them through to a successful conclusion. Cancer workers who have to attend places of regular employment will have to make an extra effort to keep their minds from wandering. Lack of concentration would have serious consequences. Parents or family members may bring good luck and happiness.

6. SUNDAY. Good.   This will be an important day for attending to family affairs. Cancer people will probably be at their happiest staying at home today. There will be much to attend to, keeping you meaningfully occupied within your own four walls. It should not be necessary to spend a great deal of money. You can get the best that this day has to offer doing relatively simple things like walking or visiting a museum. There is not likely to be a great deal of pressure put on you by loved ones. You and your mate or partner should find that your relationship has very much improved. It should be a good time for deepening ties of affection between you and current romantic partners.

7. MONDAY. Good.   You should have plenty of energy and zest for your job, after yesterday's restful and enjoyable break. Get off to an early start. It would be a good idea to throw yourself wholeheartedly into your work first thing. Outstanding affairs that were left over from last week can be successfully concluded within a short time. You should be looking for ways now to put more cash to one side over the next few weeks. Bills will be increasing to meet the additional expense of the coming festive season. The holiday season is not very far away now. Some Cancer people may feel that a relationship is coming to an end. They should have the strength of character to call it a day.

8. TUESDAY. You appear to be slap-bang in the middle of a very important period. You must do all that you can to push yourself harder. Let influential people be aware of your natural talents. You should have no difficulty in expressing yourself well when it comes to making a good impression on superiors. You may have the chance to streamline mundane jobs and show off your natural inventiveness. This is a period for buying surprise gifts for loved ones and intimate friends. It is favorable also for buying clothes and perhaps some special treats for children. Partners or spouses who have earned a break can perhaps be given an extra vacation or an occasional day off.

9. WEDNESDAY. Good. Today could see the culmination of all that you have been striving so hard to achieve. You should be well pleased with the progress that you have been able to make. Everything seems to have gone very smoothly for you so far this week. Push hard while your luck is in to get influential people to accept your ideas for change and progress. Meetings with influential people under social conditions should go especially well for you. Do not be reluctant about coming forward with your ideas. Lay the groundwork for new speculative enterprises that you have to launch very soon. Cancer people should consider trying their hand at a new outdoor sport.

10. THURSDAY. Variable. Romance is likely to be uppermost in your mind. This looks like a favorable day for contacting someone whom you recently met socially and would like to see again. Cancer people should show more confidence in their dealings with the opposite sex. Intimate evenings out can be arranged. The Crab will find it easier than usual to make the right impression. Your efforts will be noticed and appreciated at your place of employment. This could lead to promotion in your particular field of endeavor. But there is a risk of such success causing hostility and envy among co-workers. Nothing should be done that could stir up such emotions.

11. FRIDAY. Good. This will be a good day for putting the pressure on. You should do what you can to speed things up. There is extra money to be made today. Don't allow yourself to be sidetracked. Friends or loved ones will play an active role in helping Cancer-born people to meet deadlines in work situations. You should be able to give all of your attention to your job. Family members and close associates will be willing to deal with smaller routine jobs. You will then be able to get immersed in affairs that you consider to be of major importance. Even activities will be enjoyable because associates will be in a cheery mood.

12. SATURDAY. Disquieting. This last day of the week is likely to be something of an anticlimax. You will have problems in getting along with the very people with whom you had been hoping to join forces. Even old friends will be unpredictable and irritable. The sort of jobs that you should concentrate attention on are those which do not require any outside assistance. Cancer people must avoid too much self-imposed strain, whether physical or emotional. Unorthodox methods of treatment may help alleviate ailments where the more usual methods fail to have any effect. Partners or spouses may appear deliberately uncooperative. Quarrels should be avoided, however, if at all possible.

13. SUNDAY. Deceptive. Don't allow yourself to be hoodwinked by people who have the gift of gab. So-called friends may be trying hard to get you to invest in their schemes. But you must not part with money to back ventures where there is a high degree of speculation. The risk of loss could be great and definitely not worth it. When dealing with loved ones, it is essential that you demonstrate your own good intentions. By doing so, you should discover that your nearest and dearest will be more willing to make some sacrifices. But marital affairs are likely to contain some degree of intrigue and deception. More attention should be paid to youngsters. Take children on outings to visit close relatives.

14. MONDAY. Variable. Legal problems that may have been giving you a headache should only be discussed with people whose professional expertise could be helpful. Influential associates will be willing to give you the benefit of their experience. The advice that you receive may be a little difficult to follow. If you can exert the necessary discipline over yourself, however, it will be well worth heeding. Those people who are in the driver's seat will be willing to give official backing to teamwork and other cooperative endeavors. This will also include speculative schemes. Children may cause panic all of a sudden by disappearing. Words need to be chosen with more care. A careless remark might be misinterpreted, causing unnecessary hurt or resentment, perhaps both.

15. TUESDAY. Variable. In many ways you will have a somewhat frustrating time of it. You seem to have been making excellent progress in certain areas of your life, but all that is likely to come to a dead stop now. Partnership resources must not be tapped to back extravagant or unrealistic living standards. You may not be able to afford the luxury entertainment that friends want you to become involved in. When it comes to dealing with your regular job you are likely to be more than usually successful. Cancer business and career people can make valuable strides forward in their chosen fields of endeavor. This is contingent on your obtaining the goodwill and assistance of people behind the scenes.

16. WEDNESDAY. Variable. Find out what has been going on behind the scenes. Secret enemies may become converted into actively helpful associates. You should spend more time dealing with background figures. This is an important day for readers who are involved in the world of the arts or entertainment. This time should be favorable for setting up home with a loved one. You may be making an important decision about your personal life today. A friendly agreement with a financial partner can help to reduce unnecessary or unwise expenditures. It is a good time for dealing with all outstanding matters connected with alimony payments. Try to establish rapport with whoever is involved.

17. THURSDAY. Good. After a brief marking-time period, you seem to be back in the saddle. This is an important day for catching up with jobs that you had been hoping to start work on much earlier in the week. You should be willing to accept overtime work. The payments that your receive for additional output are likely to be much improved. Show more interest in your regular job. If there is greater enthusiasm on your part, it should be possible to win over superiors. Cancer people will tend to be more intuitive and even prophetic. Dreams should be recorded as there is a greater chance than usual of their coming true. It is good for study and academic pursuits with the help of others.

18. FRIDAY. This is another favorable day for going on trips. You should try to broaden your horizons. Readers who are involved in the business of buying and selling should be able to drum up business in distant parts. There will be little to hold you back. Cancers who earn their living on a commission basis should be able to increase orders. It looks as though you will be earning some sort of promotion very soon if you carry on as you are now doing. This is a time of the year when you will certainly be grateful for any extra cash that is coming in. It would be a good time for starting vacations or obtaining extended vacation leave from superiors and employers. Children will appreciate being treated with authority and also with respect.

19. SATURDAY. Variable. If there are jobs that you need to carry out in seclusion, the morning period will be the best time for doing this. Work that requires you to consult with people who operate way from the public eye can also be carried out first thing. You may have to make a journey at a moment's notice. This is not a day when it would be a good idea to plan too far ahead. You will have to go more on your intuition. Do not worry about that as it is not likely to play you false. Where ambitions are concerned, Cancer people should not try too hard. Do not bother influential people when they are at home if you can just as easily get in touch with them at the office or work place on Monday.

20. SUNDAY. Quiet. This weekend day is likely to be just what the doctor ordered. You should not have to expend a great deal of energy today. This is likely to be one of those days that will allow the Cancer-born person extra time for pursuing his or her own activities. Catch up with hobbies and pastimes that take your mind off problems connected with the work-a-day week. Loved ones are unlikely to be putting any special pressure on you, for a nice change. It should be good for giving some attention to writing letters in order to promote your career prospects. But people with bad names and reputations should be avoided at all costs.

21. MONDAY. Good. This will be an up-and-at-'em day! You should have plenty of energy. There are not likely to be any problems over getting into high gear. There will be lots of jobs to deal with, both at home and at your place of regular employment. The possibility of earning extra money will give you all the incentive that you require. The period up to and including midday will be helpful for establishing ongoing talks with business colleagues. These relate to joint financial ventures and activities. The experience and know-how of such people can be invaluable to you. Later in the day you will have the chance to spend more time with loved ones. The company of mutual friends is likely to appeal to you.

22. TUESDAY. Variable. Business financial problems that have been nagging away at the back of your mind are likely to let up of their own accord. Some news that you receive from your accountant, or from some similar professional advisor, is likely to ease your mind on this score considerably. It will no longer be so difficult for you to concentrate on routine affairs. Be more adaptable and flexible. In this way, you can boost your efficiency as well as increase your earnings. But superiors may be tight-fisted and hold back bonus payments until later in the year. You may feel that people in authority are keeping back a greater portion of the profits than they should. This will be hard to challenge.

23. WEDNESDAY. Variable. The Crab is likely to feel very optimistic today without really knowing why. But some fortunate developments are likely to be just around the corner. You will be filled with feelings of eager anticipation. Your confidence will rub off on others. You should be able to bring a positive influence to bear on associates at your place of employment. Some of them seem to have been a bit down in the dumps lately. There may be extra work loads imposed on you by your boss. You are probably going to have to work flat-out if you are going to achieve all that is expected of you. Good for furthering hobbies and all ambitious schemes that you can squeeze into your leisure time.

24. THURSDAY. Good. This will be a very important day. It would appear that you will have plenty of opportunities to further your career interests without having to be too pushy. This will tend to be a more relaxed and peaceful day. Cancers will find that they are allowed extra opportunities for privacy, quiet and seclusion. Problems connected with love and romance are likely to solve themselves. Love interests with people older and more mature than yourself are likely to blossom. You may find that you are leaning toward a particular type of person to whom you have never been attracted before. This will be rather exciting for you, as well as for the other person. Do all you can to keep this friendship.

25. FRIDAY. Disturbing. You appear to have had things go pretty well your own way of late. All that is likely to change today, however, and you may be brought down-to-earth with a bump. Cancer people must avoid jumping to conclusions. Although your intuition is usually on target, this is one of those rare periods when it is likely to be playing tricks upon you. Go on facts and facts alone. This applies especially when it comes to making decisions that would affect the future well-being and security of you and yours. Health can suffer due to overexcitement and nervous tension. Partners and loved ones may make what seems to you to be unreasonable demands. Try to reason with them without losing your temper.

26. SATURDAY. Good. Everything points to your being back on the right track. In fact, yesterday's difficult trends may have done you some good. They stopped you dead in your tracks. After Friday's experiences you will take your time when you have to make a decision affecting others. It might be best to sleep on any important ones that you have to make with regard to your career. This will be especially true if you have been thinking about changing your job. You must give more thought to what your nearest and dearest feel if you have been contemplating a move to another town or city. This is a pleasant day for entertainment and for your search for pleasure.

27. SUNDAY. Excellent. Coupled with what took place yesterday, this has all the hallmarks of a memorable weekend. You should be feeling fairly pleased with yourself and the progress that you have been able to make. Cancer people may well have been able to put enough cash to one side to fund a dream holiday this Christmas. You will certainly want to do all that you can to make people close to you happy and contented. The nice thing about today is that you will have much more choice as to how you spend your leisure time. This is also an excellent time for attending to practical matters. Being able to get hold of usually unobtainable people can bring financial gain. It should be a good time for taking advantage of intrigue and double-dealing.

28. MONDAY. Variable. Improved reputations can bring financial gain. For Cancer readers there is a possibility that you will be able to get involved socially with influential people. You have longed to meet such community leaders and discuss matters affecting everyone. At your place of employment it would be a good idea to take a firmer stand with difficult people and known troublemakers. Cancer workers may receive substantial bonuses or pay raises. Any extra cash that comes in should be plowed into savings schemes and not frittered away. Resist the desire to be extravagant in your search for romance and pleasure. Thinking should be kept practical and to the point.

29. TUESDAY. Quiet. There will not be anything particularly exciting taking place today. In fact, this is a period that is almost certain to be marked by its lack of activity. There are not likely to be any difficult or exciting developments. Routine activities are best. There will be a number of desk jobs to attend to. Included are letters to be written that you will be pleased to get rid of before November comes to a close. Some budgeting may be the best way of preserving incomes and boosting personal resources. Have a quiet evening at home. Family relationships will benefit from your giving more attention to domestic issues; this could be vital.

30. WEDNESDAY. Variable. An original or inventive move on the part of Cancer workers may bring them rewards. Don't be afraid to speak up if you see a way in which routine affairs can be streamlined. Superiors will encourage you to take advantage of your specialist skills and abilities. These could be of great value to you in increased responsibilities and income. Trial and error can indicate to the self-employed the best and the easiest ways to maximize earnings. It is far better for you to experiment today than merely to follow old patterns. Romance can be truly romantic. Dreams may at last come true. Readers who are unattached may bump into the man or woman of their dreams.

DECEMBER

1. THURSDAY. Good. You will begin the last month of the year feeling fairly confident. This is a good day for pushing your new projects hard. You had hoped to launch these before the end of December and get them accepted by people who have the influence and power to help you. It will be easier to track down people in other towns and cities whose support would be beneficial to you. This is a favorable time for creative writing and all mental endeavors. You will not have so many interruptions to contend with. Associates will be more communicative and can be persuaded to state their intentions in clear and straightforward terms. You may not agree, but now you know what they are planning.

2. FRIDAY. Variable. Good news is likely to come your way through the mail. Correspondence will be important. Letters that you write today to business people in other towns or cities could save you a journey later on. Relatives will be instrumental in bringing about the realization of secret hopes and dreams. This is going to be an important day from the point of view of close personal relationships. You ought to be able to straighten out just where you stand with a member of the opposite sex. You may have felt that the person has just been playing with your feelings. It is essential that you do not neglect routine or monotonous tasks that come around on a regular basis.

3. SATURDAY. Deceptive. Be far more careful who you trust, especially where money is concerned. Do not part with cash to back the speculative schemes of friends. Close associates will be trying all sorts of ploys to get you to dig deeper into your reserves. With Christmas not so far away you really cannot afford to gamble on half-chances. Domestic obligations can conflict with business or career activities. You will have a lot of pressure to cope with at home. Your opposite number will be making demands on you that conflict with your own ideas. It will be difficult to prevent serious arguments from erupting. Insufficient attention to detail can leave Cancer people open to severe criticism and even some reproof.

4. SUNDAY. Deceptive. This will be another tricky day from the point of view of all personal relationships. Watch your temper first thing. Silly bickering with other members of the family could result in big arguments breaking out. These, in turn, could lead to walkouts. There will be a number of duties that you have to attend to that may conflict with your plans for seeking pleasure and entertainment. This will not be a particularly demanding or strenuous day. But from the mental point of view, you are likely to be in a state of inner turmoil. Bring outstanding affairs to a conclusion as soon as you can tie up all loose ends. With another year not far away, you must make preparations for a new cycle of activity.

5. MONDAY. Good. This will be an extra-special day. You will be feeling full of the joys of spring even though it is nearer to Christmas. Loved ones will be easier to get on with and that will make you truly happy. There will be good opportunities to work, in a way that will bring you in extra cash. It will be favorable for furthering hobbies and spare time interests. Cancer people will be in a creative and artistic mood. Original work will be highly appreciated by those people who are in a position to be of assistance to you. Financial backing is likely to be forthcoming. Treat your mate or partner to a special surprise. An unexpected gesture will cheer them up if they are down in the dumps.

6. TUESDAY. Disquieting. Children and youngsters need to be treated with more care and consideration. Parents should become aware of the desires and spiritual needs of their brood. Spare time should be devoted to family affairs. You must watch your temper today. You appear to be in an emotional mood and this could cause you to act out of character. You may even have to impose stricter discipline on teenagers for their own good. Be sure that you do not backslide out of your responsibilities. A friendly chat will also help relatives to see reason. It will also give them greater insight into your motives and into the reasons for acting the way you do. This could clear the air and allay ill feelings.

7. WEDNESDAY. Disquieting. Speculative ventures can spell bad news for the Crab. This is certainly not a time when you should gamble or take chances with your hard-earned cash in any other way. You will lose your standing with people in powerful positions if you become enmeshed in risky enterprises with shady characters. Friends are likely to behave irresponsibly. People with whom you have made certain arrangements are likely to let you down. You may have to reassess your opinion of people who you thought you could trust. Cancers may be left holding the bag for the mistakes of other people. Accusations must on no account be made before you are sure that you can justify them, however.

8. THURSDAY. Good. Extra exertion put into routine or occupational affairs can be instantly rewarded. This is one of those days when you can earn more money if you are prepared to exert yourself. You will have to put more time in at your place of employment. You may be asked to work through your lunch hour or put in some overtime. It will be well worth your while, however, to give up leisure hours. The cash that you can make today will be extremely helpful for covering extra Christmas expenditures. Ambitious urges may be gratified through promotion. Employees will be responsive to the urgings of the Cancer boss to increase productivity and efficiency.

9. FRIDAY. Good. This will be a pleasant routine day. You are more than likely to find time to squeeze in many little chores that you have been putting to one side. Come to grips with desk jobs like accounting. This is also a good period for using your lunch hour to buy Christmas presents and cards. You and your mate or partner may be making the final arrangements for however you wish to spend Christmas. It may be that you are going to have a much larger number of people over to your home than usual. It would be a good idea to extend invitations now so that those you invite do not get tied up in any other way.

10. SATURDAY. Deceptive. Watch your step. So-called bargains may not be worth the cash that is being asked. Make sure that any goods you buy from door-to-door salesmen or street merchants are guaranteed. Do not be taken in by smooth-talking people who have the gift of the gab. Partners and associates can be devious and even resort to deception. This pertains especially if they are unwilling to admit to their inner confusion. You will also

become extremely annoyed with loved ones who are so opinionated they refuse to listen to reason. Legal complications can cause
impatience and even loss of temper. This will do nothing whatso-
ever to speed matters up. You may as well try to push water uphill.

11. SUNDAY. Good. There will be a feeling of excitement and
general optimism within your home. Loved ones will be in high
spirits. It will be possible for you to get your plans for pleasure and
entertainment accepted by other people. You should not need to
spend lot of money to extract the best that this day has to offer.
Romance is highlighted. This is a lucky day for the Cancer person
who is in love. You will feel far more sure of the emotions of a
person who you have been keen on for some time. This is an auspicious day for making relationships that mean a lot to you more
permanent. Now is the right time to commit yourself more
definitely to a new relationship.

12. MONDAY. Good. Go all-out for what you know you can
achieve if you really put your mind to it. This is a very favorable
period for research into current business ventures. You may be
able to find ways to realize greater profits from projects that are
already under way. You should have no difficulty in getting on
with influential people. Your boss will have time and the inclination to listen to what you have to say with regard to creative enterprises. Information and data gathered in connection with other
people involved can give the Cancer person a head start over possible competitors. Take advantage of any such opportunity and put
it to good use.

13. TUESDAY. Variable. Cancer women readers are likely to
have a lot to cope with. You must not work yourself up into a
state. Deal with one job at a time. You will probably be trying to
get ahead with lots of little jobs. You certainly do not want to have
to cope with these when the Christmas rush gets under way. Be
sure to send your Christmas cards to people in faraway places early
so they will arrive on time. Parents may be making demands on
you and you may have to run certain errands on their behalf.
Influential people, especially bankers and employers, can help to
improve the future economic outlook of the Cancer native.

14. WEDNESDAY. Fair. This may be a so-so day. It looks as if
you will have the opportunity to make certain gains through the
extra cash that comes in. But that is likely to be swallowed up in
the payment of regular bills and Christmas expenditures. This is
quite a good day to get in some Christmas shopping before the

rush gets into full swing. This is an important day for teamwork and cooperation. People at or from a distance can be especially helpful to your plans. The recovery of debts can be ensured by legal decisions. Loved ones will come up with original and novel ideas for having a good time that would be worthy of careful consideration. They will be delighted to have you accept their ideas.

15. THURSDAY. Good.   Today you are likely to be full of the joys of the festive season. For you, at last, the Christmas spirit will be very much in the air. You and your loved ones will be making plans to turn this special time of the year into a memorable period. The morning should be favorable for confirming vacation or holiday reservations. Affairs or events at a distance may provide opportunities to make gains through speculation. Money for investment will be easier to get hold of. This is a good period for study and academic pursuits. It will be easier to concentrate on details, especially those that give scope for personal self-expression.

16. FRIDAY. Variable.   People or events at a distance will continue to be particularly important to you. It will be a good day for travel. You will feel inhibited if you have to spend too much time at home or at your place of regular employment. Secret hopes and wishes can move a step nearer to realization. You will be able to have favorable meetings with influential people behind closed doors. Some information may be passed on to you that will save you a lot of time and trouble. But others may let you down by failing to honor verbal commitments or even contractual obligations. Loved ones can overreact and make mountains out of molehills.

17. SATURDAY. Disturbing.   Cancer business or career people are advised not to take any chances. Nor should they place too much hope in the speculative schemes of others. This is the wrong day for gambling. You should try to keep as much money as you can to one side to pay for unexpected expenditures which are likely to be cropping up. This will not be an easy day for the Crab who has had to leave it until this weekend to do the bulk of his or her Christmas shopping. The crowds will undoubtedly get on your nerves. It will not be easy to find the gifts that you want for people who are difficult to please at the best of times. But the day will be good for clearing up any obstacles connected with desk jobs.

18. SUNDAY. Good.   You will enjoy today because you will be feeling much more relaxed. You will get plenty of enjoyment out of giving more time to family affairs. It should be an exciting day for discussing Christmas plans and for getting your presents wrapped. Try to fit in visits to people who you will not be able to see on Christmas day. Take a trip to call in on old friends and relatives who may be alone and feeling a bit down in the dumps. Although this is a Sunday, contacts with influential people can bode well for occupational and career affairs. You may have the opportunity to discuss your future at the home of your boss. You should be feeling a good deal more secure.

19. MONDAY. Disquieting. This could be a tricky time for you. You may be feeling a little tired and drained of energy. Something inside of you is likely to be fighting against carrying out routine chores. It may be that all of the excitement of Christmas has wound you up into a highly nervous state. There are also likely to be constant interruptions at the office or work place. You should double-check all accounting work that you are responsible for. Mistakes made now in accounts will be difficult to rectify at a later date. Business finances can be subject to severe loss through speculation. Club and group activities may interfere with the personal lives of the Crab.

20. TUESDAY. Variable. Romance may be an area about which you will have to do some serious thinking. You may have good reason to be worried about your feelings for a person who has been playing an important role in your life for some time. You may even be a little afraid to commit yourself to a long-standing relationship. Do not make promises that you may not be able to keep. But good luck can come to Cancer people through the activities of friends and acquaintances. Close associates will rally round and do what they can to cheer you up and to boost your confidence. This should be a good time for channeling business profits into new, expansive schemes.

21. WEDNESDAY. Good. Thinking will tend to become more imaginative. You will be coming up with some good ideas any day now. They will be likely to get the support for Christmas events from loved ones. This is an important time for dealing with little jobs. You surely do not want to have them hanging over your head when you are determined to give yourself and your loved ones a good time. Get involved in routine jobs. There will also be better opportunities to deal with affairs like the wrapping of Christmas presents. Make sure that you send off cards to your friends. Do not forget a person who always remembers you with a little gift. This is a favorable time for dealing with secret enemies.

22. THURSDAY. Disturbing. Perhaps you have bitten off rather more than you can chew. Whatever it is, you may want to whittle down your program. Get your priorities straight. There will be difficult conditions to cope with at your place of employment. Your boss may quite unrealistically expect you to attend to more work than you had realized. You maybe required to put in some overtime and this could hamper your social plans. Your boss may not be clear in his or her own mind about whom to bestow favors on. It will hardly be surprising then that their actions appear unpredictable to you. Loved ones and dependents may go out of their way to prove their so-called independence and freedom.

23. FRIDAY. Deceptive. Be careful what you purchase, especially if you are in a hurry. Remember the old adage that all that glitters is not gold. Door-to-door sales people may try to impress on you the value of their wares. Just be sure that whatever you purchase carries a guarantee. This will be a tricky day for dealing with difficult and highly strung people. Parents and other older relatives may be making demands on you that you regard as little short of emotional blackmail. Colleagues and associates cannot be relied upon to honor their commitments. In legal affairs there is a risk of double-dealing and deception. But the day is favorable for trips in connection with partnership affairs.

24. SATURDAY. Variable. You will be rushed off your feet today. As this is the last shopping day before Christmas you are not likely to have a spare moment to yourself. It would be wise to keep your schedule uncluttered and manageable. Conversations with partners or loved ones may become unexpectedly heated. Little differences could develop into full-scale rows. Try to keep control of your emotions and your temper. This is definitely not a day for rushing into new business commitments. Important agreements and negotiations would be best postponed until after the New Year. The evening will be an especially cheerful period. Friends will make congenial company.

25. SUNDAY. MERRY CHRISTMAS! This will be a relaxed and enjoyable Christmas day. Whether you are spending your leisure time at home or at the home of friends, you will enjoy yourself. It should be possible for you to do whatever you like. Loved ones and friends will not be putting any pressure on you. There will be the opportunity to attend some social gathering later on. This will appeal particularly to the reader who may have had enough of cooking and similar chores. But Cancer people who are looking for excitement and distraction are likely to be disappointed. Gifts of money may be received or gift certificates.

26. MONDAY. Variable. Don't waste money on gambling. You appear to be in an impulsive mood when you would be likely to take silly risks. Curb the impetuous streak in your nature. Do not mix with people who could have an unhealthy influence on you. You should be seeking ways to plow more cash into your bank account. There surely will be hefty bills to pay early in the New Year. Don't spoil children. Make sure that youngsters appreciate the simple things in life. Generosity is not always the best way of showing care and affection for youngsters. Routine career activities are likely to offer opportunities for gain. But influential people will tend to be cold to the basic needs of the Cancer native.

27. TUESDAY. Variable. You may be finding it somewhat difficult to get back into the swing of things. Do not try to rush through jobs just because there is quite a backlog for you to cope with. Cancer readers are probably going to be snowed under at home. There will be plenty of tidying up to do. It would be a good idea for those who have been overindulging to get onto some sort of diet. Cut back on your intake of starchy foods and alcohol. Finances require more careful handling than usual. Go over accounts. Be sure that you are not charged twice over for goods or services that have recently been rendered.

28. WEDNESDAY. Fair. Get around and meet people as this can lead to the forming of unexpected and long-standing friendships. It should be a good day for teamwork and all cooperative endeavors. See what you can do to clear up any legal confusions that have recently arisen. See professional people such as your lawyer or accountant if you are at all unsure about where you stand in the eyes of the law. Loved ones may be hard to get through to. They are likely to be placing work before romance. Do not press your affections on people who seem to be cold. The Cancer-born will be left very much to fend for themselves. The evening is good for pursuing hobbies and other creative work.

29. THURSDAY. Good. It should be possible to get back into top gear. Teamwork will be important today. A job shared will be a job halved. Try to get associates to join forces with you. That will help you to get rid of dull routine desk jobs far more quickly and efficiently. This is an especially important day for entering into new partnership agreements. Links that are forged today augur well for the future. Influential people will be helpful and will encourage you to go further with your original and artistic ideas. It should also be good for the signing of agreements and official documents. Casual acquaintances can be especially good-natured and generous. Be sure to respond in a sincere and warm manner.

30. FRIDAY. Disturbing.   A letter that arrives today or possibly a telephone call that comes in could be rather upsetting. There will be news from a distance that could cause you to change your plans for today. This is definitely not a time when you should take anyone or anything for granted. Other family or household members can strongly oppose the introduction of changes that you are keen to put into practice in the home. It would be better to bide your time just now. Wait for a more favorable day before you try to alter the ways by which day-to-day events are handled. This is not a time for borrowing money in order to finance property moves. Cancer people may be unable to pay back their debts.

31. SATURDAY. Variable.   Routine and other occupational work is likely to contain fringe benefits. The effort to meet deadlines will bring job satisfaction as well as financial gain. The week and the month and the year should come to an end with your feeling a good deal more optimistic about what the future holds for you. Loved ones will be willing to fall in with your plans for seeing the New Year in. But influential people should not be relied upon too heavily. Their promises should be taken with the veritable grain of salt. Your bosses' memories will be vague and may desert them. Social activities will be memorable. There could be romance in the air for the footloose and fancy-free reader. Whatever else you do, see the New Year in with some merrymaking.

October–December 1987

OCTOBER

1. THURSDAY. Satisfactory. Active cooperation is what you need. Without this a great deal of your efforts can be wasted. Recognition will not come easily, but that is not your main focus at the moment. It would be much better to maintain good relationships with your everyday contacts. In this way you can build up your resources on a reliable basis. Partners in business may not see eye-to-eye with you. Let this ride for the moment. Do not trust such people. They may put appearances before essential cooperation and achieve nothing. Rely on your own judgment and on the friendship of those you meet every day. Relatives are friendly.

2. FRIDAY. Manageable. Seek the advice of a parent or senior member of the family. You do not like to take family business out of the nest, so listen to wisdom at home. If you are having a problem meeting family commitments, remember this is nothing new. Provided you keep your head there is no fear of wasting money. But you will need to discipline yourself. It is all too easy to give in to the demands of children. Arrive at a working agreement that will make your family income more secure. It may be a good idea to have insurance premiums paid in advance at their source. This can save you worry over missing a crucial date and expense. Look for a permanent arrangement to free you from such aggravation.

3. SATURDAY. Good. Spend some money on brightening up the home. This will be a good investment and will add to the value of your property. Take note of family views on investment. Get an all-round opinion for future transactions. It seems an appropriate time to do some research with an open mind. Methods and rewards should be considered seriously before action is taken. Property matters can be settled without disagreement. You should find happiness in the company of someone well-known to the family. Entertain at home. A trip to see someone you admire may follow later in the day. Prepare the way with a bit of self-promotion. This will do no harm and could even help you.

4. SUNDAY. Harmonious.   Get moving early in the day. If local interests kept you at home yesterday, make an early start. The wide-open spaces beckon you and yours. Visits to family can be undertaken. Equally important, you are also in a position to entertain. The main thing is to meet friends and family you see infrequently. Look up travel schedules for future vacations. it may be wise to plan ahead in order to get the best treatment. Students should have a good and productive weekend. A break from regular studies will prove beneficial. Develop your interests and broaden your mind generally. There is nothing like travel to do this.

5. MONDAY. Sensitive.   Nothing fits into place today. You may be glad to avoid routine and long for the open road. But even that can provide its quota of problems. Traveling will not be the pleasant pastime you had expected it to be. Working conditions create problems. Imported material is not up to usual standards. A deal with an overseas firm is more trouble than it is worth. Try to keep emotions under control, although that will be difficult. A working relationship can save the day. You should be able to resolve a lot of problems in the quiet and peace of home. Security is strengthened by a rearrangement of your working routine.

6. TUESDAY. Strenuous.   You are full of ideas. Concentrate on those that seem to offer the most reward and have a sound basis. Creative urges are strong, so you could be a bit wayward. Opposition may be met from a parent or senior member of the family. If you seek to show off too much you are likely to be brought back to earth quickly. Family ties may prove to be overriding. A partner could let you down. You have your own ideas and this may rule out cooperative action. So do not expect help from others. It is usually best to go your own way. Consider your reputation in all aspects. There are some who would like to get you down off your pedestal. See to it that your position is secure.

7. WEDNESDAY. Productive.   It should be a happy day to be away from home responsibilities. Business will be much more attractive and work more stimulating. You can make a lot of headway and be given the room to develop and expand your efforts. Concentrate on the job at hand. Do not waste any time on trivialities. It may be difficult to include some things, so ignore them and get on with something else that fits into place. This is a day of opportunity. You cannot please everyone, even those who depend on your labors. But despite this, you should be able to make a great deal of progress that is essential to your future prospects. If the family feels neglected, try to explain the pros and cons to them.

8. THURSDAY. Difficult. You can get carried away with idealistic plans. Seek the cooperation of willing partners in whatever
you contemplate. Only genuine support will be offered, so you
need not be suspicious. Opposition to your aims will have to be
faced. A deep-seated resentment may be stirred up in some areas.
Be firm in your reaction. Try to guide your personal talents for the
benefit of people who can be steered toward a humanitarian goal.
You may have to choose between using such talents for purely personal or social advantage. If a balance cannot be struck, something
may have to go by the board. You might rationalize the choice. If
you opt for social advantage, you will be apt to reap benefit.

9. FRIDAY. Disconcerting. This would appear to be an
uneventful day. You could have difficulty in getting any idea or
project accepted that you think is worthwhile. Dumb insolence or
a blank stare might greet you. For those involved with children or
education this can be frustrating. Try to forge ahead anyway and
remember that you are trying to improve the lot of someone who
needs help. No one is particularly reliable. You will be far better
off on your own, keeping your distance in company and remaining
friendly or somewhat aloof. Avoid intimate involvement. You
may be misunderstood and that would not benefit you.

10. SATURDAY. Rewarding. Make the most of weekend privacy. Settle down to interests that have been neglected too long.
You will be energetic and so can make adequate plans for work
that will benefit the whole family. Take into consideration all matters connected with the home that you can handle yourself. Where
you need advice, a member of the family with more experience
will be ready to oblige. A parent can be extra helpful and set your
mind at rest. Consider a long-term contract for house maintenance. This seems like a good time to make firm arrangements.
Lay plans for a lengthy schedule that will attend to the basic needs
of the family. Their hard work should be recognized.

11. SUNDAY. Pleasant. Collect your thoughts. Planning is essential while you have peace and privacy. Opposition to some
scheme may make you ponder the pros and cons of the present
situation. Take note of any advice or support offered by someone
of importance. It would be sensible to entertain such a person in
order to cultivate a private source of strength for the future.
Should you take life too seriously, this could be a worrisome day.
You may try to do too much or think you are hardier than is the
case. Avoid taking on too heavy a responsibility and thus endangering your health. A friend in need may be glad of your attention.

12. MONDAY. Uncertain. It will be a day of changing emphasis. Workaday problems make life uncertain early on. Be prepared for changes and erratic behavior from your colleagues. An opportunity to make headway can come later. Someone may pass the word to you in private. You seem to be in favor with the fair sex and at war with men in general later in the day. This may mean a complicated evening for you, so play your cards with care. Romance seems promising and this will suit you. Your ego can be boosted. Look out for squalls at home if you disturb the family. A member of the family may take a dim view of some of your activities, and you must expect some criticism in the process.

13. TUESDAY. Exciting. Something you started yesterday may build up today. Your lovelife can become more and more interesting. Emotions may run high, but you will find this exciting. If you are married there is a possibility that your partner may take a poor view of your manner. For those without ties, this could be a day to develop a new relationship. Be on your guard that you do not misjudge your opposite number. You could get carried away and perhaps lose out if you are not honest with yourself and your new-found friend. You might wind up behind the eight ball or may be led up the garden path. So be romantic, but avoid entanglements. Make good use of your artistic and creative talents.

14. WEDNESDAY. Strenuous. Do not push your luck. The urge to go your own way can be strong. Given a bit of rope, you could hang yourself, figuratively speaking. You could be tempted to seek public favor. What you have to propose to any backer or business friend will not be received well. It is too risky at the moment. Your security can be threatened if you take on too much and do not heed the advice of people with influence. This may be frustrating. Stay away from any property deals for a week or so. You can do a lot of homework in the interim. Look for moral support or just comfort from a partner who has helped you before when you were in trouble. This will help you cope.

15. THURSDAY. Sensitive. You could feel like splashing your money around. Your first priority should be the home. You may not be looking for bargains, but you should have a clear idea of what you are after before you hit the stores. Deal directly and you should get your money's worth. The young and unattached may have more problems. You are eager to please. What you wish to do can be very expensive. Try to impress someone you admire with your natural talents. Should you have to resort to buying your favors, this will cost you a bundle. There is a possibility of going too far, in some respects. But if you are making someone happy, you will take it all in your stride.

16. FRIDAY. Satisfactory. You will be aware of your true worth. Take a good hard look at yourself, your prospects, and your abilities. This should give you heart and confidence. Apply yourself to whatever has to be done and see that you get due reward for your labor. No one will sell you short today, possibly because you have made your mind up to get your rights. Your finances should be sound. You will feel you are getting somewhere. You may be tempted to sign away some asset. Someone could try to talk you out of hard-earned cash. Keep clear of such temptation. Children may be expensive. If you have to pay a school fee this could be unavoidable.

17. SATURDAY. Promising. Make the most of public popularity. You who are in the business of merchandising should have a great day. Any way in which you can demonstrate your talent or your potential should pay dividends. Show-biz folk will do well. Though some influential people may consider this is not your true future, they will give you support that will encourage you. As long as they understand what it is that you are seeking and the financial background, this is all you need expect. What you do in public is your own affair. Security can be slack in some way. Look after property if you have doubts about the safety of valuables. A partner may be a weak link in any property transaction.

18. SUNDAY. Useful. An obsession of yesterday may seem less important today. You could feel more relaxed or uplifted, and so able to think more clearly. Disbelief or confusion can be clarified if you apply your mind to some outstanding problem. Be patient in handling anyone who has got it wrong. Activity in your neighborhood should be good for you. A relative can be thoughtful or you, in your turn, can be extra considerate of a relative in need. Plans can be made for future family travel. These are early days, but you should be prepared. You may have two or three relationships going at the moment. Stop to think if this is wise. You can waste time and talent by spreading resources too far.

19. MONDAY. Demanding. Traffic problems can delay your start. Try to be patient, for this could be the pattern for the day ahead. As the day progresses you can become more and more frustrated. Being an emotional person you will soon get uptight. Think about those stomach ulcers in the future and let things take their course. If you can get things organized, all to the good. It may be difficult to stick to a schedule. Try to avoid wasted journeys. You could be distressed by news of a sick relative. This is one of the areas where you can use your sympathetic talents constructively. If others want to be contrary, let them go their way.

20. TUESDAY. Satisfactory.   Make your holiday arrangements final. Come to an agreement with other friends who share your recreational interests. Take up a new hobby that will give you more contact with artistic and articulate people. Some may start another collection if one is nearly complete. Avoid dealings in property. You may think you are on to a good thing, but there will be flaws in your reasoning. At the moment you could be very sure of yourself. This can blind you to other issues, some of them quite serious. When you are quite satisfied, you can take the initiative. Sharing responsibility, however, is not recommended. A partner or opposite number is likely to let you down.

21. WEDNESDAY. Good.   Complete arrangements for a family get-together. You should know how many you can accommodate, so can arrive at a firm estimate for food and beverages. Stock up, if necessary, and put enough aside for the unexpected guest who will be made welcome. Consider the impact of your efforts on society. You could go overboard and make a splash, or you can restrict your operations to manageable proportions. Be conservative and you will not lose your good reputation. House reconstruction can go ahead. This could be part of a long-term project. It will add to the size of the structure and provide needed security to weak spots. Get modern safety equipment installed.

22. THURSDAY. Challenging.   Some of you may be starting another chapter of life. This can be a most important step. For some it can mean a new home and fresh responsibilities. Your maternal instincts can be stimulated, as home means so much to you. Think of your background, the past, the stock you came from. As this is a year of opportunity, consider what you want to make of the future. But remember how much depends on your understanding of the past. It is a day, therefore, on which to be optimistic. If your nearest and dearest finds you a little distant, be loving and kind. You have all to gain and nothing to lose by sharing with those you love.

23. FRIDAY. Uneventful.   Concentration on a personal interest can keep you from general activity. Some may be obsessed with their children who could need special attention. Others can be intrigued by the power and ability of a child they meet. Young lovers may be deeply moved by the thought of becoming parents. Try to be constructive when in such a mood. Make plans if that is all you can do. Pay some attention to little ones if it is within your power. Use your intuition to advantage and get what you are after. You can be a step ahead of those who have to reason logically. Later on you may appreciate how much you can enjoy yourself by being interested in a great variety of subjects.

24. SATURDAY. Enjoyable. Once more, Saturday gives you a chance to show off your skills. Business and shopkeeping should be good for those who live by their own efforts. The public will be enthusiastic and should appreciate a novel approach if you have the good sense to experiment. Your lovelife should be active. You can have more than one iron in the fire. This can keep you very busy as well as lending variety to the weekend. See that you get your fair share of publicity. You might be given a pleasant social outing to keep you in a good mood. If you feel adventurous, you should be glad to show off your talents. A meeting with someone in the law profession or government service is possible.

25. SUNDAY. Rewarding. You will not have any time to waste today. The remainder of the weekend should be gainfully occupied in doing those outstanding chores in and around the home and the premises. Ladies will straighten out the home while menfolk get on with heavy-duty jobs of repair that have been left untended for too long. There could be some hitches. Do not take things too seriously or you will make yourself miserable. By the end of the day you should be well satisfied with your progress. Consider seriously a proposal regarding a property transaction. Look into the mechanics of buying and selling. Get yourself acquainted with all practical aspects. Consolidate any gain you have made.

26. MONDAY. Productive. There will be a lively start to the working week. Your services may be in great demand. Rise to the occasion and you will gain in prestige. Reputations can be made today if you care to apply yourself. No doubt you may feel a little adventurous again, so can experiment in order to broaden your horizons. If you have prepared your ground carefully there will be no fear of failing today. So go ahead and have faith in yourself. You should be able to enlist some support before the day is over. The cooperation of important people in show-biz or of those who understand the market will help, once you have broken new ground. Your enthusiasm and know-how will inspire confidence.

27. TUESDAY. Tricky.   Reach an understanding with someone who is willing to cooperate. This is a good time to talk and arrange joint affairs. Plans must be laid prior to any action. You could be very sensitive to whatever is going on around you. Use this in a positive manner and sound out any situation before you commit yourself to action. Should you be fearful and act in a negative way, someone could quite easily play you for a sucker. You would then lose out altogether. All people do not think as you do, although you may think someone in particular is perfect. If your kind feelings are reciprocated, this will be fine. Avoid arguments in the home.

28. WEDNESDAY. Sensitive.   Patch up any disagreement you have had recently. There is no need to have family quarrels. A recent hitch in a relationship can be put to rights. Some of you will be considering marriage and getting organized for the great day. Others may be even further advanced toward the altar. By now you should have been able to reach an understanding on important details. Business partnerships which have been through a trying period lately may receive a boost. This is something you should treat with some reserve. Someone at the top could be setting a trap. Risk at the moment is unlikely to pay off.

29. THURSDAY. Worrisome.   An influential person in fashion or show-biz may apparently be of help and wish to cooperate. There are two sides to this coin. You may gain a friend who carries weight, but you could easily lose money or risk family funds. Try to judge which is more important. Consider the timing of any such proposal. There could be a substantial loss of revenue if you are too immersed in one aspect of a joint venture and so miss its deeper implicatons. Someone may be looking for an opportunity to cooperate, or may be more inclined to gain control. Be on your guard. Look after a long-term asset. Consider reinvestment if you have money to play with.

30. FRIDAY. Manageable.   You are determinedly poised ready to promote the family funds. This is the time to come to a fair decision about joint resources, based on sound working practices and public reputation. Look ahead with confidence. Be happy to improvise after due consideration of all important facts. Take advantage of a progressive offer from someone who knows the legal position in business. A public official could be of assistance and should be welcomed. A great deal of joint monies may have been spent recently on entertaining, hobbies, and other pleasure projects. This is the time to put your foot down.

31. SATURDAY. Exciting. Hit the road with close friends and family. This is a day to get clear away from everyday chores. You should be feeling great and at peace with everyone. Some will travel far to join the one person in their lives. Love blossoms in all corners of the globe. Partnership interests are promoted by the friendly attitude of all sorts of people. Good publicity comes for those in the theater. A top-rank promoter can do some of you a power of good. Do not be too shy to advertise your talent. Be happy to travel if you are given the opportunity. Students with hopes for the future should be able to put across their truly creative ideas. Children and young people should have a good day.

NOVEMBER

1. SUNDAY. Upsetting. You could be feeling under the weather a bit. A journey planned earlier may have to be postponed until you are able to cope. It is just one of those things, so do not get in too much of an uproar. Practicalities may weigh heavy on you. While you have great ideas for the future, you are obliged to think of the everyday responsibilities and chores that seem to restrict your progress. There could be news of a near relative, possibly an in-law, that arouses your compassion. Do something practical rather than just worry. Students could find this a frustrating weekend. Preparations for future examinations can be more than usually burdensome. Stick to it.

2. MONDAY. Demanding. Stand on your own two feet. Public appearances count for a lot. You should seek recognition in your own right while being aware that someone else may be giving you a push. Influential people can be forceful or persuasive. If you are looking for progress, you may be wide open to exploitation. Your judgment is all-important, so do not put too much trust in any partner or intimate friend who offers advice or assistance. A partner may be rather confused. Your aspirations may not be fully appreciated or shared, so a loved one may be upset. There is little hope of changing your attitude. The bit is between your teeth now and there's no stopping you. Make good use of your talent.

3. TUESDAY. Useful. Taking chances may pay off. Even so, all will not be plain sailing. You could get an opportunity to make good. Prestige can rise if you time things well. Opposition from home may upset your schedule. Try to avoid friction, even if you have to bite your tongue to keep quiet. Should you have to make a major decision, take time to consider the pros and cons. Patience and consideration are on your side though you may be impatient for results. If engaged in any bargaining, have your groundwork done previously. A well-prepared case will win the day. Positive action will overcome any argument. Be careful in the home. See that all is secure.

4. WEDNESDAY. Variable. It is hard to satisfy everyone. Though you may be feeling it is time to relax, there may be many details to tidy up. Arrangements can be upset. Your point of view will not be acceptable to someone who is concerned with the way you handle your public affairs. Take on no transaction connected with property if you want a quiet day. Such business is likely to be complicated. Previous property deals may have complications you did not see earlier. Be on your guard for someone who will try to talk you into something you can do without. Your partner may have ideas that help you out of a difficulty. When the business of the day is through, this is a good time to enjoy social activities.

5. THURSDAY. Difficult. Watch your step or you can overdo things. There is a temptation to go all out in order to make a point. This attitude will arouse opposition from people in authority. Show-biz people should avoid confrontation with producers and other influential top brass. Be content to please the public without thinking too much of your own self-satisfaction. Social life can be upset by the interference of people who could control your destiny or have the power to block your plans. Humanitarian interests may turn you on at the moment. You will not get far with your plans until you can enlist the help of the big boys with the money.

6. FRIDAY. Ordinary. Make a list of things that need to be done. Get on quietly with your work. The upsets of yesterday may have left you a little shattered, so do not push yourself. Life is rather like a jigsaw puzzle at the moment. Before you break for the weekend see that you are prepared for the jobs you have in mind. Be sociable without getting out of your depth. Business finances will need to be put straight today. Do not attempt to start any new venture. You should be buttoning things up rather than looking for new business. Though you may have a busy day, you should not become too involved with people. Try to get some privacy, especially later in the day. Above all, keep cool and calm.

7. SATURDAY. Good. Now you will have the time to get on with your own private jobs. An early start will help if you have weekend shopping to do. You will not want to be involved in hustle and bustle today. Quiet efficiency should be your goal. With a fair bit of work to do around the house, you will appreciate the opportunity to be left to your own devices. Feelings may be touched if you are separated from a loved one. Others may have to leave you on your own, which is what you want. But you will become somewhat nostalgic if you are not fully occupied. You can't have it both ways, so buckle down and get on with your good deed for the day. Don't lose sight of those private jobs you had lined up.

8. SUNDAY. Mixed. Look for a change if you are getting bored. A little bit of public excitement should break up any feelings of isolation you may have. Should you be behind schedule with your efforts of yesterday do not take it too seriously. Somewhere along the line there is likely to be a stoppage. So make the day one you can enjoy. There will be another day tomorrow or next weekend. Think of a friend who may be in need. Your sympathy could be aroused for an older person who has fallen on hard times. You should be able to cheer someone up if you use your initiative and act informally. Don't be a stuffed shirt.

9. MONDAY. Misleading. You may feel uncertain about a relationship. Be cautious rather than adventurous. A close associate may not be everything he claims to be. Look after your own interests as a main priority without being selfish. Cooperation may be hard to come by, so you are better off making your own decisions. If you have a legal matter to contest, be well prepared. The opposition is likely to produce something out of the blue. You could be involved with a slippery client or customer if you are engaged in a business deal. Consider the needs of your true partner. If there is a genuine need to comfort and support someone you love, make a good job of it. Make your feelings clear.

10. TUESDAY. Challenging. Personal desires can be fully expressed. Look for genuine support from influential people if you have something creative to offer. The business side of the coin may be more heavily involved. You might have to choose between security at home and possible personal development in public. Encouragement from those who know your inner potential can lift you high enough to handle any problem. But guard against taking too many risks or becoming too sure of yourself. Pride can go before a fall. The family may have their own interests and be involved in making progress in a way different to yours.

11. WEDNESDAY. Worrisome. Involvement in family affairs can lead to complications. The small print on any agreement can be more important than you think, so take care of details. A certain amount of haggling can throw you off your guard and waste a lot of valuable time. You have personal matters to complete. Do not get rattled by the chatter of people who have little appreciation of your needs. Business expansion has been threatened recently and will still remain uncertain today. You need to think clearly before making any decision. Be as tactful as you can. Remember you are in the driver's seat and should be able to control negotiations.

12. THURSDAY. Productive. Use your charm and you will get all you deserve. Work should be a pleasure. Some will meet a new friend at work and from this beginning a romantic experience can start. Given the right approach, you should be able to make money. Be prepared to spend wisely if you are looking for a bargain. Your taste should be especially good today, so get something nice for the home if you see it. Provided you use judgment, you are on a winning roll. Be cooperative and obliging to get the best out of the staff at work. Should you try to push your luck or exercise too much pressure, you will fall apart. Your cash flow will suffer if you gamble immoderately.

13. FRIDAY. Encouraging. An influential person who should know better may wish to receive financial backing. You should have things going for you today. This could attract a lot of attention and someone may look to you for the go-ahead or financial support. Do not allow yourself to be forced into doing a service in order to gain a favor. You are being taken for a sucker by someone who is lazy or not a true friend. If they want to get ahead, let them take the risks along with you. But do not ever accept the burden on someone else's behalf. You will get a long way on your own because family will cooperate actively. Business friends and fellow workers, who have a sense of originality, will also pitch in.

14. SATURDAY. Good. The weekend will get off to a good start. With free time you can make the rounds among relatives and neighbors. Get up-to-date with all you have missed in the past week. Enjoy your natural pleasure in the company of children. Their activities in local affairs should give you a feeling of warmth. Any activity that brings you in contact with articulate people should be encouraged. The local paper may report something to your advantage. Intimate ties are especially meaningful. You will want to do things together with your partner. Be gentle and relaxed. Use your imagination. Seek to develop relationships within the family by keeping in touch with a wider circle.

15. SUNDAY. Disturbing.   You may be surprised at the attitude of a relative. Perhaps a shoulder is needed to cry on. There may be some unhappiness in others that you can help clear up. Health problems can come to the fore. Use your versatility to cope with any problem that arises during the day. It may be necessary to change your diet, which may currently be out of balance. Someone you are fond of may have to work today. This will throw your anticipated schedule right out of whack. Don't worry too much. It could be worse. You may be inclined to get upset and do too much running around. This will be fruitless and could give you ulcers.

16. MONDAY. Mixed.   Early travelers can have problems. Overnight delays will take some time to clear up. Be prepared to improvise. Try to keep your cool if you hear upsetting news. First impressions are not always right. Though you may appear to start out on the wrong foot, you will get organized eventually and all will be well. There could be some trouble with employees right at the start of the working week. No one is very happy on a Monday morning. Avoid early negotiations with discontented staff. They will be more cooperative when you can produce a workable proposition. That should give them more scope and basic security.

17. TUESDAY. Good.   There should be a much better start to the working day. After the pressure of yesterday it can be a pleasure to be with your colleagues. They will also be in a much better frame of mind today. Domestic conditions should be considered. It may be a good time to select material for decorating your home in the future. Prepare quietly for entertainment. You may wish to invite a colleague home for a meal. As you are feeling friendly, you should share your goodwill. Think ahead to the holiday period at the end of the year. Try to be prepared in advance by getting the basics organized. Use your charm to get the family on your side, so that you are not left with too much to do.

18. WEDNESDAY. Demanding.   You are in the mood to get your house in order. An early start will give you the headway you need for coping with a busy day. Positive thinking is required and you are ready for action. Organize your day. Be prepared to stick to your schedule. Despite some interruptions later in the day, you will get straight to the point in whatever you do. Business interests may be distracting. Remember you are dealing primarily with basic matters on which your security depends. You therefore cannot expand too much at the moment. Once you have made your position secure, you will be more free to develop at will.

19. THURSDAY. Productive. A regular engagement comes round again. You will concentrate on one interest for a part of the day. If you decide to focus your attention on one subject, some people may feel they are being ignored. Use your good judgment as to your priorities. A child or children may take up much of your time. There could be a need to concentrate on some creative venture that you feel should be interpreted or publicized. Loving support can come from a partner who is on your wavelength. Because you are particularly sensitive, you could be either vulnerable or totally impervious to outside intervention. Be cooperative if you want best results. Your creative talents could be in heavy demand.

20. FRIDAY. Strenuous. Though work still goes on you will want to enjoy the day. It will offer a good time for shopping. You can be well employed in selecting presents and other goods for the Christmas period ahead. Get out of the house and travel a bit more than usual in search of whatever may have special appeal. You may be inclined to spend a little more than usual. Try to be practical without losing that taste for which you are noted. Children may have to be excluded from today's operation. They are likely to make their presence known, so you should be firm if you hope to get anything done. Reach an early and firm understanding with them before you set out. They will repay you in kind.

21. SATURDAY. Pleasant. Put your best foot forward today. If you are obliged to work today, do so with high hopes. You have a need to put all of it to good use. Many outlets will interest you. The boredom of work will be lessened by the variety of occupations you handle in just a few hours. Artistic interests come naturally. You can apply yourself with purpose, so you are not likely to lose an opportunity to do yourself some good in the bargain. Use your judgment. Your reputation depends, to a good deal, on the reliability of your work and your sense of service. Honesty will be rewarded. For those dealing with the public, this is particularly appropriate. If you have a free day, enjoy a public outing.

22. SUNDAY. Productive. Carry on with the good work. This looks like a weekend in which you will get a mountain of work done. You can also lay the foundations for the holidays at the end of the year. Cooperation comes easily. Every one of the family should pitch in with whatever has to be done. If you are in charge of operations, allocate the jobs. Otherwise you will have more helpers than there is work to do and something will get missed. Leave no stone unturned, as they say, and no task untended. This could be the last chance many have of getting things shipshape this year. Make good use of the opportunity.

23. MONDAY. Deceptive. This will be a day of surprises. You will find little is likely to go according to schedule. Follow your hunches in some cases. A relationship can take on unexpected importance. You may find that working conditions are unpredictable. Look on the bright side and with a bit of polish or diplomacy you can have everyone eating out of your hand. Personal ties can be strengthened if you use your good sense and tread carefully. A partner may be very loving or hypersensitive. You will have to gauge the situation for yourself. It would pay you to be considerate and loving with intimates. A business partner may be trying to pull the wool over your eyes.

24. TUESDAY. Satisfactory. Someone may encourage you to be extravagant. Take no notice of business acquaintances who have little idea about family commitments. Cooperate with those who matter to you. Pay attention to the young members of the family. It may be a youngster's birthday and you should show your love. Arrange a family outing. You may hear of a forthcoming engagement in the family. Take the family out for the day if you get the chance. If not, take your loved one to a show later on. There are lots of things you can discuss with partners. See that everyday matters are attended to down to the smallest detail.

25. WEDNESDAY. Mixed. Conserve the family funds. Discuss with your employer any matter that can increase the family income. Pension rights may need to be considered. Your bank manager can give sound advice if you have additional income to handle. Self-employed folk should be able to button up important contracts with the person they report to. Do not waste time with an assistant if you can get hold of the big chief. Having made ground, do not lose everything by being careless or stupid. You may be tempted to let yourself go. This will be selfish. Think of those who depend on your goodwill for their sustenance.

26. THURSDAY. Useful. Business prospects look good. Make the most of your chances and this will fatten up the family coffers. Work with a purpose and to a pattern. There is little time to spare for pleasure or recreation. Any time taken off will undermine your main ambitions. While you have the active cooperation of partners and colleagues, it would be unwise to divert your activities. Someone may try to talk you into a deal that will have no future. Keep away from any investment dealing in sporting goods or pleasure outlets. Talk about future holiday arrangements is untimely. Deal with matters of the moment which need your direct attention.

27. FRIDAY. Successful. You are now in a better position to talk over holiday plans with the family. See that passports are up to date and other necessary matters are taken into consideration. You should be able to make the complete arrangements tomorrow if all goes well. Before committing yourself to any family expense, get your partner to agree and involve the family in your deliberations. A family powwow can resolve a lot of questions. Your friends at work will be interested in your plans, even if they are not also involved. On the other hand, your employer may take a dim view of your ideas if it will upset schedules. Your first consideration should be for the family, however.

28. SATURDAY. Disquieting. Stick to your original plans. This will not be easy and you may think everything is stacked against you. But it is better to try than be frustrated through inactivity. Students could be faced with last-minute hitches as they seek a free weekend. Many of you will find you have to work after you had expected to be enjoying a free day. Traveling can bring problems. There could be delays at airports. Customs people can be uncooperative. Stick it out if you want to see some result for your labors. Do not expect good publicity if you have plans for self-promotion. Health problems may interfere with your early plans. An in-law may be feeling down in the dumps.

29. SUNDAY. Disconcerting. You may have had a restless night. Do not expect sympathy. Perhaps everyone else has had a bad night also. If you are tense there may be little you can do about it. For some there may be a continuing need to work. This is probably because of some emergency that throws everything out of schedule. Try to keep your cool insofar as possible. There may be little reward at the moment for your efforts. Family or loved ones may be missing when you return home. There will be good reason, no doubt. An engagement may have to be overlooked and this could disappoint your partner. You could wind up in the doghouse until you can come up with a way to make amends.

30. MONDAY. Quiet. You will start they day off under mixed influences. Feel optimistic. This is a day to straighten out your business life. So take time to reflect and look around you for those indications of the prosperity you expected last January. Take stock while everyone is getting back into the swing. Frustrations of the weekend may have given you food for thought. Possible emergencies which may have arisen can sharpen your mind to future prevention methods. At times you may wonder if you should have taken a certain course of action. Fate will sort things out as they should be. You may be thinking of future business combined with social matters. Make provision for everything as best you can.

DECEMBER

1. TUESDAY. Encouraging. Your stock should be high. If you play your cards right today you have much to gain. You will learn that you're popular with all. Relationships should prosper. A lively interest in someone of the opposite sex will do wonders for both persons. Look after a friend who may become a partner. Your better half will be feeling warm and loving. Start the day on an unconventional note. The early bird catches the worm at business as well as in the park. Work will go with a swing if you are allowed enough freedom to do your own thing. It is a day to improvise or try something different.

2. WEDNESDAY. Fair. You can be bursting with love and goodwill. Nothing is likely to stop you if you feel you are on the right track. Emotion can be your strength, given a happy response. You seem to be in tune with the one you hold dearest. You also have time for most other people you call friends. If there is a division of interests or someone thinks he or she is being neglected, make them feel at ease. There is no reason to doubt your sincerity. Passions can run high. You may have a new friendship that is developing rapidly into a much closer tie. You will know in a little while whether or not you are infatuated or really in love.

3. THURSDAY. Worrisome. Someone may think you are an easy touch. If you are handling business finances hold to the traditional values and try nothing that could be open to doubt. You may think you are on to a good thing and can be misled. Partners may be very loving. They will probably have ulterior motives. Among friends you will not mind, but beware of those who flatter in business. A legal wrangle can work against your interests if you have been deceived. It may be possible to mislead some folk, but not all. The attention of friends may leave children at a loss to understand you. Club activities should be enjoyable.

4. FRIDAY. Mixed. Look for a quiet spot. You may find it difficult to get away from people who talk too much. Working conditions can be made miserable by the gossip and interference of inquisitive and malicious people. Do not have your resolution undermined by a careless word. Keep your own counsel. Traveling may be disrupted by a detour due to repair work on the road. Trying to keep aware of all that is in progress can be very tiring. Use modern methods to keep up with the times. If you do not have modern tools available, don't start complaining. You will get nowhere by trying to persuade employers of their shortcomings.

5. SATURDAY. Demanding. You may very well have a headache. Irritation due to the recent past events could cause you a sleepless night. If you took any pill to combat this, you could have a sort of a hangover. A friend may offer to do what you had intended to, out-of-doors or at business. This will give you a break. Rest may do you good. On the other hand, you may feel it only right that you attend to the needs of others who have problems. Do not take life too seriously. Any frustration will bring a challenge you should meet. All your resources may be tested before the day is out and you will then know where you stand.

6. SUNDAY. Challenging. You could feel much relieved, but not quite up to par. Have a lazy day if that is possible. Otherwise, you may attempt something and fail. This will make you feel inadequate and deflate your ego somewhat. As the day progresses you will gain confidence and soon be back in fighting trim. Enjoy some energetic pastime which should liven you up and make you much more compatible. It is essential that you get on your feet as soon as possible. This is a day for personal interests. No one else is going to care very much about them. You cannot survive on sympathy, but will soon put that right. That will serve as a challenge to you.

7. MONDAY. Changeable. Others do not understand the way you feel. A major disagreement could be brewing. You should try to keep out of their way and follow your own interests. No good can come from disagreeing with those you would expect to show compassion. If you have to meet someone halfway, be as dignified as possible. You have to keep up appearances no matter what the differences. Some respite can be had through sport or active interests. Make full use of your talents. At some later date you will be in favor and must not let yourself get rusty. To avoid sharing is no sin, especially when you feel you should go it alone.

8. TUESDAY. Uneventful. Get on with your own life in whatever way you choose. Make the most of any opportunity that comes your way without expecting too much. Personal affairs need to be considered in some detail. You have your own plans to set in motion for the remainder of the year and will not have another opportunity like this again before the Christmas break. Get yourself organized. After all, this has been an eventful year and you want to end it with all flags flying. Look ahead, considering your financial state first after you have fully collected your thoughts. Working conditions are complicated at the moment.

9. WEDNESDAY. Changeable. Put your wits to good use. A working condition can be turned to your advantage if you are on the ball. Just spot the opportunity and say the right word at the right time. If you are thinking ahead about a wage increase, prepare your plans now. Do any talking or writing you feel is necessary. You will be better organized for a direct approach tomorrow. But today you must prepare the ground and sow the seeds. You can be a bit heavy-handed if you have had a night out enjoying yourself. Getting near the holiday season puts pressure on the checkbook, especially if you are spending on children.

10. THURSDAY. Encouraging. This is the day to make a hit with the boss. Bonus day is here. Some will be told they are being promoted. It will also be a good day for business. Hard work eventually pays off despite the gloomy predictions of some people. Influential people know what is going on and will look to the future with optimism. You should feel this also. Some people believe in luck. It often strikes where least expected. If you feel you have earned your keep this year, it is partly the result of good judgment, but more perhaps, of application to your work. Your bank manager will be glad to help with any plans you have for your savings.

11. FRIDAY. Satisfactory. It will be a day of mixed blessings. Progress should be made at work with the active support of your employer. Business can prosper, given the full cooperation of people who rank high in industry. Personal problems can occur through children who may be a bit of a handful or unwilling to listen to parental reason. You should be able to cope with any problem if you use your good sense and allow for the vagaries of humanity. An active mind should keep you ahead of the field. You may hear romantic news about a neighbor or near relative. This could make you think of the past and your own relationships.

12. SATURDAY. Pleasant. Play it by ear for a change. Whatever the day brings, you can count your blessings with respect to the less helpful possibilities. Superiors or people with influence are still feeling helpful toward you. Take advantage of their aid if you have something to promote. Others in the working situation may be less cooperative. Bad feelings can be caused through gossip or idle talk. Try to avoid unnecessary travel. If you have to get around, take a friendly companion. Your lovelife should be good and this will brighten the day. Your partner should be extra cooperative and any recreation should be shared.

13. SUNDAY. Challenging. Don't take life too seriously. If you feel you have a rough day ahead, spend an extra hour or two in bed. There is probably no need to bother yourself too much. Workaday worries can bother you if you have time on your hands. When you are emotionally upset, you can become despondent quite easily. Perhaps you can turn this to advantage by doing a bit of careful and constructive preparation for the coming week. Some of you will be expecting to take on added responsibility in the next day or two. Look forward with conviction and be prepared to welcome this essential recognition of your worth.

14. MONDAY. Misleading. Domestic chaos may get you off to a poor start. Do not take this to heart. If there are problems at home you will be able to master them in due course. Try to keep yourself organized, as it is possible that others who depend on you could be in a bit of a flap. Look after basics. Despite the unreliability of those who are supposed to cooperate with you, it is essential to keep your feet on the ground. Have no dealings in real estate, despite whatever the temptation. Avoid legal encounters in this respect. Nothing will be clear and you could end up making absolutely no progress. A romantic episode in the family may cause some domestic bad feeling.

15. TUESDAY. Important. Prepare for a day of decision. You are likely to take on added responsibility. This may be due to pressure from an employer or because you are taking over from a senior who cannot handle it. Accept such responsibility in a positive way. This could be an important day in your life as it affects your career or business prospects. Keep in touch with the outside world. There are opportunities which give you a chance to put a word in the right ear at the top. Your activities may not find favor with a loved one. Perhaps you cause others to worry if you press yourself too hard. Do not let this deter you.